Best w
K

CLOGGER OF THE YARD

Apologies for the delay!

J. M.KNOWLES

J. M. Knowles

29. 10. 2005

LIST OF CONTENTS

1   FLASHING MATTER

Set majestically on a series of hills, the City of Durham is the historical and cultural centre-piece of a traditional mining county, ravaged by industrial decline. Despite inevitable road development, the old stone bridges of Elvet and Framwelgate still access a cobbled island of university buildings and quaint shops. Dominating the skyline, the cathedral and castle tower over the meandering River Wear with its deeply-gorged and heavily-wooded loop.

By day the well-worn towpaths are the domain of educated men on clapped-out pedal cycles shouting instructions to sweating oarsmen in tones that set them apart from the less refined local population. At night the same area transforms into a stage for courting couples, strolling beneath a back-drop of impressively spot-lit, dark-stone fortifications. Apart from an occasional high-spirited student celebration and the annual Durham Miners' Gala, the City is a relatively quiet place in terms of policing. Deriving status from the cathedral, it is merely a sub-division of the greater Durham Division, itself statistically less troublesome than towns like Gateshead, Sunderland and South Shields. But it wasn't always that way; well, not in 1969!

One of the few public houses in the city to remain unaltered for the last thirty years is *The Shakespeare* in Saddler Street. Most casual visitors to the premises are intrigued by the original spit-and-sawdust conditions and the labyrinthine panelled rooms at the rear, but few understand the real reason for the ageing, wood-grained decor. It's true of course, the museum quality has impacted favourably on beer sales over the years, but the big snug is also headquarters for the little known B-Relief Action Committee. It meets annually on the 1st April and was constituted for the purpose of drunken debate into a phenomenon of Durham Police history known as the Catchpole Crisis or the Three-Week-War. As a gesture of support, the owners of *The Shakespeare* vowed never to re-decorate the hostelry until the mystery surrounding the destruction of the City's police station was finally put to rest.

Convened specially at lunch-time, many anticipated the 1999 reunion would be the last. Under the thirty-year rule the three surviving members of the original B-Relief were convinced the release of official government papers, emanating from the Wilson administration, would reveal all. Each carrying a crystal-clear pint of good northern ale, with a slopping ice-cream head, the retired trio filed from the bar into the inner-sanctum, ready to be locked-in for the day. The speech-impaired chairman, who as a much younger man survived and documented the worst of the atrocities, removed an official brown envelope from his leather-elbowed, tweed sports-jacket and pondered the Home Office logo.

"Wight chaps, this is it," he announced, plonking his glass down to rip open the correspondence with his thumb.

The three-line reply to a three-hundred page document thirty years in the preparation, and worthy of a literature prize, was a gut-wrenching blow to the plight of the police pensioners.

"Breakdown in recruiting procedure, my arse," said one, slumping into a chair with his head in his hands. "Brushed out of history by MI6 more like it. Now we shall never know!"

On Tuesday 1st April, 1969 Police Constable 1328 Roger Catchpole transferred to Durham City from Bishop Auckland, accompanied by a nondescript but curiously extensive personal file. At the ripe old age of twenty-two it was his fourth posting. When he passed out of the regional police training centre at Newby Wiske Hall as a nineteen-year-old, the commandant there described him as academically borderline but very enthusiastic, with an ability to entertain his peers. Under normal circumstances his first station ought to have encompassed his two-year probation, but after one year an enterprising superintendent suggested his colossal energy needed the stimulation of a busier division. The second superintendent to command him observed that while he was not destined for high rank he was potentially an effective police officer, and should be accepted as a fully-fledged regular on the condition he received close supervision during the formative years of his career. Coincidentally, a sergeant with the right attributes was not available in that division and

Constable Catchpole was packed-off to Bishop Auckland where a third superintendent in as many years found him a little accident prone, but only requested his immediate transfer on the grounds that an indiscreet personal relationship was affecting operational efficiency.

The latest sub-divisional head to experience the enemy-within was a tall, slim, greying man with an abnormally bulbous blue-veined nose, who had no connection with prize-fighting. Known affectionately as Gentleman Jim, he happened to be pondering the cryptic personal record of Constable Catchpole at his first-floor office window when the latest addition to his sub-divisional complement raced his car into the rear yard of the detached police station from the direction of Court Lane, contravening a No Entry sign. The minor traffic violation, especially by a stranger to the one-way system, only warranted casual advice by a lower rank, but the smile on the face of the Morris 1000, and the cloud of blue smoke in its wake, tempted the superintendent even closer to his office window.

Looking-on wide-eyed, Gentleman Jim watched the vehicle clatter into a position totally obstructing the sub-divisional petrol pump. Then he observed a fully-uniformed giant elbow himself awkwardly from the driver's door, holding a chrome-topped helmet in one hand and something the size of a tea mug in the other. The newcomer dropped the item inside the headgear and screwed the loaded bucket firmly into place on top of his head. After slamming the car door shut, he walked to the front to contemplate a tattered piece of rope connecting the bonnet to the bumper. Loosening a hitch in the trailing end, the stranger then pulled hard on a slip-knot, restoring a serious expression to the vehicle's face. Satisfaction was just discernible beneath his helmet when he tied-off the rope with a gentle pat.

By now the mild-mannered blue nose was oscillating between the window and the telephone on his desk, experiencing a perplexing moment of indecision. It was flashing light-green socks, as Constable Catchpole bounded from the car to the back door of the police station, that forced Gentleman Jim into a rare bout of front-line leadership. Struggling urgently with the frame of a cumbersome, grime-impregnated sash-window, the senior officer launched his white-shirted torso into the cool spring air just before the giant disappeared into the Victorian building below.

"You!"

The newcomer stopped and looked up at single, chrome shoulder crowns. "Me!"

"Yes, you. My office, now."

"Right, boss," responded the surprised transferee, seconds before the heavy sash crashed-down onto Gentleman Jim's back.

Entering the rear door of Durham City police station, PC Catchpole tackled a shallow flight of three stairs in a single leap, before turning left into a corridor and poking his bowed head around the first open door, marked; Policewoman's' Department. Only one of four wooden desks was occupied. A slightly surprised but very pleasant round face looked up from her deliberations, loose strands of long, brown hair falling gracefully from a carefully constructed walnut-whip. Fixing his eyes firmly on a fully-inflated and precisely-ironed white shirt, Constable Catchpole grinned lecherously, exposing a full set of perfectly arranged, large white teeth.

"Where's the boss's office, sweet-face?" he asked, the grin subsiding into suggestive pouting.

"Up the staircase, turn right and it's at the end of the corridor," answered the young policewoman with a badly concealed giggle.

"Thanks," winked the transferee, turning to attack the stairs in the minimum amount of strides.

When the new addition to the sub-divisional strength eventually squeaked to a noisy halt on the highly-polished brown linoleum outside the superintendent's office, he found the door partially open. Screwed to the magnolia-glossed wall beside the heavy blue door, a defunct electronic contraption with a red and green light momentarily confused the young giant.

He can't be engaged he thought, daring to knock on the woodwork.

"Come," commanded a voice from inside, seated and ready for action.

Without his helmet Constable Catchpole could only just pass through a standard door frame, upright and unhindered. As he pushed open Gentleman Jim's office door with one hand, he instinctively grabbed the little peak of his helmet with the other and swung-off the headgear a split-second before his huge, beaming face crossed the superintendent's line of vision. The result was an entrance befitting a music hall performer. With perfect trajectory, a brown-crusted pork pie, factory wrapped in cellophane, careered straight into the corner of the sub-divisional commander's office. It glanced-off the edge of a regulation square carpet, immediately in front of his ornate desk, then picked-up speed on the linoleum to skid into the deep, white-painted skirting board between a carved-oak bookcase and the station safe. The refined host flinched when the hand-grenade thudded into its target, but then his mouth opened in astonishment when his guest lumbered down onto all-fours to recover the popular north-east delicacy. His socks were not only light-green, but they had a luminous property too!

"Oh, terribly sorry, boss," blurted the honey-monster. "Emergency provisions, you know what it's like in this job!"

After Constable Catchpole carefully re-shaped the bruised pork pie, he wedged it back into the pointed-end of its receptacle. The superintendent sighed, contemplated his retirement date, and then made an observation to the effect that most officers under his command were the proud owners of a conventional sandwich-box.

"Tupperware is very good," he suggested, pointing to his own container standing air-tight on top of the adjacent bookcase. "Now, let's start again, should we?" the superintendent continued, taking a deep breath to reinforce his characteristic patience. "What's your name?"

"PC 1328 Catchpole, boss."

Glancing down at the puzzling personal file topping-off some other papers on his desk, Gentleman Jim went on with remarkable restraint.

"Don't call me boss young man, sir, or if you prefer, superintendent. Both are acceptable modes of address."

"Yes boss...I mean superintendent. You can call me Clogger if you like, everyone else does!"

Gentleman Jim grimaced, put both elbows firmly on his desk-top, and then rested his chin on his interwoven fingers to look away from

9

his guest, towards the array of memorabilia adorning his office walls. Anxious to maintain his composure, he focused for a while on a framed-photograph of himself in full uniform and took another deep breath.

"Is that you superintendent? Very nice. Where was it taken?" asked Clogger, noticing his host's attention was elsewhere.

"Oh, the staff college at Bramshill," Gentleman Jim inadvertently replied, before stepping up to the next octave. "Never mind the photograph, is that your blue Morris 1000 parked in my yard?"

"Well, yes and no, superintendent."

"What do you mean, yes and no? I watched you park it there!"

"Well it belongs to my brother actually...and it's not really blue. It's a two-tone, blue and rust."

By now Gentleman Jim couldn't decide whether he was being ridiculed or subjected to an elaborate seasonal wind-up. He glanced at his desk calendar then his wrist-watch.

It's gone twelve he confirmed, slapping his clammy palms on either side of Clogger's paperwork to stare menacingly at the notionally upright hulk, cuddling an inverted police helmet loaded with a cold pork pie.

"Is it roadworthy? Does it comply with the Construction and Use Regulations?" the sub-divisional head demanded.

"Well, just between you and I boss...I mean superintendent," confided Clogger, leaning forward to place a supporting hand on the corner of the superintendent's desk, "I don't think so, it could do with four new tyres and an exhaust."

Not quite as tall and certainly not as bulky, Gentleman Jim levered himself up out of his chair, re-planted both of his own palms on the desk and confronted his subordinate blue nose to square chin.

"Well, just between you and I, Clogger, if that car is in my yard when you start duty tomorrow it will be inspected by a qualified vehicle examiner, and I will prosecute you personally."

"Does that mean you want me to come on my motorbike in future boss...I mean superintendent? By the way, you've got a dirty mark on the back of your shirt."

Clogger's final remark broke the camel's back. Gentleman Jim snapped for the first time in living memory. He picked up his robust twelve-inch office ruler and whipped the white plastic against the back of Clogger's supporting hand.

"Get your fucking hand off my desk," the superintendent screamed, circumnavigating the furniture to engage the enemy.

Still cuddling his bucket of pork pie, Clogger rubbed his stinging knuckles against his tunic and retreated across the carpet in the shadow of a swashbuckling pirate.

Jenny, the superintendent's prudish, middle-aged secretary, slotted her head out of the small office next door.

"What's going on?" she inquired, just in time to witness a flashing light-green giant scarper back along the executive corridor.

"And move that fucking heap away from the petrol pump...and get those fucking socks off," the raging bull bawled from his office doorway, still brandishing his ruler.

"Oh, superintendent, I've never heard you use language like that before," declared Jenny, slamming her own door shut in disgust.

When the escaping imbecile descended the main staircase, using every third step, he coincidentally bumped into the same busty policewoman scurrying along the ground-floor corridor with some papers.

"Where's the parade-room, sweet-face?" he called.

Secretly impressed with Clogger's rugged looks and black, spiky crop, she pointed to another closed blue door and smiled.

How can hair point in so many different directions?

It was two o'clock exactly when Clogger barged into the stark sub-divisional parade-room bringing the occupants to an abrupt silence. A long rectangular table with carved feet and a badly scuffed, in-laid green-leather surface, dominated the centre of the floor. Five constables, sitting unevenly on either side, immediately rotated their heads, and the shift patrol-sergeant at the head of the table looked up from a black, lever-arch file.

"Constable Catchpole, I presume! We're so grateful you could come," the three-striped supervisor quipped, with a presence honed over twenty-nine years in the gutters of every County Durham town.

"In this division we parade fifteen minutes before the start of duty. Go home and come back at nine-forty-five, in good time for the night-shift."

Clogger analysed the instruction for a few seconds, tilted his head to one side, smiled broadly, then declared, "Oh, you don't really mean that, sarge," bouncing towards a vacant chair on the right-hand-side of the table.

When he kicked the table leg, a cup in front of the sergeant rattled violently and spilled brown liquid into the saucer. Dropping into the spare pew, Clogger went on to bang his loaded helmet onto the table, adding to the saucer's limited capacity. After a perfectly choreographed ripple of grimaces, a pregnant silence prevailed while the two men stared at each other, the audience panning like spectators at a tennis match.

For his part Clogger continued with his innocent grin to contemplate the sergeant's hair. A thickly-woven ginger rug was sitting neatly on a base of greying wisps, forming an unnaturally distinct hair-line across the top of a screwed-up face and a button nose. Provoked beyond the point of reaction with his fists tightly clenched, the supervisor's forearms were beginning to ache and beads of sweat were gathering beneath his toupee when the stand-off suffered a timely interruption.

"Stand," the sergeant called, responding to a youthful shift-inspector, who entered the room without warning, sporting a white shirt with shoulder pips.

"Sit," instructed the dashing blue-eyed blond, before the contingent had time to unfold their full height. "You must be PC Catchpole," he continued, extending his right arm in the direction of the only unfamiliar face.

Clogger rebounded to his feet and shook the shift-inspector's hand vigorously. "Yes, boss...I mean inspector," he replied enthusiastically.

"What's your first name?" enquired the well-spoken university graduate.

"Roger, but everyone calls me Clogger"

"Well Woger, welcome to B-Welief."

"He was late for parade, inspector," the miffed sergeant interrupted, anxious to restore his credibility among the rest of the team.

"Oh, I don't think it was intended sergeant, he went up to see the super first... to intwoduce himself," ventured the inspector, tongue-in-cheek.

"Oh, yes," Clogger confirmed, with an apologetic glance at his new patrol-sergeant. "He's a proper gent the super, he wanted to talk to me about my motor car."

"Yes...and Woger, don't forget to move it away from the fuel pump," the inspector insisted, recalling the mauling he had just received from the temporarily insane sub-divisional head. "If you have any pwoblems whatsoever, you must wemember to seek advice from the sergeant or I. Do you understand?"

"Yes, boss...I mean inspector," Clogger agreed, thundering back down onto his chair.

The apparent misunderstanding restored the sergeant's pride and returned the atmosphere to some sort of normality. After carefully fingering the position of his toupee, the supervisor pointed out that he would brief Constable Catchpole on his duties later, and then he invited the inspector to take the floor with his more general daily contribution.

"I only have one item," announced the dynamic team-leader who didn't bother to sit down. "It concerns a small piece of new legislation, called the Tattooing of Minors Act. In the statute book next year. Particularly intewesting because it emanates from a test-case in this force awea. Briefly, we no longer charge assault in the case of minors tattooed without pawental consent, the new legislation pwovides a specific offence. There's a pwovisional copy of the Act in the tutor sergeant's office. Have a look at it when you can."

Daily announcements of this nature by the fast-track inspector were intended to keep B-Relief at the cutting-edge of policing, ahead of its rivals. To this end the well-educated inspector would often encourage healthy debate on current issues, but the tattooing of children was far from controversial and he was about to formally dismiss the assembly when Clogger's fixed grin subsided.

Fidgeting with the pork pie in his helmet, the newcomer dropped his eyes, adopted a very concerned expression, and then uttered his opening address in what was to become one of the most profound legal debates of the century.

"I think this new law is unfair."

"Weally!" the inspector replied, bursting to hear Clogger's thoughts on such a stale piece of news. "Cawwy on."

"Well, in my opinion it's like that homosexual bill, it's discriminatory."

"Oh," the academic said, trying desperately to determine Clogger's line. "Why do you think the legislation legalising homosexuality is discwiminatory?"

"Because it exempts merchant seaman," asserted Clogger.

A thread of logic stimulated the inspector's appetite for constructive debate. "You're wight, of course," he enthused, "but in that case parliament democwatically decided it was unhealthy to permit homosexual activity in the confines of a ship."

"Well, I wonder what my landlady will think when she finds out," retorted Catchpole QC, plunging the whiz-kid back into darkness.

"Has your landlady got an opinion on this?"

"No, but her husband was a miner!"

His head on one side, penetrating blue eyes screwed-up, the inspector was wrestling with the subtleties of Clogger's argument when the budding Lord Chancellor closed the debate with devastating clarity.

"Why has parliament democratically decided to continue charging assault when engineers and bricklayers are tattooed?" he concluded, nodding his head triumphantly in all directions.

The sergeant, still sitting at the head of the table sighed loudly, closed his eyes and exposed the top of his ginger wig.

They've sent me a divvy!

The rest of the parade, including the inspector, wandered out of the room in emotional turmoil. Nobody could decide whether to laugh or cry, but something told boy-wonder his high-flying career was about to lose momentum.

The independent briefing of Clogger followed a bawled instruction to the Elvet beat officer to wait in the corridor. For some reason the sergeant felt unable to deliver his orders at normal speed and what ought to have taken two minutes stretched to five. With the slow, deliberate emphasis of a school teacher coaching a difficult pupil, he repeated every instruction and didn't move on until the giant's head nodded in acknowledgement.

"Right, get on with it," the ginger-wig concluded, rising to his feet with his lever-arch file tucked neatly under his left arm. "And don't forget to take spare batteries; communication is paramount in the city-centre."

It was two-fifteen before Clogger finally joined forces with his tutor for the day. Equipped with a freshly charged pocket-radio and extra batteries, drawn against signature from the communications-room hatch, the new member of B-Relief stepped out of the front door of Durham City police station with his fully-charged helmet hovering eight inches above that of his colleague.

"Prison and assize court," the Elvet beat officer clipped, once the pair had cleared the steps.

Clogger looked down at a cocked right arm and followed it skyward to an adjacent, sinister-looking multi-storey block of barred windows. Below, a very high stone wall topped with nasty barbs, enclosed the Victorian fortress, its line broken only by two huge, arched wooden doors, complete with bobbled-steel reinforcement and twin turrets.

"Its got a high security wing," continued Clogger's tutor. "Holds the most dangerous criminals in the country. Causes all sorts of problems!"

"Right," the lumbering pupil acknowledged, pondering the top of an adjacent chrome-ridged helmet.

Must have been wearing thick socks when he was measured!

Shoulder to ribs, the two-man patrol strode away from the front of the police station along the asphalt path that twists through St. Cuthbert's churchyard into Old Elvet. Hands clenched behind their backs, the pair then turned left and headed towards Elvet Bridge at the regulation foot-patrol speed of two miles per hour, which in Clogger's case meant a slow goose-step.

"What did Bald Eagle tell you to concentrate on today?" the established constable asked, craning his neck in the direction of his pet gorilla.

Reference to the sergeant's toupee exaggerated Clogger's natural, silly grin. "Said I've got to walk the Elvet beat with you and make myself familiar with the judge's post and the cathedral tower, then at four you've got to show me the traffic warden's box, just in case I ever have to relieve her. Is it a medical problem?"

Totally confused, Clogger's minder shook his head and led the way across the picturesque Elvet Bridge hovering in one of the recesses to look down on the slow-moving, rich-brown water.

"Big problem with flashers," advised the tutor, pointing to the beautiful tree-lined towpaths below. "In the summer we have to turn-out policewomen in plain-clothes."

"Really," Clogger replied, unable to see any navigation lights among the smattering of hired rowing boats.

Just before Little and Large reached the Market Place, Little turned sharp-left into an earlier century. He led the pair along Saddler Street to the Baileys, passing the access to Palace Green and the architectural splendour of the Dean and Chapter buildings. At the southern end of the narrow street, directly beneath the historic arch, the cobbled road surface petered out into an unmade track, dropping down onto the river bank. A white-painted wooden post padlocked into the ground, prevented vehicular access to the ageing Prebends Bridge.

"Judge's post," Clogger's tutor snapped. "Only circuit judges are allowed to use the bridge...to get to their residential accommodation. If you're on this beat when the assizes are in session you must carry the key at all times and remove the post to let the limousine through."

"How will I know when the judge is coming?" queried Clogger.

"Radio," his minder answered, patting the receiver part of his pocket-set clipped to the inside of his lapel. "Don't forget to replace the post afterwards...and don't forget to salute as he passes."

"Right," Clogger responded, bemused by the thought of the unsafe bridge crumbling under the weight of a heavily-regaled red-robed judge, sitting like royalty in the back of a chauffeur-driven limousine.

Lesson one complete, the two-man patrol retraced its steps and climbed to Palace Green with an unconscious co-ordination stimulated by the gentle pulse of stereophonic pocket-radio receivers.

"This is where the Durham Light Infantry was formally disbanded," the Elvet beat officer announced, when a beautifully manicured green patch appeared between the castle and the cathedral on the imposing summit of the ancient city. "I was on duty that day," he continued proudly. "We all received commemorative mugs to mark the occasion."

Once his handshake with the Lord Lieutenant of the County had faded from his mind, the experienced constable pointed to the ornate cathedral entrance in the opposite corner of Palace Green, then tilted back his head and gazed at the very top of the square tower.

"See over every wall in the City from up there," he advised, with a well-timed dramatic pause. "Including the one around the prison. Ideal spot for a sniper to nest!"

"Oh," replied Clogger, the notion of a hairy-arsed police ornithologist crossing his mind.

"Very sensitive, especially since John Mc Vicar's escape from E-Wing last year. You'll often get a call to evacuate all tourists from the tower...when something unusual is happening inside the prison."

Turning on his heals to march on more of the City's key facilities, Clogger's mentor for the day concluded the second lesson with a general piece of advice.

"Elvet is the most important of the city-centre beats," he insisted. "Never lose contact with the communications-room, and always carry spare batteries."

By the time the unevenly balanced pair had strolled the remaining main streets of the Elvet beat and engaged in statutory small-talk with familiar faces, it was ten minutes to four.

"Better show you the traffic wardens' box," remarked the low-flying helmet, glancing at his wrist-watch to set a slightly brisker pace towards the hub of all traffic activity.

Dominating the centre of the granite Market Place, an hexagonal structure constructed in well-maintained hardwood, housed a shabby, swivelling high-chair that faced a semi-circular closed-circuit television console, complete with well-worn knobs and switches. Half glass, the turret resembled the body of an ungainly giant spider with connecting, single-carriageway cobbled legs. It confronted a very light traffic flow from the university buildings in the narrow Saddler Street and on the extreme left access to Claypath was similarly less problematic. Between the two a much heavier snake from the south of the county, lurked out-of-sight behind traffic lights on the other side of Elvet Bridge. To the right Silver Street burrowed its way down onto Framwelgate Bridge, beyond which another column of revving motors waited on a distant grid, formally called North Road. The rest of the partially pedestrianised focal point was a bustling grandstand for cogitating students, browsing tourists and determined local people anxious to buy fresh fruit and vegetables from the covered market.

"We all have to know how to operate this, in case of emergency," the Elvet beat officer boomed as the pair marched on the weather-proofed installation in yellow, watery sunlight. "I'll let the Painted-Lady teach you the ropes. I must go to St. John's College. I have an appointment with one of the god-squad about a motoring offence."

Abandoned at the rear of the traffic control box, Clogger was confronted by a stable door. Firmly bolted from the inside, the bottom section served as a leaning rail and the smooth, raw wood shone like the proverbial netty-door. Always slightly ajar for ventilation purposes, Clogger pulled open the top-half with typical enthusiasm, nearly dislodging a yellow-trimmed hat hooked to a petite uniform tunic swinging pendulously beneath. When a startled pyramid of pinned-up, greying hair swivelled round to face him, Clogger was assailed by the sickly compound smell of cheap perfume and fresh perspiration.

"Oh, you must be PC Catchpole," declared the red-lipped mask. "Bald Eagle said you would be here at four. I have to teach you the controls until five, and then you're on your own while I take my break. The rush-hour should get you up to speed!" the buxom traffic

18

warden continued, her facial rendering sufficiently durable to withstand the stresses and strains of a complex sentence.

"Okay," replied Clogger, triggering a second, more urgent, one-hundred-and-eighty degree rotation of her well-proportioned body.

Once the yellow peril had returned to her proper operating position, with her back to the stable door, Clogger adopted an appropriate rural posture and leaned over his new tutor's shoulder with his forearms positioned along the top of the gleaming wood-barrier.

"Bridges are the problem!" she clipped, talking to a column of vehicles advancing on her from the direction of Elvet. "Patterns are irregular during the day, got to rely on the cameras and change the lights accordingly," she continued, switching the southern approach into the stop sequence while she glanced at the gently flickering black and white image of the busy North Road.

"What happens during the night?" Clogger asked, contemplating the line of an over-stretched bra strap, just visible underneath the back of a white, uniform shirt.

"At ten o'clock we lock-up and switch to automatic until eight the next morning. The automatic mode copes okay during the silent hours and sometimes on Sundays, but not during the week," she advised, pointing to the largest switch on the console.

For thirty minutes or so the Painted-Lady continued to demonstrate her expertise, flicking switches and rattling out guidance with the speed of an auctioneer. Predictably, Clogger's attention waned very quickly and his fascination with the back of her mammary support tempted his head even further into the capsule. Just beyond the yellow-flash on her right epaulette, the newcomer could see an unfastened shirt button. While the traffic warden's torso necessarily rotated through her panoramic field of vision, the edges of the fine nylon material the button was supposed to be holding together, opened and closed in unison, like the shutter of a camera. By trial and error Clogger established the optimum viewing point and immediately after a tiny area of wholesome bare cleavage received maximum exposure, he used the down-time to scan two black-silken knees.

She's wearing a skirt today, can't see her box. I wonder if she really is a nymphomaniac!

The sincerity of the inference was just starting to confuse the young constable when a convenient lull in traffic conditions catapulted the Painted-Lady towards the side of the console where she rapidly picked up a small sandwich-box and both halves of her pocket-set.

"Come on, your turn," she insisted, spinning towards the bolt on the bottom-half of the stable door.

Clogger straightened-up and stepped back allowing the masked invader to launch herself from the capsule's hot-seat onto the market cobbles.

"It's like a furnace in there," she quipped, maintaining momentum in her wobbly bosom to grab her hat and tunic from behind the upper section of the door.

The traffic warden's urgent approach to the change of rocket command stimulated Clogger's impulsive streak. Moving up a cog he tossed his own radio onto the side of the control panel and threw off his tunic.

"Put it inside, on the floor," rattled his instructor, when the small self-adhesive hook refused to accept the additional weight of Clogger's loaded helmet, suspended by its chin-strap.

By the time Clogger had fully stress-tested the swivel-chair's footing, the Framwelgate screen was full to hazy capacity.

"Close down Elvet," the Painted-Lady insisted, resting her substantial swimming-aid on top of the stable door while she leaned over to secure the bolt. "Never let either direction build-up to the point where you can't see the end of the queue. Clear North Road," she further advised, buttoning up her tunic to bring some discipline to her unruly breasts. "That's right, back to Elvet, but don't forget you've got one in Saddler Street, don't let him sit there all day."

Straining on her tip-toes to see beyond Clogger's huge shoulders, the traffic warden was impressed with her student's understanding of the closed-circuit television equipment and began to make final, ritualistic adjustments to her headgear in readiness for a well-earned

20

refreshment break. A last glance at the state-of-play confirmed her protégé was well positioned to tackle his first solo flight.

"Never take your eye off the bridges," she concluded, pushing the stable door to a position where the cockpit would receive essential ventilation. "I'll be back in an hour or so."

"Okay, sweet-face," replied Clogger, turning in time to catch his first glimpse of generous buttocks bouncing enticingly across the Market Place.

Take-off was smooth enough and the climb-out was going well, but before the new pilot reached the stability of cruising height he spotted the blurred outline of a disorientated heavy goods vehicle waiting in North Road, like a saddle on a snake's back.

He'll never get up Silver Street, Clogger thought, facing his first untimely emergency with limited training.

Switching Framwelgate Bridge into the green sequence, the leading three or four cars raced into the Market Place and cleared the control box efficiently, leaving the tortoise to crawl beneath Clogger's electronic field of vision.

At least he's moving, Clogger consoled while the mechanical tail slithered out of sight.

The deserted cobbled carriageway on the right-hand-side of the vibrant Market Place had an eerie feeling to it, made worse by the onset of the evening rush-hour. Beads of sweat began to form on the trainee pilot's brow lifting the temperature in the cockpit to an uncomfortable high. Nervously he watched the flickering image of nose-to-tail traffic flood Elvet Bridge and the main southern approach of New Elvet beyond. In the midst of the proverbial lull, a mental contingency plan began to occupy Clogger's thought processes. While he waited for the Framwelgate monster's head to appear at the top of Silver Street, he rapidly chopped off its slow-moving tail with a clear, red stop signal, then turned his attention to a clutch of boffin pedal-cyclists waiting patiently in the tranquillity of Saddler Street.

They can come through, Clogger decided, while I'm waiting for the lorry. When it comes, I'll pull it over onto the market cobbles and clear Elvet with an extended green sequence.

The plan would have worked had it not been for a sudden, cutting draught from behind the pilot's head.

"Don't worry sweet-face, everything is under control," Clogger rattled, thinking his buxom tutor had returned prematurely to bail him out.

"Officer, officer," a distraught young female replied, "he's over there."

"Who is?" demanded Clogger, swivelling one-hundred-and-eighty degrees to frame himself in the wide-open upper section of the stable door.

"The man that exposed his body to me last week," whispered a very agitated science student, swaddled in a university scarf.

"Exposed his body!" Clogger smiled. "What's wrong with that?"

The freckled face leaned into the aperture and stared earnestly at the six-feet-five spaceship commander. Twisting her lips to blow aside a flimsy long fringe, she glanced behind before silently mouthing the sordid detail.

"He exposed himself. You know...his erect penis."

"What!" Clogger blurted, lip reading a series of exaggerated facial expressions while he urgently unbolted the bottom section of the control box door. "Where is he?"

"He's standing in Woolworth's doorway with some other men. I made a full statement to a policewoman last week. It happened while I was sitting on the river bank, reading."

"Okay, sweet-face," asserted the friendly giant, vacating the turret in his blue, long-sleeved uniform shirt and black clip-on tie. "Point him out to me."

Carelessly leaving his tunic suspended inside the wide-open stable door and his loaded helmet underneath the control console, Clogger abandoned his post and marched across the deserted carriageway to the busy slabbed-pavement on the opposite side of the Market Place, with his chief witness in tow. Although potentially serious, such a lapse would normally have been forgiven in the prevailing circumstances, but the time had gone five and both bridges were on red. The fact that his pocket-radio was also in the control box talking to itself didn't help, but the situation only passed through the critical stage into melt-down when Clogger started to conduct a well-intended street identification.

Perfect, lots of people about, the officer enthused, remembering his training-school days. Only take a couple of minutes. I'll report him for summons and get straight back to the box.

"When we reach the doorway love, look at everybody in turn, then indicate exactly who you think is responsible for the offence. Leave the rest to me."

When the shirt-sleeved giant pushed his way through the pedestrian cross-flow, parting the waters so that his prosecution witness could do her stuff, he was confronted by half-a-dozen local layabouts sucking slyly on cigarettes in the deep recesses of the shop front. Ushering the university student to the mouth of the doorway, Clogger spread himself across the rest of the entrance to protect the identification from the clot of rubber-necked spectators, rapidly gathering in a circle behind him. Exactly on cue, Clogger's petite companion started to look over the motley crew, but before her eyes settled on the rodent-featured suspect panicking deep in the clutch, his small primate body dropped into a crouch and tunnelled on all-fours between Clogger's open legs.

"Stop him," the giant screamed, as one side of the fickle audience dissolved as readily as it had congealed. I'll get the bastard!

Clogger urgently turned and anteloped after his lean, leather-backed quarry, reaching the mouth of Silver Street just in time to see the birth of a creeping monster. While the agile rodent bobbed and weaved through the pedestrian traffic on the left-hand-side of the wagon, Clogger took the other route with the finesse of a sixteen-pounder. An apologetic collision with an elderly skittle momentarily delayed his progress, but once he was satisfied the freshly-seated pensioner and her walking stick were unscathed, he emerged from the other end of the bowling-alley, his head rotating like a stalked deer. A couple of other pedestrians, bent double below him, were rummaging in the steeply descending gutter trying to trap escaping apples, when Clogger's radar locked onto the skinny back of the over-sized rat.

Driven by blind determination, Clogger ignored his twenty-second disadvantage and skidded around the bend at the bottom of Silver

Street, just in time to see the fugitive disappear down the stairway at the Silver Street side of Framwelgate Bridge.

The bastard's gone to ground, he thought when he paused to look down on the apparently deserted, but densely-wooded lower towpath.

Undeterred the giant negotiated the historic stonework with a series of ungainly vaults, using the black-iron handrail as a fulcrum. Assailed by the pungent smell of wild rhubarb, he thudded onto the hard-packed earth and startled a middle-aged couple approaching with a small, unleashed dog. Punctuated by the occasional impatient car horn on the bridge above, the pursuer then moved stealthily into the undergrowth on the river-side of the well-worn path.

He can't have gone very far, Clogger deduced, digging his feet into a carpet of wild ivy.

While the canine Hoover sniffed in from the other direction, the earth-mover tore through the foliage ripping away tangled, woody stems with his size fourteen, black-leather boots. The cross-fire was clearly too much for the over-sized rat with the showbiz penis. When Clogger made a concerted effort to reach the trunk of a weeping willow tree, leaning gracefully towards its own reflection in the still, brown water of the River Wear, the little dog started yapping with excitement. From a hastily burrowed den in the centre of a reed bed, up popped a frightened, mud-stained primate. It bounced back across the undergrowth, like a child on an inflated play-castle, prompting Clogger into a similar high-stepping routine. After cannoning apart the middle-aged billiard balls, the suspect sprinted-off along the towpath, into the fading evening light, closely followed by the flashing luminous-green gait of a cumbersome giant.

Unlike Clogger, the denim-legged suspect was built for speed. He also had the advantage of baseball boots and made substantial ground on his pursuer along the straight, beneath the castle and cathedral. At the half-mile mark, where the river loops acutely back on itself, the race-horse was enjoying a comfortable two-hundred-yard lead over the camel, whose armpits were discharging copiously into a hard-wearing, royal-blue shirt. The Kingsgate footbridge between Chads and Hatfield colleges marked the three-quarter-mile point and the first indication that the rodent's turn of speed was beginning to submit to

24

Clogger's superior stamina. By the time the quarry had circumnavigated the old city boundary and reached Elvet Bridge, at the neck of the mile-long river loop, his backward glances were becoming more frequent. Shirt almost completely saturated, Clogger chased up another stairway to a crescendo of variously pitched motorcar horns and zigzagged between the grid-locked traffic on the narrow carriageway.

Bridge seems very busy, he noticed, glancing into stationery infinity through a gently simmering carbon-monoxide haze.

On the other side of Elvet Bridge the tiring sprinter dropped again into the relative isolation of the river bank and followed the asphalt path east, passing the swimming baths to reach a series of wide-open sports grounds, known locally as the Racecourse. Maintaining his pace, the determined policeman pounded after the suspect reducing the lead with every stride. The College of St. Hilda and St. Bede came and went, then at roughly the two-mile point, the exhausted flasher succumbed. In shear desperation he veered-off to his immediate left and made a token attempt to cross the river, finally stumbling into a prone position in the cold, stony shallows of the shoreline.

"Don't scud me," the flasher gasped, turning onto his back to beg to his towering captor.

"You're nicked," panted Clogger, splashing towards the swaddle of wet denim and leather.

Equally saturated in perspiration, stone-age man grabbed a generous portion of collar, shirt and string vest, then dragged his captive backwards, on his bottom, to the sanctuary of the grassy shore. Although not Home Office approved, the restraining technique was effective. When Clogger finally paused to recover his wind, his prisoner was firmly bound around the thighs, just below two bleeding wet buttocks and a tiny, wrinkled penis.

She must have been carrying her microscope! Clogger mused, while his breathing pattern wound-down. What's that noise?

Immensely satisfied with his first-day achievement, Neolithic man rested for a few minutes then began the long haul back across the Racecourse towards Old Elvet, his trophy partially suspended by the neck. The effect of Clogger's enormous stride, to the tune of assorted car horns and chopping helicopter blades, forced the performing penis into a song and dance routine that involved a permanent single-handed grip on the waste-band of his soggy jeans.

Something heavy must be going on in the City! the giant concluded, catching his first glimpse of a huge, military bird hovering patiently five-hundred feet above Her Majesty's Prison.

It was five o'clock exactly when Bald Eagle left his office to boil the kettle in the unmanned station canteen. Timing their in-bound journeys to perfection, the three early-break patrol constables would normally have joined him within seconds of the late-day ritual, but on this occasion the facility remained ominously deserted for all of five minutes with only the yellow-peril turning up dead on time.

"Traffic's bad!" the Bowburn panda-driver announced, when he eventually barged through the canteen door holding his flat driving cap and a bulging, plastic sandwich-box. "Where is everybody?"

"No idea," answered the sergeant, munching at a table, his head in the Daily Mirror and his spare hand hovering close-by with a round of thick-cut bread ready for destruction. "Brew the tea."

When the other two members of the early-break contingent banged through the canteen door together, moaning in unison about deteriorating driving conditions, the sergeant temporarily abandoned his reading matter and lifted his perfectly aligned toupee in the direction of the Painted-Lady, sitting opposite.

"Who's in the box?"

"New boy," she muttered, nibbling on a dainty quarter-slice with its crust removed.

"Ah, yes," Bald Eagle replied, recalling his start-of-shift briefing. "Can he manage?"

"Should be alright!"

The sergeant sank back into his newspaper while the Bowburn mobile wrestled with the corner of an unopened milk carton. He was standing behind a serving-hatch lined with four standard-issue tin mugs and an elegant china cup, all steaming with hot tea.

"I wish they'd get proper bottles," blasted the budding mother when the wall-mounted telephone disturbed his manipulation of the hand-crafted spout.

"Canteen."

Slopping milk carton in one hand, grey telephone receiver in the other, the tea-maker spent ten seconds nodding to the equipment before lifting it away from his ear to focus on the preoccupied sergeant.

"Communications-room. Say they've had several calls about heavy traffic."

"Tell them to send the Elvet foot-patrol straight to the control box, Catchpole must be struggling," Bald Eagle rattled over the top of his newspaper.

"Did you hear that?"

"Yeah."

Clunk.

Fed and watered, a sticky, dog-eared pack of playing cards appeared from somewhere and the men started a four-handed game of brag while the lady traffic warden clicked out a tune on her latest knitting project.

"Sarge, you'd better come quick," blasted a very concerned communications-room anchor-man, banging through the canteen door to bring all refreshment activity to an abrupt halt. "Civil war has broken out at Nevilles Cross! The section office is under siege from angry motorists."

Bald Eagle slammed his fan of playing cards onto the green, Formica-topped kitchen table then scraped his tubular chair to one side to follow the radio operator out of the room. "Stand-by here, until further notice."

Off limits, the communications-room door was normally kept locked with general access restricted to the hatch, but in his panic to get to the canteen the anchor-man had ignored the convention. Wupert, the young fast-track inspector was already deep inside the facility, having stormed in from his office following a telephone call warning him that the adjoining sub-division of Chester-le-Street was also descending into unaccountable chaos.

27

"Situation weport, chop, chop," Wupert demanded, while the anchor-man resumed his prime seat in front of the radio consoles.

"City's at a standstill," rattled the second radio operator, desperately trying to communicate with the Elvet beat officer. "You're breaking-up," he moaned, frustrated by the intermittent nature of the reception."

"Elvet beat officer to foxtrot bravo control."

"Loud and clear, go ahead."

"PC Catchpole is not in the box, repeat not in the box."

"Who is in the box?" the inspector and sergeant demanded, pushing themselves between the shoulders of the side-by-side communication-room crew as if they were preparing for a group photograph.

"Nobody, sir," crackled the Elvet beat officer, responding respectfully to the change in transmission voice. "Door's wide-open, but there's nobody here."

"Where's Catchpole?"

"No idea," the sub-divisional radio console continued. "Wherever he's gone he's left his tunic, pocket-set and helmet...oh, and there's a pork pie in here as well, sir."

"Bleep, bleep, bleep."

A full year of special training at the police staff college had equipped Wupert with instant and decisive leadership qualities that kicked-in as soon as he was confronted with the emergency. He turned to face Bald Eagle, rapidly marshalled his thoughts, and then rattled out a series of strictly prioritised orders.

"How many men are in the canteen?"

"Three and the traffic warden."

"Send her to the Market Place to help the Elvet beat officer with the twaffic. Detail a man to each of the bwidges with instwuctions to stand-by. Tell the wemaining officer to open the major incident box and set up a tempowary command centre in the pawade-room."

While the communications-room duo looked over their shoulders in awe, the seasoned sergeant pondered the possibility of over-reaction.

"I think we should conduct some cursory enquiries first, Inspector," he ventured sceptically. "There may be another explanation!"

"No," Wupert asserted, "it's definitely abduction. Perfect diversion for a pwison bweak! Oh, and contact the supewintendent pronto."

Not having the benefit of razor-sharp powers of deduction, the second element of Wupert's proposition stunned his audience into action. With the haunting memory of John McVicar's breach of the apparently impenetrable E-Wing fresh in his mind, the sergeant jogged from the communications-room to the canteen with his hand on his head. The senior radio operator reached for a bright-red emergency telephone standing proudly on its own desk-top plinth and secured immediate contact with the force-wide control-room at nearby Akley Heads.

"Durham City here, implement Operation Drawbridge, duty inspector's instructions."

The order not only scrambled a search and rescue helicopter from R.A.F. Acklington in Northumberland, but it was also responsible for the re-deployment of the entire county contingent of on-duty police officers. As they hurried to every major road and rail terminal, the momentum of panic spread to the prison itself. Dog-handlers began to scour the perimeter wall, and the prison population were urgently banged-up and counted, accelerating the unstoppable force to top speed.

By the time the inspector reached the temporary command centre, Bald Eagle and his assistant were re-arranging the office furniture. Wupert duly took his place in the most comfortable chair at the head of the parade-room table, alongside a dedicated telephone extension and a thick pad of blank task chits. The sergeant sat on his superior's right-flank, adjusted his toupee then penned the date on a special log-sheet.

"Eighteen-hundred-hours, incident post established," dictated the dynamic leader of B-Relief, while the dog's body circled on his other flank, ready to run the first errand.

Feeling proud to be part of the lightning response to such a serious emergency, the sergeant finished scribbling the opening log-entry, then chirped, "All set, inspector."

In anticipation of another opportunity to demonstrate his command capability, Wupert's ego was also soaring when a peculiar dragging sound turned his attention to the partly open parade-room door. In such a highly-charged atmosphere, someone passing in the corridor ought not to have been significant, but a luminous-green flash was sufficient to disturb the equilibrium of the coiled-spring.

"Who was that?" Wupert demanded, urgently abandoning his comfortable chair to race across the floor.

An irregular, elongated wet smudge had dulled the buffed, brown linoleum in the corridor outside the major incident post. Carefully tracing its meandering route, the inspector lifted his disbelieving gaze just in time to see another flash of luminous-green, apparently towing a wet sack into the charge-room. The sinking feeling in his abdomen preceded a violent anal contraction as boy-wonder skidded after the vegetable merchant, marginally ahead of a tilting toupee.

"Where've you been?" Bald Eagle bawled before his gob-smacked leader could string a sentence together.

"I've made an arrest," declared Clogger. "Obstructing a police officer in the execution of his duty and indecent exposure," he continued proudly, holding a large, half-drowned rat aloft by its collar.

"But we thought you'd been abducted!" spluttered Wupert.

"Oh, no inspector, obstructed."

Overcome by competing emotions the inspector dropped his head and tried unsuccessfully to remonstrate.

"I thought a pwisoner had escaped from E-Wing," he sniffled defensively.

It was probably the sight of a grown man crying that triggered the giant's compassion. He instantly released his grip on the obnoxious rodent, allowing its limp skeleton to thud onto the wet, slippery floor. Then he put his arm affectionately around the senior officer's shoulders and squeezed reassuringly.

"Don't worry boss...I mean inspector. If anyone is over the wall, I'll help you find him."

2   SUDDEN LIFE

In the years since the Catchpole Crisis various barrack-room analysts have felt that April 1st, 1969 was not a complete success. Bent on softening-up the entire B-Relief command structure at an early stage, the KGB planners failed to take into account the sub-divisional superintendent's home address. Although he was called-out to take part in the debacle, the location of his comfortable semi on the outskirts of the City meant his usual ten-minute journey home in the family saloon, shortly after five o'clock, took over an hour. Convinced a road accident somewhere was to blame, he had just closed the up-and-over door of his detached, red-brick garage when his wife approached him. At that time of the year the couple would normally wander their budding garden for a few minutes before sitting down to an evening meal, but the detail of an urgent telephone message prompted the senior police officer into a military-style about-turn.

Fastidiously ignoring persistent queries from stationary motorists, he doubled back through the noisy City streets to the police station in full uniform, where unfortunately his arrival only coincided with the aftermath of Clogger's first strike. In some quarters this strategic slip is blamed for phase-one of the campaign moving into a second day, which in the interests of momentum, ought to have been consecutive. Whether the theory is valid or otherwise, the fact is that Clogger left the clock ticking through two inconveniently rostered rest-days and returned to duty riding an elderly, 250cc Royal Enfield motorcycle.

Gentleman Jim, strictly a nine-to-five Monday-to-Friday man, spent most of Wednesday and Thursday at his desk fending-off offensive telephone calls from anonymous Headquarters' staff, all of whom wanted to point out the cost of resourcing an aborted Drawbridge operation. Occasionally the sub-divisional head managed to focus on prosecution papers awaiting clearance, but his concentration soon reverted to his blotter where an extensive and elaborate series of doodles confirmed a preoccupation with his new problem-child.

Mentally prepared and determined not to over-react, at one-forty-five on Friday 4th April, Gentleman Jim was nevertheless startled by

31

the incredible noise of an approaching machine and rushed to his office window. Being careful not to reveal himself, he peeped down into the police yard to witness Clogger negotiate the ungated entrance from the direction of Elvet Crescent, in compliance with the one-way system. A tentative feeling of relief rippled through the superintendent's veins as he watched the transferee dismount the cumbersome motorcycle, then haul it onto its stand in the corner of the yard. More concerned about the machine's sensible resting place in relation to the fuel pump, Gentleman Jim could not see the steadily leaking sump and focused instead on the giant's choice of stocking-wear. Clearly not regulation black, royal-blue was a distinct improvement on luminous-green. When Clogger opened a pannier to remove his new plastic sandwich-box, albeit of gigantic proportions, the sub-divisional head's relief turned into a deceptive sense of progress.

I just need to persuade him to wear a proper crash helmet, Gentleman Jim pondered, returning to his desk with his own packed-lunch looming on his mental landscape.

Clogger also lulled Bald Eagle into a sense of false security when he was the first shift-member to enter the parade-room, exactly fifteen minutes before the start of his second tour of late-duty. Under the cautionary gaze of a synthetic thatch, the lumbering monster lobbed his helmet and sandwich-box onto the end of the big table, grinned broadly, then took pole position close to the sergeant's left shoulder.

"You should fit it with casters and tow it to work!" quipped a bemused colleague when he took his seat in the shadow of Clogger's refreshments.

After thirty seconds of shuffling and chair scraping, a deathly silence befell the room. Cocooned at the head of the table, Bald Eagle glanced at six, pen-poised faces and silently confirmed B-Relief was all present and correct. Then with appropriate dramatic effect, he threw back the hard, black cover of the lever-arch file in front of him and read out a synopsis of every incident since the relief was last on duty. Not bothering to look up, his machine-gun monotone continued until he reached a piece of key information such as the registration number of a stolen car or the description of a suspect. At that point a conditioned reflex kicked-in. Like a lorry driver changing gear, Bald Eagle lowered his voice, slowed his delivery and simultaneously raised his head to check on six busy pens.

Part one of the start-of-shift briefing over, the sub-divisional incident log was duly initialled and flicked shut.

"Right, allocation of assignments," the button-nosed supervisor continued, moving swiftly into the second-half of his daily routine.

Looking at each of the established members of B-Relief in turn, Bald Eagle rattled out two or three numbers then paused momentarily while they were also written down. The first represented the ground he wanted patrolling, either in the form of a city-centre foot beat or a peripheral panda area. The second was the start of the officer's break time, which on late-day alternated daily between 5 and 6 p.m. Finally the sergeant gave out to panda-car drivers a police service number of up to four digits, identifying an officer who required transport to the police station in time for night-duty at 10 p.m.

Recognising that Clogger was still unfamiliar with the sub-division, the tufty thatch left the newcomer's assignments until the end.

"PC Catchpole, I've given the city-desk constable four hours time-off, so that he can take his wife to hospital. I want you to cover for him and take your break at six. It will give you a chance to get to know our desk procedures, then you can double-up with the Framwelgate beat officer and continue your familiarisation of the city-centre. Do you understand?"

Clogger had just finished a zealous head-nodding sequence when the parade-room door opened and the not so bright-eyed inspector entered the arena to conduct part three of the ritual.

"Wemain seated, just a couple of items," he muttered without his characteristic vigour. "The superintendent has asked me to speak to you all about the twaffic contwol box. He wants me to wemind you to exercise extweme care on those occasions you are wequired to opewate the equipment. If something woutine is weported while you are otherwise engaged, it should be welayed by wadio to the communications-woom for allocation to another wesource. If immediate action is wequired, the console must be switched to

33

automatic before the box is vacated and a situation weport made by wadio at the earliest opportunity...needless to say loose items of police equipment must never be left unattended anywhere."

The sermon according to Wupert brought the eyes of the entire room down on Clogger. An uncomfortable silence persisted that seemed to demand an urgent explanation for reckless conduct that would ultimately reflect on the whole shift. Expecting a series of convoluted excuses and a strenuous denial of responsibility, the audience were completely wrong-footed when Clogger rose to his feet unsolicited, his hands in the air like a cornered gun-fighter.

"Sorry boss...I mean inspector, all my fault, I take full responsibility," the giant proffered with endearing sincerity. "My mother always said I was daft!"

A second pregnant pause ensued while the confused jury rapidly re-aligned their sympathies and considered the verdict.

"Well, I suppose you're not entirely to blame," Bald Eagle announced in a strange, fatherly tone. "The system is unique, perhaps I expected too much of you on your first day!"

"And let's not forget your awwest, Woger," sang the inspector, feeling obliged to reinforce the supervisory support Clogger was receiving. "Wan him into the gwound after a perfect stweet identification, jolly good show!"

As if to toast Clogger's health, glances were exchanged amid general nods and murmurs of agreement, then the briefing was dismissed with a rallying-call from a revitalised shift-leader.

"We should all learn a lesson from this and be couwageous enough to admit to our mistakes...oh, before you all go, one final thing. The Boy's Bwigade are wehearsing on Palace Gween this afternoon, it may cweate some parking difficulties."

An internal expression for the enclosed public counter, the city-desk was just inside the main door of the police station. It formed an ante-room to the parade-room and was manned on a twenty-four-hour basis by a series of elderly constables. Apart from dealing with the general public the post had a variety of other miscellaneous responsibilities, including the management of all lost and found property. When Clogger crashed into the chamber from the internal

34

door, he was greeted by a silver-haired lived-in uniform waiting patiently by a solitary desk.

"Nothing outstanding. Key to the cupboard," the officer rattled, pointing to a chrome key prominently positioned on the desk-top, in front of an Imperial typewriter and a wire document tray. "Do you want to check the contents, before I go?"

"No, I trust you," grinned the friendly giant while the maturing constable threw himself into a civilian Macintosh ready for his trek to St. Margaret's Hospital.

Alone in his turret, Clogger surveyed his grey, nicotine-stained surroundings and the equally drab office furniture. Apart from the desk and typewriter, the brown Marley-tiled floor supported a wardrobe-sized grey metal locker, marked; Transit and a free-standing unit of similar design that held the full range of day-to-day force stationery.

Mmm, pondered the hulk, lowering his eighteen stones into a creaky wooden chair. Seems like a cushy job!

Give or take a few local differences the function of a police station counter is fairly standard, but in the case of Durham City the isolation of the building away from any main thoroughfare, left it prone to long periods of inactivity. After bouncing his helmet on top of some miscellaneous papers in the wire tray, Clogger tackled his first spell of boredom by prising the lid off his lunch-box with his fingernails, to examine the bulky contents. Unable to resist the delights of a grossly over-filled beetroot sandwich, he had just managed to compress two crusts of brown bread between his big teeth when he was disturbed by a frustrated knock on the counter.

"Oh, terribly sorry, I didn't hear the buzzer," Clogger blurted, pebble-dashing the typewriter keyboard with particles of blood-red flesh.

"Buzzer ain't working," advised a casually dressed American gent, his head bowed under the weight of a bazooka-sized telephoto lens. "Can you direct me to little old Finchale Abbey, officer?"

The black-serge bear conscientiously leaned out of his cage to see if anybody else was waiting before taking a give-away tourist map from the top of a neat pile in the corner of the windowsill. Chewing

35

vigorously to clear his mouth, he searched for the popular attraction then ringed it with his pen and handed the sheet to the grateful explorer.

"Thank you officer. Have a nice day!"

"You're welcome," the public relations specialist replied after a final swallow.

A second period of calm allowed Clogger to finish his between-meals snack. I wonder what's wrong with the buzzer, he mused, squeezing the air-tight lid back over the remaining wedges of wholemeal bread.

A brief journey through the bowels of the ship and Clogger was in the police station foyer on the public-side of his counter, repeatedly pressing a bell-push screwed to the green-painted woodwork. Unable to get a tune out of the damned thing, the enterprising newcomer returned to his den scooping up a loose sheet of plain paper as he passed through the unoccupied parade-room. An extended rummage in the top draw of the city-desk uncovered a black felt-tipped pen and a roll of sticky tape. Meticulously, the budding commercial artist scrolled a temporary notice in his best copper-plate writing; Buzzer Out Of Order. A final flourish and he was back in open territory taping his handiwork next to the broken teat.

Perfect! he relished, stepping back to admire the creation.

The trickle of customers that afternoon all complied with the temporary sign, attracting Clogger's attention by knocking on the counter or the enclosing woodwork. A few minutes after five, he had just finished taking down details of a student's driving licence, test certificate and insurance cover, in response to a chit issued in another force area, when a well-dressed lady approached the fortification carrying a brass bugle.

"Found it on the pavement in the North Bailey," she said, thumping the highly-polished instrument down onto the counter in front of Clogger.

"It probably belongs to the Boy's Brigade," proffered the giant, "they've been practising on Palace Green this afternoon."

Snapping up a blank found property form from the stationery rack, Clogger recorded details of the find, then thanked the lady for her public-spirit with a suggestion that if the item was not claimed within three months she should consider taking music lessons and joining a brass band.

Smiling broadly the finder disappeared through the front door of the police station leaving the over-grown schoolboy to tinker with his new toy. Alone in his sentry box, he stood smartly to attention and lifted the gleaming bugle to his lips with the precision of a soldier. Intent on mobilising the entire police station at his very first attempt, Clogger's initial blast only produced a faint gurgling sound. A second effort sustained by abnormal lung capacity, resulted in a fragmented, farting rendition of the Last Post and a rapidly reddening complexion. When Clogger's ballooning cheeks turned shiny blue, he abandoned his music career in favour of mundane desk duties and marched on the property transit cupboard brandishing the little key. Just about to put the mysterious instrument to bed for the night, the telephone disturbed his train of thought.

"City-desk, PC Catchpole."

"Is that the police station?"

"Yes."

"I've lost my bugle!" a distressed youngster declared.

"Where did you lose it?"

"In the Bailey I think, after the parade."

"Don't worry, I've got it here."

"Oh, great," the caller concluded, relieved of the potential impact on his pocket-money. "I'll collect it as soon as I can."

In anticipation of the anxious youngster attending the police station at break-neck speed, Clogger quiet reasonably decided to leave the bugle handy in readiness for its imminent collection by the rightful owner. He placed the found property form face down on the public counter with the receipt section fully exposed and ready for completion. Then, to hold the paperwork firm, he plonked the salivating bell-end of the instrument on top of the document and resumed his seat with the satisfaction of having finalised another major enquiry.

At six o'clock, after a tedious afternoon with his wife in out-patients, the regular city-desk officer resumed duty just in time to witness his stand-in give another object lesson in public relations.

"Calm down love, don't panic," Clogger reassured a distressed eighty-year-old on the telephone. "Read out what it says on the front."

When the caller's whoops of sobbing subsided into heavy sniffing, Clogger solved his second important case of the day.

"Its from the tax office, darling" he advised, "take it and show your neighbours. If they don't understand, bring it in here and we'll have a look at it for you."

An extended silence punctuated by milder sniffs of agreement seemed to suggest that Clogger's technique had impacted favourably. "It's not the end of the world, sweet-heart. Don't forget, if you have a problem bring it in here. Ask for the city-desk."

"Matter of life and death! I'll see to it," Clogger's relief said warmly, recognising the nature of the crisis while he levered himself out of his Macintosh. "Anything else?"

"Only that bugle," answered Clogger, pointing to the counter while he replaced the telephone receiver and vacated the hot-seat. "The owner is coming in to collect it."

Burdened by helmet and sandwich-box, Clogger made his way to the canteen at the back of the building to find Bald Eagle and the rest of the early-break contingent still playing cards. Nodding and clicking on the periphery of a smoky mushroom, the Painted-Lady occasionally scrutinised the outstanding double-kitty at the centre of the extended proceedings. It had somehow interfered with the sergeant's obsession for punctuality, and allowed the traffic warden to finish the left sleeve of a chunky sweater she was knitting for her son.

"Shush," demanded the four-handed chorus when Clogger slammed into what was essentially a family-sized kitchen and dining room.

The Framwelgate foot-beat officer and a panda-car driver were already on the other side of the serving-hatch, washing tin mugs and refilling the big, chrome kettle at the stainless-steel sink unit next to the cooker.

"Tea, Clogger?" asked the foot-patrol officer, designated to look after the giant for the rest of the day.

"Yeah, please," he grinned, attracting a second unanimous call for quiet.

While the custodian of Framwelgate used the hissing chrome kettle to charge a metal teapot, an almighty roar signalled the end of the nail-biter. Beaming from ear to ear the Bowburn panda-car driver cupped his hands around three pounds in mixed coinage and an IOU scribbled on a dismembered cigarette packet.

"Needn't go to the bank this week," the delighted winner declared, prompting the Painted-Lady to return her knitting to its paper carrier bag.

The sergeant glanced uneasily at his wrist-watch. "Right, back to work," he instructed, triggering the speedy exodus of half of his operational team.

Once the ear-piercing sound of scraping chair legs had subsided, the late-break constables were assailed by sudden tranquillity. As the Framwelgate beat officer led three slopping tea mugs from the kitchen area to a dining table, mention of the bank made him reflect on the state of his own finances.

"I preferred it when we were paid fortnightly in cash," he grumbled. "My money never seems to last the full month under this new system."

Opening his sandwich-box Clogger gazed at the remaining door-stops. "It was the same for me last month," he confided, lifting a beetroot briefcase to his mouth. "Got a letter from the bank manager saying that he wanted to see me."

Temporarily mesmerised by the size and choice of his new colleague's menu, a few seconds elapsed before the late-break panda-car driver contributed to the conversation.

"What did he say to you?"

"Said I was over-drawn by seven pounds," the friendly giant announced.

"Did you have to pay it back?"

"Oh yes, there and then," asserted Clogger, drawing the undivided attention of his two financially naive workmates.

39

"How did you manage to do that before pay-day?"

"Easy, I wrote him a cheque," concluded the City whiz-kid, his mouth releasing a chunk of beetroot to its own devices.

The high-flying financier tackled the rest of his sandwiches with the enthusiasm of a hungry dog devouring broth, but his two colleagues were more hesitant. A recurring preoccupation with the mechanics of the banking system to which they had only recently been introduced, dominated their thoughts for the rest of the forty-five-minute break. When Clogger finally gnawed clean the core of a Granny Smith and launched it roughly in the direction of the pedal-bin, his Framwelgate minder was still scrutinising a network of ceiling cracks, and the panda-car driver was gently sipping tea trying to remember the guidelines printed on the inside cover of his own, newly issued cheque-book. Even the giant's clumsy attempt at shuffling the sticky station playing cards didn't tempt the pair from their deliberations, so Clogger abandoned the idea in favour of a dog-eared copy of Men Only that was part of the canteen furniture.

It was a touch chilly and the light was beginning to fade when Clogger and his colleague donned their chrome-topped headgear and marched out of the front door of the police station, casually admiring the new ornament on the public counter. Radio receivers pulsating in unison, the duo strode the well-trodden path through St. Cuthbert's churchyard onto Old Elvet, then they crossed Elvet Bridge into Saddler Street and the Market Place. The rush-hour traffic had dissipated, noticeable by the laid-back rotations of the Painted-Lady in the lunar module. Even with the delicate nature of her mask, she managed a careful smile when Clogger's rugged bone structure crossed her line of vision. In slow deliberate step the Framwelgate foot-patrol moved on Silver Street and over Framwelgate Bridge into its assigned territory.

"Fighting Cocks is heaving, as usual," Clogger's minder remarked, as the couple approached the vibrant frontage of a popular student haunt. "Let's show our faces, then I'll take you to the bus and railway stations."

40

Seconds later the familiarisation plan was thwarted by the stereo effect of side-by-side pocket-sets. "Framwelgate foot-patrol from foxtrot bravo control."

"Go ahead."

"Make your way to forty-two, four two, The Avenue, treble nine call."

"Received, what's it all about?" queried the regular beat officer, urgently leading the way up the steep cobbles of Crossgate.

"Concern about neighbours, wants to see a policeman."

"Roger."

"Bleep, bleep, bleep."

Not as savage as Crossgate, The Avenue was also a five-minute test of cardiovascular fitness. When the out-of-breath uniformed twins arrived at their terraced destination a wholesome lady wearing a floral pinny gasped a sigh of relief from behind a tall, Victorian bay window.

"I think there's something wrong next door," she mouthed desperately, when the robust front door opened of its own volition.

"Take your time, and tell me what you think is wrong," Clogger's colleague insisted, ushering the matriarch backwards into her own high, stained-glass lobby.

"They're both in their eighties and he's a bit, you know. She has difficulty controlling him. I've told her to get help, but she won't..."

"Carry on," interrupted the regular beat officer, sensing a time-consuming side-track.

"Well, about half an hour ago I heard a terrible commotion, you know, shouting and banging, and then it all went quiet. I've been round to see if everything is alright, but I can't get an answer."

"Which part of the house do they live in?"

"The kitchen, at the back. Come through and I'll show you."

The concerned informant opened a delicately leaded internal glass door and led the way along a never-ending strip of hall carpet, edged with yellow linoleum. Passing through a factory for the production of home-made preserves that doubled as the family kitchen, the intrepid law-enforcers crossed a small concrete yard into a narrow cobbled

41

lane. The adjoining yard gate was standing open, but the rear door of the next door neighbours' house was firmly locked.

"Can't see a thing, the light isn't on," Clogger advised, peering through the kitchen window.

"They definitely didn't go out?" asked Clogger's colleague, seeking confirmation while he considered the best means of gaining access to the property.

"Oh no, they hardly ever go out. I do all their shopping."

Like the starter at an athletics meeting, the floral pinny flagged an assault on the rear door of number forty-four that would have made an international second-row forward proud. Head to one side, Clogger stepped back a couple of yards, dropped his right shoulder and bulldozed into the barrier with the finesse of a rampant bull. Had it not been for the elderly couple's obsession with security, and the array of internal bolts and chains added to periodically over the years, Clogger's strategy might have proved successful, albeit expensive. In the event he rebounded back to his exact starting position only this time his bottom took the brunt of the impact. When the search and rescue expert eventually got to his feet, slightly winded and bruised, his colleague was drawing his truncheon from its special trouser-leg pocket. Like the Monarch appointing a new knight, the other constable broke a pane of glass in the kitchen window, poked away the jagged left-overs then put his hand through and released the catch.

"Give me a leg up," he instructed.

Some items of crockery on the draining board immediately underneath the kitchen window, presented a minor problem in the dark, but that apart entry was relatively straight-forward and within a couple of minutes Clogger's colleague was feeling his way through a contemporary metallic melody behind the back door.

"Where's the light-switch?" he asked the anxious neighbour, as soon as he reappeared in the small yard.

The neighbour pushed by the officer and flicked on the kitchen light. "Oh, Albert, are you alright?" she called, shaken by the silent presence of a hollow-featured old man sitting motionless at the kitchen table.

Clad in blue-striped pyjamas and completely unaware of his surroundings, the disorientated eighty-something-year-old had his gaze fixed on a meat-hook, the only item on the table in front of him. His deep sunken eyes were dilated and strangely unresponsive beneath a spray of wildly erect white hair.

"Albert, what have you done? Where's Mary?" the neighbour demanded, trying desperately to make contact with another planet.

The old man grunted incoherently, then started to tremble with cold.

"Put a blanket around him," ordered Clogger's colleague, prompting the floral pinny to sprint back to her own house.

With one arm resting compassionately on a frail shoulder, the regular Framwelgate beat officer contemplated the meat-hook. Naturally it didn't take long for the personal safety of the householder's elderly wife to enter the equation.

"Search the rest of the house, Clogger," he urgently instructed.

Abandoning his helmet on the cracked, plastic-coated tablecloth, Clogger barged out of the kitchen into the hall and fondled the bulbous, porcelain light-switch. It illuminated a dark, wood-grained door surrounded by brown-varnished wallpaper, in vogue a century earlier. The door led to a cold living room appointed with ageing furniture that smelled faintly of mildew.

"She's not in here," called Clogger, before tackling the standard-sized staircase with his customary triple leap.

On the landing another period light-switch with a tiny brass pin exposed a series of four identical wood-grained doors, only one of which was closed. Instinct steered the lumbering hulk towards it. He twisted the spherical handle and fondled again for illumination. Another click and the circumstances of the domestic drama were apparently complete.

"She's up here," Clogger shouted, his eyes scanning the gruesome crime.

Dominated by a thickly-blanketed double bed complete with ornate brass head-board and four acorn-shaped knobs, the master-bedroom was lit by a pink globe suspended from the ceiling on three chains. It was sufficient for Clogger to see the lower-half of a human

43

leg protruding from underneath the iron-work. Knee down and shoeless, a loose, unsuspended nylon stocking partially covered a crepe surgical bandage bound tightly around an ageing calf.

Being careful not to disturb the murder scene, the first officer stepped cautiously forward, bent down on a thread-bare bedside-rug and made a further visual examination. He could just see a network of varicose veins and the elasticated bottom of a blue bloomer. The rest of the motionless body was jammed between the bed springs and the cold linoleum floor.

Serious incident! Clogger decided, carefully retracing his steps to switch off the light and close the door.

When he turned to stand guard on the bedroom and properly protect it from unauthorised or unnecessary interference, the Framwelgate beat officer was already at the stair-head having left the prime suspect in the custody of the caring neighbour.

"What's the score?" he asked with deep concern.

"Body under the bed, elderly female," answered Clogger, removing his note-book from his breast pocket to scribble a contemporaneous record of events.

Clogger's positive assessment somehow deterred the regular man from giving a non-essential but often advisable second opinion. Instead he pressed the button on the transmitter part of his pocket-radio and released the short telescopic aerial.

"Framwelgate foot-patrol to foxtrot bravo control."

"Go ahead."

"Forty-four The Avenue, suspicious death, request the attendance of supervision."

"Roger, stand-by."

Bleep, bleep, bleep.

Once he'd set the ball rolling, Clogger's partner then identified his own immediate role in the affair and hurried back down the stairs into the kitchen to supervise the elderly man. Although mentally disturbed, he was the most likely person to have committed the crime and should not be in the hands of an untrained civilian.

A few tense minutes elapsed before Clogger heard a car screech to a halt at the front of the house. At the suggestion of his colleague the friendly neighbour was waiting at her own front door to pilot the sergeant and inspector to the scene of the tragedy.

"Up the stairs, sir," the Framwelgate beat officer rattled, when Wupert and the walking haystack appeared in the kitchen doorway.

Leaving Clogger's colleague to pacify the elderly suspect, the supervisory duo climbed the main staircase in order of seniority and confronted the sentry.

Clogger looked efficiently at his wrist-watch, lifted his pen to his note-book and wrote; 8pm - arrival of sergeant and inspector.

Suitably impressed, the inspector said, "Give me a situation weport, Woger."

Paraphrasing the contents of his note-book, Clogger continued to impress his shift-leader. "Body of an elderly female under the bed, boss...I mean inspector. Husband is apparently senile. He was sitting downstairs in the kitchen with a meat-hook when we forced entry."

"Vewy good, Woger. Let me see the body."

Clogger made another efficient entry in his note-book then opened the bedroom door and switched on the light. "Don't touch anything," he cautioned.

"Bad show," the senior supervisor concluded, after a thirty-second scan of the protruding surgical bandage. "Sergeant, call out the police surgeon to certify death, then inform the CID and Technical Aids...oh, and get someone to telephone the supewintendent."

Bald Eagle checked his thatch, then wandered slowly back down the staircase rattling the inspector's instructions into his radio transmitter.

"Well done, Woger," the inspector praised, as Clogger turned off the light and secured the bedroom door again. "Second most important wule in these sort of situations; pwotection and contwol of the cwime scene, otherwise it becomes a circus and we all end up chasing our tails."

It wasn't long before the circus started to assemble. Tasked by the communications-room anchor-man, acting on his own initiative, first to arrive was a plain blue utility van carrying a full range of miscellaneous equipment, including portable flood lighting. Bitter experience had taught Bald Eagle the importance of establishing a

45

forward control point. He had just managed to open the extensively bolted front door of the house for that very purpose, when he was confronted by a civilian handy-man called Walter, drawing a robust, general purpose, fibreglass coffin from the wide-open rear doors of the vehicle.

"Not yet," the sergeant shouted, in full view of a steadily building circle of rubber-necks.

Second to arrive in the wrong order of priority was a similarly plain Hillman van filled with aluminium carrying cases of every size and description.

"Photographs only at this stage, the police surgeon isn't here yet," Bald Eagle called to another technical zealot, dressed in white, disposable overalls.

Meticulously recording details of the unknown spaceman, Clogger had just allowed him and his lens into the master-bedroom when Gentleman Jim climbed the staircase in civilian clothes.

"Who was first on the scene?"

"Me, boss...I mean superintendent, death hasn't been certified yet," Clogger advised, diplomatically discouraging the sub-divisional head from forensically contaminating the crime.

Equally impressed with Clogger's management of the situation, Gentleman Jim moved a few yards along the landing to receive a verbal briefing from Wupert in typically clipped, machine-gun rhetoric. Adopting the posture of a guardsman, the friendly giant posed proudly in the bedroom doorway with his pen and note-book at the ready, while the white ghost moved stealthily around the protruding leg, flashing from every conceivable angle. In the kitchen the Framwelgate beat officer placed a loose sheet of clean newspaper over the meat-hook, to preserve any traces clinging to its surface, then encouraged the fragile suspect to sip tea prepared by the friendly neighbour. At the front door, Bald Eagle presided over the source of a cutting draught that penetrated every corner of the dwelling. He was subconsciously checking the alignment of his thatch, after an abortive attempt to disperse the growing army of rubber-necks, when a Rover 90 tagged onto the end of the line of Police vehicles parked on the road outside.

"Doctor's here," the sergeant shouted, preparing everyone for a sudden break in the procedural stalemate. "Would you take a look at the suspect first, sir?" Bald Eagle asked, assailed by the smell of malt. "He's in the kitchen and appears very distressed."

"Yes," the white-haired professional snapped, steering his leather bag along the long, narrow hall.

Two minutes later the police surgeon emerged from the kitchen as positively as he had entered and stormed back towards Bald Eagle.

"Dementia," he blasted, "I know the family. Where's the body?"

"Straight up the stairs, sir."

When the doctor reached the master-bedroom, Clogger had already recorded his presence and efficiently pushed the door open to allow the medic immediate access. The photographer stopped what he was doing and took a back seat while the superintendent and Wupert lined-up on the doctor's flank.

"Only saw her last week," the police surgeon remarked, abandoning his bag on the bed-side rug to get down on all-fours. "Diabetes was playing up."

"Try not to disturb anything, doctor," Clogger cautioned head and shoulders above Wupert in the back row.

Right-hand on top to support himself, the police surgeon put his left-hand underneath the bed to probe for and confirm the absence of a pulse. Almost immediately the down-turned knee-joint of the protruding surgical bandage flexed and lifted the calf muscle out of its feeding position, like the neck of a swan. The foot rotated momentarily as if to assess the intruders, then thudded back down onto the floor, shaking a dishevelled nylon stocking further down the leg.

"Fucking hell, doctor," Clogger barked, astonished that the police surgeon should be indulging in medical trickery at such an inappropriate time.

"Coma," diagnosed the doctor. "Probably the diabetes! Help me get her out."

For the second time in a week Gentleman Jim lost his characteristic calm and turned on his inspector. "She's still alive, you bloody fool," he snarled, inflicting debilitating embarrassment on the university graduate.

Gobsmacked, Wupert turned sharply around to stare up at his incompetent first officer.

"Don't look at me," insisted Clogger, shaking his head from side to side. "I never said she was dead."

Chaos ensued thereafter. The superintendent assisted the police surgeon to carefully pull the elderly pensioner from underneath the bed. Then the doctor administered an injection while the sub-divisional head unhooked her right index finger from the handle of a china chamber pot. In the meantime Wupert anteloped out of the bedroom to the stair head.

"Chop, chop, call an ambulance," he bawled to Bald Eagle, who was preoccupied at the front door with an inquisitive flock, and a civilian handy-man proudly stroking his number-one transit coffin.

When the paramedics finally arrived and stretchered the casualty down the stairs and out of the house, the detective inspector and the detective sergeant joined the entourage. Cloned in blue Macintosh coats and Trilby hats, with the smell of cigarette smoke and beer encircling them, they looked-on in bewilderment while one of the ambulance crew slammed shut the rear doors of the white Bedford and ran to the driver's seat.

"We were told it was a suspicious death," puzzled the senior detective, his face flashing to the rhythm of a blue strobe disappearing in the direction of County Hospital.

"Oh, don't worry...that isn't for another ten minutes yet," Gentleman Jim growled, vacating the front door of the dwelling with the departing police surgeon. "Thank you, doctor," he continued, his blue-veined nose locking onto Bald Eagle. "Finish up here sergeant, and get social services out to the old boy. Where's the inspector?"

The superintendent urgently rotated his head to find Wupert standing sheepishly behind him, in Clogger's shadow. "Put him under house arrest and bring him straight to my office."

Police discipline regulations don't provide for house arrest, but Gentleman Jim's uncharacteristic finger-wagging discouraged the academic from pointing out his error.

The sub-divisional head left the scene in his private car, closely followed by Wupert driving the supervision vehicle with his unofficial prisoner hunched in the front passenger-seat. The sergeant and the Framwelgate beat officer hung on for social services and the emergency glazier, while the technical aids officer moaned to the detective inspector about the roll of film he had wasted.

"Only glad I didn't get round to taking forensic samples," he muttered, before driving off.

Last to disperse was Walter who didn't seem to understand why he'd been marginalised. Unable to show-off his neatly labelled equipment, it was only when the sergeant closed the front door in his face that he realised his services were no longer required.

By the time Gentleman Jim weaved his way through the single-file, cobbled city-centre streets and reached his designated parking place in the police station yard, Wupert and Clogger were on his immediate tail. Apart from a silly grin and a suggestive grunt from Clogger, when the supervision car was acknowledged by the Painted-Lady in the traffic control box, perfect silence prevailed throughout the journey.

"I suggest you be open and fwank about your mistake, Woger, like you were about Tuesday. You know you must always check for a pulse first, when dealing with a suspicious death," the inspector advised, decamping the little Mini saloon to follow the superintendent.

For reasons of convenience the three men filed around the side of the building towards the traditional blue lamp illuminating the front door. In order of seniority Gentleman Jim was the first to encounter the steps and barge purposefully through the inner swing-doors into the public reception area. Intending to march straight to his office, he was fazed by the sight of the city-desk constable crouching over the prostrate body of another elderly lady, lying on the floor immediately below the counter. A surge of adrenaline propelled the sub-divisional head to the side of the resuscitating officer, who was making a final concerted effort using the mouth-to-mouth method.

When the inspector came on the scene a split-second later he was similarly fazed, but Clogger instantly seized the opportunity to redeem himself. He pushed past Wupert, lurched to the other side of the body and dropped onto his knees beside an abandoned set of dentures and an official looking letter from the Inland Revenue. While the city-desk officer supported the patient's tilting head and frantically puffed air into her lungs, Clogger carefully lifted a wizened hand from the floor and released a vice-like grip on a Boy's Brigade bugle.

"Oh, this one is definitely dead, boss...I mean superintendent," he sighed with two fingers expertly positioned on the patient's inner wrist.

3   SUMMARY INJUSTICE

Gentleman Jim's plan to give Clogger the mother of all bollockings in the presence of Wupert didn't materialise. After the really dead body was removed from the reception area, he was overcome by a strange, physical weakness that forced him to make his way tentatively across the yard to the adjacent police club and consume two large whiskies. The medicine had some remedial effect, although it didn't completely relieve a nasal tremor that impacted adversely on his normally confident delivery. Consequently the highly-regarded superintendent wasn't able to indulge in customary small-talk with his off-duty colleagues, and went straight home amid a flurry of whispers.

After a restless night, the zombie returned unexpectedly to his office early on Saturday morning and shut himself inside. Divorced from the telephone and day-to-day trivia, he began to frantically draft and re-draft a lengthy coroner's report. By lunchtime his waste paper basket was overflowing with crumpled foolscap and the more pronounced facial tremor had travelled to both hands. No matter how many times he tried, he was unable to pen any justification. The cold realisation that a bugle, provided in place of a broken buzzer, had contributed to the death of an old lady with a heart condition, pushed Gentleman Jim into total body spasm. Today the experience would warrant professional post-trauma counselling, but all those years ago the notion was an admission of incompetence and the symptoms simply marked a personality change that would stay with him for the last weeks of his life.

Being a younger man, the impact of phase-one on the inspector was less acute. He also had the advantage of an academic wife who helped him analyse and understand his predicament, nevertheless there was a noticeable deterioration in his approach to leadership, particularly his vitality and enthusiasm for decision-making. Mental trauma strikes different people in different ways. Conversely, Bald Eagle started to lose his obsession with the alignment of his ridiculous toupee, but the behavioural improvement was short-lived. He bought a state-of-the-art pocket calculator and spent every free moment crunching numbers relating to his personal finances, in an attempt to determine the optimum hour of his retirement.

Over the years at the annual get-together in *The Shakespeare*, the B-Relief veterans have proposed and debated numerous explanatory models to account for Clogger's infiltration into the fabric of British society. By 1999 though, through the natural wastage of drunken participants and shear theoretical exhaustion, one formula became dominant. Indeed, it was the basis of the three- hundred page letter sent to the Home Office by the action committee chairman, but it was far from perfect in terms of empirical explanation. The softening-up of the command structure was straight-forward enough, but phase-two has always been ill-fitting and contentious, not least because it seemed to be an unnecessary diversion. B-Relief personnel, sub-divisional resources and other hardware were all outstanding targets when Clogger temporarily veered-off in the direction of the judiciary and the church, taking full advantage of a phenomena known as quick-change-over.

In most conventional three-week shift systems, operating on eight-hour tours of duty, the month consists of a week of earlies, a week of lates and a week of nights with nine rest-days dispersed between. Inevitably, at some convenient point in the pattern, the Relief must forgo their normal sixteen hours down-time and return to duty after only eight hours rest. In the case of Durham City it occurred at the end of the late-shift week when a ten o'clock finish on Sunday evening was followed by a six o'clock start on Monday morning. Another factor supporting the proposition phase-two was opportunist emanates from a local policing policy. It involved two men crewing a large, blue Commer van for the last four hours of each late-shift on Friday, Saturday and Sunday evenings. The function continued into the first four hours of night-shift and was officially referred to as team-policing, but expressions such as pub-patrol or meat-wagon were much more common.

Following Clogger's sub-divisional debut, the consensus of opinion at all levels of management was that he should be confined to the limits of the police station for the rest of his natural life, and never again thrust on an unsuspecting public. However, in the absence of a firm order on his future deployment, he was Bald Eagle's automatic choice to take-over in the meat-wagon with a seasoned and trusted constable who normally manned the Ferryhill panda-car.

At least I've got him marked, grimaced the ginger wig after he briefed Clogger, while they find him a position in the used envelope department!

The ploy very nearly worked. Assisted by the most effective policeman in the history of the service; heavy rain, the meat-wagon had a very quiet Saturday, but on Sunday 6th a break in the traditional April weather was the catalyst for some high-spirits.

Clogger and his new minder were scheduled for an early refreshment break on their last 2pm-10pm tour of duty that week. At six o'clock prompt, the duo left the canteen and wandered out of the back door of the police station, across the yard to the big garage. While his colleague carefully reversed the meat-wagon out of its special bay and manoeuvred towards the ageing fuel pump, Clogger lurked in the middle of the yard cuddling his helmet, contemplating the improvement in weather conditions.

"Where's all that oil come from?" the giant's immaculate colleague muttered, elbowing himself carefully from the driver's door to avoid a sticky, black patch on the crumbling, asphalt surface.

Clogger was still engrossed in slow-moving cumulo-stratus when the meat-wagon commander zeroed the clockwork gauge on a green, free-standing contraption that resembled a nineteenth-century post box. Signalling for full steam ahead, he pulled the brass handle back and forth a couple of times, kicking the equipment into life. Petrol filler-cap in one hand, medieval hand-gun in the other, Clogger's new minder casually scanned his surroundings while the pump laboriously churned petrol from an elevated storage tank somewhere.

"Something is losing oil!" remarked the tidy-minded driver, unwittingly plotting the parking habits of a nearby Royal Enfield while the pump continued to chug and vibrate.

"My motorbike uses a lot of oil," Clogger confirmed, finalising his meteorological deliberations to take his seat in the cockpit. "I don't know where it all goes," he pondered as his colleague slammed the monotonous fuel pump into silence and screwed back the vehicle's filler-cap. "I've even tried a longer dipstick, but I still can't find it!"

On week days socialising in Durham City was limited to university students and local people, but the complexion changed dramatically at weekends. Hard-working, hard-hitting miners and their womenfolk, from peripheral pit villages, tended to descend on half a dozen well known public houses by service bus. The purpose of the special weekend patrol was to support the city-centre beat officers by responding rapidly to reports of disorder, and to maintain a high police profile in the vicinity of the bus station. Apart from the deterrent value, the latter function also provided an opportunity for the meat-wagon crew-members to gather vital intelligence about the arrival of likely troublemakers. Clogger and his colleague were conspicuously parked in North Road, apparently engaged in the secondary role, when their observations were interrupted by the radio.

"Turn yours off," instructed the meat-wagon commander, screwing-up his face in response to ear-piercing feed-back.

"Elvet foot-patrol, location?" the remaining receiver crackled.

"New Elvet"

"Confer with supervision, one zero minutes"

Bleep, bleep, bleep.

"Bald Eagle's out and about," Clogger's partner advised, anticipating the start of a series of routine supervisory checks.

Another twenty minutes of serious surveillance and the meat-wagon crew were nearing the end of their early evening intelligence gathering exercise.

"Elvet foot-patrol from foxtrot bravo control."

"Go ahead."

"Is the sergeant still with you?"

"Affirmative."

"Make your way to number eleven Hallgarth Street, report of excessive noise in student accommodation."

"Do you want us to attend?" interrupted Clogger's colleague, anxious for some action at the end of a quiet week.

"Negative, two en-route, stand-by for a situation report," the communications-room operative decided, knowing that if he moved a resource unnecessarily sod's law would kick-in.

Bleep, bleep, bleep.

Clogger's conscientious approach to note-taking continued to impress, but the team-leader noticed the use of a numerical technique to replace traditional descriptive jargon. Uncomfortable because he wasn't up to date with the new system, presumably developed in Bishop Auckland division, Clogger's minder remained in the dark until a group of mini-skirted adolescents alighted an in-bound bus from Coxhoe. After totting up columns of figures, Clogger was clearly satisfied with the result of his research.

"Definitely the Kelloe girls," he glowed.

"Go ahead, Elvet foot-patrol"

"You're breaking-up, I can't hear you, which college?"

"Understand you want a key-holder called-out from St. John's"

"Affirmative."

"Stand-by."

"Bleep, bleep, bleep."

"Two points clear on tits," the social researcher continued, double-checking his calculations to justify his earlier conclusion.

"Team patrol from foxtrot bravo control."

"Go ahead," answered Clogger's colleague, simultaneously reaching for a special switch on the dashboard.

"Better make your way to eleven Hallgarth Street. Elvet foot-patrol and the sergeant are struggling to gain entry and we've had a second report of masked men decamping by a side window."

"Roger."

Fully charged with adrenaline, the meat-wagon commander raced the vehicle towards Framwelgate Bridge discharging blue flashes across the roof tops. When one strobe ricocheted off a wall-mounted closed-circuit television camera, the traffic warden in the control box immediately switched the lights to green, clearing the vehicle's path through the Market Place and over Elvet Bridge. Screaming to the top of New Elvet it was Clogger, riding shotgun in the front passenger-seat, who first noticed a distinctive cardboard hat staggering across the road at the junction of Church Street and Hallgarth Street. With the stability of a newly dropped foal his heavily-buttoned and very colourful eminence was a serious traffic hazard.

"What's he doing off his column?" Clogger queried, stepping out of the meat-wagon to investigate.

Encouraged by a very appreciative student audience queuing outside Sweaty Betty's fish and chip shop, the famous historical figure whisked-off his headgear with a flourish, then bowed in front of the lumbering, uniformed giant.

"Good evening ossifer. Admiral Lord Nelson," he greeted incoherently, amid loud cheering.

While the illustrious seafarer was returning to an unsteady upright position, Clogger whisked-off his own headgear with an equally energetic flourish.

"Good evening, PC 1328 Catchpole at your service," the giant responded, before the chrome knob on the top of his police helmet connected with the top-dead-centre of a noble head, reproducing the sound of a dropped coconut.

When his lordship shuddered to a sitting position in the middle of the carriageway repeatedly rubbing his scalp, traffic stopped in both directions in awe of Clogger's technique. In the presence of a significantly less enthusiastic chip-shop audience, he opened the rear doors of the Commer van with one hand and applied an ear-lock and screw to the prisoner with the other. Anti-clockwise manipulation of the lobe encouraged the admiral to his feet then an opposite and equal force, intended to re-tighten the entire hearing organ in its socket, secured him pole position on one of the wooden bench seats. After he launched the cardboard headgear at its owner and slammed shut the meat-wagon doors, Clogger took a second bow in the direction of Sweaty Betty's and reduced audience participation to a stony silence.

Continuing along Hallgarth Street with the groaning Sea Lord safely behind the dividing grille, the meat-wagon next encountered the Elvet beat officer. Surrounded by the usual clutch of rubber-necks, he had the caped-crusader's assistant, Robin, firmly pinned against a garden fence in a more traditional arm-lock and bar.

56

"I can manage here, give Bald Eagle a hand," the foot-patrol shouted, as Clogger leapt from the passenger-door and waded into the fray.

Clogger turned on his heal to antelope a further twenty yards along the street towards an all-in wrestling bout officiated over by Kent Walton and a string of volunteer referees and seconds. During the first round Batman had obviously been deprived of his super-human powers. A very bald, fourteen-stone challenger sporting three stripes, who Clogger didn't immediately recognise, was sitting patiently on the caped-crusader's sternum having won by one fall and a thoracic rupture.

"Oh, it's you boss...I mean sarge," Clogger blurted. "You'll catch your death like that," he continued, his surprise turning to concern as he barged across the pavement towards the gutter.

Rolling gently along a path of least resistance, Bald Eagle's helmet was home to a small rodent with a ginger-brown synthetic coat. Scooping up the receptacle he leapt back to the panting victor and promptly plonked the animal wrong-way-round on Bald Eagle's gleaming scalp. Then, to secure the insulation and keep out the cold, he leaned over his supervisor and pushed and twisted the headgear firmly back into its proper position. The cracking and grinding of vertebra at the base of the skull prompted a very technical and extremely succinct verbal command that even took the squadron of rubber-necks by surprise.

"Clogger," the sergeant screamed, "fuck off. Go and check the house."

Miffed by Bald Eagle's lack of gratitude in the cool evening air, the giant dropped his head, pushed his way through the audience and ambled a further thirty yards along the street.

Can't do right for doing wrong he sulked, approaching a shabby three-bedroomed house, clearly pivotal to the evening's events.

It had a small uncultivated front garden with no gate. The front door was standing open and all the lights were burning. When the giant stepped over the threshold to investigate he was consumed by a warm, smoky atmosphere with a pungent after-taste of beer and perspiration. Only an open window, creaking on its hinges

57

somewhere, broke the deathly silence of a recently abandoned ship. Stealthily negotiating a trail of empty beer bottles, Clogger viewed a series of giant pumpkins, hand-painted on the walls of an otherwise drab hall. At the end of a short passage a wall-mounted Keep Left sign pointed to the communal mess deck where Admiral Lord Nelson had presumably entertained the dynamic duo before he and the rest of the crew took to the lifeboats.

They've got more No Parking cones than the police, Clogger pondered, scanning a ground-floor lounge furnished with a battered three-piece suite, an old television set and a full range of local authority road signs.

While he contemplated an intriguing trail of real, black-painted foot-prints, up one wall across the ceiling and down the other, Clogger was startled by definite movement on the upper-deck. Frozen to the spot, he listened intensely to the staircase creaking under the strain of descending body weight. Then the dull thud of wood against wood suggested that the hitherto gently swinging window was now being deliberately manipulated. Like a tiger stalking its prey, Clogger turned and crept out of the lounge across the hall to the galley. Amid precariously tall columns of empty take-away cartons, sitting like tin-foil stalagmites on every available kitchen surface, a black clerical torso was leaning over the sink unit, wrestling with the fittings on a stubborn casement window.

The ship's chaplain has just sobered up! He's also taking to the lifeboat, Clogger suspected, pouncing to thrust his huge, left paw in behind the back of a heavily-starched, white dog-collar.

In characteristic style, the Neolithic law-enforcement officer dragged the apparently mature student backwards out of the house into the darkness of Hallgarth Street.

"Please, please officer, you're making a terrible mistake," the prisoner begged, his hollow rhetoric falling on deaf ears as Clogger hauled him towards the hovering meat-wagon.

When they reached the vehicle it was already loaded and waiting to go. The pub-patrol commander was in the cockpit twitching impatiently on the throttle. The Elvet foot-patrol was leaning against the closed rear doors with Bald Eagle crouching beside the near-side wing-mirror making a final adjustment to his toupee.

"Where've you been?" the supervisor blasted, pumping himself fully upright to replace his helmet.

"Last one," Clogger declared proudly. "Caught him escaping through the kitchen window."

"He looks a bit old for this sort of thing," the sergeant observed when four flailing limbs were towed by, amid indignant protestations of innocence.

Curious about the authenticity of Clogger's fancy-dressed troublemaker, the sergeant followed the captive to the back of the meat-wagon and was ready to intervene, but by then Clogger's life-threatening grip on the vicar's dog-collar had taken its toll and rendered him incoherent.

"Pissed out of his head, just like the rest," Bald Eagle concluded, signalling for the Elvet beat officer to re-open the meat-wagon doors so that Clogger could sharpen-up on his caber-tossing technique. "Bang them all up, we'll wait for the key-holder."

With that the Elvet foot-patrol slammed the doors shut again and walked into the centre of the carriageway to stop the light traffic flow. To reach his place in the co-pilot's seat, Clogger strode back along the near-side of the meat-wagon and deliberately smashed into the last of the pack of rubber-necks.

"Come on ladies and gentlemen, help the police!" he pleaded, beat yourself up.

Once it was safe to manoeuvre Bald Eagle clattered on the side of the van prompting a three-point-turn and the start of the team-patrol's short journey back to the police station. Securely caged on board were three seriously drunken celebrities and their half-strangled spiritual advisor.

In those days it was customary to search drunks for anything potentially harmful, then incarcerate them in separate cells until they were sober enough to furnish full particulars and understand the intended charge(s). In the knowledge that there was a regular magistrates' court sitting the following morning, and Bald Eagle and the other arresting officers would resume duty within eight hours, the late-shift gaoler took a practical approach to his responsibilities. When Clogger and the meat-wagon commander lined the unsteady quartet in front of the charge-room counter, he used a light pencil to initiate individual entries in the station record book. Searched and stripped of their belongings, including belt and tie, the items were recorded in the appropriate column alongside their respective owner; Nelson, Batman, Robin and finally, Vicar.

Extremely distressed and typically dishevelled, it did occur to the officiating gaoler that Vicar was more collected than the rest of the fancy-dress-brigade and probably sober enough to be fully processed by the sergeant, especially when he demanded that his college be informed of his whereabouts, and a lawyer called.

"St. John's are already aware of the situation," the tidy-minded custodian assured, anxious that nothing mundane should interfere with his regular late-evening drink in the police club. "You'll have access to a solicitor in the morning, before you appear at court."

Five-forty-five the following morning (Monday 7th) a bleary-eyed B-Relief trickled back into the parade-room for an unusually relaxed formal briefing. Wupert had taken four hours time-off, effectively leaving Bald Eagle in charge of the station until nine. Without the pressure of an officer on his shoulder, the sergeant up-dated his team on the events of the last eight hours, allocated responsibilities and refreshment times, then turned to Clogger brandishing his recently acquired pocket calculator.

"Catchpole, you can assist me prepare the prisoners for court," the supervisor instructed, seizing another opportunity to keep Clogger out of mischief.

"Right," grinned the newly appointed deputy sergeant, convinced his performance the previous evening had propelled him into Bald Eagle's good books.

Smug with his meteoric rise in the shift pecking-order, Clogger removed his hands from the plastic sandwich-skip on the table in front of him, and folded his arms across his chest. Scraping back in his chair, he uncoiled his right leg out from underneath the parade-room table, radiating satisfaction in all directions.

"Can someone give him a bootlace?" Bald Eagle sighed, when a matt-black size-fourteen police boot crossed his line of vision, bound from toe to ankle in low-grade white string.

As soon as B-Relief dispersed to their allocated ground, Bald Eagle went to his own office to finalise a couple of trivial matters left over from the previous shift. Alone in the parade-room, Clogger was about to make a premature assault on his refreshments when the departing Framwelgate beat officer returned with a black lace.

"I want it replaced," the officer demanded after he launched the squirming baby eel in Clogger's general direction. "It's my only spare."

The new bootlace took Clogger's mind off his beetroot door-stops. "Oh, thanks," he said, bending to unpick his improvised fastening.

When Bald Eagle returned a few minutes later, unnaturally groomed and ready for action, Old Mother Hubbard was mid-way through the remedial process. Competing in size with his emergency provisions, a gigantic police boot of incredibly knobbly form held centre-stage on the parade-room table. Permanently dulled by frequent contact with motorcycle engine oil, it was subject to a clinical threading technique.

"Right, let's go and see what we've got," the sergeant called, urgently turning in the direction of the charge-room. "As soon as you can," he continued less enthusiastically, the pungent smell of a sweaty-socks reaching his nostrils. At least they're black!

Re-booted, the monster joined his supervisor at the hub. The gaoler had already produced the first customer of the day from the cell block. Nearly upright but very bedraggled, a research fellow in the guise of Admiral Lord Nelson was apologising profusely across the big wooden counter while Bald Eagle rattled off an allegation of drunk and disorderly.

"I'm very sorry," the sergeant repeated, formally noting the defendant's response before handing him a copy of the charge sheet. "Ring Nottingham and verify his name and home address, then do a check with criminal records," he instructed, spurring Clogger into action. "Next."

Batman and Robin turned out to be second-year under-graduates at the same college whose birthday coincidentally fell the previous day. Similarly remorseful they too were subject to telephone enquiries by Clogger who confirmed their true identities and previous good character. Vicar however was a different kettle of fish. He turned out to have an unreasonable and arrogant attitude of a type frequently encountered by meticulous, hard-working policemen. Mentally composed and physically erect, he readily furnished his personal particulars, but then looked-on in disgust when Bald Eagle politely asked him whether his college status meant he too was a post-graduate theology researcher, like the noble Sea Lord.

"I want to see a solicitor," Vicar boomed, unable to enter into conversation with a complete moron.

"You are not obliged to say anything unless you wish to do so, but anything you do say will be taken down in writing and given in evidence. You are charged that you did..."

"Suffice to say, I'm a tee-totaller," the prisoner formally responded, watching carefully to make sure the sergeant made a precise written record of his reply.

"You will have an opportunity to consult a solicitor in due course," Bald Eagle concluded with reciprocal arrogance. "Bang him back up, gaoler. Look up the word bursar in the dictionary, Catchpole."

Aware that Monday's court was guilty plea only, which meant that any disputed case would be stood-down to another date for a full hearing, Bald Eagle retired to the tranquillity of the parade-room to pen a précis of evidence, sufficient for the presiding lay magistrates to pass sentence.

"He must be studying church finance," Clogger advised, bouncing the station type-writer down on the other end of the parade-room table.

"Ah, right," Bald Eagle flinched. "Start typing-up this lot."

Nearly two hours of one-fingered clunking and half a ream of typing paper later, Clogger stapled together the three-page provisional case papers and proudly dropped them before his preoccupied supervisor, who by then had completed a second thorough scrutiny of the Daily Mirror and was tapping personal data into his pocket calculator.

"Oh, good," Bald Eagle declared, "you've finished. I'm going to retire at the end of the year! Lets get some bait."

Standing on its own some three or four hundred yards away from the police station, Durham City Magistrates' Court dominated the junction of Green Lane and Whinney Hill. Unlike its learned clerk it was a relatively new, low-rise building with modern light-oak furnishings and an asphalt apron to accommodate police and other official vehicles. Presiding in No.1 Court with a rod of iron, a gowned and balding Dickensian character approached his responsibilities with the precision and discipline of an army general.

At ten o'clock exactly, complete with bushy sideburns and gold-rimmed spectacles, the portly clerk to the magistrates sprang to attention in his slightly elevated chamber and barked, "Court stand."

The only other people in the room at that early stage in the proceedings were a robed, lady usher with sharply contrasting white hair and a youthful, very shy police prosecutor. Standing inside the main door, the usher instantly turned to face the front, her arms flowing at her sides. The dark-suited pencil abandoned his front-line pew and shot to his feet with one eye trained nervously on the Führer. Immediately above the clerk's head a door opened in the main gallery and an elderly lady wearing a navy-blue two-piece and a plumed hat, strode majestically to the central throne. Two equally well-dressed middle-aged gents brought up her rear and politely took less imposing seats on each flank, against a back-drop of the City's coat of arms.

"Court sit," the Führer bawled reflexively. "Not you," he continued impatiently, when the only person able to respond began to lower his bottom. "Licensing applications, motoring offences, overnights, then crime."

Abruptly reminded of the clerk's strict running order for plea-only hearings, Hapless Harry straightened-up again. "There are no licensing matters today, sir."

"Traffic then, get on with it...appearances first, then letters...address the bench, not me."

63

The timid young solicitor turned to two piles of buff-folders arranged neatly on the bench seat beside him and lifted the first set of case papers up to his chest.

"Your worships, there is only one motoring appearance this morning," he quivered, looking over the top of a shiny, bullet-shaped head to face three stern faces in the royal box. "The defendant declined to respond to his summons by letter, wishing instead to attend the court personally. Call Godfrey."

Leaving her sentry post at the back of the court, the lady usher pulled on a robust brass handle and wrestled with the hydraulic resistance from an automatic door-closing contraption.

"Godfrey," she shouted into the smoke-filled corridor.

A slimly built thirty-something-year-old, with neat black hair, cautiously entered the room wearing a prominently logoed brown dust-coat and a straw hat. As he removed his headgear and tried to orientate himself, his oscillating torso flashed the Milanda trademark into every corner of the courtroom.

"Over here," the lady usher whispered, opening the gate to another slightly elevated hardwood chamber, in the very centre of the floor, immediately behind the prosecuting pencil.

Ensconced on his feet with his hands gripping the symbolic brass rail, the defendant peered over the round-shoulders of his reluctant accuser to face the formidable clerk and the glowering faces in the terrace above.

"Is your name William Godfrey?" the clerk growled, referring to his own list of runners and riders.

"Yes, your honour."

"On February 10th this year, in Gilesgate, you are charged with driving a Thames Trader bakery vehicle in excess of the 30 mph. How do you plead?"

"Oh, guilty, your honour."

"Don't call me your honour, address their worships," the Führer instructed, stabbing his finger above and behind. "Brief facts, if you please."

"Your worships," the prosecutor chirped, "the defendant is a delivery driver based in Darlington. At 11am on the day in question he was followed by a patrol car for over half a mile. Speeds of up to 53 mph were recorded. The police speedometer was subsequently checked and found to be accurately calibrated. Mr Godfrey is of previous good character."

Relieved that he'd got his opening lines out of the way, the pale-faced solicitor flopped back down onto his bench.

"What do you want to say to the court before their worships pass sentence?" the clerk rattled, easing his spectacles onto the end of his nose to improve his vision.

"Well, em...I'm not of previous good character, that's the problem."

"What on earth do you mean?" snapped the clerk.

"Well, em...I wasn't going to mention it, but my wife insisted. She said you would find out anyway."

"Insisted on what?"

"I'm already disqualified from driving."

Perfectly choreographed, the mouths of the three presiding gargoyles dropped open in unison prompting the stunned prosecutor back to his feet, trembling his way through more papers. The Führer was momentarily fazed, but then he analysed the situation. Never before in his thirty-five years experience had the police made such an elementary mistake. Patiently he waited for Neville Chamberlain to find what he was looking for.

"Your worships, I have here written confirmation from the North Eastern Criminal Record Office that the defendant has no previous convictions," a very relieved young prosecutor announced, waving the form above his head.

"Mr Godfrey, there must be some misunderstanding. Let me see your driving licence."

"But I haven't got it," the defendant retorted, triggering the first symptom of the clerk's recurring congestion.

"Where is it?" demanded the Führer, his delivery interrupted by a tickly cough. "You were told to bring it with you. Their worships may wish to endorse it."

"It was taken from me when I was disqualified," the bread man explained.

The clerk's feeble throat problem developed into a splutter and there was a discernible change in his complexion. "Mr Godfrey," he asserted, "you've heard the prosecution confirm to the court your previous good character. Now, where is your driving licence? Have you lost it?"

"Certainly not," the defendant replied, offended by the suggestion he'd been careless with an important personal document. "It was taken from me six months ago, when I was on the Bishop Auckland run."

The bread man's persistence preceded an uncomfortable silence. The three hopelessly confused beaks looked at each other in turn while Hapless Harry ventured a glance behind at the judicial gremlin leaning over him in the dock. Vastly experienced in summary court procedure, the clerk knew the criminal record system relied essentially on dates of birth, with names and addresses being of secondary importance.

Clearing his throat again he contemplated the only possible explanation; the police patrol car driver has taken down a wrong date of birth culminating in a check of another man with the same name.

Feasible, the situation was nevertheless extremely serious. Since his disqualification by Bishop Auckland Magistrates' Court the defendant had evidently continued in his employment as a driver, circumstances that warranted a more serious charge of driving while disqualified.

He's probably driven to court today thought the clerk, the colour of his face beginning to move through the spectrum.

"What's your date of birth?" the Führer spat, startling the young solicitor back into the real world.

"Err...9th of May, 1936," answered the bread man.

"Well!" the clerk blasted at Hapless Harry, whose mental journey hadn't encompassed the same line of reasoning. "Check the case papers."

When the prosecutor produced for a second time the all important criminal record form, the reddening missile-shaped head of the clerk strained forward in anticipation of the discrepancy.

"Nine...five...thirty-six," the solicitor announced, carefully running his finger across the paper.

Confirmation that the man before him had no official previous convictions, adversely affected the clerk's already suspect blood pressure and deepened his complexion to a shiny, reddish-blue. Swinging-off his spectacles with one hand, he banged down hard on the woodwork with the other, frustrated by a serious lapse in strict procedure that defeated his razor-sharp brain.

"Get the duty-inspector," he bawled, sending a terrified usher scurrying out of the main door to the nearest telephone.

The initial thud on the court-room super-structure startled the royal box, but it was only when the Führer made a second assault on the fittings that the lady chairman decided to lean over the top of her rail and visibly check the sanity of her learned advisor. Suddenly aware of the frowning face above him, the clerk remembered his station in life and uttered his apologies.

"I'm so sorry, your worship," he whispered, glancing to the ceiling. "This is a most unusual turn of events. You may wish to adjourn the case for one hour while the circumstances are investigated."

"Case adjourned for one hour, take a seat at the back of the court Mr Godfrey."

Before he replaced his glasses, the clerk produced a white handkerchief from somewhere and wiped his gently perspiring brow. His complexion subsided to a more normal hue, but a dryness in his voice persisted well into the next session.

"Motoring letters," he rasped, prompting the young solicitor back into action armed with his traffic bundle.

It took about half an hour for the summary machine to weigh-off the rest of the dozen or so uncontested speeding offences. Knowing the clerk's obsession with efficiency, Hapless Harry outlined the facts of each case in the minimum amount of words, before the Führer expertly paraphrased letters containing the regular list of imaginative excuses. For their part the three beaks made use of a spread-sheet correlating levels of excess speed with monetary values, and rattled out fines and endorsements accordingly. The solitary bread man, sitting at the back of the court in the corner of the public gallery, soon tired of the entertainment and dropped his head in the direction of a tabloid newspaper concealed on his lap. It wasn't long before the lady usher crept back into the room. As instructed she'd summoned Wupert to the helm, but being an old hand and a calming influence on her temperamental boss, she'd also taken the opportunity to warn the charge-room of the likely time the overnights would be called. Coupled with the speed at which No.1 Court was now operating, the pre-emptive action helped contain the clerk's hypertensive tendencies and bring some sort of normality back into the summary justice system.

"That's all the traffic matters, your worships," said the clerk, rolling his eyes to the bench. "Have you called the duty-inspector?" he continued, moving his attention to the dashing lady usher.

"The inspector will be here in a few minutes, sir," she replied, "and the overnights are waiting outside, under escort."

"Good, have them brought in."

Before she had time to make a formal call in the corridor Bald Eagle marched into the room with a folder of papers, just ahead of the fancy-dress troupe. Handcuffed together and launched onto the stage by Clogger, the concert party stumbled about the floor like competitors in a three-legged race with Batman and Robin somehow knotted face to face.

"Over here," the usher whispered.

Under the bemused gaze of the clerk, three glowering oriental gods and a re-vitalised bread man, the grinning ring-master unravelled the elephant trail and chivvied it into the pen, taking over as sentry on the outside of the dock gate. While the immaculately turned-out sergeant, resplendent in his ginger thatch, approached the master of ceremonies with four charge sheets, a second pin-striped pencil slid into position on the opposite end of the front bench.

"Are you involved in this case, sergeant?" the clerk asked.

"Yes, sir," Bald Eagle replied, "I'm the senior arresting officer."

"You may feel it expedient for the sergeant to present the facts, your worships," the clerk remarked, before Bald Eagle had a chance to pass the précis of evidence to Hapless Harry.

"Yes," the lady chairman agreed, equally anxious to avoid the monotonous ramblings of an unprepared youngster.

Brimming with expertise honed over twenty-nine years, Bald Eagle remained on his feet in the aisle, tilted back his head and looked directly at madam chairman and her two colleagues.

"Good morning, your worships," he said. "As you can see the charges in this case all emanate from an unruly fancy-dress celebration last evening that spilled into a public thoroughfare."

Delighted to receive a professionally delivered cue, the clerk responded quietly, "Thank you, sergeant," then turned his attention on the concert party. "Name?" he growled in the direction of Admiral Lord Nelson.

The first bedraggled and very subdued theology researcher confirmed his personal details.

"You're charged with drunk and disorderly conduct in Hallgarth Street, Durham City last evening. How do you plead?"

"Guilty," the noble Sea Lord replied, dropping his head in shame.

Equally hung-over and remorseful, Batman and Robin also acknowledged their student status and pleaded guilty, but when it came to Vicar the summary session started to veer off course again.

"I represent this accused," the duty defence solicitor announced, bouncing to his feet at the other end of the front bench, immediately after the clergyman had confirmed his personal details.

"How do you plead?" the clerk asked.

"Not guilty," answered the defence lawyer, pre-empting his client. "If the court pleases, I would appreciate an adjournment for one month so that I can take full instructions."

"Agreed," rattled the clerk with the speed of an auctioneer.

While the Führer fingered his calendar for a suitable hearing date, the clergyman fidgeted at the other end of the dock. Dark rings around his eyes contrasted sharply with his pale, drawn features. Trying desperately to groom his dishevelled brown hair with his only available hand, the unlikely member of the concert party turned unexpectedly to mouth something to his lawyer. The action had a knock-on effect that rippled through three sets of shackles and pulled the noble Sea Lord into an unscheduled hopping routine.

"My client realises that he will have an opportunity to defend himself fully at a later date, your worships, but he wishes this court to know how distressed and hurt he feels by the police reference."

"What reference?" the clerk asked impatiently, looking up, ready to stifle any unnecessary presentation during a plea-only session.

"Fancy-dress," advised the defence solicitor.

The Führer would normally have dismissed the comment out of hand at that stage, but something made the street-wise master of ceremonies pause and scan the faces before him. Temporarily unoccupied, the junior prosecuting pencil was sitting with his head on one side fantasising about his go-carting skills, while Clogger grinned incessantly, apparently without a care in the world. The eyes of the equally street-wise police sergeant however, were closed-tight and a deep cringe exposed an almost full set of big, brown-stained teeth. The facial expression triggered a peculiar feeling of insecurity that rippled down the clerk's spine and reversed the downward trend in his blood pressure.

"The court notes your client's objection," he told the defence lawyer with uncharacteristic hesitancy. "He will be bailed in his own surety to reappear before this court on a date to be fixed. The usher will prepare the paperwork. Release the prisoner, officer."

Back into action, Clogger leapt to the other end of the dock and leaned over the rail to unlock the handcuffs securing Vicar to Robin. With one eye firmly fixed on Clogger the cowering clergyman rubbed away the stiffness in his left wrist and walked behind the other three accused to exit the pen.

"Take a seat at the back of the court for a few minutes, while I prepare your bail form," whispered the kindly usher as she led the flinching defendant away from the shackle-swinging monster.

"Salient points if you please, sergeant," the clerk continued.

Armed with his précis of evidence, Bald Eagle related the circumstances of the first three arrests, carefully avoiding any reference to Vicar who would be the subject of a separate hearing and have the pleasure of Clogger as the principal prosecution witness.

"Those are the facts, your worships," Bald Eagle concluded. "All three accused study at St. John's College and are of previous good character."

"Thank you, sergeant. Have you any questions for the police, your worships?" the Führer continued.

"Just one thing, officer," came a very refined reply. "Has the university been informed of this extra curricula activity?"

"As you are no doubt aware ma'am, it is sub-divisional policy to take such action, but in this case the college in question failed to respond. I personally waited over an hour for someone to attend, finally securing the accommodation myself."

No sooner had Bald Eagle delivered his closing syllable than the recently liberated clergyman, sitting close to the bread man in the public gallery, recovered sufficient composure to publicly interject.

"That's incorrect," he called. "I was there within a few minutes."

"But you are one of the accused," the perplexed clerk insisted, his congestive cough returning with vengeance.

"I'm also the bursar of the college," shouted Vicar from his soapbox. "I'm responsible for all outside accommodation."

"But what were you doing at the birthday party?" the clerk spluttered.

"I wasn't at the party, I was closing the kitchen window when that oaf arrested me."

Reference to Clogger prompted him to about-turn and face his accuser, but before he could respond the bread man was on his feet waving his straw hat in response to the preacher's rallying-cry.

"And he's the one who took my licence off me and disqualified me from driving...he also fined me three pork pies."

Blue in the face, the clerk's coughing bout had escalated into life-threatening breathlessness by the time bright-eyed Wupert appeared on the scene thirty seconds later.

"Got here as quickly as I could, sir," he rattled, approaching the incoherent clerk. "How can I help?"

"Call an ambulance, inspector," the alarmed lady chairman insisted.

71

4   RIVER TRIAL

Clogger's unique and simplistic approach to the rule of law probably created a legal precedent, although nobody took the trouble to conduct the relevant research. When the acutely agitated master of ceremonies was finally stretchered-off to accident and emergency, wrestling with a portable oxygen mask, the lay chairman and her colleagues finalised the day's proceedings without the support of a legally qualified clerk. After the inevitable mayhem, she fined the remaining members of the fancy-dress-brigade five pounds each.

"Fourteen days to pay. I don't want to see you in this court again," she insisted, in rhetoric appropriate to the occasion. "Release them."

Clogger leaned into the dock and unshackled the trio. Then, oblivious to the bemusement of everyone left in the courtroom, he opened his tunic and carefully suspended two more pairs of borrowed handcuffs from his already burdened waistline. With the comedy act out of the way her worship called the bread man to the front of the court, and as a gesture of good-will dismissed the case against him. Disbelieving his luck, he immediately pocketed his newspaper, donned his straw hat and scarpered. Unlike his counterpart, the college bursar still felt aggrieved after his unconventional acquittal, but when the understanding lady chairman added a profound apology for the distress caused, his professional sense of forgiveness kicked-in. Intending to march straight to the police station and lodge a formal complaint against Clogger, the cleric hesitated at the entrance, then decided to return to his quarters and clean-up first. By the time he reached the tranquillity of the Kingsgate footbridge, the complaint had taken second place to a pressing college commitment and was destined to drop-off the end of his priority list.

"The rest of today's cases will be adjourned until next Monday," the plumed chairperson announced, standing to leave the bench. "Inspector, I trust you will take appropriate action to prevent such a fiasco happening again," she finally scowled, before turning elegantly to lead her two male colleagues out of the chamber by the special door.

The adjournment of the court, mid-session, was an unexpected windfall particularly for the hard-pressed legal contingent, but the speed of their departure didn't properly reflect their delight with an early finish. Entranced by a struggling tugboat, Hapless Harry watched Bald Eagle pull, push and nudge the clanking uniformed giant towards the court door, while his defence colleague stared at the ceiling for a few minutes contemplating Darwin's Origin of the Species and the theory of natural selection. Having waited nervously for the court-room to clear, Wupert cornered the usher and looked on in amazement while she related to him, in emphatic detail, every scene from the judicial pantomime.

"I don't know what we're going to do with him," the inspector sighed, shaking his bowed head in despair."

In the absence of a formal complaint the whiz-kid had several courses of action open to him, but after walking the short distance back to the police station he was still undecided. Intending to finalise his thoughts over a cup of tea in the canteen, the inspector entered the premises by the most convenient route. Turning into the station yard, heading for the rear door, his mind was quickly made-up. The meat-wagon that Clogger and Bald Eagle had used to take the overnight prisoners to court, was positioned awkwardly in the middle of the yard with the sergeant standing next to the wide-open driver's door. Indifferent about a puddle of engine oil at his feet, the shell-shocked umpire was fingering his primitive pocket calculator with a tent-sized police tunic draped over his left arm.

"I told him to check at the city-desk first," Bald Eagle muttered in a defensive monotone, "but he doesn't listen," he continued without formally acknowledging Wupert at his side.

Open-mouthed and in awe of his physical strength, the leaders of B-Relief watched the chain-mailed gladiator squat in front of a smart, yellow Morris 1100 for the third time and lock his forearms underneath the gleaming bumper. With his enormous sweat-soaked back to the audience, Clogger adopted a modified snatch-and-jerk position, growled at the radiator grille then grunted his legs straight. When his knees locked, the front-end of the medium-sized family saloon was clear of the ground and its wheels were hanging limply, suspended by the very latest in hydro-elastic technology. After a deep-throated grunt, accompanied a stylish, clanking side-shuffle, superman abandoned his load with the agility and precision of an Olympic weight-lifter. The hydraulically assisted triple-bounce that followed sent an in-board nodding-dog into raptures and stress-tested every piece of linkage in the state-of-the-art transverse transmission system.

"Once more, and that should do it," Clogger gasped, making his way to the back of the unfamiliar private car to repeat the process on the substantially lighter rear-end. "Bloody lunatic, ought to be prosecuted!"

In the privacy of the police station yard Clogger's unrealistic quip would normally have gone unnoticed, but for some reason it conjured a sinister image in Wupert's mind and panicked him into the simplest of his disciplinary options. By the time Clogger had cleared the obstruction from the meat-wagon parking bay, admired his handiwork and returned to collect his tunic from the wigged-umpire, the inspector was hot-foot through the back door of the police station, by-passing the canteen on his way to the superintendent's office.

Confronted by a closed door, Wupert checked the sub-divisional head's mini traffic-light. While it flickered confusingly between engaged and green, Jenny's head slotted out of the office next door.

"It's broken again," she advised efficiently. "He's in a meeting, is it urgent?"

"Oh, wather!"

"What should I say it's about?"

"An incident at court this morning, involving Catchpole."

"Wait a moment."

Thirty seconds later the inspector received a verbal green light and tapped delicately on the superintendent's door.

"C...C...Come," Gentleman Jim stuttered in barely audible tones.

The inner sanctum that morning contained everyone except the Almighty himself. Looking pale and nervous, the sub-divisional head was sitting at his desk on the other side of the room, facing the door. In need of some support, his big blue beak flickered with relief when Wupert stepped over the threshold into the jaws of two other comfortably-seated bundles of braid.

74

"Oh, tewwibly sowwy sir, I didn't wealise...," the humble inspector proffered, about to beat a retreat under the penetrating gaze of the divisional chief superintendent and a headquarters-based assistant chief constable.

"Take a s...s...seat inspector, you've come at just the right time," insisted Gentleman Jim. "We are discussing Catchpole."

Although Clogger was capable of starting world war three, he was only a lowly foot soldier.

Why such a high-powered summit? Wupert pondered as he cautiously pulled a third comfortable chair into the conference circle.

"Unfortunately we've been overtaken by e...e...events," Gentleman Jim said, up-dating the new delegate with typical courtesy. "After the coroner's scathing comments this morning, the chief superintendent kindly agreed to create a new sub-divisional post; station u...u...utilities officer."

Proud of his initiative, particularly the imaginative label coined for a skivvy, the divisional head soaked up the patronage of his number-two, nodding confidently to the assistant chief constable.

"Oh, after what happened in court this morning sir, I totally agwee," Wupert chirped, relieved that positive action had already been taken to limit Clogger's operational freedom.

"But that was before the c...c...club steward brought the accounts to my attention," continued Gentleman Jim with an uneasy flick of his rudder.

Unable to make a connection between Clogger, the police club accounts and the presence of the assistant chief constable, the young academic frowned while the sub-divisional head painted the rest of the alarming picture.

"The g...g...gaming machine didn't make a profit last week. Someone tampered with it when the bar was closed. It seems strange that after all these years the problem should coincide with the transfer of Catchpole."

"Oh, sir," replied the inspector indignantly, "Woger may have a diffewent appwoach to his work, but I have no weason to believe he's dishonest."

"I hope you're right, inspector," the chief superintendent added, stirring the assistant chief constable from his deliberations. "But we are given to understand the machine is fully functional and the only feasible way of removing money without the key is to physically turn it upside down and shake the coins out."

"That's the part I have difficulty with," muttered the assistant chief, making his first contribution in front of Wupert. "Are you sure the key procedure is water-tight? That old thing has been in the club since I served here, it must weigh a ton. I doubt anyone has that sort of strength. What's your opinion, inspector?"

Wupert's heart sank as the gravity of the situation dawned. A thief in the service was bad enough, but a member of the elite B-Relief, well! "Yes, I have to say sir, he is vewy, vewy stwong."

"Alright then," concluded the assistant chief constable, imposing his authority over the meeting. "You have my permission to install covert photographic equipment and catch Hercules in action. In the meantime do nothing to enhance his opportunity. It could be construed as provocative later. Catchpole will remain on normal duties until further notice. Let's give him the rope to hang himself!"

Decision made, the busy chief officer bounced to his feet triggering a respectful ripple reaction among his colleagues, then he picked-up his bulging, black-leather brief case and marched out of the superintendent's office.

"Keep me informed," he called, before strutting down the staircase to the back door.

The scene in the police yard was confusing even for an alert, prospective chief constable. The meat-wagon occupied the slot where his yellow pride-and-joy was originally parked and the car next to it was concealed by Goliath and a handful of miscellaneous station rubber-necks, tutting through the advantages and disadvantages of modern suspension.

When Moses panicked and screamed, "Where's my car?" the waters parted revealing a very sad looking canary with both its front legs splayed wide-open, like a police dog responding to trouble on Durham ice-rink.

"It's only a month old, it's not even run-in," the heavily-braided chief officer gasped, scattering the mice back into the station woodwork.

"Don't make them like they used to boss...I mean superintendent...I mean emperor," Clogger advised.

The decision not to put Clogger into a position with unlimited access to the police club was legally sound, but in the grand scale of things it was also a missed opportunity. As station skivvy his campaign would have been seriously thwarted, probably requiring fresh consultations with his handlers and a radical change of tactics. While the appointment would never have totally destroyed Clogger, the delay may have given the police command an opportunity to come to terms with the true extent of their problem. Ironically, history demonstrates that phase-two involved a further attack on the clergy and judiciary that not only went ahead unhindered, but was also inadvertently aided by the assistant chief constable's instruction on Clogger's future.

On his second early-day shift the suspected gaming-machine bandit appeared in the parade-room shortly after 5.45am Tuesday 8th April, lunch-box under one arm, up-turned helmet under the other. Anxious that nothing should jeopardise any subsequent criminal or disciplinary proceedings, Wupert had joined the briefing early and was sitting next to Bald Eagle at the head of the table. The rest of B-Relief were seated along the flanks, instinctively hanging onto their personal bits and pieces in anticipation of Clogger's usual contact with the table leg. On this occasion though, the master of the unexpected seriously wrong-footed his colleagues. He gently placed his provisions in front of the last available chair and grinned. While a discernible sense of relief rippled through the audience he used his spare hand to fish in the bucket he called a helmet, then in the true spirit if his nick-name, he lobbed two pairs of steel handcuffs at their respective owners.

"Thanks," the giant called when one colleague with a delicate disposition, dived for cover and catapulted the sergeant's lever-arch file into orbit.

After he retrieved the occurrence folder and found the relevant page for a second time, part one of the start-of-shift briefing went ahead without further incident. While Bald Eagle rattled off the events of the last twenty-four-hours, the foot soldiers laboured in their pocket note-books.

"Right, assignments," the sergeant said, as the last ballpoint stopped rolling.

Already in the habit of leaving Clogger until last, Wupert waited patiently for his deputy to make the all-important operational decision.

"Catchpole, double-up with the Elvet beat officer," Bald Eagle barked, securing a reliable marker for the most dangerous striker on the team.

"I think he's had sufficient familiawisation, sergeant," interrupted the inspector. "He can cover Elvet on his own."

It was the very first time Wupert had stepped into Bald Eagle's traditional territory and he was seriously miffed, but entrenched discipline prevailed.

"I don't think he's ready yet, inspector," the sergeant strained, twisting his face at the thought of Clogger being left to his own devices.

The effectiveness of the planned internal surveillance relied on absolute secrecy, so Wupert had to draw on all his management skills to impose his apparently irrational will.

"Familiawisation doesn't normally run into a second week," he observed, "I don't see why he should receive pweferential tweatment."

"But inspector, the assizes are on," Bald Eagle mouthed emphatically, turning his face away from Clogger to hide his objection.

"He can handle it," the young shift-leader responded confidently. "Oh, and everyone else should note, the Bishop of Durham is entertaining foweign guests in the cathedwal today. There are no special awwangements, but it's as well you all know."

A final, concealed attempt to respectfully mouth some sense into Wupert resulted in a quick shake of the head and the whispered words, "I insist."

Dejected, the sergeant leaned forward, plonked both elbows on the table and dropped his head into his hands. A fractional forward movement of his toupee failed to receive immediate and careful attention, dispersing the embarrassed audience, with the exception of the ever-considerate Clogger. He waited until the room was almost empty, then walked over to his supervisor, eased the thatch back into position and patted it.

"Don't worry boss...I mean sergeant, I'm sure the Elvet beat officer can manage on his own."

Awarded his wings, Clogger's first official solo flight in the Elvet district of Durham City started well. At six o'clock on the dot, hands clenched behind his back, he began to slowly pace the ancient streets enjoying the tranquillity of the early morning air and the soft dawn light. A kindly milkman, rattling along the cobbled North Bailey in an electric cart, pulled up alongside and leapt out of the open cockpit brandishing a free, pint bottle of fresh milk. Expecting to engage in a few seconds of introductory conversation, while the early morning newcomer tackled his traditional liquid refreshment, the dairyman could only gape in amazement.

"Thanks very much, boss," Clogger responded, picking off the yellow tin-foil to down the entire cream-rich contents in one visit.

When a shovel-sized right hand pressed the returnable empty into his chest, the milkman's thoughts turned to irony. Bloody hell, I'm glad he's on our side!

Eight o'clock signalled the end of the lull. Gently building traffic began to flow with new impetus through the network of single-file city-centre streets, prompting the Painted-Lady to wobble her way into the command module. Shortly afterwards, Clogger's jaunt in the North Bailey was interrupted by his first radio call.

"Elvet foot-patrol from foxtrot bravo control," his lapel mounted receiver crackled.

"Go ahead," Clogger replied, releasing the little aerial on the other bit.

"Make your way to the newsagents shop in Saddler Street, proprietor requests assistance."

"Received."

Bleep, bleep, bleep.

Only a two-minute goose-step away, Clogger dropped his broad shoulders and barged through the tiny door of the premises, helmet first. A black-fingered local businessman, wearing an equally ink-smudged fawn dust-jacket was cowering at the other side of a wooden counter, rippling with daily titles. Disturbing the precision of the painstaking arrangement, a denim-clad miniature Joe Frazier with cropped, black hair and a broken nose gestured menacingly across the barricade.

"Oh, thanks for coming, officer," the very relieved newsagent blurted when Clogger peered down on a human form, wide-inches-tall. "I've already served him cigarettes, but he's demanding alcohol from the off-licence counter and it's closed."

"Don't worry sir, I'm sure we can sort this out sensibly," Clogger reassured softly, as he confronted a brown-skinned man with the pallor of a sub-mariner.

"Just a small bottle, I haven't had a drink for ten years," the awkward customer continued to remonstrate.

"Now listen to me very carefully, sir," advised Clogger, as he tightened his vice-like grip under a bulging bicep. "You're in white man's land now, you must take orders from the white man."

The politically incorrect advice preceded a sort of crude shot-putting action that launched the undesirable muscleman towards the open shop door. It wasn't a clean delivery though. The frame took a glancing blow that shook the quaint Georgian frontage and diverted the reject across the narrow pavement, directly into the path of an oncoming metal lamp-post. A concussing sound, resonating all the way to the Market Place, confused the smattering of intellectual foot-passengers outside. While some glanced towards the cathedral belfry, others felt the Church of St. Nicholas was the early morning offender.

"Fuck-off, and don't come back," were Clogger's final instructions, delivered to a disorientated bundle of denim obsessed with a rapidly developing lump on the side of his head.

"Elvet foot-patrol to foxtrot bravo control."

"Go ahead."

"Dispute with a customer, all quiet on departure."

"Roger, Elvet foot-patrol."

Bleep, bleep, bleep.

Brimming with a sense of efficiency, Clogger checked his wrist-watch. Eight-fifteen, nearly bait time he relished, trying to recall whether it was beetroot sandwich or pork pie day. I'll have a few minutes with the Painted-Lady before I head back.

The thought of the buxom older woman stirred his manhood as he strolled across the bustling Market Place at the onset of rush-hour. Leaning over the stable door to taste the sickly fumes of plastered make-up and cheap perfume, Casanova delivered his standard chat-up line to the back of a fully inflated swimming-aid.

"Morning, sweet-face," he said, noticing the outline of a heavy-duty bra-strap beneath a crisp, white uniform shirt.

Exposing the up-lifted profile of her right mammary gland as she swivelled towards the Framwelgate Bridge monitor, the preoccupied traffic warden muttered, "Oh, hello," then rotated the equipment back out of sight.

Ten minutes later, Clogger was still engrossed in the mysteries of the front-end when the whole of the right gland appeared below his chin and stopped dead.

"Where's he going?" the Painted-Lady protested pointing to the blunt nose of a single-decker service bus emerging from the mouth of Silver Street. "Newcastle is in the other direction."

The antics of an apparently disorientated bus driver didn't distract Clogger from his fantasy world until the red monster growled to a halt on the cobbled parking area behind him.

"Officer, officer," a spindly, wizened conductress called as she alighted the rear door and marched on Clogger.

When it dawned on the Elvet foot-patrol that the bus driver wasn't lost but desperately searching for a policeman, he lurched into the upright position and banged the back of his helmet against the top of the door frame.

Temporarily blinded by the rim of the headgear, superman took a few seconds to respond. "What's the problem, my love?"

"He's refusing to get off the bus."

"Who is?"

"The man at the front. He wants to go to Newcastle, but he hasn't got enough money. He says he's spent it all on cigarettes."

"Oh, don't upset yourself, darling," Clogger insisted, putting a comforting arm around Olive Oyle's shoulders. "I'll soon sort him out."

Followed by the feeble frame of the conductress, and a driver who had reluctantly abandoned the safety of his enclosed, single-seat cab, the giant grabbed the shiny-steel pole at the back of the bus and vaulted across the open platform into the narrow aisle.

"Which one?" he demanded, urgently scanning the mix of randomly seated passengers.

"Him," responded the timid support party, pointing in unison to a denim-clad back dominating a forward-facing dual-seat at the very front of the vehicle.

Head bowed, Clogger ploughed up the aisle amid a stream perfectly synchronised turning faces and tapped the dumb-insolent on the shoulder. When Joe Frazier looked up in horror, Clogger brought all of his interrogative skills to bear.

"What part of fuck-off didn't you understand?" he queried, engaging the suspect with his favourite ear-lock and screw.

"Get him off me, get him off me," screamed the pugilistic captive as he was dragged through the gaping audience.

Had it not been for a stubborn streak, little Joe Frazier's constitution would probably have survived the second encounter more or less intact, but when he decided to grab the shiny-steel pole at the back of the bus, just as super-sleuth was preparing for his javelin throw, the instincts of a life-time left him for good. A hug that any self-respecting grisly would have been proud of, was Clogger's preferred method of tearing the troublesome passenger's body away from its arms at the shoulder joints. Ultimately unsuccessful, the excruciating experience prompted a rapid re-evaluation of life-style and Mighty Mouse was last seen bolting down Saddler Street in the direction of Elvet Bridge.

He must have changed his mind and decided to go south to Darlington thought Clogger while the grateful bus crew tried in vain to straighten the new longbow, so essential to the safety of boarding passengers.

Under strict instructions from Bald Eagle, Clogger timed his return journey to the police station to perfection and entered the canteen at nine exactly. First in, he complied with tradition and filled the kettle. The rest of the early bait crew drifted in a few minutes later, but the sergeant himself was unusually late. It was ten-past nine before he arrived, chuckling his way to his usual seat at the kitchen table.

"What's so funny, sarge?" one officer persisted when Bald Eagle's preoccupation became irritating.

"Never heard anything like it before," the smiling supervisor announced, halting the jaws of all but Clogger. "I've just been chatting to a prison officer in Court Lane and he tells me the jail is in turmoil this morning. Nobody knows what to do."

"About what?" asked the Sherburn panda-driver.

"A Newcastle gangster called Darkie the Dagger was released at eight o'clock this morning. He got parole after a big stretch."

"And?"

"By quarter to nine he was banging on the main gate demanding to be let back in. He insists he's not suitable for early release and refuses to accept the parole board's decision."

"Never!"

"Yes," the sergeant insisted, tackling his first sandwich.

Amazed that in Clogger's case his revelation had failed to compete with the delights of a second pork pie, Bald Eagle's thoughts turned abruptly to a potentially more disastrous precedent.

"Catchpole, whatever happens, be in the vicinity of the South Bailey by ten-fifteen...and don't forget he's a representative of the Queen. He must not be held up."

"Yes, boss...I mean sergeant," replied Clogger, looking up to randomly pebble-dash his colleagues with gelatine.

"And don't forget to take the key...and don't forget to salute," the flustered supervisor ordered, his mind now completely void of the legal conundrum within the prison service.

At nine-forty, five minutes before the end of the regulation refreshment break, Clogger tried to inject some confidence into Bald

Eagle and make him more at ease with his Daily Mirror. He stood up, hauled his tunic off the back of his dining chair, shook the dandruff from the black serge collar, then threw himself into the garment. Painstakingly fastening each chrome button in turn, Clogger straightened his belt and clip-on tie before collecting his helmet from the kitchen draining board. Under the gaze of Bald Eagle and half of B-Relief, the grinning giant went on to remove both halves of his pocket-set from the chrome-topped pail and clip the receiver part to the inside of his left lapel.

"Elvet foot-patrol, radio check"

"Loud and clear, Elvet."

Bleep, bleep, bleep.

Communications in order, he pushed home the aerial on the blue plastic transmitter then with a twinkle in his eye, confidently produced spare radio batteries from his trouser-pocket, together with a small key, tagged; Judge's Post.

Finally, his chin-strap resting comfortably below his bottom lip and all his appointments intact, he left the canteen contingent with a very worrying reassurance. "Leave the judge to me!"

I'm going to live to regret this day, thought Bald Eagle, straining to control a toupee-threatening scowl.

About ten o'clock that morning, when Clogger strode across the Kingsgate footbridge on his way to the Baileys, his attention was drawn to the rich-brown water of the River Wear, flowing through the spectacular tree-lined gorge below. Deep and reflective, it normally appeared perfectly still, but inclement weather conditions somewhere in the depths of Weardale were beginning to take effect.

Lot of water in today, pondered the uniformed giant as he stopped briefly to gaze down into the broad meandering mirror, its surface breaking occasionally over a moody, cloud-studded image of leaning trees.

At the Norman heart of the city, Clogger gave a new meaning to the notion of positive policing when he bounced from the North to the South Bailey in the very centre of the cobbled carriageway. Giving no ground whatsoever, an oncoming clutch of two-wheeled boffins were forced to wobble precariously around his towering frame. Only the

84

arrival of an Austin A40 blunted his cutting-edge and forced him onto the narrow pavement directly outside St. John's College. The casual appearance of the dog-collared bursar at a quaint window coincided with the frantic and unnecessary closing of a series of ground floor sun-blinds, but Clogger didn't notice his petrified second scalp and continued on regardless.

The chunky little post, preventing four-wheeled access to the ageing Prebends Bridge, was firmly clasped in its metal housing when the judge's illustrious assistant reached the eroded stone arch at the end of the South Bailey. An anxious glance at his wrist-watch prompted him to rummage in his trouser pocket for the key and remove the padlock in readiness. Pacing at random to pass the time, and alert to the appearance of any unauthorised obstructions of a mechanical nature, the intrepid law enforcement officer was called into action at exactly quarter-past ten, fifteen minutes before the start of the morning session at the assize court.

"Elvet foot-patrol from foxtrot bravo control," Clogger's receiver crackled.

"Go ahead control."

"Judge en-route."

"Received."

Bleep, bleep, bleep.

Pushing his transmitter back into his trouser-pocket, Clogger leapt towards the post, pulled it out of the slot in the centre of the road and carried it into St. Cuthbert's doorway, out of sight. Wiping road grime from his hands, the sentry then stepped out of the college entrance and stood to attention on the narrow pavement, facing Prebends Bridge and the stately accommodation beyond. When the leading motorcycle outrider growled through the historic arch, Clogger forced his shoulders back and pressed his forward-facing thumbs hard against the side of his big thighs. A nod of acknowledgement from the first black-leather spaceman was followed by the appearance of a highly-polished, chauffeur-driven black limousine with a rotund high court judge sitting alone on the back seat. While the chrome-nosed car carefully twisted its way through the arch, Clogger waited until he could see the flowing grey wig and red body-sash of the quasi-royal passenger. Then, his huge right palm fully exposed, he threw an electrifying salute. Typically, the stone-faced member of the judiciary purred past, apparently ignorant of Clogger's effort, but a second nod of recognition from the trailing spaceman, signalled a successful outcome to part one of the daily operation.

Pleased with his very demanding contribution to a highly publicised murder trial, Clogger returned the mini railway-sleeper to the hole in the road and snapped it firmly into the upright position with the padlock.

"Elvet foot-patrol to foxtrot bravo control."

"Pass your message."

"All clear."

"Received and understood," responded the radio operator, radiating his obvious relief across the sub-divisional air waves.

Apart from an eccentric academic on a monocycle and the still firmly closed sun-blinds at St. John's, Clogger's half-mile trek back to the Market Place was uneventful, albeit a storm was brewing. Occasionally interrupted by a tourist seeking directions to the castle and cathedral, he managed to spend the next hour or so rocking on his heals outside Martins Bank, ogling the Painted-Lady from a discreet distance. It was the appearance of Wupert and Bald Eagle on routine walk-about that eventually reduced the bulge in his trousers. Having successfully delivered one salute that morning the black braid on the inspector's cap triggered a second regulation greeting that caught Wupert by surprise.

"Thank you, Woger," the embarrassed shift-leader chirped, reciprocating with a feeble, inward-facing palm reminiscent of an American GI. "The judge commented on your smartness when he awwived at the court building this morning. Good show! Let me examine your pocket-book."

The unexpected complement caused a dangerous surge in Clogger's ego. When the inspector handed back the dog-eared document with his signature recorded at twelve noon, its beaming owner took the initiative.

"Is that the time? Do you want me to cover the box while the warden takes her refreshments?"

"Oh, no no," Bald Eagle gasped, left cold by the terrifying image of a circuit judge marooned in traffic. "Her relief is already arranged, you stay available for the lunch-time adjournment. Have you still got the key?"

"Of course boss...I mean sergeant."

"Foxtrot bravo control to Elvet foot-patrol."

"Pass your message."

"Request from the prison, evacuate the cathedral tower until further notice, activity on E-Wing."

"On my way," Clogger blasted, proudly striding away from his supervisors.

Brimming with efficiency, the Elvet foot-patrol raced along Saddler Street towards Palace Green and the eleventh century shrine of St. Cuthbert. When he charged through the enormous wooden door of the World Heritage Site he was assailed by an atmosphere of solemn tranquillity. Stopped in his tracks, Clogger respectfully removed his helmet and scanned the lofty architectural splendour for signs of life. Apparently deserted, he cautiously made his way to a partially open oval-topped internal door and peered into a cold, sparsely furnished vestry. An elderly verger, sitting alone at an antique desk, was speaking quietly but purposefully on the telephone under the straining glow of a single light bulb, high in the ceiling.

"Got to close the tower," Clogger mouthed.

Preoccupied with constantly changing transport arrangements for his special guests, the church official pointed impatiently to a key-rack fixed to the wall and continued with his conversation. Clogger responded by stealthily removing the appropriate lump of shiny-iron. Then, anxious not to further disturb God's transport manager, he crept out of the room and made his way to the tower staircase. He had just started to climb the ancient stonework when his pocket-set spluttered into life and comprehensively tested his ability to keep two balls in the air at the same time. In the confines of the mighty cathedral the transmission was severely distorted, but among the staccato jumble of broken jargon Clogger unfortunately recognised his own call-sign and the word urgent. Wrong-footed by the radio black-spot, he thudded back onto the flagged base of the staircase in one jump, pulled the access gate shut, turned the key, and ran out of the cathedral into the wide-open space of Palace Green.

"You're breaking-up control, repeat the last message," the breathless Elvet foot-patrol blasted.

"After you've closed the tower return to the Market Place. Traffic warden requests urgent assistance. Did you receive?"

"Roger, loud and clear."

Bleep, bleep, bleep.

Now in possession of two important keys, and the Painted-Lady in some sort of trouble, our over-zealous hero turned on his heals and sprinted back into Saddler Street towards the Market Place. In the few minutes he'd been away from the hub, Wupert and Bald Eagle had gone elsewhere in their quest for an incomplete pocket note-book and the Framwelgate foot-patrol had taken over from the Painted-Lady in the hot seat. Intending to make her way to the station canteen, she was crouching outside the Victorian indoor market with the head of a twelve-year-old boy in her vast bosom.

"He's been playing the wag from school," she called as Clogger weaved his way across the crowded market cobbles.

"What's urgent about that?" asked the sweating giant when two tearful eyes flashed in his direction.

"They've been fishing and his pal is stranded on the pebble island near the ice-rink."

"How did he get over there?" Clogger queried, dropping onto his haunches to engage the emergency at eye-level.

"We waded out this morning," sniffed the truanting juvenile, "but the river came up and he's stuck. It's still rising, he's going to drown."

When the weeping boy turned again for the comfort of the traffic warden's tear-stained headlights, Clogger bounced to his feet and applied lightening logic to a potentially life threatening situation.

"Forget your lunch, sweet-face" he ordered, "take the boy back to the scene and pacify his pal from the shoreline. I'll be with you in ten minutes."

Besotted by Clogger's command of the situation, the Painted-Lady cuddled her charge towards the public steps by the Church of St. Nicholas, while he cannoned off again through dense pedestrian traffic towards Elvet Bridge. Charging down the steps on the west side of the river crossing, with one hand on his helmet, Clogger advanced on the staved profile of Brown's boathouse and the crocodile of varnished rowing-boats moored tightly alongside.

"I'm commandeering a ship," he bawled to a man idly sweeping the concrete landing.

"We're closed for the day," the boatman replied. "The river's in spate."

"It's an emergency!"

"Take the big one on the end," conceded the employee, temporarily abandoning his sweeping-brush to untie Dunelm.

Clogger threw his unwieldy helmet into the bow, then clambered aboard the wobbly planking with the assistance of a firm shoulder. Inexperienced in single-handed marine exploration, he lost vital seconds trying to slot the bulky oars into rocking brass rowlocks from a very precarious standing position.

"Sit down first," the boatman insisted, fearing decapitation. "Which direction are you going?"

"Down stream."

Once Clogger had stabilised his centre of gravity on the broad, central cross-plank and adjusted the footboard to its extreme, his on-shore assistant threw the trailing end of the bow-rope aboard, then launched the expeditionary force with his all-purpose sweeping-brush, pushing the pointed-end firmly towards the main current. Swinging the little rescue boat in the direction of nearby Elvet Bridge, Sir Francis was more concerned about his first obstacle than the boatman's final piece of advice. Urgent glances over his right shoulder and the thrashing of oars successfully aligned the vessel with the central arch, but marginalised a lifetime's experience on the river.

"Don't go beyond Prebends Bridge, it's dangerous!"

As the crow flies the scene of the emergency was about four-hundred yards away, but to get there by river Clogger had to negotiate the mile-long loop and circumnavigate the castle and cathedral. Assisted by a strong current he rowed his clinker-built galleon towards the Kingsgate footbridge under the curious gaze of a group of academics taking their constitutional on the towpath. By any standard

Drake's rescue plan was a brilliant piece of initiative. Indeed, it may have qualified for some sort of award had it not been for a breakdown in communications. Sweating profusely, Clogger was cruising at five knots confident of reaching the little island within the allotted ten minutes, when his slavish rowing style was interrupted by the radio.

"Elvet foot-patrol from foxtrot bravo control."

"Go ahead."

"I've got someone from the cathedral screaming on the telephone. Have you got the tower key?"

Oars trailing, the single-handed explorer drifted off-course while he rummaged through his trouser-pocket.

"Oh, yes, terribly sorry," Clogger panted.

"Get it back there, pronto," the irritated controller blasted. "Someone is locked-in"

"Committed at the moment," apologised Clogger. "Tell them I'll return it as soon as I can."

Punctuated by a gently pulsating receiver, a pregnant radio silence prevailed. While Clogger hauled himself through a curtain of weeping willow back into the mainstream, and prepared for the hair-pin at the half-way point, the busy communications operative paged his records to discover that he had not been updated on the progress of Clogger's last detail.

"Elvet foot-patrol."

"Go ahead."

"What exactly are you doing?" the controller quizzed, revealing to the whole sub-division that he had failed to live up to his title.

"Mobile on the river," Clogger transmitted, sculling the bow into line with his free hand.

The declaration prompted a second more extended radio silence at the flummoxed communications hub. Ruling out the possibility that Christ had been issued with a pocket-set, the puzzled operative contemplated the territorial boundaries of the river police.

Perhaps they are no longer restricted to the tidal reaches, he thought, glancing at Sunderland on a huge, wall-mounted map. No, he must mean he's engaged on the towpath.

Anyway, before the controller had time to disentangle the conundrum and up-date his log, he was faced with another priority telephone call, this time from the assize court building.

"Elvet foot-patrol from foxtrot bravo control," he called urgently.

"Go ahead."

"Exact location?"

"Approaching Prebends Bridge," answered Captain Catchpole, glancing over his shoulder.

The fact that Clogger was apparently where he should have been at that hour of the day caused the controller to exhale pure static over the air waves.

"Judge en-route," he sighed again.

"But..."

"Priority," the controller insisted before engaging another resource in conversation.

His arms and legs were pumping like well-oiled machines when Clogger sailed under the typically deserted Prebends Bridge into the watery sunlight of the final straight. With his back to his objective it was a faint call from heaven that first attracted his attention, not the little sign nailed to the trunk of a towering Elm; No Boats Beyond This Point. Less than half a mile from home a second distant cry caused the lone oarsman to miss a stroke. Temporarily disengaged, he scanned the tree tops on both sides of the river before homing in on the Almighty. With his head screwed round hard to the left, Clogger's eyes followed the imposing stone profile of the cathedral all the way to the cloud-base. Frustrated by the verger's inability to secure the prompt services of a medieval locksmith, the Bishop of Durham and his distressed VIP entourage had returned, appropriately enough, to heavenly territory in their quest for freedom.

Nobody should be up there! Clogger pondered failing to recognise the desperate plight of a small group of flailing arms at the base of the flagpole.

Having successfully interned the region's leading churchman, Captain Catchpole adjusted his centre of gravity and got back into his stroke. In the broken waters of a quickening current, he was rapidly putting distance between his stern and the majestic Prebends Bridge, when a more readily identifiable figure stormed across his line of rear vision. Sandwiched between a pair of two-wheeled robots with his grey locks and black robe bellowing in the breeze, the face of the rotund circuit judge was the same colour as his crimson body-sash. Albeit under motor cycle escort, never before had a visiting high court judge walked home for his lunch.

Clogger's next course of action is open to conjecture. One view is that he panicked when he realised he was free-wheeling out of control, while a second more likely theory points to his rekindled interest in saluting. Whatever the reason, under the disbelieving gaze of a senior member of the judiciary and his mummified bodyguards, Clogger shipped oars and stood-up smartly on the fast moving approach to the old Fulling Mill. Seconds later, alongside a renowned cathedral viewing point, occupied by a clutch of tittering Japanese, the little rowing-boat nose-dived over the swollen weir and discharged her cargo arse-over-tit into the drink. When the army helicopter eventually arrived from Catterick Garrison the population of the tiny pebble island near the ice-rink had doubled, qualifying for its own foot-patrol.

5   BUDGERIGAR-WORRYING

The point where the opportunistic phase-two of the offensive gave-way to the sustained and gruelling phase-three has always been a source of speculation. Before Clogger had completely side-lined the clergy and judiciary he was embarking on the longest part of his three-week campaign; the systematic destruction of B-Relief's resources, both physical and human. Ship-wrecked, with a judicial loose-end still to tidy-up, he comprehensively disproved the Pye Telecommunications' sales-pitch that secured the lucrative contract for the first police pocket-sets. The equipment turned out not to be constable-proof after all. It could be destroyed by a series of underwater boulders, bounced over at speed. Police helmets were similarly vulnerable, although the tattered shell of Clogger's bucket served for many months as a keep-net for a snotty-nosed Newton Hall angler, conducting secret life-expectancy tests with decapitated eels.

Ironically the only hardware to survive the disaster more or less intact was H.M.S. Dunelm herself. Up-turned and oarless, she was decommissioned from crown service in shallow water near The Sands, then man-handled back to base for a refit. After a final coat of varnish sea-faring superstition kicked-in and today she's available for charter, to a maximum of four camera-wielding rubber-necks, in the name of Clogger's Folly.

Phase-three was the back-bone of the offensive, designed to render an elite team of front-line policemen ineffective in the fight against crime. Starting as it did, when serious civil unrest was brewing in Northern Ireland, the notion that Constable 1328 Catchpole was really a republican agent has dominated many a subsequent multi-lateral summit in the back room of *The Shakespeare*. Timing though, has always been a difficult aspect to theoretically accommodate in the light of Clogger's three years unbroken police service. Ignoring the biological contradiction in terms, it meant he was a highly-trained sleeper at a time when the republican movement wasn't that well organised, although it's possible his sympathies were stirred by daily media coverage giving the activists an anonymous, but effective early presence on the mainland.

Scheduled to commence at 6.0 a.m. on Wednesday of early-day week, the ground assault was delayed by a compulsory two-hour sub-divisional training session, hastily organised by the tutor sergeant on the direct instructions of Gentleman Jim. For reasons beyond Clogger's comprehension, the focus was on inter-organisational co-operation, public relations and the handling of the elderly and recently bereaved. Given the trend-setting title of a carousel course, it ran continuously for three days between the hours of 8.0 am and 6.0 p.m. Too little too late, the desperate sub-divisional head ordered the attendance of all ground-cover constables, including policewomen, under the guise of voluntary vocational training.

The ploy, to make staff attend in their own time, was an attempt to safeguard against the counter-productive effect of under-manning at a time when operational efficiency was at a low ebb, but Bald Eagle successfully applied a perverse logic to the situation. In a whispering interlude during the start-of-shift briefing, the sergeant seized the opportunity for a respite from the rigours of supervising Clogger, convincing Wupert that in his case under-manning would enhance operational efficiency. As a consequence Sir Francis was the first student to arrive for the first session. Typically disobeying the laws of human nature, he plonked himself on the very front seat in the small classroom, and in duty-time conscientiously absorbed material invaluable to the elimination of his feathered, judicial loose-end.

It was after ten that morning when the real action began to unfold. Clogger had hastily disposed of two pork pies and half a pint of tea, returning to the Framwelgate foot beat where it was felt he could avoid a chance meeting with the still motorised circuit judge. Apart from the fact the senior law officer had expressed concern when he learned of Clogger's survival, another glimpse of the moron was likely to diminish his lordship's ability to clinically sum-up, provoking a costly re-trial. In the event the old sea dog was standing on the corner of North Road and Neville Street in his spare uniform, making-up a duplicate pocket note-book issued in exchange for a block of papier-mâché.

"Framwelgate foot-patrol from foxtrot bravo control," the hitherto auxiliary pocket-set crackled.

"Go ahead control."

"Have you had your refreshments?"

"Roger," said Woger.

"Make your way to three zero South Street, report of a sudden death."

Now an expert in this particular field, Clogger had an advantage over his communications-room colleagues and arrogantly asserted his authority.

"From whence did this report come, control?" Clogger queried.

"Telephone," answered a curious radio operative.

"May I ask who took the call?"

"I did. What do you want to know that for?"

"Was the caller male or female?"

"Clogger, it's an emergency, just fucking get on with it."

Ironically the unusual lapse in the radio operator's polished broadcasting style was an involuntary reaction to the trauma of controlling a maritime disaster for which he ought to have received time-off and or professional counselling. Anyway, the terse instruction stunned the entire sub-divisional radio network into silence. Momentarily halted, units everywhere turned their receivers to full volume and listened intensely for the outbreak of war.

"Control, I have to remind you that this is not an emergency in the ordinary sense of the word," Clogger advised, quoting verbatim chunks of the tutor sergeant's thoughts on the subject. "Clearly there's nothing we can do for the deceased, but we can minimise the distress suffered by loved ones. Now, was the caller male or female?"

Embarrassed by Clogger's polite dominance of the intellectual high-ground, the operator reluctantly replied, "Female."

"What's her relationship with the deceased?"

"Wife."

"How did she sound to you?"

"She was sobbing."

"Was there anybody else in the house with her?"

"How do I bloody know, I haven't got a crystal ball."

"Control, you'd better send a policewoman to accompany me."

95

Assisted by the Painted-Lady's recognition of the spare panda-car on the closed circuit television monitor, a policewoman appeared in North Road within five minutes and stopped her little two-tone blue Mini van at the kerb, immediately in front of the Framwelgate giant. Not having seen him since his first day in the sub-division, she was overcome by a hot flush as Clogger swept-off his new helmet and crossed the path of a determined column of ants, hauling shopping bags towards the city-centre.

"Ah, it's you, sweet-face," Clogger chirped, swinging open the passenger-side door to squeeze his huge frame into the sardine can. "You'll have to turn round, we're going to South Street."

With one admiring eye on Clogger's rugged features, the faintly-perfumed young policewoman threw the vehicle into a nifty three-point-turn bringing the light, two-way traffic-flow to a respectful halt.

"What's it all about?" she asked, while Clogger's eyes browsed her black-silken knees.

"Sudden death, but the wife could be distressed," he advised, passing across two uniformed bumps to the long, trailing roots of a black-capped walnut-whip.

"You must have been on the course! I'm going to attend tomorrow afternoon," she swooned, racing the panda-car back down North Road to the junction with South Street.

Severely hunched with his helmet on his lap, he was about to answer when his attractive chauffeur swung the little van violently to the right and exaggerated the effect of the centrifugal force.

"Thirty," instructed Clogger, his driver reluctantly easing herself off his log-sized right arm to get to grips with the street numbering.

When the little van came to a body-lurching halt twenty seconds later, Clogger experienced a romantic urge that forced him revisit the adjacent silver-nippled twin peaks.

She's gagging for it!

Number thirty South Street was an elegant, middle-class Victorian dwelling with a medium-sized Mercedes parked on the inclined carriageway outside. An immaculate gloss-painted, black front door with a highly-polished brass knocker, sat between two broad bay windows facing onto a small, well-kept front garden, enclosed by iron railings. While Clogger banged the knocker the policewoman carefully closed the garden gate and brought up the rear. She was standing shoulder to waist on his right flank when the door opened and a maturing, silver-haired lady wearing an embroidered satin housecoat, appeared.

"Oh, come in," she sobbed, her swollen eyes red and tearful.

Clogger hadn't bothered to replace his headgear after alighting from the panda-car, but the policewoman respectfully removed her's before following him over the threshold into a tasteful, high-ceilinged hall, adorned with delicate watercolours of Durham City.

Each carrying their headgear like church collection plates, the police team followed their host along a classically-patterned thick red carpet to a door at the far end of the passage.

"Through here," the lady of the house wept, trying desperately to maintain her polished vowels.

The large, bees-waxed living room was dominated by a chunky, black-leather three-piece suite positioned around a rectangular, glass coffee table. When Clogger saw the magistrates' clerk sitting in one of the armchairs, his head resting serenely beneath an ornate, free-standing budgerigar cage, he was confused. The Times, limply suspended across the deceased's lap, added to the impression he was just napping.

"Oh, sorry to disturb you boss...I mean sir," blurted Clogger, anxious not to provoke another congestive attack.

Had it not been for the presence of the policewoman Clogger would probably have switched into disaster mode there and then, but fortunately she was able to kick him without the next-of-kin noticing.

"Oh, what a tragedy!" Clogger blasted, recovering just in time.

"He took ill at court on Monday," the distressed wife explained, between a flurry of sobbing gasps.

The giant put his lumbering right arm around the bereaved's satin-clad shoulder and reassured her. "I understand," he whispered economically. "It was my inspector who called the ambulance."

"Came out of hospital yesterday," the lady of the house continued to sob. "He seemed perfectly alright until just after breakfast, then he said he felt tired and went to read the newspaper. Then, this!"

Unable to carry on, Clogger ushered his distressed host to the sofa and guided her onto a soft, bulbous leather cushion. Acting instinctively the policewoman sat beside her and replaced Clogger's comforting arm with her own.

"I have to call-out the police surgeon, to confirm death," the newly qualified counsellor quietly advised, searching his dedicated right-hand trouser-pocket for his radio transmitter.

"There's no need, officer," sobbed the clerk's wife, "I've already called the family doctor. It was he who told me to ring you."

"Then tell me where the kitchen is and I'll make you a nice cup of tea."

When Clogger returned five minutes later with a mug of hot sweet tea, the policewoman was gently encouraging the deceased's wife to look at her beloved husband and openly grieve, not bottle-up her feelings.

"That's right," Clogger confirmed, "don't worry about us, cry as much as you like, it's good for you."

There was a strange, surreal pause at that point. The well-groomed lady wiped tears from her cheeks and sipped Clogger's concoction with a sad but grateful glance into his towering eyes. The attractive policewoman relaxed her embrace and pondered the content, podgy blue features of the dead clerk and the build-up of frothy residue in the corners of his mouth. Still on his feet, Clogger was eyeball to eyeball with a nodding green budgerigar, proudly perched in its pendulous conical cage.

"What's its name?" Clogger asked, breaking the silence with a genuine interest.

"Joey," said the lady. "He's six years old."

"Nice bird! My dad breeds budgies."

"I should have known something awful was going to happen. When Jack didn't come home from court on Monday, Joey stopped talking. He's talked ever since we got him"

"Really!" Clogger said, peering into the cage.

"Birds sense these things you know," asserted the deceased's wife, her hands cupped around her tea mug

"No, I think it's just a coincidence," Clogger diagnosed. "When was his beak last clipped?"

"Can't remember. I don't think it's ever been clipped," answered the bereaved, her mind skilfully diverted from the crisis in hand.

"Have you got a pair of nail-clippers handy? I'll have him talking again in no time!" the self-appointed veterinary surgeon assured, under the gaze of two cuddling females.

"Oh, it would be nice if he could talk like he used to," said the lady. "Now that Jack's gone, he's the only thing I've got left in the world."

Suddenly enthused by the possibility of her beloved pet recovering his prolific conversational skills, the clerk's wife untangled herself from the policewoman's arms, stood-up and scurried into the kitchen with her empty tea mug. When she returned brandishing a pair of chrome nail-clippers, Clogger already had his enormous hand in the cage, coaxing the patient out into the operating theatre. With a skilful snatch learned from his father, the bundle of green feathers was locked tightly in his left palm, its innocent little head peering over the top of a formidable, ink-stained thumb.

Adequate light was the next problem. Clogger moved into the corner of the room next to a netted sash-window, then took the clippers from his operating assistant. Seconds later the family doctor arrived and tried to awaken the magistrates' clerk with an assault on the front door knocker. With Clogger at a critical stage, he was forced to continue the surgery while the policewoman took command of the other, less pressing matter.

"Oh, my condolences," uttered the grey-suited, bag-wielding GP, pulling off the clerk's gold-rimmed spectacles to make a routine examination of his lifeless eyes. "His heart wasn't strong, but I'm afraid there will have to be a post-mortem examination," he continued, turning his attention to the grieving widow.

The peripheral veterinary surgeon, anxious not to miss anything, was trying to keep two balls in the air at the same time when a surgical complication presented itself. Applying additional manual pressure to hold the bird perfectly still, at the third attempt Clogger successfully snipped away a particularly tough piece of cuticle to complete the routine procedure.

"Now, what about you?" the kindly doctor queried, addressing the clerk's wife. "You should have somebody with you at a time like this. Who can you call?"

"There's nobody really, only Joey," replied the red-eyed widow. "Our son lives in Australia."

"Then I think you should let me give you a sedative."

The other clinician opened his left hand at this point and exposed a green budgerigar with every ounce of life squeezed out of it.

"I think so too," he said, offering an unsolicited second opinion.

A short, disbelieving silence sucked all the players into various states of indecision. Electrically shocked, the clerk's wife threw a tantrum then chose to collapse in the armchair opposite her dead husband. Clogger went to put the bird's body back into its cage, but something told him otherwise and he settled for his trouser-pocket. Astonished, the policewoman oscillated between the deceased and the living room door while the family doctor rummaged in his black bag for suitable medicine.

I must switch-off the supply first he subsequently decided, pushing Clogger out of the room with both of his open palms. "You can get all the details you need from my secretary later. There's nothing suspicious here. I'll call the undertaker."

Demoted to the street outside, feeling very uncomfortable, the policewoman was on the driver-side of the panda searching her pockets for the keys, when Mr Sensitivity recollected a particularly laboured point during the tutor sergeant's two-hour sermon.

Always keep the communications-room up-dated with developments, operational efficiency depends on it he recalled, resting his elbows on the passenger-side roof of the Mini to ogle the new barmaid. She's definitely gagging for it!

"Do you fancy a drink after work, sweet-face?" Romeo ventured, just before she climbed in behind the wheel.

Perplexed but still predisposed, the policewoman leaned over to release the passenger-side door lock and was confronted by a glazed midriff. Two searching paws appeared at each side of a bulging-crotch and clawed at the taught, dark serge. Had it not been for the temporary removal of a limp budgerigar from prime trouser-pocket space, her appetite might have been kindled there and then.

"Framwelgate foot-patrol to foxtrot bravo control," called Clogger, once he had re-arranged his accessories.

"Pass your message, Framwelgate foot-patrol."

"Reference three zero South Street, no suspicious circumstances. Inform the coroner's officer that full details will be available from Doctor Ridsdale's surgery later in the day. Oh, and you'd better inform the superintendent out of courtesy. It's the magistrates' clerk."

Suitably impressed with the completeness of Clogger's situation report, a short radio silence followed while Clogger leaned on the blue-tin work-top and the controller up-dated his records.

"Last message received Framwelgate, what is your exact location?"

"Still in South Street."

"Make your way to the junction of Crossgate and Allergate, report of a road accident," rattled Clogger's receiver.

Mr Efficiency was just about to acknowledge his latest detail when the little machine fired-off a sarcastic after-thought.

"The call came from ambulance control and the operator sounded normal," the radio advised, providing more general entertainment over the sub-divisional air-waves.

"Received," Clogger blasted, lumbering into the passenger-side of the sardine tin. "Did you hear that, sweet-face?"

"Yeah," she chirped, throwing the little van into another nifty three-point-turn. "I'm not sure!"

"You're not sure about what?"

"Whether I should meet you after work."

"We can have a quiet drink in the County for half an hour, can't we?"

"I'll think about it."

When the dynamic duo rumbled up the shiny cobbles of Crossgate to the point where the equally steep Allergate sweeps in from the right, a clutch of pensioners were clucking like hens beside a forlorn Hillman Imp. Facing downhill, the little rear-engined saloon had mounted the near-side kerb and was embracing the base of a metal lamp-post with its slightly crumpled bonnet.

"Anyone injured?" Clogger called, leaping from the upholstered roller-skate while his chauffeur struggled with the last notches on the handbrake.

"She's gan to hospital," replied a cloth-capped question mark, with a gnarly walking stick. "Young'un, brok her leg."

"Anyone else involved?"

"Nar," said the lived-in face with a blue-seamed scar indicative of a roof fall.

While Clogger looked urgently up Allergate then into Crossgate, the policewoman trotted to his side. "How did it happen?" she asked.

"No idea," muttered the puzzled giant, failing to identify anything untoward in either deserted carriageway. "Did anyone see anything?"

"Nar," the retired miner responded, his eloquence affording him natural chairmanship of the elderly audience.

"Probably swerved to avoid a stray dog!" deduced Clogger.

"Nar, yon is an Imp. Much use as an ash-tray on a motto-bike."

Despite the reputation of the crashed vehicle, particularly its propensity for stalling at inopportune times, the accident investigator chose to ignore his technical advisor when he up-dated his base station.

"Framwelgate foot-patrol to foxtrot bravo control."

"Go ahead."

"One vehicle involved, front-end damage. Lady driver already taken to hospital, probable cause; evasive action. Arrange recovery."

"Stand-by Framwelgate, while I contact casualty."

Bleep, bleep, bleep.

Aware that he was now responsible for the submission of a detailed road accident report and supporting sketch-plan, Clogger jotted down the registration number of the damaged car then rummaged in his left-hand trouser-pocket for his regulation block of weather-proof yellow wax. Together with his Swiss army knife and some other essential nick-knacks, the road marker was obstructed by his latest acquisition; an automatic rubber-neck disperser. When he inadvertently removed the limp, feathered equipment to access the depths of his secondary trouser-pocket, all but the pirate-faced spokesman scurried away from the scene.

"Not a lot of meat on yon," the ex-pitman quipped. "Thou needs half a dozen for a nosh."

The accident investigator scored the ground at the four corners of the little saloon under the undecided gaze of the policewoman, but the mention of food brought on his regular late morning hunger pangs. Standing together in limbo, waiting for further information over the radio, Clogger was contemplating the proximity of the nearest butcher's shop when his female colleague finally made up her mind to meet him socially after work.

"Framwelgate foot-patrol from foxtrot."

"Go ahead"

"Driver is receiving treatment for a broken tibia and bruised ribs, I haven't been able to ascertain her preferred means of recovery. Is the vehicle serviceable?"

"Course it's gannable," the eavesdropping technical assistant interjected. "Motto is in't back."

When Clogger swung open the driver's door and leaned into the crashed car to reach the pendulous ignition keys, the engine fired into life immediately. A push and heave on the steering wheel, resisted by squeaking rubber, completed his exhaustive serviceability examination.

"Affirmative, control." he transmitted, while the little car confidently ticked over.

"Then bring it into the station yard for safe...stand-by Framwelgate, incoming treble-nine call."

Bleep, bleep, bleep.

Come on, come on, I'm starving.

"Is Policewoman Watson still with you, Framwelgate?" the radio resumed.

"Yes."

"Ask her to drive the car to the station yard, you go immediately to Brasside in the spare panda-car, report of gunfire," instructed the controller, naturally protective of a female colleague.

103

"But it's not my area," Clogger protested in the sure knowledge there wouldn't be a pork pie vendor in the environs of a female prison.

"Nobody else to send," sighed the controller. "Local unit is already committed."

"What about my accident enquires?"

"Don't worry, I'll ring the hospital again and ask them not to discharge the injured party until you get there."

Clogger's final pathetic obstacle gave the radio operative the opportunity he had been waiting for all morning. "But I don't know where it is!"

"If you don't know where it is ask a policewoman," the delighted controller chanted, restoring his audience rating with a new rendition of an old music hall favourite.

Comprehensively out-manoeuvred, Clogger listened while his female colleague gave him directions, then he strode to the front of the throbbing Hillman Imp and dropped into a scrum position, shoulder to shoulder with the lamp-post.

"Get in, sweet-face," he called to his mystified companion. "Put it into neutral and make sure the hand-brake is off."

Disbelieving her eyes, the hesitant policewoman obliged and watched the ever reddening complexion of her new suitor straining at the end of the crumpled bonnet. Inch by inch the little saloon defied the gravitational forces of Allergate until there was about a yard of clearance between it and the lamp-post.

"Right, turn the wheel," Clogger spluttered, his leather-soled boots starting to slip under pressure.

When Mr Universe eventually released his grip and leapt for cover, the little car rolled back onto the carriageway narrowly avoiding the improvised buffer.

"See you later, in the County," shouted sweet-face, slamming shut the driver's door to disappear down the steep cobbles into the bowels of Crossgate.

"Right," the satisfied giant replied, striding towards the spare panda-car. Definitely gagging for it! Let's find a butcher's shop and get out to Brasside.

"It's all ganna end in tears," observed the solitary technical consultant as he turned to hobble about his business.

Helmet loose on the passenger seat, Clogger squeezed into the tiny cockpit of the 850cc formula-three racing machine and charged to the top of Crossgate. With the aid of the flashing blue light he bullied the little van into Alexander Crescent and circumnavigated the north-west corner of the city to reach the viaduct at the top-end of North Road. Once through the notional city gate it was 60 mph plain-sailing to Framwelgate Moor, a sprawling new council estate on the outskirts of town. On the broad, undulating sub-urban straight, just after the fire station, Clogger was forced into an unscheduled pit-stop. A service road alongside a parade of shops provided an ideal re-fuelling point for his flagging motor. With the blue strobe still stabbing at regular intervals, Clogger made a record-breaking three-stride dash across the pavement into the baker's shop, and barged to the front of a bewildered queue.

"Give me a pork pie, love," he demanded, cracking a coin on top of the glass counter.

"We've only got mince and potato left, but they're just out of the oven."

A sudden excess of saliva forced the giant to swallow. "That will do," he spluttered. "It's an emergency!"

When the white-coated assistant turned to open a heated stainless-steel display cabinet, Clogger was assailed by a savoury smell that triggered a second surge of oral enzyme.

"Don't bother to wrap it," he insisted, anticipating a life-threatening delay.

Convinced she was somehow assisting the police in the line of duty, the public-spirited bakery assistant handed the culinary master-piece to the ravenous constable, along with his money.

"On the house," she called, as he turned to race back to the grid.

The final lap was skilfully negotiated, through the private Newton Hall Estate towards the green fields of Brasside, with one steering hand, the other being permanently engaged in the frenzied supply of cockpit nourishment and the removal of occasional gravy spillage. Peppered with pastry particles, Clogger had devoured the pie and was picking the front of his tunic when the chequered flag finally came into view. On the narrow country road just beyond the female penitentiary, he could see the tell-tale signs of a rural lynch-mob. A battered green Land Rover and an old blue tractor, abandoned carelessly on the grass verge, were the backdrop for a portly farmer brandishing a shotgun and bawling incomprehensible instructions over a five-barred gate.

Nice, but I still prefer pork, the connoisseur concluded as he extinguished his emergency blue light and approached Buffalo Bill.

"Don't discharge that weapon on the highway," Clogger warned. "What's going on?"

"Five lambs down," growled the irate farmer. "Fucking Dalmatian."

"Where's the dog at now?"

"Gone to ground," the weathered-face answered, pointing to a copse at the side of the pasture where two more double-barrelled bounty-hunters were recklessly probing dense undergrowth.

"They're too near the road," the replenished giant advised. "Call them over."

Another series of incomprehensible commands reinforced by the distant sight of a police uniform, persuaded the advance party into retreat. When the two woolly-hatted rural gorillas slouched reluctantly to the other side of the gate in their shit-caked Wellingtons, Clogger demonstrated the full extent of his ordnance expertise.

"Break those weapons," he commanded, "before someone gets their fucking head blown-off."

With two out of three double-barrels pointing safely to the ground and his platoon standing at ease on either side of the gate, Clogger continued with his investigation.

"Did anyone actually see the dog attack the sheep?"

"No, but it's covered in blood," the farmer replied, adjusting the balance of his unbroken shotgun, resting backwards across a broad, tweed shoulder.

"Has it got a collar?"

"Yeah," a second trooper confirmed, "it's a thoroughbred, probably strayed from Newton Hall. All gob and no knickers, that lot!"

"Can it be caught?"

"No, no, definitely not," Clogger's second-in-command asserted, supported by the shaking heads of his vastly experienced farm-hands. "Tasted blood, anyway it's already had one barrel in the hind-quarter."

"PC Catchpole to foxtrot bravo control."

"Pass your message."

"Sheep-worrying in progress at Brasside, the animal will be destroyed under my supervision. Would you inform the prison, and tell them to expect further gunfire."

"Roger, PC Catchpole."

Bleep, bleep, bleep.

Straight into action, Colonel Catchpole leaned over the five-barred gate and addressed his motley front-line team. "Keep your backs to the road at all times and don't fire directly into the wood," he instructed. "You come with me."

Bearing his sky-ward pointing shoulder arm, the rotund farmer followed Clogger to the panda-van and realised he was required to board the tiny tin-box by the front passenger-door. Weaned on bigger more robust forms of transport, he would normally have made safe the cumbersome .12 bore and nursed it in readiness for the task ahead, but the confines of a Mini were too restrictive. A combination of anxiety and unfamiliarity prompted the farmer to open one of the two rear cargo doors first, then adjust the positions of an emergency blanket and a first-aid box. After that, with his chauffeur oblivious to the concept of safety catches, he carelessly laid the weapon across the low floor of the vehicle, between the wheel arches. When Clogger clambered into the cockpit and urgently lobbed his helmet from the passenger seat into the back of the van, to make way for his guest, the hair-triggered tendencies of the family heirloom should have been apparent, but fate allowed him to continue with his action plan.

Clogger intended to drive the short distance down the country road passed the stationary farm vehicles to the edge of the copse, park the police van with its blue light running as a warning to others, then, with the assistance of his armed agricultural advisor, flush the offending Dalmatian out of the wood into the path of the ground troops. Had it not been for the appearance of the local postman pedalling his bright red cycle in the opposite direction, the strategy would probably have taken its full course. In the event Clogger's concern for the safety of the civil servant caused a chain reaction reminiscent of cascading dominoes. The catalyst was the vehicle's braking system. Intending to warn the unsuspecting postie of the potential danger, Clogger was almost alongside when he stabbed the pedal and shunted the cannon across the tin floor of the van into the path of a series of rivet heads.

Facing forward at an angle, the blast of spread shot blew a chunk out of Clogger's second helmet before penetrating the base of the driver's seat and tearing a large, jagged hole in the bodywork, directly behind the driver's door. The first domino to fall was the postman himself. Although there was no real contact, the explosion secured him, and his bag of letters, exclusive accommodation in the muddy ditch at the base of a gnarly hedgerow. Clogger and his unofficial crew-member responded in perfect unison, each departing the freshly opened sardine can like launching sky-divers. On the near-side of the vehicle the temporarily deafened farmer belatedly cupped his hands over his ears, and on the off-side Clogger graphically outlined the symptoms of a superficial buttock injury to the prostrate postie.

"My bloody arse is on fire!" he bawled, rubbing a tattered area of dark blue serge.

Anyway, despite its unconventional nature, the flushing-out procedure was an unqualified success. The sonic boom resonated through the copse and disturbed a domestic dog, rendered insane by a diet of raw lamb. With its jaws and snout caked with blood it dragged a paralysed hind-quarter out of the dense undergrowth, across the pasture and into the deadly crossfire of Jed and Jethro Clampet. Five minutes later the duo appeared, ironically with their guns properly broken, and formerly handed over their trophy in strict accordance with the law; a thick leather collar with a clearly engraved identity disc.

"PC Catchpole to foxtrot bravo control."

"Go ahead."

"Operation at Brasside complete."

"Is the dog dead?"

"Affirmative...and the panda...and my arse isn't all that healthy either."

"PC Catchpole, what is your ETA at casualty."

"Fifteen minutes."

"After you've completed your road accident enquiries confer with Policewoman Watson and take her home."

Clogger hesitated. "Roger," he transmitted, quizzically. *I meant the County Hotel, not the County Hospital! What is she thinking about, passing personal messages over the radio?*

With his platoon demobilised, the journey back into the city was a lonely, painful affair. Apart from having to regularly shift his body weight from one buttock to the other, there was a displaced spring trying to penetrate the base of the driver's seat. A cutting draught from the new emergency exit didn't help, but it wasn't until Clogger slipped into the grounds of County Hospital from North Road that the full extent of the damage became apparent. A group of bemused student nurses gazed at the aneurysm in the once perfectly rectangular Mini van, then the war veteran alighted and their curiosity turned to open amusement. With broken glass in his trousers and the latest system of helmet ventilation, Clogger slammed shut the ill-fitting driver's door and marched on the entrance of casualty just in time to see a young lady being wheeled to a waiting ambulance with her leg in plaster.

"Excuse me," he called, "is this the lady who had the road accident this morning?"

"Yes, one of them," the escorting nurse replied, turning her attention to the incontinent robot with a hole in his head. "Are you alright?"

"Well, not exactly, I've had a slight accident myself, but I need to get some details before she goes home."

"Already been spoken to by a policewoman, she's in with the doctor at the moment."

"Ah, right," the relieved investigator sighed, resolving the mystery of his last radio message. *Sweet-face has completed the enquiry for me and is waiting for a lift. Definitely gagging for it!*

109

After the nurse had secured the first accident victim in the back of the ambulance and handed over to the driver, she noticed Clogger grimacing and pulling gingerly on the damp serge around his bottom.

"There's a toilet inside," she scowled, cautiously sniffing downwind of the stiff-legged giant.

"Oh, it's nothing like that," Clogger asserted. "Shooting accident!"

"You mean, someone has shot you there."

"Well, sort of."

Convinced she had identified entry and exit wounds, the authoritarian snapped, "Come with me," and led Lurch down a heavily disinfected green corridor to an equally pungent examination room. "Undress and lie on the bed," she ordered, scurrying off to discuss the medical impossibility with a doctor.

Safely ensconced behind a closed door, Clogger suspended his headgear from a drip-stand, then slowly surveyed his new surroundings while he unbuttoned his tunic. He was about to unbuckle his black-leather belt when the weight of his over-filled trouser-pockets threatened a painfully rapid decent, so he decided to unload the tools of his trade onto an instrument-laden side-bench. From his right-hand pocket the all-important radio transmitter was given pride of place next to a blood pressure machine, and from the other side a battery of miscellaneous secondary equipment conveniently filled two white-enamel kidney-dishes. When the nurse reappeared towing a young houseman in his sixteenth hour of duty, Clogger was lying face down on the single bed, with his hairy buttocks exposed.

"What happened?" said the bleary-eyed clinician, ignoring a bloody, red-kipper on Clogger's arse.

"Accidental discharge," the giant muttered into a crisp white pillow.

Acting on seriously defective information, the doctor made a cursory examination of Clogger's spiky scalp then glanced quizzically at his attentive assistant. The concern in her big brown eyes steered his attention to the ruptured ornament adorning the drip-stand and prompted a second cerebral scrutiny.

"Other end," Clogger advised, as the exhausted medic felt his way more thoroughly across the yard broom.

"What type of weapon was it?"

".12 bore."

The answer coincided with the doctor's gaze falling on the side-bench and the dubious contents of twin kidney-dishes. Clogger's all-purpose Swiss army knife and block of yellow wax didn't present a problem, but the shrivelled, speechless body of a recently manicured budgerigar added to the clinical conundrum.

"Don't you think you were using too much fire-power?" the doctor queried, staring vacantly at the deceased.

"Oh, no," the half-naked policeman insisted, "it was attacking sheep."

"Attacking sheep!"

"Yes, killed five."

"Antiseptic dressing please nurse, I must go and get some sleep."

The careful removal of a few pieces of lead shot with a pair of twizzers was not nearly as painful as the copious application of iodine by a humiliated nurse. Intent on retribution, she managed to induce violent anal contractions and a series of contorted facial expressions before taping a wad over Clogger's war wound.

"Get dressed," she snapped, flushing spent cotton wool into the sluice. "Do you want me to get rid of this?"

A preoccupied grunt from Clogger signalled the hasty disposal of a treasured family pet, in a manner unbecoming its station in life. When the wet and bedraggled ball of feathers swirled down the plug-hole to that big birdcage in the sky, the miffed nurse scurried out of the room.

"Your colleague is in reception," she ordered. "See your own doctor if you have any further problems."

The walk from the examination room to the waiting area in full battle-dress was a tentative affair. Although decidedly more comfortable in terms of pain, his new undergarment felt like a reverse sanitary towel and added a wide-legged dimension to his already stiff-legged gait. Despite a low box office turn-out Clogger's rendition of tin man in the Wizard of Oz received rave reviews from a bunch of randomly bandaged critics. It was this undivided attention, while he passed his personal details to the casualty receptionist, that distracted him from the condition of the policewoman, who was sitting quietly on the end of the back row nursing something.

"Thanks for completing the accident enquiry, sweet-face," Clogger enthused, rolling towards his latest conquest. "What did she say happened?"

"Intermittent brake failure," Policewoman Watson replied, void of her customary black stockings.

By then the towering robot had noticed a sparkling white plaster cast, but the revelation the accident had been caused by mechanical failure dominated his procedural thoughts.

"Oh, we must get independent confirmation," Clogger advised, suspecting that the lady driver was unlikely to be suitably qualified.

"I've already done that," the policewoman scowled, levering herself onto her feet with a pair of brand new National Health Service crutches.

6   THE FISHERWOMAN

In terms of the destruction of human resources, phase-three of hostilities opened with only moderate success. Although a serious knee injury confined the policewoman to sick-leave for nine weeks, Clogger had intended to ground her for the best part of nine months and ultimately secure her resignation. The plan however was misjudged in the embryonic stages. Unable to keep their tryst after work, Clogger still had a curious but impossible twinkle in his eye when he drove Long John Silver home to her flat on one not so painful cheek. Stiff-legged and chivalrous, he guided her shapely, pendulous body along a crumbling garden path, up three nasty front door steps and into a nicely furnished ground-floor lounge. A whispered suggestion that there was time for coffee before he returned to the police station, sent Lurch pounding into the kitchenette with bulges fore and aft.

When he returned with two slopping mugs he found the little beauty relaxing on the wrong end of a hard Chesterfield sofa with her plaster cast elevated provocatively on a matching pouffe. A flash of bare upper-thigh confirmed his prognosis and prompted the salivating, coffee-balancing conqueror to gently lower himself down beside her. Encouraged by an inviting smile, Clogger leaned towards her unbuttoned tunic brandishing the hot beverage and steam-rolled over his nappy and the big red kipper it was protecting. Apart from christening her new surgical appliance, the excruciating pain kick-started side-by-side pistons into unsynchronised action. She urgently wanted to stand but couldn't, and he wanted to sit but; well, suffice to say the episode wasn't conducive to romance and the relationship never developed into a full foetus.

On the hardware front though, the situation was an unqualified success. When Clogger logged off-duty at two o'clock, not only was the panda-van taken off the road but the ground was expertly prepared for his next initiative. Police standing orders stipulate that all road accidents involving police vehicles are dealt with by an officer not below the rank of inspector. Following the chain-of-command, Bald Eagle properly reported Clogger's mishap to Wupert whose academic mind was already preoccupied with technical definition. He was still undecided about the policewoman's accident. She had been driving in the lawful execution of her duty, but the vehicle didn't belong to the police. In Clogger's case there was no dispute about ownership, indeed there was damage and an injury, but no collision. After failing to find any precedent, Wupert decided it was an opportunity to impress headquarters. He would investigate both accidents personally and submit an in-depth, all-embracing report worthy of any murder enquiry. Using Bald Eagle as his assistant the decision effectively left B-Relief with diluted supervision for the rest of the Three-Week-War and it also submerged the blown-up panda-van into a sea of time-consuming bureaucracy.

Enthusiastic use of state-of-the-art electronic gadgetry at police workshops identified a chassis misalignment that made the vehicle technically unsuitable for police purposes, a repair insurers were unwilling to fund. Three months later, after a plethora of inspections and reports by every conceivable council department, the war relic was stripped of its livery and sold at auction to a self-employed painter and decorator who, rumour has it, was subsequently forced out of business by soaring tyre costs.

Clogger departed the mayhem that afternoon standing astride his oily 250cc Royal Enfield with his ruptured second police helmet strapped to his chin and a noticeable lump on his bottom. He intended to make the mile journey to his digs in the only comfortable riding position available to him, but the feat proved difficult. Although he cleared Elvet Bridge easily enough, the Painted-Lady was struggling with traffic backed-up in Silver Street and congestion had developed in the busy Market Place. Rather than make a painfully inconvenient dismount, the upright trials rider decided to show off his manoeuvring skills on the cobbles behind the traffic control box. By the time he'd completed his third time-wasting figure-of-eight a crowd had gathered to watch the student charity stunt. Sandwiched between his audience and the tail of a traffic jam, Clogger re-enacted the famous motorbike scene from the Great Escape. Unlike Steve Mc Queen though, he managed to penetrate the Silver Street barrier, albeit under a hail of small coinage.

Despite almost zero audience ratings, the return journey at five-thirty the following morning was even more bizarre. Bad weather in Weardale the previous week had descended on the city and brought with it heavy overnight rain and strong winds. Under the cover of darkness and wearing his bombed-out police helmet, Robocop roared back through the deserted city streets standing beneath a ballooning yellow oilskin with a fully inflated moped inner-tube around his neck and a billiard cue under his arm. Only a milk delivery boy and an early morning bus crew saw the apparition, but in the interests of preserving their personal integrity all three chose never to speak of it again.

It was anticipated Clogger would take three days uncertified sick-leave while the hole in his arse healed-up, but B-Relief didn't appreciate the absolute dedication of secret agents. A strange combination of surprise and disbelief befell the parade-room when the uniformed robot plodded gingerly through the door on Thursday 10th, the last day of his early-week. He had deposited the water-proof in the pannier of his leaky steed and dumped the billiard cue in the social club ready for night-shift, but he was still sporting a black rubber garland, a huge sandwich-box and a flak-ridden helmet.

"Fucking hell Clogger, you shouldn't have..." Bald Eagle spluttered, unable to finish his sentence.

"Wouldn't let you down, boss," the stalwart replied, "I mean sarge."

When Clogger peeled-off his wet head and neck gear the bleary-eyed audience took their usual, perfectly choreographed reflexive action and shielded their note-books and personal clip-boards from the liberal spray of surplus rain water.

"I think this should do the trick," Clogger muttered, carefully placing the stout inner-tube on a vacant chair. "Yes, perfect."

Once his bulbous nappy was comfortably inside the rubber ring, relief permeated the entire room, but by then Bald Eagle was perplexed.

What the fuck am I going to do with him today?

In such admirable circumstances it was customary to assign the walking-wounded to light station duties, but that was impossible in

Clogger's case. The stammering reaction of the now seriously reclusive Gentleman Jim, when he appeared in the building at nine o'clock, was unthinkable, and in any case it would disrupt the efficiency of the administrative machine from the top down. The Elvet beat was also a non-starter while the assize court was still in session. Another confrontation with the circuit judge was bound to bring the division unwelcome attention from the Lord Chancellor's Department, not to mention the effect a robotic foot-patrol would have on already shaky public relations. Then of course there was the issue of Clogger's exploded helmet, which had to be replaced immediately if he was to be assigned an operational role. With an unusual preoccupation, the ginger wig muddled his way through the events of the last twenty-four-hours and was still undecided when a timely intervention saved his supervisory bacon.

"Excuse me sarge, before you do the assignments, I wonder if I could walk the Framwelgate beat today?" the Meadowfield panda-driver asked, with a sincerity that radiated some important reason.

"Have you got enquires to make in that area?" Bald Eagle quizzed, suspecting that his most conscientious and talented officer had a lead on something juicy.

"Oh, no sarge, nothing like that, it's personal, but it would set my mind at rest."

"Do you want to talk to me in private, son?"

"No sarge, I count everyone here as friends. It's my wife you see."

"Is she alright?" Bald Eagle inquired, slipping into his welfare role. "I thought she had just had your first baby."

"She has sarge, but she's been doing some odd things lately. The doctor thinks it's a touch of post-natal depression."

"Where do you live?"

"Redhills. I could get home quickly if anything was to happen."

"Better than that," the sergeant asserted, suddenly noticing light at the end of the tunnel. "Patrol Framwelgate and visit your home every hour, tell the communications-room you have my permission. Clogger, can you drive on that thing?"

"Oh, yes boss...sarge," Clogger insisted, proudly rolling his bottom in the inflated inner-tube to demonstrate its effectiveness.

"Then take the Meadowfield panda...and call in at stores as soon as they open at eight," he instructed, glancing at the bullet hole prominently displayed on the parade-room table.

"What about my sheep-worrying enquiry in Newton Hall, boss...I mean sarge? I still have the owner of the dog to interview."

"Don't worry about that," snapped Bald Eagle, experiencing the onset of palpitations. "It will be taken care of by the Inspector and I."

The menacing thought of Clogger continuing where he'd left off the day before hadn't fully subsided when Wupert made what is now regarded as his historic parade-room entrance. In Churchillian style he carried a buff-folder with a discreetly hand-written working title; Catchpole Crisis. Containing a wad of notes and other relevant documentation, it was intended to encompass two dubious police accidents and an ancillary sheep-worrying, but what the young academic didn't realise was the file would never close for thirty years. Like Topsy, it would grow and grow until it became a definitive account of an ill-fated twenty-three days in the life of Durham City sub-division.

"Don't stand up," the inspector ordered, pre-empting a noisy and unnecessary interlude. "Just a couple of things!"

A nervous glance at Buddha, worshipping a burst bucket from the vantage point of an inflated rubber inner-tube, was all that Wupert could manage. Recognising direct eye contact would adversely affect his confidence, he continued with his gaze firmly fixed on the sergeant's artificial hair-line.

"Make a note," Wupert went on, prompting everyone to their pocket-books. "Female, five-feet-four, slim build, shoulder-length bwown hair, wearing a wed anowak and gwey twousers. Missing from the Lampton Ward of Winterton Hospital since twenty-one-hundwed yesterday. Sedgefield sub-division have information that she caught a bus into the City in search of a late dwink. Eyes peeled please, she may be wandewing locally or sleeping wough."

Thirty seconds of frantic clerical activity preceded the young shift-leader's second visit to the despatch box.

"Finally, I must wemind you all of the escalating conflict in Northern Ireland and the possibility that it may soon extend to the mainland. Headquarters are cuwwently dwawing-up guidelines for the secuwity of all police stations, but in the meantime it is up to each and evewy one of us to be extwa vigilant. That's all," he concluded, hastily leaving the chamber for the safety of his own office.

Despite heavy rain lashing onto his black Gannex overcoat and a wet, burning sensation in his face, the meticulous Meadowfield panda-driver was content to forfeit the comfort of his dedicated and well-ordered unit vehicle in the interests of his beloved wife and family. When Clogger drove out of the police station yard in the immaculately maintained two-tone blue van, abnormally hunched over the steering wheel, he passed the temporary Framwelgate foot-patrol battling his way through the storm along the dark and deserted Court Lane. Although both officers were entering unfamiliar territory in the quiet hours, the law that prevents a member of the public from ever seeing a wet policeman still had to be complied with.

"Get in," Clogger shouted, leaning precariously from his bouncy rubber throne to open the passenger-side door, "I'll drop you off at the bus station."

"Thanks," replied a very grateful ex-colleague designate. "You ought to get a cuppa from the duty-engineer at Broompark pumping station. He doesn't finish until eight."

"Where is it?" Clogger asked, hissing through a yellow sodium haze with the windscreen wipers at full stretch.

"Turn right at Stone Bridge, before you reach Langley Moor."

When Clogger pulled-up outside the rain swept bus station and pointed out the gently stirring crew room, his heavily padded passenger alighted with well intended words of advice.

"Look after the motor," he said, carefully pushing the passenger door closed from the outside. "It's the best on the fleet...and don't forget to refuel it before you go off-duty."

An hydraulically assisted wave from Clogger, as he sped up North Road, was the very last expression of comradeship that passed between the two men.

Clogger's two-mile journey to the Meadowfield section took him west up Crossgate Peth to Nevilles Cross, a landmark junction with the Great North Road. As he waited at the notoriously busy traffic lights, while giant goods vehicles ploughed by in both directions, the rubber-arsed panda driver noticed the oily forecourt of Ansa Motors strategically positioned on the south-west corner of the crossroads. Renowned locally for expertise in heavy recovery, the exact location of the garage was of interest to Clogger because of the company's status as a preferred emergency contractor to Durham Police. Had it not been for the inclement weather conditions, the open garage door and burning light would have prompted Clogger to follow convention and call to introduce himself, albeit such action was duplicitous and unnecessary at that early stage in the day. Content that he was now familiar with the site of the emergency service depot, the Michelin Man continued to the ungated entrance of the National Coal Board installation at Broompark.

The stark brick building stood alone like a haunted house on the bleak, barren foothills of a recently landscaped slag-heap. Set on a concrete raft beside a Portakabin, it housed heavy pumping equipment vital to the control of water levels in the labyrinthine mine-workings below. The gently ascending narrow drive, also made of concrete, was perfectly straight and normally distinct from the rest of the black, dusty lunar surface. When Clogger turned into the private road though, about twenty-past six, eight hours of overnight stair-rods had taken their toll. Rivulets of black water were cascading across the path and blurring the sharp edges, although his head-lights quickly picked-up on a large, red reflective triangle. It was thirty yards ahead and had been inconveniently placed in the very centre of the drive, making life difficult for four-wheeled vehicles and their saddle-sore drivers.

Who's put that there? Clogger wondered, unable to think beyond his first mug of piping hot tea.

Alighting from the little van and braving the storm was a painful affair, but the new Meadowfield mobile managed to carry the collapsible warning sign and re-position it properly, behind the police vehicle. Glad to be back in the comfort of his rubber ring, he was wiping surplus rainwater from his spiky, black crop when a second identical piece of Ansa Motors equipment caught his eye, another thirty yards further on.

What the fuck is going on? Clogger cursed as he motored his way through ever-deepening surface water towards the next obstruction.

This time when he rolled gently off his rubber throne into the cold wet conditions, he did notice a black lava-flow following a path of least resistance at the side of the concrete drive. It seemed to be emanating from a volcano near the pumping station, where an amber strobe was competing with the moody light of dawn.

Another short cruise and Clogger was at the front of the pumping facility panning his head-lights across the duty-engineer's empty Portakabin. He must be round the back, Clogger concluded, sliding open the driver-side window to peer into the wide-open cabin door. The sound of a growling engine with a weak, orange pulse confirmed the robot's deduction, so he splashed the little panda-van to the side of the red-brick bunker only to be confronted by another initiative test. A gnarly builder's plank was bridging two up-ended oil drums.

My arse is on fire, Clogger complained, as he eased himself from the driver's door again to prop the cement-caked cross-member against the rain-lashed wall. Bloody obstacle course!

Being careful not to stray from the slushy concrete apron, the Meadowfield mobile reached the back of the isolated pumping station to come face to face with a specially adapted long-wheel-base Land Rover sporting patriotic livery. Two men wearing identical red, white and blue waterproofs were standing on the truck's rear platform operating independently powered lifting equipment. A third man, swaddled in black leggings, a donkey jacket and oily cloth cap, was standing beside the recovery vehicle watching a marooned emergency generator being dragged to the safety of the shore.

Why wasn't I told about this? Clogger fumed, accelerating to take charge of the situation.

When Clogger raced to the side of the tow-truck and swerved dramatically to his left, to create the right impression, not only did he strafe the enemy with dollops of black slurry but he also slid neatly off the edge of the concrete deck into a gently curdling eddy. Anticipating the next assault, the battle-hardened Ansa crew took immediate cover on the other side of their crane, but the inexperienced duty-engineer hesitated in open territory and was exposed to Clogger's frantic run for shore. Maximum pressure on the throttle pedal pitched the miniature front-wheel-drive submarine ready for a full-blown dive. Then, extreme manipulation of the steering wheel aligned the unsuspecting foot soldier with the back of an acutely-angled front wheel. Like sparks from a grindstone he took the full force of a black porridge side-winder, forcing him into a defensive foetal position against the body-work of the Land Rover.

"Sod it!" Clogger bawled when he realised he wasn't equipped with a periscope.

Once the cease-fire was called the Ansa team ventured stealthily from behind their barricade and switched on a powerful emergency search-light. It was trained on the double rear doors of the Mini-van just in time for the audience to see the defeated U-boat commander abandon his ship on all-fours, with the mobility of a clockwork toy.

"I know this is a private road, but you really should cordon-off the hazard," Clogger advised, standing knee-deep in jollop.

This official advice served to disprove a theory widely held among the duty-engineer's work colleagues. His listing, oily cloth cap wasn't moulded to the top of his bald head after all. It could be removed without surgery. Indeed it could be trodden into a totally new form.

It took Sid and Dick of Ansa fame ten minutes to complete the job they'd been called in to do; rescue the emergency generator from the rigours of a mini land-slide. After that another valuable hour was wasted fishing Clogger's panda-van out of the drink in conditions that only lifeboat men occasionally experience. Although formal introductions were never made, by the time eight o'clock arrived the duo felt sufficiently familiar with their new associate that both were independently contemplating the profitability of their special relationship with Durham Police. The duty-engineer on the other hand spent the time scraping himself clean in his heated Portakabin and had mellowed somewhat when Clogger barged in to help himself to the very last communal tea bag. In the cold light of day it spawned a conscious decision to purchase a pair of second-hand binoculars. They would afford him advance warning of undesirable site visitors and provide an opportunity to lock-up and hide.

Largely due to the honed skills of Sid and Dick, the Meadowfield unit van escaped without damage and remarkably, the little engine started first time. Only a new three-tone livery; light and dark blue with a front-end pebble-dash dip, suggested it may have submersible properties.

Must wash all this shit off, Clogger grimaced as he deliberately splashed through a series of large puddles on his way along Newcastle Road to the independently sited County Headquarters at Akley Heads.

The short journey did serve to remove some surplus insulation, but by the time Clogger reached the access road to the newly commissioned complex, the torrential rain had given-way to progressively strengthening wind. Coupled with increasing heat from the engine the nose of the little panda had developed a dark-chocolate crust, although it was the dollops of black porridge flailing onto the freshly laid asphalt drive that first attracted the attention of the heavily-braided chief constable.

By then it was eight-thirty and he was alighting his red, chauffeur driven Jaguar on the covered forecourt of the main entrance, with the presence of a film star arriving at a five-star hotel. While the driver lugged two heavy briefcases in the Almighty's wake another smart uniform opened the main door from the inside and snapped a salute. A reciprocal half-hearted gesture and a polite greeting would have routinely followed had it not been for Clogger's unfortunately timed circumnavigation of the main entrance, on his way to the force stores and workshops wing at the other side of the building. Perched on his inflated inner-tube the hunched giant splattered by the gob-smacked trio with seriously defective camouflage. If he'd taken the trouble to carry a ladder or a plank say, protruding rigidly from the rear cargo doors, the king-sized ice-lollipop might have gone unnoticed.

"Find out who is driving that," the chief constable boomed, before making his way to the internal lift.

In retrospect the encounter served to focus attention on an old chestnut, debated frequently in management training circles. What is the difference between a good leader and a great leader? Hard to define, it may have something to do with thoroughness, because while the constable on reception duty diligently scoured the headquarters car-parks and recorded the registration number of the offending pleasure-beach ride, the chief constable became embroiled in an extended early morning meeting with his lieutenants and refused to be disturbed. Had the issue not dropped off the end of his priority list, a degree of tenacity at that level of command may have uncovered a soviet agent and prevented the subsequent neutralisation of an entire sub-division, not to mention the bestowing of a KBE.

"Give me another helmet boss, eight-and-a-quarter," the stiff-legged giant instructed, lobbing his bucket at a recently appointed civilian storeman preoccupied with papers on the other side of a long counter.

"Not you again!"

"Shotgun damage, sergeant's instructions," Clogger insisted, poking his finger through the cork shell.

"Shotgun damage! The other day you were ship-wrecked!" scowled the astonished brown dust-coat as it disappeared into a jungle of racks and shelves.

"By the way," Clogger called, in the wake of the pint-sized swaddle, "someone said you have a high-pressure car-wash here?"

"Yes, but it's out of order," the storeman retorted.

"When will it be fixed?"

"The engineer is coming out this morning."

"Can you get a message to me?" asked Clogger, lowering his voice when a sparkling, new eight-and-a-quarter emerged from the main warehouse.

"You must be desperate!"

"Yes, got caught in an avalanche."

"An avalanche!"

When Clogger departed force headquarters that morning equipped with his new helmet, the traumatised little dust-coat rushed to the telephone at the end of the counter, dialled nine for an outside line and disturbed his wife, still idling in bed.

"Darling," he whispered urgently, before she had time to acknowledge the call, "ring the estate agent and cancel the deal, I'll commute. This place is far too dangerous for the children."

Driving his blue and white rock-cake south down Framwelgate Peth, Clogger turned right into the litter-swept and overcast top-end of North Road, glancing at his wrist-watch as he did so.

Ten to nine; by the time I get through the city centre it'll be bait time.

Unusually his thoughts were not totally dominated by food. Gently easing his weight from one buttock to the other, on his make-shift rubber ring, the new Meadowfield man was contemplating an opportunity to adjust his hospital-issue sanitary towel in the privacy of the police station toilet, when a middle-aged lady waved him down. She was near the gates of Wharton Park, diagonally opposite the junction with Redhills, riveted into a wide-rimmed plastic rain hat, although by then only the gusting wind was a problem.

"Officer," she insisted, when Clogger gingerly levered himself onto the wet carriageway into the jaws of a young hurricane. "I've just come through the park and there's a lady lying on one of the benches. She doesn't look like a vagrant. I think she's ill!"

"Right madam, leave it to me," the stiff-legged stalwart asserted, after scribbling the informant's name and address in his note-book.

While a stream of city-bound cars hissed around the choc-ice, and the public-spirited citizen went about her business, Clogger poked ungainly between his legs then waddled into the steeply ascending little park close to the railway and bus stations. In the bleak, deserted conditions it didn't take long for Robocop to scan the broad staircase of sprouting spring bulbs and lock onto a horizontal red coat, huddled in a foetal position on a damp, green-painted bench.

"Are you alright, love?" Clogger spluttered, reaching the elevated perch slightly breathless from his laboured walking technique.

The lack of response, verbally or physically, prompted the razor-sharp law-enforcement officer to reach immediately for the lady's petite and well-manicured right-hand. While he was urgently feeling for a pulse her head rotated and a pair of glazed eyes burned directly into his own.

"What's the matter, darling?" Clogger asked, relieved by the signs of life.

124

The gargled and totally incoherent reply followed by a strong smell of alcohol, triggered super-sleuth's powers of deduction. Noticing her grey pyjama bottoms, carpet slippers, brown hair and slight build, he glanced in the direction of the bus station and sighed.

It's that mental patient, she's been out all night!

"Come on sweet-face, let's get you home," Clogger sympathised, as he picked up the prostrate rag doll and carted it off like an animated knight in shining armour.

To be fair to our hero, while descending to the foothills of the little park with the bedraggled princess in his arms, it did occur to him that her nicely cut outer clothing was relatively dry, but the anomaly was quickly negated by the close proximity of both major transport terminals, where shelter from the torrential overnight rain had been readily available.

"That's it, love," Clogger panted, when he reached his slurry-caked unit vehicle parked in North Road. "Hold on to the side of the van while I find the keys."

In the partially camouflaged circumstances, especially during morning rush hour, the single-handed contortion that followed could have easily been mistaken for criminal abduction, but was nevertheless remarkable in its execution. Silently suffering pain from his backside, Clogger managed to keep his burning buttocks apart, prop Sleeping Beauty notionally upright with his right-hand, and rummage among the junk in his left-hand trouser-pocket, all at the same time. Apart from a moment of tension when the patient seemed to slither out of control down the side of the panda-van, Clogger managed to bundle the drowsy, slip-of-a-lass into the safety of the front passenger-seat. It wasn't until he'd carefully covered her shoulders with the emergency blanket that he reached into his other trouser-pocket for his transmitter.

"Meadowfield mobile to foxtrot bravo control," he blasted, leaning on the relatively clean vehicle roof to tug at his nappy.

"Go ahead, Meadowfield."

"Wharton Park. I think I've found the missing Winterton patient."

"Pass her details."

"Unknown, she's intoxicated."

125

"Is she carrying any identification?"

Reluctant to intimately search the clothing of a semi-conscious female, Clogger glanced at her neat three-quarter length red coat before he answered.

"No," he asserted, "all she's wearing is a coat over her night clothes, and it's got false pockets."

"Does she fit the description circulated?"

"Affirmative."

"Stand-by Meadowfield."

Bleep, bleep, bleep.

Recognising that he was required to wait while the controller rang the psychiatric hospital, Clogger made a matronly adjustment to the emergency blanket before slamming shut the passenger-side door and lumbering around the front of the vehicle to the driver's seat. Slowly and painfully he found the most comfortable position on top of his improvised cushion, restoring equilibrium to the vehicle's suspension just in time to receive further instructions over the radio.

"Meadowfield."

"Receiving."

"Hospital confirm the patient is still missing. In the interests of expediency keep her warm and return her immediately to the ward. She's severely disturbed with a liking for alcohol."

"Really!" Clogger declared, glancing across at the delicate features of his slumbering passenger. Butter wouldn't melt in her mouth.

"Oh, don't worry," the radio operator interrupted. "Harmless! Apparently she's convinced she's a Lady-in-Waiting to the Queen."

Clogger smiled. "What about my bait?"

"I'll re-schedule you for ten."

"Roger."

Bleep, bleep, bleep.

With the heater fan whipping up the pungent smell of stale alcohol, Clogger skirted the city-centre via Quarryheads Lane and joined the A177 road on route to Winterton Hospital, situated in the adjoining sub-division. When he raced his little panda-van through the villages of Coxhoe and Bowburn he was frequently forced to counteract pressure on the steering wheel, although apart from a couple of salivating moans and groans, the tremors caused by the gale-force wind didn't seem to unduly disturb his passenger. The unmanned gate to the huge, rambling hospital complex had one low-profile sign backed by a 5 mph speed restriction, so, uncertain of his bearings, Clogger made his way cautiously into the mysterious heart of the region's biggest psychiatric institution, unaware of the open-management policy in some areas.

At the end of a broad drive further conservative signage led him inadvertently into a relatively sheltered plaza, milling with people. Set between three Victorian low-rise blocks it radiated a strange community spirit, centred around a small shop and garden.

"Excuse me!" Clogger shouted to a group of thick-set men as he slid back the driver-side window. "Can you tell me where I can find Lampton ward?"

Sporting a hospital-issue red anorak, an erratically groomed eighteen-stone monster stopped chatting, peered at the dirty police car through one eye, then approached Clogger with the stealth of a deer poacher.

"Who're you?" he grinned, exposing three randomly positioned black teeth.

"PC Catchpole, I'm looking for Lampton ward."

"You're not a policeman," the man insisted, "it's Thursday, you're the pox doctor. It's the pox doctor, it's the pox doctor," he continued to chant.

Suddenly realising that he had ventured into the wrong area, Clogger fought to engage reverse gear but the ranting attracted thirty or so other men and women who swarmed to the vehicle.

Fucking hell, Clogger thought, forgetting about the pain in his arse. What do I do now?

With his window firmly shut and both doors locked from the inside, Clogger was contemplating the sea of vacant expressions pressing against the muddy windscreen when his hitherto docile passenger stirred from her drunken stupor and let out an ear-piercing scream. It rallied her contemporaries into a full scale assault on the dirty little van and was so intimidating that Clogger decided to abandon ship. With the suspension rocking violently in all directions, the Meadowfield mobile leaned from his rubber ring and was shouldering open the driver's door when a white-coated general hacked his way into the mayhem.

"No vehicles in this area officer, are you lost?"

"Yes, boss," Clogger replied, relieved that professional help was now on hand. "PC Catchpole from Durham City. I'm returning this patient to Lampton ward."

"You've come in the wrong gate," advised the male nurse as he pushed away the last of the marauders to take a cursory glance at the wayward inmate. "No matter!"

For some reason the sight of the psychiatric carer's white coat at the passenger-side window produced a second head-splitting scream from Clogger's charge that seemed to put extra body into her lank, brown hair.

"Wait here," the nurse instructed, recognising that he needed assistance. "I'll be back in a minute."

A short time later the helpful professional returned with a colleague. His junior was pushing a wheelchair loaded with a hospital blanket and a small, white enamel dish. Despite a third extended shrill and a total body spasm, when the white-coated duo opened the passenger-side door they were able to execute a well rehearsed restraining procedure and inject a standard sedative with the speed and efficiency of a lizard's tongue.

"She'll be alright now," reassured the senior carer. "Don't worry, we'll get her back to her ward."

"Thanks, boss," Clogger replied, catching his emergency blanket while Sleeping Beauty was wheeled away into the enigmatic depths of the asylum.

It was a few minutes before ten when Agent Catchpole crossed the city boundary again on the return journey to his home station. Unable to prioritise between ravenous hunger and the need to adjust his anal dressing, he cut through a ferocious cross-wind into Hallgarth Street, then turned right along Court Lane towards the police yard. Clogger was carefully negotiating the narrow entrance in his freshly pebble-dashed unit vehicle when he came face to face with a very harassed

Gentleman Jim, leaving in his private car to attend yet another meeting with the coroner.

I'd better explain, thought Clogger, before he gives me a bollocking.

With perfectly honourable intentions, Clogger waved vigorously at the sub-divisional head and pulled up alongside his family saloon in the jaws of the gateway.

"Don't worry boss...I mean superintendent, I've already made arrangements to have it cleaned," the rubber-arsed giant mouthed through a clearing in the mud.

It was recognition of Clogger as much as the gesture that caused an involuntary reaction. The sub-divisional head instantly cowered in the driver's seat of his immaculate Ford Escort and slammed his foot hard down on the accelerator pedal. Unfortunately the rear drive wheels happened to be on an area of asphalt previously treated with discharges from Clogger's motorbike, topped off with rainwater. Instead of a tyre-squeal into the relative safety of a building hurricane, the rear-end of the car stepped-out on the mini-skidpan and side-swiped the concrete gate post. Sensibly, under the sanity-threatening circumstances, Gentleman Jim chose to ignore the mishap and drove away as though nothing had happened, albeit with a noticeable adjustment to his trendy new, lime-green body-line.

"Put the kettle on," Clogger called to the ten o'clock refreshment contingent when he saw them entering the station canteen in front of him. "I'll only be a minute."

Making an essential detour, the Meadowfield mobile returned from the toilet when the tea was brewed. Wearing his black rubber garland, he was carrying his sandwich skip under his left arm and repeatedly shaking loose the heavy serge in his right trouser leg.

"That's better," he announced, radiating obvious anal relief to his two operational colleagues and a cluster of bemused civilian office staff who ought to have been using a separate facility. "I could eat a scabby horse."

Centre stage, Clogger was rolling on his inner-tube pushing a boulder of a cold pork pie into his mouth when Bald Eagle and Wupert breezed into the room. The sergeant traditionally took his

129

break early, but it was the uncustomary appearance of an officer in the men's mess that brought the second half of B-Relief to their feet.

"Sit," the inspector instructed with his ginger-wigged lapdog at his heal. "We have a little pwoblem."

Without prompting, the administrative interlopers stubbed out their cigarettes and left the room, leaving the inspector to brief his team in private.

"I think you are all aware of a cewtain in-house domestic situation," Wupert opened, quietly.

"Oh, yes," Clogger nodded, acknowledging his temporary role in the Meadowfield district.

"Well there's been a distuwbing development," the inspector continued, "PC Fisher's wife has disappeawed."

"When?" a second panda-man gasped.

"Sometime between eight and nine. She was asleep in bed when he called at eight and missing when he went back at nine," Bald Eagle interjected. "There was an empty bottle of cooking sherry on the kitchen table."

"Now listen cawefully," the inspector asserted, closing down the sergeant in the interests of secrecy. "I want to keep the situation under waps, at least until midday. Hopefully we can find her in the meantime and avoid any embawwassment for the officer."

"What do you want us to do boss...I mean inspector," Clogger enthused, abandoning half a pint of tea and the remnants of a pork pie.

"I want you thwee to look after the sub-division. All calls will be diwected to you while the west of us search the Redhills area. She can't have gone far in her night clothes, especially in this weather."

"What about the baby?" Clogger's operational colleague asked. "I can send my wife round to help if you like, sir."

"Thank you, but it won't be necessary," Wupert reassured. "The child is with PC Fisher's mother-in-law."

Having willingly cut short his forty-five minute refreshment period in order to help a colleague, Clogger was still in the police yard using an abandoned cigarette packet to scrape flaky residue from the corners of the panda windscreen, when he received his first radio call.

"Meadowfield from foxtrot bravo control."

130

"Go ahead," Clogger replied, carefully selecting the optimum position on the driver's seat for his moped inner-tube.

"Pityme Bypass, report of a non-injury road accident. Ansa Motors in attendance"

"Roger," the giant snapped efficiently, relishing responsibility for the entire northern-end of the sub-division.

His journey to Pityme took Clogger through the cobbled city-centre. Alerted by the flashing blue light on her closed-circuit monitor, the Painted-Lady lubricated his passage with electronic wizardry, but then lapsed into a traffic disrupting sexual fantasy when she recognised the driver. Clogger had acknowledged two of his colleagues scouring the vicinity of County Hospital on foot, and by sheer coincidence was close to the gates to Wharton Park, when a slightly built female wandered across the road in front of him. Oblivious to the braking traffic, she had a vacant expression and was wearing a ballooning red anorak and flimsy trousers.

"Can I help you, darling?" Clogger asked, pulling alongside the hazard.

"Where's Her Majesty? Are you the King?" answered the lady with the coherence of an old soak.

"Ah," Clogger sighed, realising his proximity to Redhills. "I'm not the King, but I think you are Mrs Fisher. Am I right?"

Proud of his achievement and the prospect of profound gratitude from his colleague, Clogger decided to delay his attendance at the non-injury road accident and coax the distressed lady into his slurry-caked roller-skate. "Come on; let's get you home, before you catch your death."

"Where are you taking me?" the detainee asked, recharging the inside of the panda-van with the pungent smell of alcohol.

"Back to your palace," Clogger smiled, screwing the pulsating tin can into a three-point turn.

As with all of Agent Catchpole's strategies his mastery of timing was paramount. When he turned into Redhills the distraught permanent Meadowfield officer and five members of B-Relief, including the sergeant and inspector, were all out of sight frantically searching the immediate vicinity in gale-force conditions. PC Fisher's kindly next-door-neighbour, who had been recruited to stand guard in case the wanderer returned of her own volition, had popped back to her own home to take something out of the oven. Judged to perfection, Clogger was able to readily identify the police house by its standard design and usher the Queen's Lady-in-Waiting straight through the unlocked rear door and up the staircase to the master bedroom.

"Have you found her?" the returning next-door-neighbour called.

"Yes," Clogger replied, "I've put her straight to bed, I think we ought to call the doctor though, she seems a touch delirious."

"Oh, I am glad she's safe."

"Meadowfield from foxtrot bravo control."

"Go ahead," replied Clogger, while he descended the creaking staircase like a saddle-sore cowboy.

"What's your E.T.A. at Pityme? I've had Ansa Motors on the blower again, they urgently want the traffic stopped on the bypass."

"Ten minutes, control. Unavoidable delay. Would you inform the inspector that Mrs Fisher is now at home?"

"Received and understood."

"I'm leaving her with the neighbour," super-sleuth concluded, pounding out of the house to tackle his next detail.

Bleep, bleep, bleep.

Clogger was hacking his way through a vicious westerly cross-wind in the north-bound carriageway of the very exposed Pityme Bypass when the need for his presence became apparent. Lying neatly on its side, across the nearside verge of the south-bound lane, was a solitary furniture van. Hardly able to stand, Sid and Dick were in attendance wrestling with an assortment of ropes, chains and pulleys at the back of an enormous ex-military vehicle. Clogger promptly switched on his blue strobe light to signal his long awaited presence, then charged to the roundabout at the northern end of the new road to access the other carriageway. In anticipation of his traffic regulating role he raced back to the scene and parked his little, blue-flashing panda-van about thirty yards before the hazard, closing-off completely the partially obstructed inside lane of the dual-carriageway.

"Tell me when you're ready," he called to Sid and Dick as he plodded towards them with one hand on the top of his helmet and the other on his bottom.

"We've been ready for quarter of an hour," came a distant, wind-distorted reply.

With all the south-bound traffic using the outside lane, Clogger waited efficiently for the recovery team to board their red, white and blue monster before springing into action. A thumbs-up sign from Sid in the cockpit had the Meadowfield robot hovering in readiness for a suitable break in the crocodile, then, as if to further demonstrate his unique sense of timing, Clogger acted decisively to stop all the traffic for the few minutes it would take to pull the lorry upright.

Legs wide apart, he marched into the centre of the overtaking lane and raised his right hand firmly in front of the only other empty, high-sided goods vehicle in the North of England on that particular morning. Having already fought twice with the steering wheel on the notoriously exposed new stretch of road, the driver made a series of confusing gestures indicating his desire to maintain forward momentum, but they didn't register. Clogger held firm his fully-uniformed regulation hand-signal and brought the towering empty box to a grinding halt directly alongside the police van. By the time Robocop noticed the super-structure struggling to maintain its balance on all-fours, it was too late. The underbelly was exposed and the whole thing toppled over, rather dramatically, on top of the Meadowfield unit vehicle, making a sound reminiscent of the crushing machine in Charlie Newton's scrapyard.

"Meadowfield from foxtrot bravo control."

"Go ahead."

"Two outstanding messages. The storeman at headquarters reports that the car-wash is now working, if you still want to use it, and the sister on Lampton ward would like you to contact her urgently. Apparently she cannot identify the patient you returned there this morning."

"Mmm, it's all very worrying!"

Bleep, bleep, bleep.

7   OTHER OFFENCES

The continuing success of Agent Catchpole's hardware neutralising strategy needs no further explanation other than to perhaps point out that after a second hour of roping and winching, Sid and Dick managed to uncover the crushed dessert for a second time that morning. It was sitting among pieces of broken chocolate shell, topped-off with an inverted blue cherry. Apart from the extra cost to Ansa Motors in terms of man-hours, because it was a police accident Wupert had to officiate again. He hacked his way to a section of the county's primary road in biting wind, only to find a ten-mile, south-bound traffic jam and a posse of irate motorists conducting kangaroo accident enquiries. Oblivious to the punitive wishes of a critically delayed haulier wielding a large chrome spanner, Clogger was on all-fours trying to fish his trapped surgical appliance from the mangled wreckage.

"Hang the silly bastard," the grease monkey shouted.

"Oh, come now chaps," Wupert soothed, "a fellow is entitled to make a mistake."

Thinking he'd done enough to quell the rumblings of discontent, the young inspector was making notes about Clogger's apparent incompetence when he heard another profound suggestion from a second boiler-suited spectator.

"He should trade-in his brain for a new model."

"Why?" the audience jeered.

"Low mileage! He'd get a hell of a deal."

The wind-distorted laughter prompted Wupert to look at Sid and Dick for moral support, but the traditional police allies were also in raptures.

"I think you'd better go back to the station Woger, and leave me to it."

"But it's a Dunlop," Clogger protested, pushing himself back onto his feet.

"I'll see to it Woger, make your way back to the office," rattled Wupert, uneasy with the ridicule and general breakdown in public confidence.

"But boss, it may still be inflated...I mean inspector."

Realising that his refined Oxford delivery wasn't altogether effective in strong, swirling wind, the inspector reverted to colloquialism to bawl his final order.

"Piss off, Clogger...Now."

With one hand on his arse and the other on his helmet, Robocop was last seen hobbling along the south-bound verge towards the village of Pityme, where presumably he took advantage of the police concession on public service vehicles and secured an undeserved prompt finish to his 6 a.m. 2 p.m. tour of duty.

Although the demise of the permanent Meadowfield man was as comprehensive as his treasured little unit vehicle, the outcome in his case does need further explanation. It was Bald Eagle who instinctively tried to resolve the domestic crisis enveloping his star officer. While Wupert was necessarily adding yet another chapter to his ongoing investigation, the sergeant, also on voluntary overtime, drove to a local florist and secreted two bunches of flowers in the boot of the supervision car. From there he raced through the storm to the police house in Redhills and in an atmosphere of hysteria, cajoled the Queen's Lady-in-Waiting into the front passenger seat of his Mini saloon.

"Get that fucking lunatic out of my house," PC Perfect screamed, when the member of the Royal Household proved reluctant to abandon the comfort of his master bed.

"Don't worry, I'll have your wife back in no time," reassured Bald Eagle, towing the paranoid red anorak down the garden path.

When the ginger-wig eventually reached the frontier of Lampton Ward to execute the patient exchange, the first bouquet did absorb some of the ward sister's wrath, but the second cut no ice with Mrs Fisher. Now sober and mysteriously cured of post-natal depression, the granite-faced dischargee snatched her spray from Bald Eagle's grasp. In a moment of strange serenity she handed the flowers to the royal assistant and adopted a warm, caring smile indicative of first-hand experience.

"I'm going to sue," the policeman's wife growled, once the real inmate had been whisked away into the screaming depths of the madhouse. "Get me home."

On several occasions during the twenty-five minute journey back to Durham City, the patronising sergeant attempted to explain the unfortunate and coincidental circumstances prevailing that morning, but his efforts were to no avail. Like a hardened criminal, Mrs Fisher refused to speak and avoided all eye contact. Even when she was reunited with her doting husband she remained detached and failed to see the funny side of the affair, prompting Bald Eagle to take his leave. Despite the severity of the experience, it was assumed that her mental scars would heal over the course of B-Relief's long weekend, but by 9 a.m. the following morning everyone knew she definitely couldn't take a joke. PC Fisher's resignation was on Gentleman Jim's desk.

Succinctly worded, it indicated that his wife had lost confidence in his police career and he intended to make an immediate change of direction in the interests of their relationship. An offer of compassionate holiday failed to impact, then it was quickly retracted when the sub-divisional head learned the domestic deal involved Mrs Fisher withdrawing from potentially messy litigation. The only person to marginally gain from the affair was the family doctor. He wrote an article for the British Medical Journal promoting the case for short-sharp-shock treatment in instances of mild depression and alcohol dependence. It generated a certain amount of professional interest and a moment of glory, but was soon universally discredited for its lack of scientific substance.

The down time, between 2 p.m. on Thursday 10th and 10 p.m. on Monday 14th, gave Clogger's big red kipper a chance to heal. Christened 'the home of the over-filled sandwich' by his colleagues, Clogger spent most of his long-weekend relaxing in his digs. By Sunday afternoon scar tissue had begun to form and although still nappy-clad, he felt comfortable enough to help his elderly landlady clear out her late husband's tool-shed.

"Oh my God, what's this?" spluttered the rotund pinny, when her track-suited house guest returned from yet another trip to the dustbin. "And you a policeman and all."

Looking as though she'd just been confronted by a nasty reptile, the manufacturer of Clogger's daily door-stops dismantled a pile of junk and gingerly produced an old polythene bag containing a rusty service revolver.

"He brought it back from the war," she explained, holding the relic between her forefinger and thumb. "I thought he'd got rid of it years ago. What am I going to do?"

"Oh, don't worry, mar," superman reassured, squeezing a pair of podgy shoulders. "There's an amnesty on that sort of thing. I'll take it to the station tomorrow and get it destroyed."

When Monday evening arrived, Clogger's bottom was still tender but the excruciating sting had gone and he was able to replace his nappy with a thickening of antiseptic cream. At nine-thirty exactly, in full unhindered uniform, he placed the dusty polythene bag and his big sandwich-box in the pannier of his motorcycle and roared off into the darkness to start his first night-shift in Durham City sub-division. Apart from the habit of using his police helmet as a substitute for British Standard protection, the first part of his journey through the city-centre was unremarkable. The weather had long since settled, the prevailing breeze was refreshing and there was only a smattering of dipped head-lights to think about. It was probably this slightly premature lull in the evening traffic flow that encouraged the Painted-Lady to close the traffic control box early and make her way on foot to the police station, ready for a quickie.

Because traffic wardens don't operate during the night and usually have an independent shift system, it was reasonably assumed that Clogger's chugging presence in Saddler Street just as she was completing her late-day tour-of-duty, was sheer coincidence. Thirty years on of course it is empirically evident that espionage relies heavily on the manipulation of reasonable assumption, an area where Agent Catchpole had undoubted natural talent.

"Get on, sweet-face," Clogger called, standing astride his throbbing machine with renewed mobility in his huge thighs. "I'll give you a ride."

"Oh, alright then, but go easy," answered the pair of stotting buttocks.

In season and blushing behind her mask, Clogger's latest target hitched-up her black-serge skirt and cocked a bulky, dark silken leg over the pillion seat. At that stage the plot was probably flexible but as soon as Clogger reached the bumpy cobbles of Elvet Bridge, two arms wrapped tightly around his middle and a huge pair of tits rubbing on his back, things turned to concrete. Half a mile or so later in the confines of the haphazardly lit police yard, the Painted-Lady made an ungainly dismount before smoothing down her skirt into its proper position. When she wobbled across the oily Tarmac to the rear door of the station, with the agility of a beached sealion, Clogger's tongue dropped out of his mouth. He closed down his mechanical systems in record time and hauled the Royal Enfield onto its stand. Then, in search of oats, the stallion trotted after the mare bearing gifts; well a sandwich-box and a tarnished polythene bag to be exact.

Oblivious to the presence of Clogger's motorcycle discreetly discharging yet more gunge in another dark corner of the police yard, the remaining members of B-Relief drifted into the parade-room ready to spend seven nights on the graveyard watch. Traditionally it was a week of deteriorating pallor, spent in dangerous isolation shaking hands with door-knobs by torch-light. In the interests of personal safety the ritualistic production of appointments marked the start to every tour-of-duty, and in Bald Eagle's case he preferred to carry out the inspection in bulk.

"Where's Catchpole?" the supervisor queried, systematically examining a table adorned with ebony truncheons, chrome handcuffs and standard issue torches, complete with serviceable batteries.

"No idea," one of the team replied. "Had severe arse-ache on Thursday, must have reported sick."

Whether the ginger-wig agreed with the reasoning behind the assumption or was simply pursuing a policy of out of sight out of mind nobody can be sure, but the fact remains the sergeant didn't make any effort to check the station records at that early stage and decided the mundane task could wait until the quiet hours when he intended to re-calculate his optimum retirement date, based on yet another revised financial formula.

"Right then, let's make a start," Bald Eagle ordered, prompting his platoon to clear the parade-room table.

Once the noise had subsided, the sergeant started the laborious task of summarising the events of the last twenty-four hours, which of course was a misnomer after a long-weekend. Although he managed to skim-over much of the stuff relating to the latter part of the previous week, the men had only just finished scribbling when the inspector made his customary entrance. Wupert had spent his extended rest-days agonising over his problem-child, eventually deciding to take full advantage of the relatively quiet night-duty week and personally counsel Clogger on his unfortunate policing style. Because of his other extensive report-writing commitments he was anxious to organise the sessions, based on a structure suggested by his academic wife.

"Where's Woger?" the whiz-kid queried, scanning the four recoiling faces around the parade-room table. "Wemain seated."

"Fortunately or unfortunately, sir, he appears to be sick. It depends of course from which direction you are looking," Bald Eagle proffered, creaking back into his big chair.

"What's the matter with him?"

"Anal bruising and laceration I suspect, from last Wednesday."

"I thought it was superficial!"

"It was, but he may have picked-up a fatal infection," Bald Eagle gloated.

"Make a note sergeant. He must weport to me as soon as he weturns to duty."

"Right, sir."

"Before you do the assignments, I have an announcement to make. PC Fisher has left B-Relief to puwsue a caweer in teaching. His outstanding annual leave and overtime accwual mean the wesignation takes immediate effect. I'm sure we all wish him evewy success in the future."

139

Despite earlier and extensive circulation on the sub-divisional grapevine, the formal announcement generated some genuine sadness.

"How's his wife?" ventured one officer, unaware of the complexities surrounding her return to civilisation.

"Apparently she's made a full recovery," the ginger-wig grimaced, while he struggled with a new configuration of resources and refreshment breaks.

With two men and two vehicles down on a relief of six, operating two under strength anyway, eight territorial areas could be divided evenly. Three unit drivers each covering two adjoining sections and one man patrolling both town centre footbeats was the optimum solution to Bald Eagle's assignment responsibilities, although in terms of effective policing it was barely credible.

"Myself, one and five, early bait," the supervisor rattled, "three and the city foot-patrol, 2 a.m...and be careful with the vehicles, there's no spare and the meat-wagon is in for service. Have you anything inspector?"

"Yes, listen-up chaps," Wupert asserted, before the assembly was dismissed. "Firstly, there will be substantial CID activity in the sub-division duwing the course of this night-shift week. Unless specifically called to assist, you must go about your normal business and ignore the pwesence of any detectives."

"What are they doing out in the dark, sir?" came a voice from the depleted audience.

"I'm not at liberty to tell you the full detail. Appawently it's the culmination of months of painstaking surveillance and because the success of the opewation depends on absolute secwecy, it's being conducted on a stwictly need-to-know basis."

"Cloak and dagger stuff," Bald Eagle muttered, casting a sceptical glance at a nicotine-stained fluorescent tube, flickering on the shabby ceiling.

"The other item, gentlemen, concerns station secuwity," the young shift-leader continued, brandishing a copy of a two-page headquarters memorandum. "These are the new guidelines! Most of the document concerns measures to minimise the impact of a tewwowist attack, which the day-shift have already implemented. You can wead and

140

digest them in your own time. There is however, one item of immediate concern to B-Welief."

Focusing on a heavily underlined paragraph half-way through the typescript, Wupert went on, "Quote, between the hours of 10 p.m. and 6 a.m. it is the wesponsibility of the night-duty personnel to check and secuwe the wear doors to the station, together with all non-operational sections of the building. Access and egwess duwing the silent hours will be westricted to the main fwont door, under the contwol of the desk officer, unquote."

"Mmm, makes sense," someone reluctantly conceded, familiar with the convoluted and often unworkable diktats emanating from headquarters.

"The sergeant and I will undertake the task tonight and establish a key pwocedure. Thereafter it will be subject to wota. That's all, good hunting."

It was the very last time anyone used the back door to Durham City police station after 10 p.m. Once B-Relief dispersed to their assigned territorial areas, Bald Eagle closed his lever-arch file and disappeared from the parade-room for a couple of minutes, leaving Wupert engrossed in the subtleties of the new security instructions.

"Keys," the sergeant announced, when he returned shaking the miscellaneous contents of an old biscuit tin.

There was something contradictory in the fine detail of the memorandum that the inspector couldn't put his finger on, but the noise snapped him from his deliberations.

"Oh, good man," he sparked, leading the duo into the dirty magnolia corridors of the ageing building.

The entire top floor of the single-storey Victorian fortress was the domain of the nine o'clock brigade, none of whom had ever encountered an angry man in their lives (gospel according to Bald Eagle). Apart from the superintendent's office, which was locked anyway, the rest of the Dickensian complex could be secured with only three old mortise keys.

"Good show," Wupert rattled, after he poked his head around the last standard blue-panelled door to confirm the squeaky, brown-linoleum of the typing pool was free of IRA activity.

"Let's go downstairs!"

By the time Bald Eagle had struggled with the medieval key and looped it onto a separate piece of coarse brown string with two others, Boy Wonder was at the base of the main staircase contemplating his ground-floor surroundings. The robust rear door into the police yard wasn't the problem, it was the nearby CID wing. Only occasionally used during the night, Wupert nevertheless decided it was an operational part of the building.

"There's only the back door down here, the west of this floor wequires twenty-four-hour access," the inspector concluded, while his clanking, ginger-wigged deputy brought up the rear.

"What about the traffic warden's locker-room and the tutor sergeant's office?" ventured Bald Eagle, locking and bolting the big back door in a manner that was to become another night-duty ritual.

The valid observation caused the inspector to pontificate for a few seconds with his hand on his chin. "No, the tutor sergeant's woom contains important opewational weference material, but you're wight about the locker-room. We'll secure that as well."

Had it not been for Bald Eagle's eye for detail, the route into the master spy's trap would have been less direct, albeit probably just as interesting. In the event though, without a lateral thought in their respective heads, the supervisory team were sucked instantly into a finely tuned ambush with catastrophic results.

"Stwange, the door is already locked," Wupert observed, when he tried to access the converted storeroom.

"Oh, I remember now," Bald Eagle interjected, scraping around in his biscuit tin. "When this was the stolen cycle store somebody lost the key, so Walter fitted a latch. The traffic wardens have probably had some keys cut and keep it locked themselves, personal belongings and all. You know what civvies are like!"

"Best check anyway," asserted Wupert, typically anxious to execute his duties thoroughly.

The small shiny form of a modern Yale key among the rest of last century's ironmongery made its recovery from the tin a speedy affair. Like a theatre nurse assisting a surgeon, the sergeant handed the instrument to the inspector who carefully penetrated a new site above the original paint-caked keyhole and handle. Twisting clockwise, Wupert managed to turn the little key fractionally before it jammed hard.

"Mmm," he muttered, easing the scalpel out of the wound a little to make a second concerted effort. "It won't open!"

"Here, let me have a go," insisted Bald Eagle, abandoning his old biscuit tin on the highly-polished floor.

A change of surgical technique was of no consequence. The mechanism was solid in its resistance to all manner of manipulation.

"It must be locked from the inside," the sergeant suggested, when frustration threatened to shift his rug.

"It can't be," responded Wupert, glancing at his wrist-watch. "The late-day twaffic warden finished half an hour ago."

Perched on the horns of a dilemma, the duo stared at each other for a few moments before Bald Eagle broke the impasse.

"Do you want me to break the door down, sir?" he asked, gripping the handle tightly to get a feel for the likely resistance.

"Oh, it shouldn't come to that," the young inspector replied. "It's pwobably bwoken, ask the communications-woom to wing the handyman."

Recognised in the New Year's Honours List for his dedication to duty, Walter GDB (general dog's body) lived alone in a small council house in Court Lane, only a few yards from the police station. A confirmed bachelor in the autumn of his years, he relied heavily on his National Health spectacles and had just arrived home from a well-lubricated domino session in the Court Inn. Despite reacting to the overtime call with characteristic gusto, he didn't meet his usual two-minute response time.

"Some clown has locked the back door," the pristine boiler-suit asserted when it swept into the corridor where Wupert and Bald Eagle were still loitering.

"Oh, its the new pwocedure," interrupted the inspector, anxious that his miffed deputy should not be diverted from the job in hand.

"What's the problem?"

"Can't get into the twaffic wardens' woom."

"What do you want to be in there for?"

"Non of your business," the sergeant snarled, "just open it."

Still poking from the new lock, the frustrated safe-breaker carefully grasped the head of the little brass latch-key between his right forefinger and thumb, put his left ear to the woodwork, then twisted in both directions.

"Snip's down on the inside," rattled the expert, instantly providing a second opinion. "There must be someone inside!"

"Can't be," Wupert replied, looking again at his wrist-watch. "Anyway, there's no light on."

Inspired by the inspector's gaze settling on the dirty oval-topped window pane immediately above the door frame, Walter suddenly turned heal and charged off towards his heavily fortified internal lair, next to the canteen.

"Two minutes!" he estimated. "I'll have to call on support services."

When the storm-trooper returned he was swinging a pair of step-ladders like a giant shoulder-arm and carrying a flash-light any light-house keeper would have been proud to own.

"Switch off the tubes," Walter instructed in janitorial slang, before commencing his assault in an atmosphere of stale beer and impregnated industrial floor polish.

With three evenly-spaced fluorescent ceiling lights extinguished, the eerie darkness that befell the operation prompted Bald Eagle to stabilise the ancient, free-standing contraption with a size-nine boot. For his directing part, the young inspector stepped back to get an angle on the balancing act.

"Can you see anything?" he called to the silhouette of his front man.

"Give me a chance," retorted the slightly tipsy general dog's body, leaning precariously towards the glass with both hands clasped around the body of his search-light.

The initial, carefully guided pan into the murky depths of the locker-room proved fruitless and Walter's whispered assertion that the place was empty generated some relief among the special forces team.

"Lock must be bwoken!" Wupert deduced. "Come down before you have an accident."

144

Well intended, the final instruction was unfortunate in its timing because as Walter's powerful beam made its return journey across enemy lines, he thought he saw urgent movement behind a locker, at the very extreme of his limited viewing angle. Accompanied by an ever so faint shuffling sound, he lurched even closer to the ornately-framed dirty window at an estimated altitude of eight feet.

"No, I think there is someone inside," the reconnaissance officer declared, revising his earlier intelligence. "And there's a box of some kind on the report-writing table."

When Wupert queried the type of box he didn't get a reply from above. Walter's flash-light had already picked up the outline of a service revolver alongside the ammunition.

"I don't get paid for this," shrieked the mountaineer, ducking violently for cover.

Governed by the law of gravity, the heavy flash-light was the first to drop from the shadowy stratosphere. Albeit a glancing blow, the director of operations was temporarily incapacitated by the invisible meteor when Bald Eagle completely lost control of the top-heavy structure. Like a goggle-eyed bird of prey, Walter seemed to hover for a while on his rickety, wooden-perch with his wings flapping. Then he plummeted to earth, desperately locking his talons into the sergeant's wig in a futile attempt to break his fall. Audible in the next corridor, the noise of the disaster inspired the communications-room anchorman to send his number-two on a reconnaissance mission.

When the corridor was returned to full illumination, Walter and his step-ladders were prostrate beside a cuddly toy, the sergeant was sitting in the lotus position with a shockingly unfamiliar appearance, and Wupert was rubbing the side of his head.

"There's a fucking gun on the table," groaned the handyman, holding his rapidly swelling wrist.

"Stay there," the inspector screamed, resuming command of the situation with his back firmly against the gloss-painted corridor wall. "Are you weapons twained?"

"Yes, sir."

145

"Go back to the communications-woom, inform headquarters a suspected tewworist attack is in pwogwess and break open the armouwy."

"But..."

"Do it," Wupert blasted. "Is there another way in?"

"No," advised balloon-head, adopting a similarly defensive position at the other side of the heavy internal door. "There're no other windows either, it was designed as a found property store."

By the time the communications-room constable returned with a .38 Smith and Wesson police revolver the contingent were noticeably pale and Walter, still prostrate on the brown linoleum, was visibly shaking from the onset of shock.

Struggling to generate some moisture in his mouth, the inspector croaked, "Take your position."

"But, sir..."

"It's an emergency, just do it."

Squatting on one knee at Wupert's flank, the radio operative reluctantly adopted a two-handed grip on the stock of the revolver and aimed it at the offending locker-room door.

"Armed police, suwwender your weapon and come out with your hands up," the young shift-leader bawled in regulatory fashion, cautiously adjusting his defensive position to swing an awkward kick at the base of the barricade.

Having already had their carnal activities disturbed by Walter's probing flash-light, and any lingering passion quenched by the noise of the collapsing gantry, Bonnie and Clyde were more or less re-dressed and ready to give themselves up when the door stopped vibrating. The unlocking click of the Yale latch heightened the tension to fever pitch and a deathly silence prevailed as the big, blue door started to swing slowly inward.

"Weapon first," Bald Eagle blasted from his vantage point, when the aperture reached six inches.

Ten seconds later a transparent polythene bag and its rusty metallic contents skidded across the highly-polished corridor floor.

"And the explosives," added Wupert, with the smell of glory beginning to penetrate his nostrils.

146

Ten seconds after that when the familiar form of Clogger's fully charged Tupperware lunch-box followed the war relic to the feet of the reluctant marksman, it was the sergeant who was the first to express his emotion. Abandoning his back-against-the-wall cover, he slumped again into the lotus position and dropped his grey-trimmed football into his cupped hands. I fucking knew it!

Less familiar with Clogger's refreshment arrangements, Wupert was fractionally slower on the uptake and didn't drop his guard until a huge, spiky head poked out of the doorway and rotated through one-hundred-and-eighty degrees.

"Oh, it's you boss...I mean inspector!" the jackal remarked, casually rubbing patches of make-up and bright-red lipstick from his face.

With the benefit of hindsight, at that stage Walter's body trembling and intermittent groans should have been Wupert's priority, but for reasons of professional pride he chose to ignore the black and blue club on the end of the handyman's arm and pit his college-honed fast-track wits against those of a secret agent. While Bald Eagle continued to meditate and the official gun-slinger wandered the corridor in blissful relief, the inspector began one of the most penetrating interrogations in cold war history.

"What are you doing locked in the twaffic wardens' woom, Woger?"

"Extra curricular activities, boss...I mean inspector," Clogger replied, shielding the Painted-Lady's hastily cross-buttoned tunic from view.

"Where did you get the wevolver?"

"My landlady's husband, but don't worry he's dead and it isn't loaded."

"Thank God for that," the wandering marksman interjected, gazing at his own hand-gun. "This isn't loaded either."

"I don't fucking believe it," Bald Eagle sighed, looking up from his palms with his mouth wide-open. "Where are the bullets?"

"Locked in the super's safe," the sniper advised. "New procedure, must be kept separate from the weapon."

"Why?"

"Security, in case of a terrorist attack!"

Dropping his head once again in disbelief, Bald Eagle prayed to the groaning general dog's body while the interrogator-in-chief continued to nail his prime suspect to the disciplinary mast. Glimpsing a dishevelled and exhausted witch skulking with her hair down in the darkened bowels of the locker-room, he made a reasonable assumption, then continued with a razor-sharp summing-up.

"Unlike all the other incidents you've been involved in wecently, Woger, this one is a delibewate bweach of Police Wegulations. Before I weport you for discweditable conduct, have you anything to say for yourself?"

Terrorist Catchpole didn't answer immediately, he was struggling to pick a tantalising pubic hair from the tip of his tongue.

"Well?"

"Is it possible to have two other offences taken into consideration, boss...I mean inspector?"

A certain amount of confusion prevailed thereafter. On the frantic instructions of Wupert the communications-room managed to cancel a posse of senior officers, collectively known in police circles as a hesitation, but they were too late to divert a party of trained negotiators anxious to test their newly acquired skills for the very first time. After piling-up at the locked rear door, the recently conceived plain-clothes quartet came face to face with a departing ambulance crew in the foyer, very nearly dislodging Walter from his stretcher.

"Negotiation team," one of their number snapped.

"This is the police station," answered the desk constable, "County Hall is on the other side of the city."

Outside the remit of Police Regulations, the acutely embarrassed Painted-Lady disappeared into the night distressed in the knowledge that news of her philandering might one day reach her husband. Clogger on the other hand had different concerns. His misdemeanour didn't justify suspension and would typically take three months to process, but for some reason the coaching staff had sent him to Coventry, unconsciously threatening his planned research into unconventional forms of detonation.

"No more serviceable vehicles," the anchor-man advised when Cock Robin signed for his pocket-set at the communications-room hatch. "Double-up with the city foot-patrol, I've sent him to an insecure load and he may need some help."

In the light of Walter's painful but treatable shattered wrist, the senior radio operator's diplomatic initiative could not have been more fortuitous. Wrapped in the police version of an army greatcoat and wearing black leather gloves, Clogger left the front door of the station shortly after eleven. Passing beneath the standard blue lamp amid badly concealed sighs of relief, he cut a large but lonely figure on route to Milburngate on the west-side of Framwelgate Bridge. The steep commercial thoroughfare leading to Framwelgate Waterside, was completely blocked by a large, curtain-sided night delivery vehicle.

"Lost," the official city foot-patrol rattled, clapping together his identical black-gloved hands to combat the deteriorating temperature. "Tried to do a three-point turn and the load slipped...anyway, I thought you were on the sick!"

"Oh, no," retorted Clogger, offended by the suggestion he was a malingerer. "I have to double-up with you."

Destined for a supermarket in another part of the city, five-dozen crates of Tizer and a lesser number of cardboard cartons had tumbled down the granite sets at the side of the river. Confronted by the broad-side of the tilting vehicle, Clogger squeezed between the bonnet and the stone kerb to see for himself the arrow-head of debris stretching into the yellow, sodium-gloom.

"I'm ever so sorry," the worried young driver repeated. "The gaffer will do his nut."

"Council have already been called," advised the city foot-patrol before engaging his straight-man in a subtle dual-act. "The offence of insecure load is always complete when goods fall from a lorry of their own volition."

"Mmm," Clogger answered, continuing the legal deliberations in front of the nervous listener, "but there are extenuating circumstances in this case...and nobody was injured."

"Yes, you're right. I suppose I could recommend an official caution, subject of course to his documents being in order."

"Oh, of course," Clogger concluded as the penny finally dropped.

While the city foot-patrol was searching his pockets for his stationery wallet, the much relieved driver rummaged through the mountain of irregular light-weight cardboard, lobbed at random back onto the lorry's rear platform.

"Oh, thanks lads, I have a full licence," he declared, passing a small plywood box to each of his sponsors. "The corners are bruised, but the contents should be okay."

Until that point in his life Clogger had only experimented with smoking, certainly never indulging in king-size cigars of South American origin. The sophisticated smell oozing from the neat little package triggered an impulsive change of image vital to the successful outcome of his mission.

"Well done, boss," responded the giant, patting the outside of his greatcoat pocket with his right-hand. "You're a gent!"

In the chilly night air the city foot-patrol took off his gloves and scribbled out accident details, including a chit requiring the driver to produce his licence and insurance certificate, at a police station of his choice, within five days.   "Where's your nearest nick?"

"Tudhoe, no Spennymoor," the young man hesitated, mentally preoccupied with a convoluted explanation for his employer. "It's near the depot."

"Can I take a couple of bottles of pop as well?" Clogger called, crunching his way through a mound of broken glass, bleeding red fizzy liquid into a storm drain halfway down the hill.

"Help yourself, I'll probably be out of a job tomorrow anyway."

Unhindered by traffic in the quiet side street, and certainly unconcerned about the laws of physics, the assistant accident investigator descended to the very periphery of the spillage. Several bottles of the popular soft-drink had survived a gravity-assisted fifty-yard slalom and come to rest against a shop front at the bottom of the cobbled piste.

These two look alright, Clogger decided, bending to twist road grime from the stout distinctive glassware with his gloved hands. Should be okay!

Apart from being warm and durable, early greatcoats were generously pocketed. In addition to the two outer compartments, one of which was already home to Clogger's main prize, the two inner pouches were deep enough to carry litre-sized containers.

Perfect, the giant purred, re-buttoning the thick serge to return to the centre of operations, slightly broader across the beam.

Motivated by an enhanced night call-out rate, a four-man team from the Highway's Department didn't take long to arrive and insisted on doing a thorough, time-consuming job. The offending driver was discharged to face the wrath of his depot manager, leaving Clogger and the city foot-patrol to divert a virtually non-existent traffic flow at either end of the clean-up operation. It was one in the morning when the brushing and shovelling finally came to an end. With every fragment of debris in the back of a pint-sized tipper-truck, the secret agent noticed that the experienced emergency clean-up crew hadn't bothered to salvage any unbroken bottles.

Perhaps they don't have any kids, he puzzled.

"Are you finished?" shouted the anxious city foot-patrol, wringing his gloved-hands vigorously. "I'm freezing!"

"I think you should send for the fire brigade, so we can swill-down the carriageway," the foreman cash-register replied. "May be some toxicity in the drains!"

"Don't be fucking stupid, it's only Tizer."

"Ah, right, we'll be on our way then."

With Milburngate restored to narrow silent quaintness, the city foot-patrol glanced at his wrist-watch. "Another hour," he shivered, "what bait time have you been allocated?"

"None."

The flash of surprise on the chilled features of his colleague, prompted Clogger to enlarge. "Oh, there was a bit of an incident at the police station after you left, Walter got injured and the sergeant was otherwise engaged."

151

Coming from any other member of B-Relief, the city foot-patrol would have succumbed to burning curiosity and elicited the juicy details, but in Clogger's case he sensed a saga that would require another long period of debilitating inactivity, so he decided not to pursue the matter.

"We can't take our refreshments together," the official foot-patrol insisted, anticipating the reaction of Bald Eagle if the patch was left uncovered. "I'll go now and relieve you at two," he continued, exercising his seniority to take early advantage of the warm canteen.

The arrangement didn't unduly concern Clogger for a number of reasons. Apart from the fact that he'd only been exposed to the elements since eleven, it was generally known that his vast bulk had the same sensitivity to temperature as his brain had to common sense, and in any case there was a potential loose-end to tidy-up in the centrally-heated confines of County Hospital. When the two men went their separate ways, Clogger marched up North Road with a churning purpose in his stride.

I've come to express my profound apologies for your misfortune, Clogger rehearsed as he passed a rather old looking Post Office maintenance vehicle, discreetly parked at the junction of Neville Street. Lines must be down!

Once again coincidence played no small part in Clogger's plans. He cleared the railway viaduct and walked up the deserted drive to County Hospital, crossing the heavily illuminated ambulance reception area to reach the main door of casualty. Chest to face with the same emergency medical team that had treated his arse injury, the doctor scurried off into the background leaving the more forceful nurse to deal with the unexpected visitor.

"If it hasn't healed properly you should see your own doctor," she instructed, before Clogger opened his mouth. "This facility is for accident and emergencies only."

"Oh, it's not that, sweet-face," the beaming giant replied, removing his helmet to cuddle his favourite carer. "I've come to see Walter."

"Who is Walter?" demanded the nurse, shaking Clogger's lumbering arm from her shoulder.

"He's the station janitor."

"Oh, the man with the wrist injury."

"That's him! Is he still here?"

"Yes, we're keeping him overnight. He's got mild shock and the doctor wants him examined by a specialist in the morning. It's a compound fracture, there may be complications!"

"Can I see him?"

"Well, I shouldn't really, he's about to be transferred to an orthopaedic ward, but you can have five minutes," she continued, pointing to the cubicle where Clogger had attempted to make medical history a few days earlier.

Attached to a drip with his arm in a sling, Walter was gowned in a wheelchair beside a standard hospital bed, minus his familiar National Health spectacles.

"How are you feeling?" Clogger enquired cautiously.

"Oh, not too bad," replied the handyman, squinting to identify his unexpected visitor.

"I had to come straight away, it was all my fault and I want to apologise personally. If there is anything I can do, well..."

"Don't worry about it. These things happen."

Walter's forgiving attitude left Clogger momentarily speechless. Struggling for words with which to make polite conversation, he was inspired by a water jug and drinking glass, prominent on top of the bedside locker along with Walter's personal belongings.

"Oh, I forgot, I've brought you a little present. It's not much. It was all I could manage at this time of night."

"You shouldn't have bothered," the handyman responded, embarrassed by the kindness of an officer he hardly knew.

Partially unbuttoning his greatcoat, Clogger reached into the inner-pocket on the left-hand-side and produced a sweating bottle of Tizer that Walter didn't really want, but gratefully accepted in the circumstances.

"Thank you," he said, "put it with my other things. I'll have some later."

With cunning indicative of espionage training, Clogger placed the armed device in the only available space on the locker-top, directly in front of Walter's spectacles.

"I'll have to ask you to leave now officer, they're coming down from the ward to collect him soon."

"Oh, I understand nurse, thank you for letting me visit," Agent Catchpole replied with deceptive politeness. "Look after yourself Walter, and get well soon," he concluded, bounding from the casualty cubicle content in the knowledge that he had made his peace with a vital cog in the police station wheel.

Clogger was hovering beneath a street-light at the main hospital gate, preparing himself for a full assault on the shop door handles in North Road, when the supervision car turned into the grounds, driven by Bald Eagle. Blinded by the headlights, he didn't immediately recognise the vehicle and continued to strap his helmet firmly to his chin and check the function of his torch.

"I thought it was only an insecure load you were dealing with, Woger. Didn't wealise anyone had been injured," Wupert queried, winding down the front passenger-side window to expose two chrome shoulder-pips.

"Oh, it's you boss...I mean inspector," spluttered the giant, cracking-off a salute. "You're right, nobody was hurt. I've just popped into casualty to apologise to Walter."

"Weally, that was thoughtful of you. That's where we're going. How is he?"

The surprise conversation extended Clogger's regulation greeting by a second or two. When he eventually snapped his right arm back to his bulky side it collided with his secreted cigar box, which in turn sent a shock wave into the remaining Tizer bottle. Exactly how he determined the lethal frequency remains a mystery, but it triggered two consecutive explosions. The first, a heavily muffled but nevertheless audible thump, attracted a second straining head to the passenger-side window, just in time to witness a pink frothy substance cascade down the outside of Clogger's trouser leg onto his boot.

"Don't need to ask you what the lorry was carrying!" Bald Eagle muttered, while the assistant accident investigator adopted a one-legged poise consistent with breaking wind.

The second blast, detonated remotely, was similarly muffled and came from somewhere within the hospital. It had different sound characteristics and coincided with Walter's fumbling attempt to recover his spectacles from the top of the bedside locker, in readiness for his wheelchair excursion.

8   NIGHT-SIGHT ROBBERY

Midway through the ground attack Running Bear had taken one-and-a-half more scalps and disposed of a piece of cherished equipment as old as the police station itself.

"They don't build them like this any more," Walter would say, patting the maturing rungs with tender loving care.

In isolation the giant wooden step-ladders were of little strategic consequence, but symbolically they marked a turning point in the war. After Walter had confirmed the aeronautical concept of drag could only be overcome by mechanically-assisted lift, the climbing frame became more versatile and developed an inconvenient tendency to execute a gymnastic manoeuvre commonly referred to as the splits. Coupled with the probability of a compensation claim, Gentleman Jim dithered over their replacement and eventually ordered a less lofty, modern aluminium pair, but in doing so sent out the wrong signal to Agent Catchpole. With phase-four and victory in sight, the freedom-fighter had taken important psychological high ground.

The half-scalp was that of the Painted-Lady, who in the midst of wildly inaccurate rumours about her cycling skills, spiralled into emotional turmoil. Dedicated to her husband and family, she couldn't resist the services of her tame bull moose and became racked with conflict and guilt. The couple found a new, much safer venue for their secret trysts, away from the tightened security of the main police station building, but her professional effectiveness soon deteriorated.

A series of traffic jams, peripheral to the city, culminated in the involvement of a militant local councillor and an investigation by the headquarters-based traffic management department. It concluded the problem emanated from the control box and the suppliers of the closed-circuit television equipment were called-in to conduct tests. When they failed to identify an electronic reason for the spasmodic congestion, the traffic wardens' duty roster was examined and a heavily made-up common denominator emerged. Although her inability to concentrate properly for long periods meant that her days were numbered anyway, she did survive the whole war, then divorced her husband and joined a convent in the South of England.

After a long period of convalescence, Walter was fully scalped. He learned from his orthopaedic specialist that he would never regain full mobility. Because Clogger had extended the problem to both upper-limbs, in the light of his poor eyesight it was abundantly clear that as a handyman he was no longer handy. An out-of-court settlement by Durham Police insurers topped-off with a disability pension and a part-time job as a lollipop man, secured Walter's early retirement to the smoky environs of the Court Inn domino league, where he would develop the big game temperament and ultimately become the undisputed fives and threes champion.

"Produce your appointments," Bald Eagle routinely ordered when B-Relief assembled for their second 10 p.m. 6 a.m. tour of duty. His eyes were fixed on Clogger who had just entered the parade-room with a giant cigar smouldering in the corner of his mouth. It was another turning point. Until then Bald Eagle harboured a secret. He rightly suspected his latest transferee was under the control of a sinister anti-establishment force, but there was always the possibility of turning his allegiance, then enjoying retirement in the knowledge his beloved sub-division was intact. The brown log Clogger was in danger of falling off began to dispel that particular notion.

"And your truncheon, Catchpole," Bald Eagle insisted, when Clogger added his bait-box, handcuffs and torch to the line.

A tightly rolled-up racing paper called the Sporting Life, reluctantly produced from a dedicated lining alongside his right-hand trouser-pocket, slammed the door firmly in the sergeant's face.

"This is not a Punch and Judy show," boomed the ginger-wig. He's definitely fucking Mafia.

Traditionally an officer on night-shift without his full appointments would be sent home to rectify the problem and have his over-time accrual adjusted accordingly, but Clogger was saved by the bell, or the parade-room telephone to be exact.

"This better be important," Bald Eagle snapped when he recognised the voice of the communications-room anchor-man. "I'm just about to start the parade."

157

A pregnant silence followed, punctuated by a series of concerned grunts. "I know Walter is on the sick," the supervisor blasted.

Rattled by the obvious, the sergeant's irritation soon subsided. "Is the meat-wagon back in the system?" he queried softly, before hanging-up. "Catchpole, take the meat-wagon to Bearpark, the late-day mobile is detained with a suspected suicide...and don't forget the cask...and don't smoke that thing in public," he continued, rapidly relieving the pain in his neck.

Certain that he was firmly established as the sergeant's preferred choice in cases of emergency, Clogger scooped up his appointments with characteristic gusto and charged out of the room brandishing a state-of-the-art paper baton. "Leave it to me boss...I mean sergeant," he shouted from the muffled depths of the main corridor.

It's reasonable to assume that in tasking Clogger with a labouring job normally undertaken by the station dog's body, Bald Eagle skilfully engineered a few more hours respite from the rigours of supervising an imbecile, but it's also worth noting the time and date. Ten to ten on the evening of Tuesday 15th April, 1969; almost a week since Clogger last attended a full operational briefing. Anyway, it wasn't relevant to his first problem. Having drawn a pocket-set from the communications-room hatch, written down the address of the incident and collected two sets of keys, Clogger reversed the meat-wagon to the doors of Walter's other sanctum in the corner of the police yard. In the shadowy glow of lamp-light, cigar protruding from his mouth, he contemplated a neatly painted sign; Special Equipment, then the temporary undertaker tackled a series of bolts, bars and padlocks to gain access to a well-ordered array of outdoor oddments, ranging from a neat stack of traffic cones to a full set of drain rods.

Occupying centre stage on matching trestles, two freshly swilled and disinfected light-weight transit coffins, illuminated by a single light-bulb, presented Clogger with a choice. For reasons of convenience and limited visibility, he ignored Walter's obsession with labelling and shouldered the nearest brown-plastic container to the rear doors of the vehicle, sliding it between the lateral bench seats in an eerie scene reminiscent of a horror movie. When he turned off the light and locked the store up again, oblivious to the popularity of the nearby main London to Edinburgh railway line as a means of suicide,, the newer more presentable utility cask, paint marked; GP (general purpose) was undisturbed.

Predictably the route to Bearpark took Agent Catchpole through the city-centre at dramatic, blue-flashing speed. Although he didn't get a chance to impress the heavily made-up light of his life, he was nevertheless able to demonstrate his ability to cope under pressure.. With the control system on automatic, he charged the big Commer van through the Market Place and up North Road, noticing for the second time in twenty-four hours, an old Post Office maintenance vehicle parked at the junction with Neville Street.

The lines can't still be down! I'll check it out later.

It took Superman another ten minutes to reach the quintessential County Durham mining village of Bearpark with its active but declining colliery, and all the trappings of a hard-working, hard-drinking close-knit community. A series of terraced bungalows, at right-angles to the main road, were at the heart of the settlement, together with a workingmen's club and a welfare hall. Clogger didn't have to look beyond the third, unmade colliery-row to find the epicentre of activity. He spotted an assorted group of chattering rubber-necks standing in the glow of a street-light close to a badly parked panda-van, and threw the meat-wagon into a sharp gravel-crunching turn, clicking-off the blue light.

Here we are, he enthused, pulling-up behind the vehicle of his late-day colleague, with a glowing pole in his mouth.

Clogger had only just swung open the driver's door when the plastic-curlered leader of the thirty-strong spectator group addressed him from her front-line position, alongside a more formally dressed man carrying a familiar, black-leather bag.

"Bloody tragedy!" declared the matriarchal battle-axe, her podgy forearms folded tightly beneath a wholesome woolly bust

"What is?" Clogger asked, making a token effort to obey Bald Eagle and conceal his cigar behind his back.

"He's club indoor games champion, three years in a row. Never been done before. Everything to live for!" the spokeswoman advised.

159

"T'other one had to break in," she continued, when the giant's gaze settled on the wide-open front door of the compact little dwelling. "Dogs have been howling all day. Smell was terrible."

"Mmm," responded the cool and collected law-enforcement officer, eyeing the spikes of raw timber protruding from the thickly-painted door frame.

"Call me, officer, as soon as it's safe to go inside," instructed the bag-carrying man in the self-evident tones of the local doctor.

The adjacent sash-window, with its typically defunct pulley system, was propped wide-open from the inside with a stout wooden coat-hanger, a tell-tale sign the first officer on the scene had decided on immediate ventilation. Feeling smug in the knowledge he was equipped with the perfect antidote for objectionable smells, Clogger pushed his Montecristo back into his mouth and puffing hard on it, entered the cramped cottage in a cloud of repellent fumes. Although effective, the strategy wasn't an unqualified success. Vigorous repetition in the short, linoleum appointed passage seemed to eliminate entirely the rancid odour of decomposing flesh, and any other smell for that matter, but it obscured completely Clogger's vision into the clean but sparsely furnished sitting-room.

I must try this when I go fishing in the summer, toyed action-man, wafting through a dense plume to peer into the unoccupied and very draughty parlour, illuminated only by the residue of the street-light outside. It should keep the midges away!

The short distance between the wide-open sitting-room door and the similarly gaping kitchen provided the fumigator-in-chief with an opportunity to wind-up his operation, indeed it was probably his impersonation of a Scottish piper that concealed the sudden increase in combustibility. It didn't escape the attention of the late-day man though who was in visual range of his fast-burning assistant, framed by watery moonlight in the kitchen doorway. When he looked up from the vicinity of the occupied gas oven, holding a wet towel over his mouth, the sight of a red-glowing torch in the blue-tinged darkness launched him into a sort of clumsy straddle dive. Intended to encourage an effective through-flow of fresh air, the sash-window in the kitchen was also propped open, but a second wooden coat-hanger from the bedroom wardrobe had all of the characteristics of a spring-trap.

When the slightly built and very agile late-day man urgently brushed the trigger to one side, the heavy frame hesitated, then slammed down just in time to trap his squirming buttocks.

"Are you alright?" Clogger queried, wafting away more smoke to get to the aid of his strangely over-reactive colleague. "What's the problem?"

"Put that fucking cigar out," the wriggling late-day man screamed, while he fought off the attentions of the deceased's two greyhounds, stalking the dark corners of the back yard.

The dogs must have been more familiar with the explosive properties of coal gas than Clogger because while the honey-monster fumbled for the cold water tap, to quench his huge weed in the stone sink, one of the racing machines finished licking the late-day man's thrashing head and took a precautionary measure of its own. It lifted its hind leg and casually pissed all over him.

Despite being made doubly safe in a rapidly stabilising atmosphere, the late-day mobile was still reluctant to withdraw his torso from the aperture and come in from the cold. Using his colossal shoulder strength, Clogger rammed the blade of the guillotine back into the cocked position and used his forearm as extra protection for his colleague's head.

"Don't worry, I've jammed it open," Clogger reassured, thinking a second accidental activation was the problem.

"Are you sure that cigar is out?" quivered the late-day man. "Yes," Clogger insisted. "Sit down over there and pull yourself together." He must have a phobia!

While the ammonia-tainted late-day mobile recovered his composure on a creaky kitchen chair, comfortable in the proven knowledge the dangers of spontaneous ignition had gone, Clogger naturally assumed command of the crisis and turned on the light. The problem emanated from the centre-piece of the tiny white-washed kitchen; a large, gnarly, blue-enamelled gas oven with its door standing wide-open. Although all the chrome control knobs were safely in the off-position, thanks to the quick-thinking first response, the elderly occupant was similarly reluctant to remove his torso from the aperture. In fact he was determined; rigor-mortis had set in.

Dressed in a white-starched collarless shirt, braces, and heavy blue trousers, the widower was in a kneeling position with his head resting uncomfortably on the base of the roasting compartment.

"Must have decided to call it a day," Clogger sighed philosophically, leaning towards the slight, silver-haired body to ponder the morbidly contorted expression on a blotchy-blue face.

"Call in the quack to certify death," advised the revitalised late-day man, rising cautiously from his chair. "There's usually a note, look for a note!"

Despite a thorough search of all the likely places in the spotless little dwelling, the police duo was unable to elicit a reason for the tragedy, albeit murder was never an option.

"Let's box him up and get him to the mortuary," Clogger's number-two suggested, sniffing his urine-soaked sleeve after the doctor prodded the corpse with his toe and nodded his head. "I want to get off home for a bath. The coroner's officer can do the follow-up in the morning."

Thundering back along the tiny passage on his own, Clogger was confronted by an even bigger crowd of bristling locals, completely encircling the front door.

"Let the dog see the bone," he called insensitively, pushing his way through the creeping throng to reach the meat-wagon.

"Is Percy definitely deed?" demanded the lady battle-axe.

"I'm afraid so," Clogger acknowledged, inflicting head-bowed silence over the entire congregation. "Move away from the vehicle please."

Forced into experimenting with a personally developed crowd dispersal technique, Clogger hauled the ageing secondary container from the rear of the meat-wagon and clumsily separated it from its close-fitting lid. With the main part under one arm and the top under the other, he left the vehicle doors wide-open for convenience, then scissored his way back through the mourners. Effective among people who maintain a natural instinct for self-preservation, the flapping technique was prohibitive in the confines of the cottage doorway.

162

After a series of ungainly, spine-jolting shunts with the already damaged woodwork, he decided to temporarily abandon the more manageable lid and haul the main part of the equipment along the little passage into the kitchen.

"Hang on, while I go back for the other bit," Clogger rattled to his pungent partner, before spinning his heels on the cracked linoleum floor.

When he returned to the front door the composition and character of the external audience had changed significantly. No longer respecting an imaginary boundary line, the lady that looked like a bulldog with a wasp in its mouth had been relegated to the second row, her position as prop taken by two suited gentlemen, bearing note-pad and camera respectively.

"Stay outside," Clogger ordered, disturbing the journalistic-looking pair from their close examination of the coffin lid on the floor of the tiny lobby.

"Can I have a word?" asked the younger more alert of the two, unfolding his full height with a pen at the ready.

"You've been clocking again," Clogger responded, referring to the practice of monitoring police messages on modern VHF radio equipment. "I'll comment later."

It was only after our hero had ushered back the front line and recovered the lid that he noticed a small, white-painted operating instruction in the limited vocabulary of Walter, GDB. With more pressing commitments to concern him, the mind-bending meaning of the succinct footnote escaped the Arctic explorer's intellect, so he towed the second six-foot sleigh to the kitchen, dropping it into position alongside the main coffin without another thought.

"Press are here," Clogger remarked, matter of fact, making an initial appraisal of the job-in-hand.

The feather-weight of the five-feet six-inch deceased wasn't a problem for the giant. Indeed, in the confines of the little kitchen a single-handed approach to the task was preferable. It was the obtuse, all-fours posture of the rigor-mortified slender frame, and the possibility the right cheek was somehow stuck to the oven, that proved potentially awkward. Standing astride the local indoor games celebrity, with his hands locked beneath a morbidly cold and lifeless rib cage, Clogger bore the weight of the corpse and gently eased the head into open space. There was a popping sound, then much to Clogger's relief the resistance abated.

"Straight into the box," the late-day man urged, impressed with the success of his assistant's first effort.

Bent double with the praying Moslem suspended between his legs, Clogger waddled into position then straightened his back to achieve more height. Like a construction site jib-crane he carefully swung over the open target and deposited his load with pin-point accuracy.

"Perfect!" quipped the late-day mobile, the very second the manoeuvre was complete. "Put the lid on!"

To avoid potentially embarrassing situations, equipment of this nature is always designed to accommodate the biggest, and in terms of capacity the old transit box was no exception. Apart from the fact that under Walter's regime it had never been used to carry a complete specimen, the preferred resting position of the deceased was inconvenient whichever way one chose to package the body. In the event Percy's bottom was necessarily protruding above the rim like the fulcrum for a playground see-saw.

"Can't take him like this," Clogger proffered, removing the rocking lid again to analyse the problem.

It was during a futile, bone-creaking assault on the forces of nature that Clogger made the discovery behind what is now widely regarded as his master-stroke. Irrespective of the pathologist's wrath had he succeeded, the giant was attempting to straighten Percy's legs when he noticed that the outer knuckle of his right ankle-bone was unusually bulbous. Without disturbing a well-worn leather carpet slipper, Clogger eased up the trouser leg and fished inside a thick woollen sock with his thumb and forefinger. As cold and hard as the limb itself, he carefully withdrew a small, gleaming ivory slab and turned it over in his hand.

"What's that?" the bewildered late-day man inquired, peering at the find.

"A domino," answered Clogger, admiring a professional quality found only in workingmen's clubs. "Must be a fanatic!"

164

Having casually abandoned the curiosity on the Formica-topped kitchen table, Clogger conceded to the superior forces of rigor-mortis and replaced the ill-fitting coffin lid.

"Come on, we'll have to make the best of it," he suggested, bending again to lift the foot of the hard-plastic container.

Prompted by his assistant's initiative, the late-day man took the opposite end and using a series of uncoordinated chin and upper-arm movements, the pair managed to negotiate the tiny passage with the coffin lid oscillating gently at chest height.

"Show some respect," Clogger called, steering his backward facing colleague between a pair of vultures, hovering at either side of the front door.

The fact that Percy was leaving home in such an untraditional manner, i.e. head first instead of feet first, was of no real concern to the press team, although it did cause a ripple of disapproving gasps among the viewing public. It was the occasional glimpse of his protruding bottom beneath an unstable lid, marked; Misfits Only, that stimulated the journalistic frenzy.

"Who is he?" the reporter demanded to know, while his colleague fired-off a series of flashes.

"You know better than to ask me that before the body has been formally identified," Clogger replied curtly, giving his partner an object lesson in on-the-hoof media management.

"Why is he in that position?"

"Stiffness!"

"Was he into depraved sexual gratification?" the interrogator continued, feverishly pursuing an exclusive.

"No, only the gas oven," advised Clogger.

"Do you suspect foul-play!"

"Don't be silly, he only keeps greyhounds and they were both locked in the yard."

"Why did you find it necessary to break down the door?"

Way below the belt the penultimate question needed careful thought, so Clogger, being a true professional, bought some time. When the late-day man rested his end of the transit coffin on the rear threshold of the meat-wagon, the police spokesman slowly pushed the overloaded bread tray between the bench seats.

"Good question," he muttered, shutting the double-doors carefully to put his hand on a damp, sticky shoulder. "My colleague here thought that if he'd knocked he was unlikely to receive an answer."

Totally exasperated by Clogger's command of the interview, the journalist's next question was delivered in a manner unbecoming his honourable profession. "Then, what can you tell me about the deceased?" he screamed.

"Well," said Clogger thoughtfully, "as yet we've been unable to establish a reason for his suicide, but we are pursuing the possibility it had something to do with dominoes."

"Dominoes?"

"Yes, dominoes."

"What is the connection with dominoes," the note-pad wielding hack enthused, feeling he was at last getting somewhere.

"We recovered the double-six from his right sock," announced Clogger, radically transforming the main body of the audience from a state of solemn deliberation to one of frenzied chattering.

By the time Clogger and the late-day mobile had secured the tiny dwelling and left Bearpark, heading in convoy for the mortuary at Dryburn Hospital, the domino revelation had penetrated every corner of the village and started a debate that would quickly divide and ultimately destroy the whole community. In retrospect it was probably an ingeniously exploited opportunity to further his master plan, but the poker-playing secret agent typically disguised his emotions with a cheesy grin.

"Get off home, I'll finish-up here," Clogger insisted, once the late-day man had helped lift snoopy-sniffer into the discreetly located, white-tiled hospital chamber.

"Thanks," replied the grateful holocaust survivor, anxious to discard his uniform to the sealed confines of a regulation laundry bag. "Don't forget to leave the paperwork for the coroner's officer."

A hospital mortuary shortly before midnight on a moonlit evening is a test of anyone's constitution, but it was the disturbance of a wide-eyed, leery-looking attendant during his packed-meal that speeded up the admission procedure. As though under scrutiny from a time-and-motion analyst, Clogger unconsciously shifted his cud-chewing, round-shouldered assistant into top gear and the pair made an unofficial attempt on the world record. Despite the obstructive effect of lingering rigor-mortis on the body-stripping section of the course, the overall aggregate was a respectable, if not a successful challenge. Clogger had already bagged the clothing and filled-out the obligatory sections of a standard coroner's report, when creeping Jesus finally emptied his mouth of home-cured ham and tied a morbidly pendulous label to Percy's big tow.

"Good night," called the relieved giant, dragging both halves of his Misfits box through the mortuary ante-room towards a short Tarmac path and the specially secluded parking area.

The farewell gesture wasn't acknowledged verbally, but when Clogger slammed the meat-wagon doors shut and noticed the chamber light go out in a tiny, grilled external window it was evident he was no average mortal. A second dose of sinister moonlight at the silent, unsuccessful end of a sprawling hospital complex ought to have proved too much. Not in Clogger's case, though. He leapt into the security of the driver's seat and raced to the niggling conundrum in North Road, suffering only a temporary loss of appetite.

Apart from a trickle into the Caprice night-club, the city-centre thoroughfare was deserted. Loaded with an empty coffin, Clogger trundled the meat-wagon under the viaduct and locked his heat-seeking faculties onto the junction with Neville Street. Unattended, the Post Office maintenance truck was still there.

That's strange, Clogger puzzled, pulling-up on the other side of the carriageway to rummage through his right-hand trouser-pocket.

"PC Catchpole to foxtrot bravo control."

"Go ahead, PC Catchpole."

"Vehicle check."

"Pass details."

Peering through the driver-side window, Clogger could just make out the rear registration plate of the specially adapted Austin Gypsy.

"Romeo papa tango, one fiver niner, B bravo, parked North Road, Neville Street," he rattled in phonetic speak.

"Stand-by."

Bleep, bleep, bleep.

Normally, the out-of-hours presence of a telephone repair vehicle would accompany a tented open manhole of some description, and a partially submerged technician wrestling with a plethora of multi-coloured wires under a feverish butane light.

Peculiar! super-sleuth pondered, scanning the vicinity with his fingers rolling impatiently on the steering wheel.

"PC Catchpole from foxtrot bravo control."

"Go ahead, control."

"Not reported stolen. Do you want me to call-out County Hall for owner details?"

"Not necessary," retorted Clogger with a readily recognisable logo in full view. "It belongs to the GPO. Give them a ring and find out what it's doing here."

"Roger."

Bleep, bleep, bleep.

It was at this point the special investigator decamped the meat-wagon and stealthily crossed North Road to circle the irregularity on foot. The bonnet was stone-cold and both cab doors were firmly locked, but the lofty, double rear doors had some give in them. Although they wouldn't open, Clogger detected a strange, dynamic resistance from the inside, made more mysterious by the absence of a padlock in the exterior hasp and staple.

There's someone inside, he puzzled, his pulsating receiver crackling into life again.

"PC Catchpole from control."

"Go ahead."

"Night-duty manager has the vehicle logged-out on special loan. No further details available until the morning."

"Received," Clogger sighed, his eyes panning back to the meat-wagon and the parade of shops it was parked in front of.

Blessed with an inquisitive mind, Agent Catchpole was understandably uneasy about the unresolved nature of the situation and made a further ponderous examination of the rear doors. When he fingered two newly installed glass studs set in tiny rubber grommets,

168

and contemplated their engineering purpose, the legitimacy of his parentage was secretly debated by the blind school. It was however the silhouette of an enormous koala bear, breaking the sky-line at the summit of a telegraph pole immediately behind the parade of shops, that fuelled his fertile imagination. The bloated Alpine figure, harnessed in a one-piece jump-suit, didn't appear to be working and had a bazooka-sized contraption hanging from his thickly-hooded neck.

Despite not being up-to-date operationally, like most other County Durham residents Clogger had read the local papers and seen the television news. He was aware of a series of undetected robberies that typically involved the abduction of a shop manager from his home during the night. Under threats of violence, one of the raiders would force the victim to open his premises and disarm the burglar alarm and safe. Then a second illusive duo would appear, specialising in pre-strike reconnaissance and the comprehensive removal of money and valuables. The realisation the parade of shops, on the opposite side of North Road, included a busy bookmaker and a high-class jeweller paved the way for another award-winning initiative.

Could be a rabbit away! Clogger theorised, fighting off the tingling onset of adrenalin to nonchalantly stride back to the meat-wagon.

Exuding the appearance of a satisfied customer, Agent Catchpole casually drove to the end of North Road, but instead of negotiating Framwelgate Bridge he turned sharp-right into the dark tranquillity of South Street, carefully secreting the stand-in hearse between two family saloons. Alighting from the vehicle, he then transferred his radio receiver to the breast pocket of his blue shirt and quietly discarded his helmet and tunic on the front passenger-seat before creeping back into the main street. Hugging the shop fronts in a manner befitting a trained sleuth, Clogger retraced his steps and flashed into the shabby foyer of the Caprice night-club.

"Members only," a surprised doorman thundered, reflexively complying with the law. "Let me see your card."

"Never mind all that," countered Clogger, "give me your jacket."

169

Despite extensive experience in the field of law and disorder, the pugilistic receptionist was slow to respond and needed further words of explanation.

"Quickly, arsehole," Clogger snapped, pulling a three-quarter length bottle-green jacket from the back of the reluctant donor.

Not satisfied with an image reminiscent of the bygone teddy-boy era, special detective Catchpole turned-up the black-velvet collar and chewed the end off a giant cigar. When he returned to the front line in clever disguise, a lamp-post next to the yellow maintenance van was his first port of call. Demonstrating true professionalism in the face of imminent danger, he decided to confirm his suspicions before neutralising part of a very dangerous criminal gang. Sporting a smouldering roll of the finest Cuban leaf, Clogger shinned up the street furnishing sufficient to see a small, partially open sky-light in the roof of the rear workshop compartment. It bore tell-tale traces of water vapour, consistent with additional humidity from a confined human presence.

Definitely a runner, the giant concluded, thudding to the base of the lamp-post like a responding fireman.

Straight into action with the ethos of the special forces, Clogger knew he had to work quickly and alone. To summon blue-flashing assistance prematurely would frighten-off the other half of the team and leave him embarrassingly short of evidence. Fearless, he glanced furtively at the elevated look-out, drew the Sporting Life from his truncheon pocket and huddled protectively into position, rolling-up the newspaper even tighter in the process. Then, grimacing through a cloud of eye-stinging cigar smoke, he clicked home the hasp on the rear doors of the repair truck and fed the compressed paper rod into the staple.

That's cooked his goose, he confirmed, twisting the stiff ends into a loose but effective knot.

With one of the would-be robbers neatly contained, the teddy-boy temporarily removed the log from his mouth and sprinted across the sodium haze of North Road, into the mouth of an alley accessing the back of the parade of shops. His spiky, black head rotated in all directions, then under the weak glow of a Montecristo, General

Catchpole penetrated behind enemy lines and tackled the near total darkness with his bottle-green back firmly against the wall. Unsure of his next move, a fortuitous stroke of luck emerged from the penumbra. The suspicious koala bear was strapped to the upper part of a knotty telegraph pole fitted with its own top-half rungs. A fully extended aluminium ladder propped against the base, was the only means of escape, so the secret agent sucked hard on his comforter then carefully lifted the apparatus away, lowering it quietly to the ground.

So far so good!

Although Clogger thought otherwise, his action hadn't really escaped the attention of the elevated mammal, but in such critical circumstances the look-out resisted the temptation to broadcast cover-blowing expletives and returned his intensified focus to the job-in-hand. In the meantime the heavily disguised SAS man crept around the block and reappeared in North Road ready to make a final dash for safety. In another scene from The Great Escape, he took a deep breath and dropped into a crouch to zigzag across the illuminated battle-zone into the seclusion of the open-planned bus station. With only a smouldering Montecristo for personal protection, the lone warrior was careful to select a suitable command and control bunker. Settling on a park-type bench beside an enormous glass-framed time-table, Clogger laid full-stretch on his stomach, peeping into the theatre of war with his cigar in one hand and his radio transmitter in the other.

"PC Catchpole to foxtrot bravo control, priority message."

The jargon caused the communications-room team to drop everything.

"Go ahead PC Catchpole," the anchor-man responded, his assistant switching on emergency voice recording equipment.

"Serious robbery imminent at the top-end of North Road, request covert support in South Street, Crossgate and Alexander Crescent."

"Stand-by, PC Catchpole," clipped the controller, leaving the radio channel open for Clogger's dedicated use.

Bleep, bleep, bleep.

Time being of the essence, in such pressing circumstances it wasn't considered good form for either party to query the other's professionalism. With one eye peering over the top, Clogger puffed thoughtfully on his cigar and held his entrenched combat posture while his communications-room colleague blindly and efficiently re-deployed key resources on a separate radio link. What seemed like a lifetime of gently pulsating silence ended after a couple of minutes.

"ETA fiver minutes, repeat fiver minutes, standing by," the controller rattled, indicating that he had sealed North Road and was ready to deal with Clogger's next request.

"All city-centre units to ground, inform supervision, ambulance crew to stand-by."

"Roger."

Bleep, bleep, bleep.

Comfortably within the five-minute margin, two sinister, black, double-crewed Austin Westminster patrol cars slipped into place in the shadows of South Street and Alexander Crescent, then slightly later, the single-crewed Sherburn panda rolled to a quiet halt at the Crossgate end of Neville Street.

"Supervision also to Crossgate" the controller advised, reinforcing the weakest link in the cordon with two more mystified participants. "Ambulance holding at County Hospital, radio to talk-through."

For twenty minutes the ambush was in place, its heart-racing combatants hovering like falcons while the scene was descended on by two unconnected private vehicles. From Gilesgate in the east, a Newcastle-upon-Tyne registered 3.2 litre Jaguar approached with five occupants, the least burly of them trembling uncontrollably in the middle of the back seat with a knife at his throat. The second more modest saloon came from the direction of Bearpark, following an extended late-night interview with one of Percy's more co-operative neighbours. When the Jaguar pulled-up outside the jewellers and two villainous-looking men urgently decamped to look-out positions at either end of the parade of shops, Commander Catchpole was slightly confused but nevertheless had the presence of mind to coin the now famous phrase.

"The eagle has landed," he announced over one dedicated radio channel. "At the ready, gentlemen."

172

Even more confused was the communications-room anchor-man who overheard a remarkably similar message on another dedicated facility, at virtually the same time.

"Subjects in situ, wait for it."

Bleep, bleep, bleep.

When a key-carrying pencil-neck, wearing only his carpet slippers, was manhandled towards the front door of the shop by a baboon the radio waves were electric, but it was full entry into the premises that triggered a stereophonic feedback in the communications-room.

"Go, go, go!"

Unleashed from the shadows, two patrol cars flashed into life and roared to opposite ends of the parade of shops, where their truncheon-wielding crew-members were released like hounds on the real, unsuspecting look-outs. Textbook stuff, both bandits were overwhelmed and surrendered without a fight. The highly-trained patrol car drivers then tyre-squealed across the bow and stern of the offending Jaguar and squeezed a third submissive robber from the sandwich. By the time the Sherburn panda-man had descended Neville Street and edged past the violently rocking Post Office maintenance truck, the last baton-swinging traffic officer was screaming into the front door of the jeweller's shop with the teddy-boy General puffing at his shoulder.

"Police, you're surrounded, release the hostage and come out with your hands up."

Brilliantly appraising the situation, the Sherburn man didn't add unnecessary weight to the seat of the action, but drove straight across North Road into the alley, intending to cover the back of the shop. Charged with adrenalin, he came to a metal-crunching halt close to a telegraph pole, and in the secluded darkness abandoned his unit vehicle ready to club to death anyone who crossed his path. The first indication that all was not as it seemed came shortly afterwards in the form of a heavenly apparition. While the Sherburn mobile was doing his night-image impression of a caged-lion outside the locked and barred service entrance, the Almighty spoke.

"Wooden-top," he called, "get your fucking car off my ladder."

Meanwhile, at the front of the jewellers, Wupert and Bald Eagle were indulging in telepathic communication in the supervision car. Descending Neville Street in the wake of the Sherburn panda, the chauffeuring ginger-wig had similar trouble passing the rocking Post Office truck, but the duo also noticed the rear doors pumping in and out like bellows, against the rapidly failing resistance of a paper truncheon.

What's he done this time? they wondered in silent unison, just as the cigar twiddling Mafioso reached over his traffic colleague's shoulder to seize the surrendering gang-leader by the hair.

There isn't space here to describe in detail the events that followed, suffice to say that when the paper bolt eventually broke it was like the referee's final whistle at a Newcastle, Chelsea game. A four-strong group of visiting supporters thundered onto the pitch in standard Post Office overalls, and steamed by Wupert and Bald Eagle in a seething attempt to reach the man-of-the-match. Being a new-boy to the sub-division, Clogger didn't recognise the raiding party but it did dawn on him, in part anyway, that he had somehow miscalculated. Momentarily releasing his double-handed grip on the ringleader's hair, Clogger engaged a paralysing, body-bending head-lock with his right arm, then turned to his left-flank to palm-off the first aggressor with the skill of a cornered wing-half.

"My fault boss, my mother always said I was daft. I didn't realise you had something on."

The immediacy and sincerity of the teddy-boy's apology temporarily took the wind out of the sub-divisional detective inspector's sails; well he stopped spitting blood and reverted to saliva. Seconds later Clogger was confronted by another party of fanatics. The presence of the press predictably suppressed the mother of all bollockings and triggered a surreal, collective ambience. General Catchpole casually released his prisoner to one of his handcuff-bearing traffic colleagues, straightened his sleeve and turned down his brushed-velvet collar, before abandoning a cigar stub sufficient to choke a donkey. With four dangerous criminals shackled in pairs, the uniformed traffic team were standing-off on Clogger's right-flank, facing their CID rivals under the distant gaze of a bewildered university graduate, a ginger-wig, the Sherburn panda-man and a deep-sea diver surgically attached to a night-sight.

"What has happened here, officer?" the same VHF equipped journalist boomed, while his colleague urgently replaced the roll in his well-used camera.

"We've foiled a daring raid on this jeweller's shop," replied the teddy-boy General, poking a thumb over his shoulder.

"Is the same gang responsible for all the other raids in the region?" the salivating young reporter continued with an erection in his pants.

"Too early to say," Clogger advised, impressing the detective inspector with his confidence.

"Officer, I now understand the body you removed late last night from a house in Bearpark was that of a serial domino fraudster. Is there any connection with this incident?"

"It's unlikely, but as always we shall be keeping an open mind," Clogger replied masterfully, while the re-composed detective inspector prepared himself for centre stage.

Anxious to take the helm and grab some credit for a protracted surveillance operation, the wide-eyed young hack's next question was an ideal opportunity for Clogger to introduce the cleverly disguised senior detective.

"I assume you'll be calling-in the CID?"

Contrary to popular belief, General Catchpole wasn't attempting to inject some humour into the proceedings when he put his lumbering arm around the overalled-shoulders of the smug CID chief, grinned warmly and said, "Oh, I don't think so, they don't seem to have caught their own robbers yet."

9   ROAD GAMES

No matter how much damage limitation, Clogger's latest strike was always going to be highly embarrassing to Durham Police, but it was aggravated by a series of unfortunate coincidences. The detective inspector, who had been a useful athlete in his day with a propensity for inter-force boxing, was also a notorious hot-head with a sense of humour diametrically opposed to that of Clogger. When he debased the noble art with a contemporary Ali shuffle, then secured the removal of Clogger's left-arm from his shoulders with a short, stabbing body-shot, he was just in time for the press photographer's first flash. Recognising the career-threatening danger, the CID team rushed to smother their leader from further exposure, but their intentions were clouded by traditional inter-departmental rivalry. It appeared to the traffic side that a temporarily indisposed uniformed ally, albeit of adequate proportions, was about to be out-numbered in a grossly unfair way, so they collectively decided on a formal scrum. During a series of skirmishes, beyond the control of Wupert and Bald Eagle, the two press representatives justified the postponement of critical deadlines and gathered material for a fully-illustrated scoop, increasing the circulation of the Northern Echo to an unprecedented level.

It was only the second time in the history of the Darlington based regional newspaper that the editor had authorised a centre-page, pull-out supplement. On the first occasion pre-referendum arguments for and against entry into the common-market were of limited viability and the idea remained in the balance. Today, thanks to the teddy-boy General, supplements of this nature are an integral part of north-east life.

Two photographs of note appeared the following morning depicting the robbers and the poor victim. Shackled together but unsupervised, the shell-shocked gorillas, afraid to escape, were snapped scrambling into the safety of the two patrol cars. The mentally-wrecked jeweller slammed shut the front door of his shop to protect himself, then reluctantly answered the newspaper reporter's questions through the confines of his letter-box. His perspective permanently distorted by the experience, he praised the relatively humane conduct of his abductors, ultimately having a beneficial effect on their sentences.

Of course Gentleman Jim saw the disturbing copy over breakfast, but by then he was a spent force. The initiative for positive action, albeit far to late, came from the chief constable's staff officer, whose first chore every morning was to read the dailies. When he saw the material and urgently rushed it into the ivory tower at Akley Heads, the Almighty was given a second opportunity to save the fabric of his most prestigious sub-division, but his reaction was fatally pedestrian. Presented with a full diary by his lap-dog, the only appointment the chief could properly cancel fell early in the afternoon of the following Wednesday, three weeks and one full shift-pattern after the Martian's arrival.

"Ring the superintendent and tell him I'm coming over there personally, to show him how to run his sub-division," the chief constable boomed, giving the infiltrator just the leeway he needed.

The next night when Clogger rode his motorbike to work he was unusually preoccupied, but not with the mammary attributes of the Painted-Lady. Approaching the critical transition from phase-three to phase-four, for the first time in the campaign damage-assessment was unclear. Sitting bleary-eyed in the living-room of his lodgings after a disturbed morning's sleep, the one o'clock television news confirmed the suspension of the detective inspector, but gave no indication about the state of morale. The picture began to clear however when Clogger rumbled into the police yard to confront a traffic patrol vehicle refuelling at the sub-divisional pump. The driver was holding the nozzle of the antique device with urinal concentration, but the soft-capped crew-member, leaning on the spot-lit roof of the black Austin Westminster, looked up from the petrol record book and peered through the gloom.

"Clogger for president," he cheered, suggesting that the traffic department were generally pleased by the demise of their prima-donna, plain-clothes rivals.

The adulation was not what Agent Catchpole wanted, although it turned out to be the only blip in an otherwise demoralised sub-division. When Clogger parked his oily-machine and hauled his bait-box through the main building into the parade-room, Bald Eagle and the remnants of a once proud relief were all engaged in silent prayer. It was disconcerting to the point that the giant managed to take his seat without colliding with either a chair or table leg, then the ginger-wigged vicar looked up and started an unconventional sermon.

"The incident-log is incomplete," he said in solemn monotone. "The events of the last twenty-four hours were too extensive to record, suffice to say the village of Bearpark is now at war, divided on domino-religious grounds. Until further notice, all available ground-cover resources will be deployed removing street barricades and quelling violence. That of course, does not include you PC Catchpole," Bald Eagle continued, staring menacingly at the enemy-within. "If you so much as set foot in Bearpark, or the city-centre for that matter, during the course of the next eight hours, I will personally castrate you. Is that clear?"

While the prayer-circle grimaced Clogger tentatively felt his private parts, analysed his supervisor's instruction, then with a quizzical frown, confirmed he had properly understood.

"You mean you want me to look after the entire southern-end of the sub-division, single-handed, boss...I mean sergeant?"

"Yes, unfortunately Clogger," Bald Eagle sighed. "You'll have to use the CID car, I don't suppose they'll need it any more during the night."

Lurching to his feet, top operator Catchpole was about to gather-up his belongings and lead his platoon over-the-top, but the sergeant's unusually brief approach to his responsibilities troubled him.

"Come on, what else have you got to tell me?" he grinned, reaching out to pat Bald Eagle's toupee.

Ducking out of range, the harassed sergeant responded with a raised arm. "Extenuating circumstances, all refreshments will be taken discretionally, on the hoof."

"And there's something else, isn't there?" Clogger continued, dummying contact with the ginger bristle.

"The inspector won't be attending the briefing, he's now permanently engaged on internal inquiries. I'm your only point of reference until further notice," blustered Bald Eagle with a neat bob and weave.

"No, no, come on, try and remember!"

Suddenly relieved of a probing shovel, the sergeant flinched as the thorn in his side drew his black, hard-wood truncheon from its trousered-scabbard and banged it onto the parade-room table.

"Production of appointments. It's night-shift, remember!"

A plain yellow Mini saloon, the CID car was fitted with force-wide radio equipment of the type used by the traffic department and other free-roaming resources. It meant that Clogger was under dual-control. Showing up on the availability-board in the headquarters command and control facility, Clogger was also answerable locally, by pocket-set, to the subordinate communications-room in Durham City sub-division. Stressed to his limit, Bald Eagle clearly hadn't given the issue any meaningful thought. If he had, reverse logic would have suggested that in Clogger's case dual-control was a misnomer, synonymous with double-trouble. Anyway, fully-uniformed but under the cover of a plain vehicle, action-man roared to Nevilles Cross and turned south on the old A1 road, gnawing into his first discretional pork pie.

Weather conditions fair, visibility good, traffic light, it was twenty-past ten on Wednesday 16th April when he overheard his first high-level conversation over the force network.

"Mike two zero from M2LA."

"Go ahead LA."

"State and location?" the in-board radio clipped in much clearer, high-frequency tones.

"State two, Scotch Corner," replied the traffic patrol driver from the southern extremity of the force area.

"Situation report, last detail, mike two zero?"

"Still co-operating with North Yorkshire, possible road-block."

"Report of an injured horse on the carriageway at Rushyford. Veterinary surgeon en-route. ETA?"

"Unknown, LA."

179

"Stand-by, mike two zero."

Bleep, bleep, bleep.

"Foxtrot bravo seven from M2LA."

Oh, that's me, snapped Clogger, checking the unfamiliar call-sign displayed on the dashboard. "Go ahead LA"

"State and location?"

"State one, Cock o' the North," Clogger transmitted, pulling the radio handset from its clip on the front parcel shelf.

"ETA, Rushyford?"

"Ten minutes, but I'm not accident equipped," asserted the giant, anticipating the next instruction.

"Make your way in any case, foxtrot bravo seven. Mike two zero attend as soon you are free. Units acknowledge."

"Mike two zero, acknowledged."

"Foxtrot bravo seven, acknowledged," Clogger said, flicking his headlights up to full-beam, ready to flog the little saloon another ten miles south down the county's spine-road.

Bleep, bleep, bleep.

Screaming through Thinford, Agent Catchpole negotiated Ferryhill Cut then descended Chilton Bank towards the big roundabout at Rushyford. Well versed in the long-range identification of unusual activity, even in the dark he spotted two private cars parked alongside a very broad, grass verge close to the Eden Arms Hotel. Marginally outside the sub-divisional boundary, other officers would have moaned about the task, but not Clogger. In the true spirit of the Office of Constable, he negotiated the north side of the roundabout and parked next to an unsuspecting man and his elegant wife.

"Oh, it's the police dear," the evening-suited bystander announced, when he saw the plain yellow Mini give birth to Clogger's uniformed bulk. "It's dead officer, the vet has gone into the hotel to arrange for it to be taken away."

Lying motionless on the verge, the sight of an enormous black horse glinting in the road lights prompted the ever-vigilant investigator to examine the front of the nearest parked car.

"Oh, no officer, nothing like that," advised the black-gowned lady, offended by the apparent degradation of her husband's driving skills.

"We were leaving a function and we found the animal like this. It's still tethered," she continued, negating the first of Clogger's options.

He was busy scouring the heavily-muscled body with his torch, looking for evidence of other forms of unlawful horse-play, when the tweeded barrel of a veterinary surgeon reappeared from the direction of the hotel reception.

"I think it's had a heart attack, officer," he advised, finalising Clogger's crime enquiries. "According to the hotel porter it belongs to gypsies. I've contacted a yard at Spennymoor and they're sending somebody out."

"Thank you, sir," Clogger beamed, delighted that most of his work had already been done. "I'll take down some details, then you can leave it to me."

The veterinary surgeon and the evening-dressed informants left the scene in their respective vehicles. Clogger was using the roof of the CID car to complete his pocket-book when the intermittent drone of light traffic gave way to a sudden burst from the force radio.

"Mike two zero to M2LA."

"Go ahead mike two zero."

"Request talk-through with foxtrot bravo seven."

"Go ahead with talk-through."

"Mike two zero to foxtrot bravo seven, acknowledge."

Leaning into the passenger-side of his car to stretch a thick, curly black wire to its limit, Clogger answered, "Receiving, go ahead mike two zero."

"I'm still tied-up at Scotch Corner, what's the situation with the horse?"

"Don't worry mike two zero, there's no traffic hazard, I can manage. I'm just waiting for the body to be towed away by the knackers!"

Bleep, bleep, bleep.

Like a guided missile, the comment wiped-out the entire force command and control system with infectious giggling. All centrally managed police activity, including the 999 answering service, came to an abrupt ten-minute halt. Remarkably the viral attack wasn't fatal, indeed it didn't even destroy any non-essential targets. The only

181

resource to suffer was the elated traffic crew, who earlier in the evening had proposed Clogger for high office. Unlike other operatives their recovery wasn't complete. A second involuntary bout seemed to impair the driver's sense of distance. At least that's what he told the duty inspector in Bondgate, Bishop Auckland, when he wrapped the jam-sandwich into the back of the last OK service bus.

Close to midnight, the men from the knacker's yard winched the unfortunate animal onto the back of their Bedford truck and took it on its last journey, to that big glue-factory in the sky. Intending to patrol the villages of Ferryhill and Ferryhill Station, Clogger was heading north back up Chilton Bank, when he was called into action for a second time. Well; volunteered his services to be absolutely correct. Interrupting the steady stream of routine messages over both radios, mike two zero's request for priority status broke the easy-listening background noise on the force-wide receiver.

"All units to stand-by," the controller announced sharply. "Pass your message mike two zero."

"Stolen vehicle, just penetrated a joint road-block at Scotch Corner, heading north into this force area."

"Description, mike two zero?"

"Red HGV tractor unit, brand new, unregistered, believed to be a Volvo."

"Where was it stolen?"

"Transport depot in Leeds, approximately twenty-one-hundred hours. Tracked through West and North Yorkshire. All attempts to pull it over have failed."

"I will inform traffic supervision, mike two zero, have you any further information?"

"The driver is an employee of the haulier, believed to be heavily intoxicated. Apparently his wife left him today, to live with a man in Newcastle. All reports suggest he is very distressed and could even be suicidal."

"Await further instructions, mike two zero."

Bleep, bleep, bleep."

As you would expect Clogger didn't need to wait for further instructions, indeed he didn't even feel it necessary to advise the force command and control centre of his rapidly gelling plan despite its undisputed brilliance. Recognising the likelihood of the stolen tractor unit remaining on the old A1 road on its way to Newcastle-upon-Tyne, he flicked his headlights up to full-beam again and raced past the junction with Ferryhill to the summit of Ferryhill Cut. Originally constructed to divert heavy traffic away from the little village, the mini-canyon was part of the Great North Road, hewn from the black, slag-heaped landscape. Before the brow north-bound visibility was restricted, and just over the top, on the north face, opportunities to deviate from the carriageway were non-existent.

Perfect place for an ambush, the Lone Ranger observed, but what can I use?"

Seconds later his master-plan was finalised. On the east side of the pass a rocky recess showed signs of life. Resembling a miniature quarry, it was probably the source of the road builder's aggregate, but had become the home of a private coach company and the traditional resting place for other forms of heavy transport. When Clogger skidded to a halt on the gravel surface beside two large tipper-trucks, he initially ignored the bemused drivers jawing over a cigarette beside an open cab door.

"Foxtrot bravo seven to M2LA, priority"

"Go ahead foxtrot bravo seven."

"Close the A1 road between Rushyford and Thinford."

Bleep, bleep, bleep.

The terse, traffic orientated instruction from a CID resource stunned the normally spontaneous headquarters' controller into a few seconds of uncharacteristic silence.

"If you are referring to the progress of the stolen tractor unit foxtrot bravo seven, be advised that mike one has command."

"Request talk-through with mike one."

"Go ahead with talk-through."

"Foxtrot bravo seven to mike one, permission to organise another road-block at Ferryhill Cut."

Scrambled by telephone, the traffic inspector and his sergeant had just rushed from their northern base at Whickham police station and boarded the latest addition to the department's prestigious fleet. For reasons that escape the author, only the operational head was capable of running-in a heavily-decorated and fully equipped, state-of-the-art, 4.2 litre Jaguar. The awe-inspiring space-ship was negotiating Lobley Hill Bank, with both crew-members struggling to find the switch for the blue light, when Clogger first made radio contact.

"Who is this?" the sergeant responded, buying some valuable thinking time for his lord and master.

"Ferryhill panda, boss...I mean sir," answered Clogger, respecting the likely rank of a call-sign ending in one.

Familiar with every inch of road in the county, the traffic inspector marshalled his thoughts on Lobley Hill roundabout, then turned to his hand-set wielding copilot and muttered, "As good a place as any, but remind him of the procedure."

"Agreed, foxtrot bravo seven," the sergeant transmitted. "At this stage do nothing to induce a head-on collision."

"Received, mike one," Clogger acknowledged, giving the headquarters' controller the green light to close the road to normal traffic.

Still pondering the identity of a plain Mini car in an isolated, unofficial lorry park, the two drivers were fazed when Clogger's helmet plate zoomed-in from the darkness.

"We're only resting officer," one said apologetically. "We're not due at the processing plant until one."

"I'm commandeering these vehicles," blasted Clogger, oblivious to a faint, but rancid smell.

"What?"

"I'm commandeering these vehicles."

"But they aren't broken!"

It's probable the technical terminology confused one or both of the duo because it wasn't until the giant grabbed the driver nearest to the open cab door, and shot-putted him back into his seat, that the other responded positively of his own volition. Fortunately, Clogger reverted to plain English thereafter and there was no further confusion, especially when he drew his truncheon.

"Back-out onto the road, shit-head."

Baton in his right-hand, torch in the left, he took the unusual step of taking his whistle from his breast pocket, popping it into his mouth. Crunching the short distance to the ungated quarry entrance, he then stood guard for a few minutes until the traffic petered out in both directions. An eerie silence befell the normally busy Great North Road when Clogger stepped out into the yellow, sodium-haze to marshal two gnarly tipper-trucks into position. Using a series of unconventional baton and torch signals, punctuated by frequent whistle blasts, he could have been mistaken for Spanish Guardia, but leading the two side-by-side HGVs in slow formation towards the summit of Ferryhill Cut a parallel with local history was more appropriate. Minus a red flag, he looked like the guard walking in front of the Rocket when it made its first commercial journey on the Darlington to Stockton railway.

Although a conventional two-way road, the carriageway was wide enough for three lanes. When Clogger reached his chosen point on the north face of the summit, the volunteer work-force were beginning to get the idea. Facing south in the north-bound lane, Clogger waved the newer of the two trucks to its immediate right and the older, second lorry to its left. The result was a V-shaped stopper, between two shear rock faces, with a gap at the narrow end barely sufficient for a small saloon car.

"Right men, secure your equipment and follow me," the giant called, retreating with the drivers to a safe distance on the north-side of the funnel.

What the fuck is that horrible smell?

The proverbial lull preceded the storm. Standing with his two cloth-capped side-kicks about fifty yards away, Clogger put his appointments back to bed and replaced the whistle with a shark-repellent Montecristo to contemplate the symmetry of his creation. He was puffing on the monster, staring up the hill at the aperture between the rear-ends of two ten-ton tipper-trucks, when the southern night-sky began to dance with blue strobe lighting. In familiar territory mike two zero had raced ahead of the multi-force entourage and stopped the traffic at Rushyford, allowing only the rogue tractor unit access to the old A1 road. Followed cautiously by half a dozen assorted traffic cars, arms locked rigid on the steering wheel, the recently estranged man from Leeds was ploughing north with grim determination. His total disregard for safety and his unscheduled appointment with his wife's new lover were only thwarted when he climbed up through Chilton and emerged on the brow of Ferryhill Cut, unaware of Clogger's new border control point.

The meat in a nasty sandwich, self-preservation kicked-in and he braked, albeit too late. Tyres smoking, the mobile wedge skidded and squirmed downhill crunching into the metallic taper with whip-lashing accuracy. The backs of both tipper-trucks rocked vigorously on their suspension. At the same time the windscreen of the tractor unit shattered, then flaked away harmlessly to the ground. Remarkably relatively little damage occurred. When Superman ran to the immediate scene, he was confronted by traditional children's entertainment. Having suffered superficial grazing, Mr Punch was visible through the broken glass trying to make his injuries worse by banging his head on the steering wheel.

"I want to go to Newcastle," the suspect sobbed.

"I shouldn't bother if I were you," advised Clogger. "It's very cold at this time of the year!"

The success of the operation can never be denied. With the prisoner neatly contained in the crumpled cab, Clogger was joined by a plethora of foreign traffic officers who could only reach him from the south-side of the road-block by crawling like soldiers underneath the two lorries. He was receiving well-earned congratulations when mike one sped onto the scene from the opposite direction and screeched to a blue-flashing halt across the neck of the mechanical sandwich. Abandoning their brand-new 4.2 litre machine with both front doors wide-open, the traffic inspector and sergeant homed-in on the only helmet among the army of soft-topped traffic caps.

"Brilliant piece of police work," the inspector boomed. "I will be recommending you for a commendation."

"Oh, it was nothing, boss...I mean inspector," replied Clogger, flicking away his cigar to receive praise from the braided warlord.

The appearance of a senior Durham County police officer on his own turf triggered institutionalised protocol. All present lined-up ready to take his instructions.

"Look after matey," he rattled to two unfamiliar faces sporting West Yorkshire livery. "Record the damage to the commandeered vehicles in the presence of their respective drivers. I don't want any inflated claims."

What is that awful smell?

There was a period of organised chaos thereafter. Unlucky in love, the prisoner was hauled from the cab of the tractor unit, via the non-existent windscreen, while other officers squeezed and wriggled into a variety of damage-assessment positions.

"Tram-lines along the sides of both trucks," one North Yorkshire officer shouted. "Superficial!"

"Tail-gate locking mechanism buckled," another called, without recognising the temporary dynamics of impacted metal.

Satisfied that Durham Police Authority were still solvent, the traffic inspector finally gave the order to clear the carriageway in time for two very relieved drivers to complete their journey to the fertiliser factory on Aycliffe Industrial Estate. Facing the wrong-way in the north-bound lane the newer vehicle, of a different high-sided design, was the first to move off. It was evident that tension was dissipating from Clogger's structure when the driver revved hard and wrestled the beast through a series of ear-piercing, metallic creaks. Unfortunately, the cloud of blue diesel fumes not only obscured a column of dark gunge beginning to dribble from the back of the older lorry, but it also masked the rapidly intensifying foul smell.

When the first truck cleared the barricade and restored equilibrium to the tractor unit's trapped suspension, the remaining flood-gate flopped open at the bottom. Expecting an immediate spillage of some kind, the traffic inspector led his men in hasty retreat without considering the laws of physics. The inclination of the older tipper-truck, coupled with the viscosity of maturing fish waste, meant the initial deposit weighed only one ton and slithered harmlessly underneath the pulsating 4.2 litre Jaguar. The second nine-ton blob however, consisting of the head, tail and gut of every sea fish caught

187

on the north-east coast in the previous forty-eight hours, was too wholesome to burrow underneath the low-slung machine. It slopped over the door-sill into the thickly-carpeted passenger-side seat-well, then hurdled the transmission tunnel to make a treacly exit on the other side.

"Ferryhill mobile from foxtrot bravo control," crackled Clogger's pocket-set.

"Go ahead."

"Report of late-night drinking in the Thinford Inn."

"Fiver minutes," Clogger responded. "Got to go boss...I mean, inspector, duty calls!"

Shimmering in the yellow darkness, Clogger weaved his little Mini north again, through a light, two-way flow of mainly slow-moving commercial vehicles. When the fully illuminated rural road-house came into view on the east side of the Great North Road, the canned-sardine glanced at his wrist-watch.

It's nearly one! What's he doing open at this hour?

Alert as ever, Agent Catchpole approached the Thinford Inn on his sidelights, then extinguished all systems to free-wheel across the carriageway into the dark, apparently deserted peripheral car park. Quietly applying the handbrake, the investigator waited for his eyes to adjust before popping from his plain pod and easing the driver's door shut. Without headgear, he lifted his hand to his lapel and thumbed down the knurled volume control on his pocket-set receiver. A furtive, round-shouldered scrutiny of his isolated surroundings revealed the familiar lines of two mud-splashed Land Rovers, in a distant corner of the car park.

Ah, a lock-in!

Clogger made his next move with textbook professionalism. Tip-toeing to the front of the building, he cupped his hands around his eyes and peeped through the lounge window. There was nothing untoward in the curtained darkness so onward he crept, beneath a brewery sign glowing prominently above the wide-open front door.

What's the silly sod thinking about. Blackpool isn't as well illuminated as this!

On the other side of the front entrance the bar window was a different story. Also curtained, a light was burning. The over-sized sleuth searched and found the inevitable chink in the publican's armour. In classic detective pose, he rested his shoulder on the glass and peered in through one eye. The balding, barrel of a landlord was behind the counter, pulling hard on a shiny-black porcelain lever with a dish-cloth over his shoulder. Clogger glimpsed a punchy, froth-covered hand pass a pint of amber nectar to a dirty, brown-overalled customer whose attention was obviously elsewhere. While super-sleuth surreptitiously adjusted his viewing angle to see what the heinous offender was looking at, the judicial bell went; well the till to be exact.

Selling and consuming outside permitted hours, the investigator correctly deduced, abandoning his vantage point with all the covert evidence he needed.

Making full use of the element of surprise, Clogger crept back to the open front door and stealthily negotiated the lobby, before bursting into the drinking den.

"Nobody move," he called, resplendent in full, but helmet-free uniform. "You are not obliged to say anything unless you wish to do so, but whatever..."

"Shush," two shit-caked farm-hands snapped, standing at either side of a bar-mounted shove-ha'penny board.

"Tripler," whispered the eliminated spectator, swilling from his straight pint glass.

His round, blood-red face nodding a statutory defence from the other side of the bar counter, the licensee agreed.

Some people suggest it was the minefield of gaming legislation surrounding the pile of crumpled notes and mixed coinage that clouded Clogger's judgement. Others are convinced his involvement in the affairs of state at Bearpark the previous evening taught him a valuable lesson.

"Oh, that's different, lock the door and turn-off the light, landlord. Mine's a pint!"

Recognising his licence-threatening slip, the grateful publican rushed to the front door and secured the big mortise lock. When he returned to refresh his new guest, the two finalists were battling through the early rounds of competition in the warm, red glow of an open fire. Bemused by the precision of huge, ingrained paws, Clogger watched the battling rough-necks repeatedly slice a tiny brass-washer down the well-worn board. Only a slight reddening on the heal of one hand suggested the tournament had been a protracted affair.

"Ordinary or best?" the landlord asked, lifting the bar-flap to squeeze back into his trap.

"Is the Pope catholic?" quipped Clogger, indicating his preference for quality.

"Shush."

The intensity of the game held Clogger's attention for four full pints of ale, which wasn't very long considering he downed the first one in two visits to the glass. In light of the copious supply of free beer, one can be forgiven for thinking the disturbance of his biological clock on night-shift and the convivial atmosphere, spurred the giant's retreat to a cosy, red-padded wall-unit beside the hearth. Sitting beneath a water-colour depicting the premises a century earlier, Agent Catchpole pondered the tournament for a while, then contemplated the intense expression on the principal spectator's face. Half-way through his fifth pint, he noticed the landlord's bare forearms resting on the other side of the bar counter, and began a detailed analysis of the ginger vegetation. When a surprisingly pleasant farmyard smell began to radiate from the fanatically absorbed trio, Clogger's head dropped over to one side and he pretended to doze off.

"Hasn't got the big game temperament!" the licensee muttered, unaware the stability of Durham Police was being secretly usurped.

ZZZ...command structure softened, church and judiciary neutralised, hardware and human resources depleted, last pocket of resistance eliminated. It's time for the final assault!...ZZZ

How Clogger managed to feign sleep through the victory celebration and the triple-kitty counting ceremony is a credit to his training. Even two departing Land Rovers, each powered by a bag of hammers, didn't disturb him and it was well after two before he opened one eye and instinctively rubbed his stiff neck.

"PC Catchpole, acknowledge," his pocket-set whispered for the third time.

Turning up the volume in the flickering embers of a pine log, Clogger whispered back, "Go ahead," and then probed the darkness for signs of life.

The room was deserted, even the shove ha'penny board was out of sight somewhere, but prominently placed on the ornate, black-iron table in front of him, a brass mortise key secured the felt-tipped scrawl of the departed landlord.

"Radio check and result of your last detail, PC Catchpole? Difficulty making contact."

Gone to bed - lock-up and put the key back through the letter-box.

"Loud and clear, foxtrot bravo control. Advice given, all in order on departure."

With less than half the shift left and over four pints of ale on board, Clogger's conscience was troubling him. He had vast territorial responsibility but hadn't examined any vulnerable property except, arguably, the Thinford Inn. Sent to the southern extreme of the area at the beginning of his tour, he had intended to work back from Rushyford through Chilton and Ferryhill towards the city, but he was now out of position.

I'll do it the other way round, the slightly mellow giant thought, glancing at his area map to race the CID car towards the unfamiliar village of Hett.

To get to the isolated rural settlement, Clogger turned off the Great North Road at a point close to the main London to Edinburgh railway line and negotiated a narrow country lane on full-beam. By now it was decidedly chilly and he was making full use of the car-heater when he came across the deserted clutch of dwellings. Set out in a traditional way, Hett is a rambling place with a vast central patch of rough, undulating common-land. Its unique character comes from the network of irregular tracks that access the peripheral stone buildings at either side of the main thoroughfare. At the dead of night, in barely adequate street lighting, the place had strange ambience. Indeed, Clogger was travelling little faster than walking-speed, in awe of his perfectly still surroundings, when he first noticed the roadworks.

A luminous white arrow pointing right in his headlights, indicated that the two-way country road had been reduced to just one lane to facilitate the installation of a new drainage pipe. All the heavy, granite kerbstones along fifty yards of the near-side verge were out of position in the centre of the road, presumably pushed there by some mechanical means. Interspersed with conventional red and white plastic cones, the blocks formed a perfectly straight line and prevented vehicular entry into the beginnings of a very nasty ditch. The Highway's Department arrangement was in compliance with regulations, and more than adequate protection in an isolated country village. In fact at his first visit, Clogger didn't have a problem. Intending to identify and shake hands with the handful of commercial premises, he passed the obstacle without incident, but was then confronted by a local resident with remarkably big ears and a similar-sized grudge.

Fully grown and mesmerised by the car headlights, the mobile radar was sitting in the centre of the carriageway about two-thirds of the way through the village. Defiant, it remained in situ until Clogger was within a few feet of its dazzling wild eyes, then it issued its first challenge in a test of rabbit against machine. Bouncing in and out of the penumbra the cheeky buck ran ahead of the CID car at a tantalising distance, exposing a new side to Clogger's tipsy character.

I'll get the little bastard, he slurred, pursuing his tormentor onto an unmade track at the right-hand side of the road.

From police-patrol to motor-cross, Clogger doubled-back on himself at an engine-growling speed. Had it not been for the spacious nature of Hett, his first fully airborne passage across an inconvenient clump of coarse grass ought to have aroused the neighbourhood, if not the local cemetery. Unobserved, he continued to rally the works-Mini through a series of suspension-creaking, S-shaped manoeuvres that any greyhound would have been proud of. The first part of the exercise confirmed the superior agility of local wildlife, because by the time Clogger reached the beginning of the village, via the network of rough tracks, the rabbit was sitting content in the centre of the main carriageway, ready for a second lap. Its eyes glinting confidently in the car headlights, it leapt off again with Clogger in white-hot pursuit.

This time it stayed on the main thoroughfare, allowing the rally-driver to demonstrate his superior turn of mechanical speed on the firm straight along the side of the roadworks. At the half-way point, totally consumed by the competition, the huntsman was within a foot of the kill when the little bunny sensed danger and kinked acutely to its left. At full-stretch, it glided between two traffic cones and over a temporary kerb-stone with the ease of a three-day eventer. Expertly lured into the snare, Clogger tried to intercept but came to a sudden, bone-shaking halt on top of the granite peak. He was forced to retire from the race with serious sump trouble and a rapidly developing bump on his forehead. Fortunately, wisps of hissing engine steam obscured a final two-fingered salute, and Clogger never saw Bugs again.

Of course in all military initiatives there are inevitable excesses, evidenced at the time by reports coming out of Vietnam. Clogger can be excused for his earlier, opportunistic attacks on the church and judiciary on the grounds that both institutions are traditional police allies, but to write-off the CID car when the department was totally demoralised and leaderless was to say the least, unnecessary and monumentally careless. In a moment of drink-muddled madness, Agent Catchpole had exposed himself to a criminal charge of dangerous driving and the disciplinary offence of damaging police property, which in his colourful case would certainly lead to immediate suspension and the collapse of phase-four. Luckily the only witness to the accident was unlikely to hop forward, but Clogger still had to think on his feet and overcome the most critical problem of his subversive career.

Like a recruit tackling his first initiative test, he threw off his tunic and began a process of logical improvisation that remarkably took only thirty minutes, time he knew he could buy in an isolated County Durham village at the dead of night. Making full use of his torch, the levering properties of his truncheon and spillage from the beams of two dislocated car headlights, Clogger laboured through the course, achieving his objective with flying colours.

"Ferryhill mobile to foxtrot bravo control," he finally gasped.
"Go ahead."

"Hett Village, request attendance of the inspector."

"Not available, the sergeant is acting-up until further notice. Why?"

"I've had an accident in the CID car."

"What have you hit?"

"Oh, nothing," Clogger puffed indignantly, "a kerb-stone stepped-out in front of me."

"Bleep, bleep, bleep."

Still patrolling Bearpark in the supervision vehicle, ironically Bald Eagle was just beginning to feel comfortable in the knowledge that his peace-keeping force had restored order, when Clogger's predicament was relayed over the local radio.

I don't fucking believe it, the ginger-wig sighed, banging his head repeatedly on the car steering wheel like an estranged husband.

With the vitality of a Sunday driver, the despondent sergeant checked his thatch, then took a further thirty minutes to descend the county's back-bone on route to another of Clogger's follies. Unfortunately or fortunately, depending on your perspective, the time factor was critical and probably saved the giant from immediate demise. When Bald Eagle's headlights appeared in the little village the profusely perspiring Clydesdale had cooled-off and replaced its rug as protection against the onset of colic. Two enormous patches of white-tinged sweat around each blue-cotton armpit, and a similarly noticeable wet line up the centre of his back, had all stopped vaporising and were concealed beneath an unruffled, blue-serge tunic. One might have expected his hair to indicate indulgence in strenuous physical activity, but as a further measure against the early morning temperature, Hercules had also replaced his helmet. In retrospect that wouldn't have mattered. His uniquely styled hair was never out of place anyway.

So, when Clogger flashed his torch to mark his position in the village, the first thing Bald Eagle saw was a closed section of carriageway, a stationary, lifeless Mini saloon and the silhouette of a helmeted giant waving a lantern. Cautiously obeying the luminous keep-right arrow, the supervisor trundled into a stretch of restricted rural thoroughfare, now extended to one and a third lanes, and pulled up behind his problem-child.

"What have you done this time?" the sergeant sighed, alighting from the supervision car with his own heavy-duty torch.

"Never saw it boss...I mean sergeant!" announced Clogger, directing Bald Eagle to the oil-capped block of granite jacking-up the front of the CID car. "Kids must have done it!"

Bending down to shine his torch on the obstruction, Bald Eagle's extensively honed powers of deduction were thrown into total chaos.

"That's too heavy for children, it must weigh over a hundred-weight."

"Well it's the only one sticking out," Clogger asserted, prompting Bald Eagle back to his feet to scan the fifty-yard stretch of temporary barrier with his powerful flash-light.

Perfectly aligned and interspersed with traffic cones, Agent Catchpole was of course correct. The only granite kerbstone out of position was conveniently underneath the CID car, albeit the cordoned-off area between the centre of the road and the nearside verge, had somehow been reduced by a full three feet.

"Contractors must have left it like that," suggested Clogger, delicately introducing the notion of mechanical assistance into the debate.

"Mmm, unlikely!" Bald Eagle retorted, scratching his chin. There's something fishy going on here! He's definitely capable, the ginger-wig concluded, scrutinising Clogger's bulk, but why would he want to move just one stone?

The conundrum remained at the forefront of Bald Eagle's mind through three more torch-lit examinations of the scene before he finally made the fatal transmission in language intended for inclusion in the official incident-log.

"Supervision to foxtrot bravo control."

"Go ahead," the local radio crackled.

"CID vehicle damaged in non-culpable circumstances, accident report to follow. Call out Ansa Motors."

"Received."

Bleep, bleep, bleep.

Although relieved by his achievement, Clogger knew that until the incident-log was factored by Wupert and the nine o'clock- brigade, Bald Eagle was in a position to change his mind, so he cleverly denied his supervisor the opportunity for further interrogation or the chance to smell his breath.

"No, I must finish what I came to do," Goliath announced chivalrously, when he was invited to join the sergeant in the warmth of the supervision car.

Not surprisingly given the lay-out of the place, the residents of Hett slept through most of the police activity. While they waited for Sid and Dick, Clogger circumnavigated the settlement on foot shining his torch into every nook and cranny, and Bald Eagle pondered the pen-picture section of an accident report under the glow of an interior map-reading light. Having decided not to further investigate the accident on the grounds that it would serve no useful purpose, the confused supervisor was marshalling an appropriate form of words when he was disturbed by a spooky, squawking sound that catapulted Clogger back onto his mental landscape.

"What the fuck is that?" Bald Eagle called, launching himself from the driver's door in the certain knowledge that, this time, Clogger really was engaged in fowl-play.

"Nothing to do with me, boss...I mean, sergeant," answered Tarzan's flickering silhouette from across the village green.

The two men were randomly penetrating the night-sky like goons in a prisoner-of-war camp, trying to identify the progressively intensifying Alfred Hitchcock sound-track, when a scouting sea gull flapped into the picture followed by a highly-reflective low-loader and a cloud of flying-squad. By the time the Ansa Motors' carnival float pulled-up behind the convoy, bedroom lights were beginning to flash and Bald Eagle's sensitive eyes had started to water in response to the acidic smell from a miserable, gunge-filled 4.2 litre jam-sandwich.

Heavily mufflered, Dick Turpin's oily cloth-cap leaned from the cab of a medium-sized recovery vehicle. "Only manage a front-end lift," he muttered apologetically, "Nevilles Cross depot threatened a walk-out when we took it there. We've had to cart it around all night!"

Maintaining a sensible distance from the stage, Bald Eagle and Clogger took their place in the stalls while the rest of the curious, night-gowned village appeared at curtained-boxes to watch Sid and Dick perform their two-man winching show. Apart from discouraging any meaningful conversation, the pungency of rotting fish guts and the aggression of swooping sea gulls continued to divert supervisory attention away from Clogger's breath, but the giant knew that at some point he would be forced to share the same oxygen supply as his supervisor in the confines of an upholstered roller skate.

"Do you mind if I smoke, sarge?" he asked, delving deep into his clothing to produce two Monte-cristos and a box of matches.

"I suppose, in the circumstances," replied Bald Eagle, secretly grateful for the sea gull-repellent smoke-pole.

Ends chewed-off, the duo were fully fired-up when the growling winch took the last of the strain and the front-end of the CID car swung free of its granite under-carriage. In the intense glow of two roof-mounted spot-lights, Dick hastily clambered back to join Sid under cover of the cab.

"Where are you taking them?" Bald Eagle called to a sky-borne accompaniment.

"Langley Moor compound," answered Dick, a split-second before the passenger-side door of the recovery truck slammed shut. "It's isolated and we get a lot of vandalism."

While Bald Eagle puffed on the crime preventative properties of rancid fish waste, Clogger watched the entourage leave the village of Hett. Captured by two industrial highwaymen, the runny jam-sandwich disappeared into the darkness towing a sad-faced CID Mini under the scavenging eyes of one hundred night-duty sea birds. Time for Agent Catchpole to play another master-stroke.

"Give me a hand sarge, I can't budge it," he declared, bending down to push the offending kerbstone back into its apparently proper position. "Don't want it to happen to anybody else!"

On cue Bald Eagle put his Montecristo firmly between his lips, bent down, propped himself against the other end of the boulder and joined Clogger in the scrummage.

"That's it," he announced, standing up with his toupee over his eyes. "Let's get back to the nick, I've got some writing-up to do."

It was close to the end of the shift when tranquillity was finally restored to the tiny settlement. Bringing up the rear, Bald Eagle chauffeured Clogger back to the Great North Road in the supervision car, then took the first opportunity to overtake the whirlwind of low-flyers on the northbound carriageway of Farewell Bank. Upwind of what had become an offensive taste rather than a smell, the sergeant flashed an acknowledgement to Sid, wound down his door window slightly and drew hard on the rest of his Cuban delight.

"Where did you get these from?" he inquired, rolling the little log between his thumb and fingers.

"Back of a lorry," quipped Clogger, prompting a suspicious chuckle.

What's he laughing at?

Both men were enjoying a feeling of well-being in the smoke-filled tin-can when Bald Eagle turned down South Road on his final approach into the city. Alone on the suburban thoroughfare, the supervision vehicle passed between the university complexes of Van Mildert, Collingwood, Grey, Trevelyan and St. Mary's, while the first signs of day-break fractured the night-sky. At the New Inn crossroads in the silent hours, Bald Eagle might have been tempted to ignore the red traffic light and sneak across Stockton Road into Church Street Head, but he was distracted by a solitary, meandering pair of headlights approaching from the opposite direction.

"He's all over the road," the supervisor observed, hesitating at the end of his cigar.

"Mmm," responded Agent Catchpole, exhaling against the windscreen as the open-topped, low-sided, ex-American Army Jeep came to a clumsy halt face to face across the junction.

Six long-haired young people of indiscernible gender were partying in the stencil-marked collector's item with the college-scarfed driver permanently engaged in an impression of one of those weighted toys usually found in the bottom of budgerigar cages.

"Students!" Bald Eagle advised, abandoning a generous, glowing stump through the partially open driver's window. "Let's get over there, before they kill themselves," he continued, accelerating across the deserted junction to block the bow of the adolescent land forces.

With well-rehearsed precision Bald Eagle ran to the front passenger-side of the restored relic. Clogger belatedly flicked away his Montecristo and anteloped to the other side just in time to push the rigid torso of the driver back over the fulcrum into an upright position. In strict order of priority the giant then turned off the engine and snatched the keys from the ignition.

"Do you mind constable, my father is a peer of the realm," protested the spoilt rich-kid, hanging-on to his vowels to the best of his intoxicated ability.

Clogger searched his breast pocket for a laminated aide-memoire. "Oh, you live at the coast then!"

"Take no notice officer," interrupted a well-spoken female from a cramped position next to the inboard jerry-can. "He's always like this when he's been drinking!"

Realising he was about to administer his first ever road-side breath test under badly formulated new legislation, Clogger glimpsed at the card, looked across at Bald Eagle's tufty wig, then walked back to the supervision car to collect his helmet and a green-plastic container similar in size to his cigar box.

Full uniform he reminded himself, pushing his helmet into place to re-engage the enemy.

"You are not obliged to say anything unless you wish to do so, but whatever you do say will be taken down in writing and may be given in evidence. I suspect you of driving a motor vehicle on a road with blood alcohol above the prescribed limit, and I require you to provide me with a specimen of breath. At what time did you take your last drink?"

"I haven't been....," the history student nearly insisted, before experiencing more problems with his centre of gravity.

Impressed with Clogger's apparent confidence in what was predicted to become a legislative minefield, Bald Eagle stood at the other side of the Jeep with the uneasy feeling he was experiencing another bout of false security. He watched Clogger force open the brand-new Breathalyser box with his fingernails and place both hinged halves carefully on the bonnet of the ex-military vehicle, ready for the operation. Like a surgeon, the giant removed a durable, transparent plastic bag from the lid part, then unclipped a sterile mouthpiece and an ampoule of clear crystals from the body of the container. The bag connected to the mouthpiece by means of the glass tube, Clogger confronted his suspect again.

"Blow into this for no less than twenty seconds," he instructed, handing over the assembled kit amid cheers from a fascinated audience.

"Go for it," the unisex front seat passenger called as the driver's cheeks bulged to exploding point.

His face deep blue, after a full minute of concerted effort the little bag failed to inflate, indeed it didn't even flicker, and the suspect was left gasping for breath.

He's taking the piss Clogger concluded, glancing at the refusal procedure on his aide-memoire.

It was Bald Eagle's grasp of the subjective legal concept of reasonable conduct that first threw doubt on the construction of the unfamiliar equipment.

"Have you removed the cellophane from the mouthpiece?" he queried from his secondary position.

"Yes, boss," answered Clogger, noticing for the first time that there was a slot in the side of the Breathalyser box which housed a tiny, metallic saw.

When it dawned on the giant that he had asked the driver to inflate the bag through a sealed ampoule, Clogger consulted his crib-card again. After a moment of legal deliberation he quite properly pointed out that a specimen of breath had not been provided, but the circumstances did not constitute a refusal and he intended to repeat the procedure. So far so good, but as every experienced police officer knows the notion of reasonable behaviour must never be over-played.

Clogger assembled a second Breathalyser kit, only this time he carefully sawed-off both ends of the sealed glass tube. Instead of passing it directly to the drunken driver and getting on with the job, he went on to dismantle the first piece of kit, broke-off the ends of the ampoule and put the demonstrator back together again.

200

"On this occasion," Agent Catchpole advised, "I want you to inflate the bag like so."

Twenty seconds later the previously useless piece of equipment was bursting at the seams and Clogger was beaming.

"It's not difficult," he suggested, pushing the contaminated balloon in the direction of the drunken driver. "If the crystals turn green beyond this line then the test is positive. Now you try with this one!"

"But ossifer, the crystals are already green!"

Things turned a bit unseemly after that. Faced with a highly embarrassing double-whammy, a three-striped madman scrambled around the bonnet of the Jeep with his arms outstretched, clearly intending to manipulate Clogger's throat. In his frenzy he disturbed the Breathalyser box and it tumbled to the ground. Even with his superior combat skills Agent Catchpole felt strategic retreat was his best option. Not bothering to recover the equipment, he turned heal and galloped down Church Street towards the sanctuary of the police station, leaving the young nobleman to seize the moment. Propelled by a rush of blood in his alcohol stream, and a certain amount of encouragement from the rest of the hairy-brigade, scarf flowing, Zorro leapt over the low-sided driver's door and comprehensively crushed Barbara Castle's brainchild in a bid to find refuge at a nearby campus.

"Supervision to foxtrot bravo control," Bald Eagle wept, sitting head-bowed with his toupee in his hand on the wall of the New Inn car park,

"Go ahead, sergeant."

"Send the inspector."

"But you are the inspector."

Out of courtesy to Bald Eagle's surviving family, it's not appropriate to document the rest of the distressing conversation here, suffice to say it constituted the only official radio retirement in the history of the British Police Force.

10   MECHANICAL LABOUR

The sad departure of the only operational toupee in Durham Police marked the end of phase-three, but it didn't signal the start of the final phase. The secret weapon called the longest cease-fire of the Three-Week-War to plan VD-Day (Victory in Durham). It spanned the last four tours of his night-shift week, spent cramped in a special bunker. The most untidy and disordered place in the police station, the teleprinter room was really a large, insulated booth. Annexed to the communications-room, it was just big enough to seat one person and house the steam-driven free-standing typewriter that accessed the national network. Dexian shelves, stuffed to capacity with uneven lengths of flimsy, coiling copy paper, lined the walls from floor to ceiling. They added to the soundproofing, but had long since lost any semblance of order. How Clogger secured dedicated use of the facility, only visited periodically by the second radio operator, is yet another matter of conjecture but it must have involved conspiracy.

Two promising constables from other reliefs were chosen at short notice to cover for Bald Eagle on consecutive days. The capacity of Acting Sergeant was an unexpected opportunity to prove themselves in the white-hot promotion stakes, but Clogger's reputation had reached tidal-wave proportions and they mysteriously decided to bury the competitive hatchet in the interests of career preservation. To suggest they acted consistently of their own volition is perhaps too simplistic in light of Wupert's full-time commitment to the Clogger papers. It's more realistic to assume a highly placed third man was involved on the inside, but he has never been identified. Whatever, in a cloud of cigar smoke, Agent Catchpole shut himself in the cupboard for four full shifts, and in an environment of toilet paper, pork pies and beetroot sandwiches, decided on a bugger's muddle for the final attack. A negative military concept, used positively it was an exceptional piece of planning, and the new filing system wasn't too bad either. A little nicotine tainted, it survived more or less intact until the advent of the Police National Computer when a printer was installed that didn't shake the entire building.

Phase-four began at eight-thirty on the morning of Wednesday 23rd April, 1969. Like a boxer preparing for a world title fight, Clogger spent Monday of that week sleeping-off his last night-shift and most of Tuesday in light upper-body exercise in the Colpits Arms. Sustained by his landlady's cooking, he had just wandered back from the evening session when he received a late telephone call.

"Turn out for nine in the morning, not two. Report to me, you're on an over-time detail. Mass meeting!" a sergeant from another relief instructed, with a terseness that indicated his domestic arrangements had been interfered with.

"Okay, boss...I mean, sarge." I'd better have an early night!

Retiring to his landlady's spare room a little worse for wear, Clogger set the alarm-clock, pushed his feet and lower legs out of the bottom of the standard-sized single bed, then dozed-off content that victory was achievable in a single day.

VD-Day started with a sentimental, but nevertheless calculated decision on Clogger's part. He wanted to protect his treasured Royal Enfield from the worst of the conflict. Having served him well throughout the campaign, he left the leaky-steed in the cobbled lane behind his lodgings and walked to work. In hindsight the move was a clear indication of his intention, but it went unnoticed in the heat of a hastily arranged and potentially troublesome gathering of the under-ground cavalry.

Fully uniformed, bearing his sandwich-box but minus a pocket-set, Clogger pounded down Hawthorn Terrace towards Alexander Crescent intending to cross the ring-road and take the most direct route to the police station, via Crossgate. It was the tailback of traffic to his left that made him hesitate. Even in rush hour gridlock was uncommon, usually the consequence of a road accident or some electronic problem in the control box. So, true to form, Clogger decided to make a slight detour and investigate. Weaving his way purposefully through a snake of frustrated commuters, he didn't get a handle on the cause until he'd cleared the bend in the road. The giant could see people knotted around stationary cars in the centre of North Road, immediately below the majestic viaduct that accommodates the Great North Eastern Railway.

Someone has been knocked down on the junction, Clogger guessed, breaking into a jog.

Barging his way to the epicentre, Lurch realised that the platoon of standard rubber-necks were all staring skyward and not at the ground as he expected.

"What's going on here?" he queried sharply, scanning the busy cloud-base for the registration number of the offending space ship.

"Yon is a pitman!" replied a British Rail boiler suit, gesturing towards the arched Victorian splendour above. "Says he's come looking for work, but can't find any. Wants to end it all."

"How did he get up there?"

"Must have walked along line and come o'er top."

"I'm ganna jump," the pale, unshaven high-wire artist shouted when he saw the ring-master one-hundred-and-fifty feet beneath him. "Divant try and stop us!"

"Stay where you are, sir," Clogger responded loudly, pushing his bait-box firmly underneath his left arm to take regimental control. "You."

"Me?"

"Yes, you. Go to the bus station and call the police."

"But you are the police."

"I'm off-duty, dick-head, do it."

Sending one rubber-neck scurrying into action, Clogger cleverly turned his attention on the apparent expertise of the blue overall. "Railway station, warn the signal box. You, help me clear the area of vehicles. Tell the drivers you're acting on my instructions. The rest, move back onto the pavement."

Suspecting they were making way for the fire brigade with some extendable rescue equipment, the operation to clear the landing area went remarkably smoothly. Indeed the regular Framwelgate foot-patrol was still hurrying to the scene from the direction of the Market Place, when Clogger took centre stage to start the delicate life-saving negotiations.

"Sir, can you still hear me?" he shouted.

"Yeah," called the distressed Geordie, "but I'm ganna de it, divant stop us."

"Okay, sir, we're ready for you now," Clogger boomed, prompting widespread gasps of astonishment. "Try to stay on the carriageway!"

With all the railway signals on red, the audience witnessed an aerial retreat reminiscent of the silent movie era. When the suicidal arse rapidly jerked back over the precipice, Clogger finalised his depression-lifting therapy. "Newcastle is to the right, sir"

Another notch on his belt, Clogger was engaged in a series of unconventional single-handed traffic signals designed to get things moving again, when the out-of-breath Framwelgate man reached him.

"Where is he?" the officer rattled, his neck arched to breaking point.

"Down," snapped the sergeant major. "Well up, to be exact. Come on sir, nothing to see now."

"Down, up, that was quick! How did you manage it?"

"Oh, just a little compassion!" Clogger glowed, patting his colleague's shoulder. "I'll have to leave you to it, I'm on the miners' detail at nine."

Marching across Framwelgate Bridge and up the winding cobbles of Silver Street, it was the first time in over a week that Clogger had seen the Market Place in the cold light of day. Typically vibrant, an unfamiliar uniformed constable was in the traffic control box and a handful of ruddy faces were gathering by the weather-eroded base of the market cross. Dating back to 1356, the Town Hall and Guildhall were resplendent behind them, but it wasn't the stained-glass windows or heraldic symbols that first caught Clogger's eye. It was the battalion of strongly coloured Tulips parading proudly in a series of carved window boxes along the entire frontage.

Nice touch! Clogger thought, passing the annual display on the other side of the road.

Agent Catchpole reached the police station yard via the grounds of St. Cuthbert's church, shortly before nine o'clock. Nearly fifteen minutes late by police standards, an operative from the communications-room had taken the trouble to inform the supervising sergeant of Clogger's whereabouts.

"No need to explain," the anxious disciplinarian snapped. "Join group two."

On a cool, dismal April morning two equidistant twelve-man squads of men, drawn from all over the division were standing at-ease facing three unfamiliar stripes and a bulging clip-board. Sandwich-box still under his arm, Clogger hurried to the only available slot in the group-two formation and stamped into position in the centre of the back row. Feet apart, hands clenched behind his back, he was helmet and shoulders above his colleagues with an arm-lock on four pork pies, when the sergeant glanced at his wrist-watch and began the special briefing.

"Group one, traffic, two, public order," he barked in typically clipped tones.

Without looking up from his operation plan, a monotonous list of police service numbers followed, coupled to road junctions on the periphery of the city-centre.

"Nothing except access and emergencies after ten-hundred-hours. Mr Gormley is due to speak at mid-day. Any questions anyone? Draw radios from the communications-room."

Noisily breaking formation, the first dozen soldiers shuffled through the back door of the main building, signed for pocket-sets then dispersed by the front door to walk to their respective traffic points.

"Group two, crowd control in the Market Place, together with the mounted branch," bawled the sergeant. "The operation will be co-ordinated by me from the communications-room. There's already a police presence in the control box. After ten the officer will switch to automatic and use the CCTV system to monitor activity and feed through intelligence. Pay special attention to the Market Tavern, it will open as usual between eleven and three and is bound to be a focal point. The meat-wagon is on permanent stand-by. Nobody to leave their post without my permission."

Not that it mattered, but the usual invitation for questions was interrupted by the arrival of a cumbersome horsebox from the Durham Police Equestrian Centre at Harperley Hall. Very expensive and about the size of a single-decker bus, the blue logoed vehicle squeezed through the ungated entrance to dominate the centre of the police yard.

"Anywhere," the sergeant shouted to the policewoman driver, "but don't obstruct the fuel pump or the meat-wagon bay."

Feeling uncomfortable in the vicinity of the tightly manoeuvring self-contained stable, Clogger and rest of group-two broke ranks without waiting for the order, converging on the communications-room hatch to exhaust the sub-divisional pocket-radio supply. As they filed from the front door of the police station, Agent Catchpole slipped unnoticed into the canteen to deposit his sandwich-box, then brought up the rear in Court Lane. He passed the vehicular entrance to the police yard just in time to see the force's only mounted policewoman coaxing two magnificent chestnuts down a straw-strewn wooden ramp, onto the oily Tarmac.

"Which one's the mare?" he called, provoking a black-gloved Churchillian signal that probably had nothing to do with VD-Day.

Striding down New Elvet, by the time the crowd control team reached Elvet Bridge it had lost any semblance of formation, sucked unevenly into a steady stream of short-back-and-sides, making their way to the Market Place. When the police contingent spilled into the main arena about nine-forty that morning, traffic was still operating normally but a crowd of about five hundred had already gathered in anticipation of their union's planned resistance to the demise of the Durham Coalfield.

"You must be Clogger!" the very alert traffic box constable shouted when the giant crossed the carriageway and passed behind the partially open stable door. "Do me a favour and check-out those two vehicles," he continued, spinning efficiently through three-hundred-and-sixty degrees to point out his problem. "They've been there ever since I took over."

The capsule commander for the day, specially selected for his manual and electronic dexterity, had not only kept the traffic flowing normally but had also managed to discourage parking on the cobbles behind him, all at the same time. So impressed with his super-efficiency, in readiness for the ten o'clock deadline, the giant enthusiastically agreed to conduct further enquiries.

"Leave it to me, boss!"

The first vehicle he tackled was an oldish Ford Zephyr with long chrome lines, a green livery and a back seat full of books. It was properly parked, but in danger of being swamped by the growing number of motley participants.

"Any idea who this belongs to?" Clogger shouted to an elderly janitor keeping a watching-brief from the Town Hall entrance.

"Woman from the second-hand book stall in the indoor market."

Five minutes later, assailed by the smell of fresh victuals, Clogger was under glass peering over a mountain of grubby paperbacks at a pink-smocked, thirty-something-year-old, sitting on a little stool with her petite hands resting gently on top of a bump, about the size of a rugby ball.

"Is that your green Zephyr in the Market Place, darling?"

"Yes, officer."

"I'm afraid you'll have to move it, there's a miners' meeting outside today."

"I know," the imminent mother-to-be replied, her sensitive eyes filling with tears. "I really shouldn't be here. I'm waiting for my assistant, she's late!"

"Put it on Doggart's car park, it should be safe there."

"But I can't walk that far," she sobbed, "and I don't want it damaged."

"Now don't get your knickers in a twist, sweet-heart," Clogger asserted, pre-empting an outburst pre-natal emotion. "I'll keep an eye on it, and if your assistant doesn't arrive soon, I'll move it for you."

"Oh, will you officer? Thank you so much, you're very kind."

Back in the cobbled stadium the public relations consultant flashed a thumb and ten fingers at the space-shuttle commander, indicating he had successfully negotiated one removal, then he threaded his way through the crowd to the second potential obstruction. Unattended, close to the Church of St. Nicholas, a battered Austin A35 was parked in an acoustically optimal position with a heavy-duty loudspeaker strapped to its patchy grey roof. Initially Agent Catchpole assumed the sound equipment had some official function, but on his approach he noticed a more centrally located temporary rostrum. Made from scaffolding poles, the structure had a thick black cable running to it and an independent microphone and speaker system.

"Does that belong to you?" Clogger called to a group of rotund, Sunday-suited men hanging around the stage like officials at a boxing match.

"Does what belong to us?"

"That, shit-face," Clogger expanded, pointing to the Austin A35 parked behind the badge-carrying delegation from the Durham Branch of the National Union of Mineworkers.

When Clogger heard a sheepish, anonymous reply, "Nothing to de with us," he knew he was onto something juicy.

"Let me put it another way," he continued, swerving off course to confront the officials chest to head. "When did you develop your taste for prison cuisine?"

A split-second before he was picked-up by the lapels in full view of a rapidly growing audience, a leather-faced man of medium height decided to elaborate.

"Its got nothing to de with the union," he blustered, "it belongs to Loco-Len. Everything we are doing here has been approved by the superintendent."

"PC Catchpole to foxtrot bravo control."

"Go ahead"

"Request a front-end lift in the Market Place."

Bleep, bleep, bleep.

"Co-ordinator wants to know the reason, PC Catchpole."

"Unattended vehicle fitted with an unauthorised public address system. Enquiries reveal it belongs to an activist."

Clogger's update brought the supervising sergeant urgently onto the network from his auxiliary console in the communications-room.

"Agreed PC Catchpole, that's all we need...well done!"

Purely as an aside at this late stage in the affair, Clogger had begun the instinctive process of luring another sergeant into a false sense of security, but much more pertinent was the question of Loco-Len's real identity. Some analysts argue that Clogger himself should have done more at the enquiry stage, but the downside of that perspective has mind-boggling implications. In the best possible scenario the giant would probably have shook the living daylights out of the union official in front of a thousand-strong congregation, counter-productive by any stretch of the imagination. On the other end of the radio, had he been armed with the well-known alias, the co-ordinating sergeant could have instigated behind-the-scenes intelligence checks to establish that Loco-Len wasn't really a miner, but a university drop-out who toured the north-east lecturing in havoc.

Widely believed to be the inspiration behind the television series Citizen Smith, he was in the habit of attaching himself to any lost cause, and in the process had become an authority on the Judge's Rules, the legal label for the police arrest procedure. From his nearby mufflered position within a huddle of rented support, Loco-Len's finely honed sixth sense locked onto Clogger's lumbering body language and recognised interest in his shabby little motor car. In terms of impact it was not an ideal time for his carefully planned sound-bite, but the professional agitator nevertheless decided that a premature contribution was better than none at all. A couple of minutes later, when two big chestnuts made their grand, clopping entrance onto the Market Place stage, Loco-Len broke cover and seized his opportunity.

"What's he called?" asked Clogger, as the black-jompered jockey approached him to take her allotted position at the north-end of the arena.

"Viceroy," she replied, her knee-length, black-leather riding boots splayed seductively at Clogger's shoulder.

"Hello, boy."

The public order expert was nose to nose with his new sixteen-hand friend, patting the side of its head, when the mood of the crowd changed.

"Brothers, brothers, brothers," a loudspeaker boomed, snapping everyone's attention away from the towering Mounties. "This government will sell you down the river if you don't take action now."

"What the fuck!" blurted Clogger, cutting his exclamation short in view of Viceroy's limited vocabulary. "Its coming from that A35."

A final rap across the horse's chops and Clogger was cutting his way towards the two-door problem, arriving at the driver-side marginally before two of his crowd-control colleagues. The potential for serious trouble was so great Agent Catchpole didn't even attempt to converse, he just grabbed the door handle intending to engage the rogue agitator in his favourite ear-lock and screw, but it was locked and so was the passenger-side.

"Bastard!" Clogger mouthed, when Loco-Len resumed his broadcast with a smug smile.

"Brothers, you must fight now, today, or you won't have an industry in ten years time," he continued across the rooftops.

The Market Place took on the acoustics of a swimming pool as the baying mob began to clench their fists and echo the fighting talk. In the heat of the moment one of the police contingent produced a truncheon to smash the windscreen and put a stop to the provocative transmissions.

"No, no, go to the indoor market and get me a potato sack," Clogger screamed, recognising the catalytic effect of such action.

"Gormley's just a puppet," boomed Loco-Len, "it's up to you to fight for your jobs, together we can bring this country to a standstill."

Well in excess of a thousand brick-shit-houses were roaring in agreement when Clogger's counterpart reappeared with the equipment he'd asked for. Snatching it towards the roof of the little saloon, Loco-Len's final thoughts on the future of the mining industry became progressively less discernible as Clogger screwed the coarse hessian sack deep into the activist's trumpet. Then, just as the traffic flow was beginning to peter out, the giant pushed his huge face against the driver-side window and issued a broad reciprocal smile.

"That's cooked your goose," he mouthed, rubbing his hands together in satisfaction.

Having effectively gagged Loco-Len without the provocative sound of breaking glass, tension in the assembly dissipated and preparations began in earnest for a series of official union speeches, culminating in the attendance of the national president. Clogger and one of his colleagues remained by the sides of the A35 as a precautionary measure, anticipating that Loco-Len would quickly recognise the futility of his predicament. Had he done so, and unlocked the car doors, he would certainly have escaped with a verbal warning. Indeed, even if he'd started the thing up and driven off, Clogger would probably have turned a blind eye, but the freedom fighter was bent on a second round. He decided to stay put and engage Agent Catchpole in a battle of legal wits the giant didn't readily identify.

"Here's Ansa," Clogger's semi clued-up colleague remarked when Sid and Dick edged their patriotic-coloured long-wheel-base Land Rover through the variously-dressed audience. "What are we going to do with him?"

"Let them tow him away in the car, it belongs to him," the giant proposed, as the mobile jib crept into position at the front of the baby Austin. "Mind your backs everyone!"

Hooked firmly by the axle, the front-end of the offending vehicle was off the ground when Clogger's legal advisor finally got to grips with Loco-Len's ploy. "If he's taken away like this, at our request, it's a technical arrest," he proffered.

"So what!"

"Well, he hasn't been told why he's been arrested."

"I'll tell him now."

"He's locked in the car, he'll deny he heard you."

Clogger's penny dropped. "Cunning little bastard," he announced, eyeing the super-smug expression on Loco-Len's face. "If the arrest is unlawful, his ride on the truck will be false imprisonment. He'll have a case for compensation!"

"Got it in one."

"Not yet," called Clogger, as Sid and Dick made their way back to the Land Rover cab. "Give me a couple of minutes."

Agent Catchpole pushed his way back through the heavily-muscled crowd and disappeared into the indoor market. When he returned five minutes later with a large piece of cardboard, a ball of coarse string and a broad felt-tipped pen, his climb onto the back of the Land Rover generated some interest. It was nothing however to the roars of laughter Sid and Dick received when they squeezed the recovery vehicle down Saddler Street against the oncoming flow of burly miners. Swinging from the crane jib, in constant view of Loco-Len, a boldly scrawled cardboard notice read; You have been arrested for inciting a breach of the peace. Inspired, Clogger had acted within the spirit of the Judge's Rules, but as we all know his propensity for falling short was an equal and opposite force. Ingeniously validating a difficult arrest, the super-star unfortunately failed to recognise that Sid and Dick were creatures of habit and needed certain specific instructions in these most unusual of circumstances.

"PC Catchpole to foxtrot bravo control"

"Go ahead."

"One prisoner, ETA fiver minutes, warn the custody suite."

"Do you want the meat-wagon?"

"No, he's already under escort."

"Who's escorting him?"

"Ansa Motors."

"Ansa Motors!"

"Yes, Ansa Motors."

"Err...err...what should I tell the suite he's been arrested for?"

"Don't worry about that, I've given him a note," Clogger concluded. "Just let me know when I have permission to return to the station to process him."

Blue touch-paper removed, the powder-keg filled with relative safety. By ten-twenty it was awash to standing capacity and the single-carriageway in-let valves were down to a trickle. Disgruntled and in no mood for pleasantries, the two-thousand-strong mass-meeting still had disorder potential, but in the absence of Loco-Len a sense of discipline prevailed. Not as packed as the Leazes End of St. James' Park on Saturday afternoon, the Market Place nevertheless resembled the platform of Waterloo Station during rush-hour. Dome-headed porters were mixing freely with closely-shorn colliery groups under the watchful eye of two sentries mounted fore and aft. Dressed in various forms of out-door clothing, the hard-working audience were gazing at the make-shift stage with a curiously infectious deportment. Collars turned up, hands deep in their pockets, all were exposing their broad, slightly rounded shoulders waiting for the first white-starched shirt to make an appearance.

Hovering close to the Church of St. Nicholas, Clogger was surveying his bustling surroundings with a sense of satisfaction when the top-half of the traffic-box door swung wide-open and the revolving intelligence gatherer gestured like the main character in a Punch and Judy show.

"What?" the giant called. "I can't hear you!"

"Green Zephyr," Clogger's colleague shouted, stabbing his finger violently in the direction of the covered market.

In the heat of his dealings with Loco-Len, Clogger had forgotten about the lady from the second-hand bookstall and thought he was simply being reminded of the continuing presence of her motor car. So when he hacked his way back to the obstruction he was surprised to find the owner supporting herself against the driver's door under the concerned gaze of half-a-dozen muscle-bound rough-necks.

"Has she arrived?" Clogger queried.

"No, but I think she's coming," replied the lady with one hand on her bulging stomach. "How do you know it's a she?"

"You told me earlier," Clogger insisted. "Do you still want me to move your car?"

"No, I think I'm in labour, officer...ouch."

"Oh, you're in good company today," Clogger quipped, putting his five-fingered shovel on the shoulder of an equally huge donkey-jacket.

When the woman answered with a horrifying groan, then doubled-up over the bonnet and pissed herself, it was Viceroy who first suspected she wasn't really interested in politics. Big, brown ears twitching in all directions, the horse side-stepped into the situation, gently nudging Clogger and the spectators to one side. With the precision of a surgeon the animal cleared just enough space for his mistress to slip neatly from the saddle and loosen her intimidating headgear, then he snorted a general warning to anyone wishing to encroach.

"Get her into the car," the policewoman instructed, her chrome spurs clanking on the cobbles. "Her waters have broken, she's giving birth."

"What!" Clogger declared. "She can't do that sort of thing here, not today."

Second fiddle wasn't Clogger's natural place in the pecking order, but on this occasion he was happy to let his female colleague take command. She cradled the reeling pink-barrel with one arm and used the other to release a key ring from a sweaty, pain-locked grip.

"Here, clear those books to one side," ordered the jockey, passing Clogger the car keys. "I'm Pam, what's your name?"

"Mar...gar...owch," sobbed the patient.

"Don't worry Margaret, everything is going to be fine. Get into the back of the car."

Having wound down the driver-side window and launched his helmet onto the passenger-side of the bench-seat, Clogger unlocked the rear door from the inside. He was still leaning over, shovelling paperbacks to one side, when the temporary midwife fired her riding-hat past him, cajoling the mother-to-be into a semi-prostrate position. With beads of perspiration on her brow, the emergency wriggled and groaned then flopped her head and shoulders back onto policewoman's lap like an exhausted limbo dancer, sighing with temporary relief.

"That's right, try to relax," advised the stand-in nurse, adjusting herself slightly to take her charge by the hand. "Get on the radio and call an ambulance."

"Arr..arr...arr," Margaret grimaced while Clogger frantically searched his trouser-pocket.

"PC Catchpole to foxtrot bravo control, priority."

"Go ahead, Catchpole."

"Request an ambulance in the Market Place, childbirth."

"Stand-by."

"Bleep, bleep, bleep."

Of course it had occurred to the police maternity team that the emergency service vehicle would be unavoidably delayed by the congestion, but it wasn't until Margaret experienced a wholesome contraction with a particularly penetrating after-whelp that the other, quicker option was considered.

"Ask them for an ETA," the Mountie ordered. "No, tell them to cancel, we'll take her ourselves."

"PC Catchpole to foxtrot bravo control."

"Go ahead."

"Advise the co-ordinator that myself and one member of the mounted section are leaving the Market Place to convey a pregnant woman to hospital by private car."

"Overheard and understood," interjected the supervising sergeant. "Keep me updated."

"Bleep, bleep, bleep."

So far so good. After Clogger started the bigish saloon and found bottom gear on the unfamiliar column-change, he was joined by the other horseman who clopped across the cobbles to the open driver's window in response to a dismounted colleague. In normal circumstances the priority is for the second rider to secure the loose animal, but like all police horses Viceroy had been specially selected for his sound, reliable nature and trained not to wander; well not too far anyway.

"Clear the way first, Burt," the policewoman called to a stirruped leather boot. "Don't worry Margaret, we're going to take you straight to Dryburn, try and relax!"

The entourage got under way just in time to up-stage the first union man. He was on the rostrum beginning his rebel-rousing opening address with a raised forearm and clenched fist.

"Comrades, comrades," he shouted as Viceroy's counterpart snow-ploughed into the mining fraternity, cutting a path to the head of Silver Street with a morbidly rigid tail.

"Dirty bastard," the splattered crowd roared to the dismayed Sunday suit.

His second attempt to get into speech-making stride was equally fouled by an extended scream from Margaret, but it wasn't until Clogger tried to move up the three-speed gearbox that he threw down his notes in disgust. The metallic grating was audible across the entire city and even rattled the windows in the traffic control box, but Clogger persisted and by the time the Lone Ranger peeled-off he was kangarooing comfortably in second.

"Thanks, Burt!"

Twisting out of Silver Street across Framwelgate Bridge into open territory, Clogger was tempted to try for top on the North Road straight but he could see a traffic-point officer standing in the middle of the road, just before the viaduct.

"Hospital emergency," called the uniformed giant through the driver-side window.

When a firm stop signal changed to a vigorous go, Clogger was catapulted into normal traffic conditions with the gearbox growling for smaller cogs.

I'll have to change up, he grimaced.

"Arr...arr...arr," wailed Margaret.

"We'll soon be there," the lady Mountie reassured.

Coincidentally, it was immediately outside County Hospital that Clogger finally ground into top. Had he chosen to be less expedient and drive to the city's casualty department, he would certainly have known his way through the labyrinthine hospital grounds. Indeed, the same can be said about the mortuary at Dryburn Hospital further up the road, but not of the maternity unit. Dropping a cog to negotiate the big roundabout at County Hall, Clogger's confidence with column-change transmissions was growing by the second.

Piece of piss! he smiled, glancing back at his passenger as he slipped down the box again to enter the sprawling, comb-shaped medical complex.

"Oow...oow."

"Everything is going to be alright, we're here," the policewoman whispered, accidentally clicking her spurs when she squeezed the mother-to-be's hand.

The series of blue fingerposts marked; Maternity should have led Clogger to the main door of the unit, and the dropping-off point for ambulances, but as he neared his target he responded prematurely to one arguably misleading sign, and turned left into a narrow cul-de-sac between two extensively glazed wards.

"Back-up," came an anxious and rather obvious instruction from the rear seat.

On his first attempt in the new gear, Clogger was looking over his shoulder when the Zephyr lurched forward in response to the savage clutch. The sight of Margaret's freshly abandoned knickers on top of the rough pile of dog-eared paperbacks didn't help Clogger's composure, but when a second equally violent leap in the wrong direction coincided with a major contraction, a degree of panic set in.

"Reverse out, arsehole," the policewoman suggested.

"I can't find the gear," Clogger retorted, grinding into another forward gate.

With a sea of miscellaneous pale faces looking on from the surrounding windows, Clogger skilfully manipulated the clutch and brake pedals to administer a series of twelve birth-inducing therapies before the crime of ram raiding loomed. While many in the medical profession later criticised his spine-jolting technique, it did have one cost-saving advantage. By the time he was in a position to install a new entrance in the side wall of the building the baby's head was exposed eliminating the need for an epidural injection.

"Push, push," urged the policewoman, prompting her profusely sweating chauffeur to ram the awkward cuss into neutral and decamp the vehicle.

That's a good idea!

There's not an awful lot more to say. Apart from nearly scuttling an urgently approaching midwifery team with the free-wheeling green monster, and a certain amount of flood-damaged stock, mother and daughter finally entered the baby unit to a rapturous round of applause and went on to do just fine.

It was about midday when Clogger's adrenalin flow subsided. For reasons that are not too difficult to understand, he shouldered the Ford Zephyr into a staff parking bay, locked it up and gave the ignition keys to a nurse, vowing never again to pilot such a complicated piece of equipment. Need a degree to drive that!

"Call for transport," the jockey suggested, replacing her police riding hat.

"Easier to jump on a service bus," Clogger replied, fixing his own headgear into position to lead the duo down the asphalt drive to the hospital gate.

With Clogger and his dismounted colleague hanging onto the chrome boarding pole on the rear platform, the in-bound double-decker growled down North Road back into the city-centre. Granted access, it wasn't stopped at the junction with Alexander Crescent and turned into the nearby bus station at a speed that allowed the police pair to hit the carriageway running.

"PC Catchpole to foxtrot bravo control."

"Go ahead."

"Hospital detail complete. Location North Road / Neville Street. Standing-by for further instructions"

"Received, PC Catchpole."

"Bleep, bleep, bleep."

Having complied with operational protocol, Clogger and his female colleague started to walk back to the Market Place confident that she had to find her horse and he would be required to return to the police station at some point to process and charge Loco-Len.

"Everything seems orderly enough," Clogger observed as the pair cut through a crocodile of prematurely departing gorillas on Framwelgate Bridge.

"Yeah," agreed the Mountie, feeling a little conspicuous in her riding breaches.

"PC Catchpole from foxtrot," crackled Clogger's lapel.

"Go ahead."

"The meeting has just finished. The co-ordinator wants you to return to your posts until further notice."

"What about my prisoner?"

"Ah...stand-by PC Catchpole," stuttered the operator, indicating to the entire local network that a cock-up had occurred.

"Bleep, bleep, bleep."

Climbing up Silver Street into the stadium, the police couple saw Burt, apparently sitting on top of the main body of the dispersing throng. Astride his own mount, he was controlling two highly trained, side-by-side chestnuts like a circus artist. When he noticed his missing colleague approaching on foot, he shunted the enormous block of twin-hulled muscle towards her, making the necessary space.

"Thanks, sweet-face," Clogger called, administering a fiercely powerful leg-up that nearly doubled her up with Burt.

"Oh, am I glad to see you!" the regular horseman announced. "He's been playing-up."

"Not like him," answered the policewoman, high-stepping away under her own steam.

"PC Catchpole from foxtrot bravo control."

"Receiving," the giant answered making for the cover of a shop doorway with his little antenna extended.

"Charge room reception team have no record of your prisoner."

"Oh, fuck!

"Did you decide on an alternative form of disposal?" the radio operator continued, using procedural terminology.

"Negative," pondered Clogger, wincing at the disciplinary consequences of an escaped prisoner.

A few seconds of pulsating radio silence elapsed before a logical solution dawned. With depots at Nevilles Cross and Langley Moor, close to Meadowfield, Ansa Motors were near to two satellite section stations, more familiar to Sid and Dick. Not an ideal scenario, and likely to cause a great deal of internal confusion, the mistake was nevertheless reasonable in the unusual circumstances.

"PC Catchpole to foxtrot."

"Go ahead."

"Check at Meadowfield and Nevilles Cross."

"Ah...right," the operator acknowledged, reaching the same wavelength.

"Co-ordinator to PC Catchpole."

"Exact location?"

"Market Place."

"Confer with the Town Hall janitor, report of theft."

"Roger."

"Bleep, bleep, bleep."

Tasking Clogger in this way was indicative of a smooth-running crowd control operation. The co-ordinator knew from his electronic intelligence source that the out-let valves were adequately subscribed and having just re-entered the tank, Clogger represented spare capacity. Consequently, the giant anteloped towards the Town Hall to find the janitor, but in the rapidly clearing waters the nature of the crime became abundantly evident. All the tulips had gone.

220

"Hooligans!" shouted a wizened blue-collared face from the Town Hall doorway.

"Did you see who did it?" Clogger asked when the dark-suited sentry ventured from his bunker.

"No, too many people. Trimdon lot likely, ought to be shot."

Although inconvenient and very annoying, in the circumstances some interference or even damage was to be expected, but this heinous offence was as comprehensive as it was deliberate. Apparently concealed by the crowd, the thief had sheered-off every free-standing guardsman exactly at the ankles.

"Remarkable!" Clogger declared, surveying the series of well constructed and elaborately carved green nail-beds.

Coupled with the absolute precision, it was the total disappearance of radiant colour; not even a petal in sight, that led to the ace-investigator's first deduction.

Someone from the indoor market has cut them to sell...cheeky bastard! he fumed.

Being a slightly impulsive type, the potential miscarriage of justice was only thwarted by contact with the residue of a public gathering. As Clogger turned to charge into the indoor market, presumably to arrest the proprietors of every flower-stall with tulips on sale, he toed through a scattering of empty cigarette packets on the stone flags beneath the window boxes. Noticeable among the debris were a few tiny pieces of trampled stalk. When Sherlock bent over to take a closer look he realised the squashed, fibrous traces were trailing-away in the opposite direction, leading to his second equally logical but contradictory deduction.

Went down the steps!

The ancient stone staircase weaves between the Town Hall and the Church of St. Nicholas providing an albeit steep pedestrian route to Freeman Place underneath and beyond Milburngate Bridge. In those days, apart from accessing the east side of the river and the manufacturing home of the world renowned Wilton carpet, it was a suitable central pick-up point for visiting coaches, but Clogger hadn't got that far yet. He was still halfway down the bulky stonework cuddling his up-turned helmet, like a peasant looking for berries.

221

Despite continual buffeting by the departing brick-shit-house brigade, the sleuth found particles of ground-up stalk on the nose of the base step, that is before he stumbled against the side of a modern, forty-two seater single-decker tour-bus. It had a card in the windscreen; Trimdon Colliery.

"Just a minute driver," Clogger called, pre-empting the hissing closure of the hydraulic door ready for take-off. "I'm conducting an investigation!"

Under the gaze of the bus driver and cloned union representatives, sitting like gargoyles in the very front passenger seat, Clogger continued his microscopic examination. Bent double without his deerstalker hat, Sherlock scrutinised the flight of three steps leading to the driver's seat and the main aisle of the privately owned coach.

"What are you looking for?" one of the bemused union men asked, gazing down on the sniffing bloodhound.

"Transference," answered the sleuth in forensic speak.

"Transference of what?" queried the driver.

"Tulip storks."

"Tulip storks!"

"Yes, tulip storks," Clogger repeated, drawing his Swiss Army knife from his left-hand trouser-pocket. "Ah...hold this!"

Lobbing the improvised specimen container into the lap of the union official sitting in the front aisle-seat, Agent Catchpole descended on the tread of the top-step like a bird of prey. Surrounded by grime, the most incriminating piece of the wet, sticky evidence yet, was clinging to the centre of the knurled, non-slip surface. About the size of a thumbnail, Clogger was on all fours teasing the trodden foliage up from the floor, with the little blade of his all-purpose gadget, when an indirect but discernible comment was passed.

"He's gone gar gar," the temporary custodian of the forensic samples observed, looking up from traces of green mulch in the bottom of the bucket. "Driver, let's gan to the club."

"Not until I have completed my enquiries," Clogger asserted, returning to his feet between the driver and the front-seat specimen collector.

"Which of you monkeys were standing near the flowers?" Clogger boomed down the fuselage.

"What flowers?"

"The ones in the boxes."

"What fucking boxes?"

"The window-boxes."

"Can't hear you at the back. Tak us to the club, driver!"

The interrogation to this point wasn't particularly penetrating but it did indicate a worrying negative trend that prompted Clogger to take the psychological high-ground and mentally revisit the technicalities surrounding his first arrest that morning. A layman may think his logic was clouded by the earlier reference to his sanity, but that couldn't be further from the truth. Expressions of disrespect are part of a professional policeman's everyday life, dealt with efficiently and instinctively when the right opportunity presents itself. No, where Clogger went wrong was in his evaluation of the suspect-base. He knew that forty-two hard-nosed, tub-thumping miners were unlikely to woo their wives and girlfriends with seasonal flora. That was traditionally done with Brown Ale and fish and chips, but someone on the bus must have been close to the crime and seen something. Every police officer knows that in the interests of justice potential witnesses often need stimulation, sometimes quite inventive, even cunning, but perhaps not the sort typically applied to naughty juveniles on a school-outing. From another perspective abuse of power could be argued, but equally potent in those hard, militant days was mining culture. It was said the community would blindly vote a donkey into Parliament if it had the right political credentials. Coupled with the curiously appropriate treasonous crime of grassing the same donkey would also enjoy unwavering loyalty.

Bloody morons! Clogger opinionated, can't speak to them all in turn, they'll string me up. "Is there a public address system in this vehicle, driver?"

Reluctantly, with the long neutral grey face of a man conditioned to delay, the blazered-driver leaned forward in his seat and unclipped a microphone from the dashboard, using his thumb to slide the little switch into the on-position. The device was about six inches long, tubular with a wire-mesh knob on the important end. When Clogger accepted the gavel and extended the curly, black wire to its limit, he cunningly flicked the machine off again.

"Gentlemen...and miners of Trimdon," he called, "can you all hear me?"

"No," roared the crowd. "Fuck off, we're ganning to the club."

Undeterred Clogger lifted the microphone closer to his mouth, blew into it then continued with a purely experimental transmission. "Testing, testing, one, two, three."

While still experiencing technical difficulties, he secretly flicked the thing on again, hammering the hard knob three times on the front-seat passenger's head. Electronically enhanced, the noise of the little mallet top-centre on the hollow coconut, confirmed the equipment was now functioning properly.

"Ouch, ouch, ouch."

"That's better," the compere continued, leaning to prevent his helmet falling from the union man's grasp.

"Collectively, you are not obliged to say anything unless you wish to do so, but anything you do say may be taken down in writing and given in evidence. You have all been arrested on suspicion of stealing tulips from the Town Hall, sometime this morning. Do you understand?"

"Bollocks," the forty-two passengers bawled, defiantly.

"If at any time you wish to reconsider your response to my earlier questions, then feel free to do so."

"Bollocks."

"Straight to the police station, driver," Clogger ordered as he returned the microphone to its clip.

Aware of the special traffic arrangements, the pilot of the tour-coach orbited the city-centre on his way to the police station, with Clogger standing in the door-well hugging his bucket of dubious fodder. Smug in the knowledge the stand-off would eventually break, the bus was in New Elvet before the giant felt the first twinge in his buttocks.

Bastards are going through with it!

"Co-ordinator to all officers engaged on the miners' detail, repeat all officers on the miners' detail. Stand-down...and thank you gentlemen."

As soon as the open transmission ended Clogger's pocket-set receiver fired into life again. "Foxtrot bravo control to PC Catchpole."

"Go ahead."

"We still haven't located your prisoner!"

"Oh, don't worry," declared Clogger, "there's plenty more where he came from!"

11   INDECENT THING

By 1-0pm on VD-Day, Wednesday, 23rd April, 1969, most military historians consider Agent Catchpole had done enough. The bugger's muddle was sufficiently complete and ready for detonation, but typical of his professionalism and scrupulous attention to detail, on the very day that Durham Police hierarchy got their act together and networked properly for the first time in three weeks, Clogger decided to spend another hour finishing-off. With a glorious victory just around the corner, this cold, clinical approach singles him out in the world of espionage, indeed some academics believe he was more than just an infiltrator from a subversive organisation. They list him as a highly sophisticated secret weapon comparable to nuclear fission.

The communications-room skivvy was first to be alerted to the size of the bomb. He had been detailed to unlock the club stockroom and was re-entering the police station yard, via the steps that lead to the detached club-house, when he saw the forty-two seater squeezing out of Elvet Crescent across Court Lane. With a police horsebox and a Vaux Brewery vehicle already monopolising the north end of the yard, the officer felt obliged to give the driver some advice before he tackled the gateway.

"Can't bring that in here," the skivvy gestured, not immediately recognising the new conductor standing in the door well.

"Prisoners," called Clogger, poking his huge, black spiky head from the hissing fold-away door.

"What, all of them!"

"Yeah, all of them."

The young officer didn't say anything. He just gazed up at the coach windows and quizzically eyed the sea of hard angular, close-cropped faces before turning heel, back into the rear door of the main building.

Seconds later two Trilby hats bailed-out of a ground floor sash window and an unfamiliar station sergeant appeared with similar urgency in his stride.

"What's this all about?" he growled when the bus rocked and hissed to a halt beside the brewery dray.

226

"Suspicion of theft!" Clogger replied, continuing with his game of poker.

"Of what?"

"Tulips"

"Tulips?"

"Yes tulips," the arresting gorilla confirmed, stepping from the vehicle to show the sergeant the inside of his up-turned helmet.

"But they're pit yakers, they don't know what tulips are!"

"Followed the trail from the scene all the way to this bus," Clogger asserted conclusively.

The supervisor looked at the evidence, stared at the arresting giant, sighed and scratched his thinning grey hair. "You must be Catchpole."

"Yes, boss...I mean, sarge, but just call me Clogger." the celebrity replied, patting three stripes on top of the head, purely out of habit.

"Well, Clogger, what do you want me to do with this lot and more to the point, where am I going to put them?"

"It's a crime, sarge, matter for the CID," Clogger advised, in a deliberately raised voice. "Put them in the cells."

"Can't do that, we haven't got the capacity."

"Leave them on the bus to await interrogation," the sleuth went on, bluffing with a second ace. "The CID will get to the bottom of it. They have their methods."

"No, the bus needs searching," the sergeant instructed. "Take them into the club and start recording their names and addresses. I'll go and speak to the CID."

Clogger climbed back into the bus and stood at the head of the aisle between the driver and the two union men. "Right, everybody off," he bawled.

"Where we ganning?" shouted the miners.

"To the club."

"But we divint like Vaux," one of the passengers declared when he stood up in the aisle and saw the open back of the dray vehicle.

"Follow me. Not you driver!"

With grinning energy Clogger leapt back off the bus and led the party, single-file, out from between the coach and the brewery dray, down the club steps to the wide-open outer swing-doors. To allow

227

officers access to the billiard table in their refreshment period, the inner swing-doors were also kept unlocked, but between the two Clogger noticed the reinforced stockroom door propped open with an empty beer crate. That in itself wasn't suspicious in light of the brewery dray, but when he held open the inner aperture to oversee the orderly entry of the underground cavalry, he was immediately confronted by two leather-clad draymen leaving the comfortable lounge area in somewhat of a hurry. As they barged by him into the path of the advancing brick-shit-house brigade, clutching their apron pockets, Clogger's underdeveloped police instinct kicked-in.

What have they been up to, he puzzled; there's no reason for them to be in here.

Feeding the hulky paratroopers through the doors, Clogger scanned the heavily grilled drinks bar to his right. Only open between seven and ten-thirty each evening, the locks and bolts appeared secure.

Must have been skiving, Clogger mused, content nothing sinister had occurred in the Georgian refuge.

"They divint have Federation," announced a neckless monster, peering through the ironwork, "but there's some bottles of broon."

"Sit down," Clogger ordered, pushing the bull towards the rest of the suspects starting to occupy the maze of armchairs carefully arranged around drip-mat studded tables.

In an atmosphere of disinfectant and stale beer, Clogger was circulating among his captives, note-book and pen in hand, when the station sergeant entered the CID wing in the main building, and poked his head into the seriously polluted detective inspector's office. Wrestling with a pile of crime files, calendar and map of the sub-division, the distraught temporary departmental head was trying to identify the pattern to an overwhelming series of undetected money thefts.

Only pubs and clubs in the city-centre. What's the common denominator? he strained behind an overflowing ashtray and half a cup of cold coffee.

"Prisoners...suspected theft," the station sergeant ventured delicately.

"Is it much?" moaned the acting detective inspector, looking up from his deliberations with the weight of the world on his shoulders.

"Tulips." grimaced the station sergeant.

"Tulips! Can uniform not handle it?"

"There's forty-two of them!"

"What, tulips?"

"No prisoners."

"Prisoners?"

"Yes, prisoners."

"Who's the arresting officer?"

"Catchpole."

The acting detective inspector's immediate reaction was to feign illness. He put his hand on his heart and was about to complain of severe chest pain, but he didn't have the bottle.

"Clogger Catchpole?" he blurted, exploring the remote possibility of two officers with the same surname.

"Yes, Clogger Catchpole," the station sergeant confirmed. "He's got them banged-up in the club."

Exasperated, the acting detective inspector waited for the station manager to leave his office before he head-butted the pile of buff crime files on the desk in front of him. At the relatively tender age of thirty-two he hoped to prove himself in the eyes of his superiors and secure a position as heir-apparent should the suspended permanent inspector never return. The statistically damaging snowball was just manageable, but another strike from the secret weapon would surely torpedo him and the rest of the demoralised department. Unable to work out what he had done to be singled out by the Almighty, he slouched to the back of the office door, grabbed his jacket and started the slow walk from the condemned cell to the execution chamber.

When the drawn, crumpled-suit reached the social club lounge, mentally prepared for his demise, he didn't confront Clogger immediately. The noise of beer crates being manhandled in the stockroom, threatened to swamp his already frail delivery, so he back-tracked and closed the doors behind him, eliminating some of the noise.

Someone's dropped some money, the acting CID head pondered, bending to scoop-up a few ten-pence coins from the thickly-carpeted floor and pile them casually, next to the blind box on the edge of the bar counter.

"PC Catchpole I presume?"

"Yes, boss...I mean...whoever you are"

"Outline the facts please."

The instruction switched Clogger into official mode. Inhaling deeply, he expanded his chest, returned his pen and note-book to his breast pocket then marched on a peripheral lounge table, snatching his up-turned helmet to his bosom like a guardsman.

"Approximately twelve-fifteen today," the sentry properly announced, in the presence and hearing of his Philistine audience, "I was on duty in the Market Place when I was called to the Town Hall where it was apparent two-hundred giant tulips had been stolen from the window-boxes. After extensive consultations with the janitor and painstaking enquires, I.."

"What exactly is the evidence?" the temporary skipper sighed, interrupting Hamlet in full-flow.

"Fuck all!" heckled the full-house. "He's a divvy."

Not to be deterred, scene-two was equally dramatic. With a broad glow of satisfaction, he turned to face his detractors, picking the green fibrous material from his headgear with his fingers.

"Followed the trail from the scene all the way to their bus," the sleuth menacingly reasserted, sprinkling the green, soggy confetti back into its receptacle. "The thief is somewhere in this room!"

"Bollocks!"

"Mmm," muttered the acting detective inspector, scanning the tastefully panelled conical ceiling. "There's been a mass-meeting in the Market Place this morning?"

"Yeah."

"Thousands present?"

"Yeah."

"Has it occurred to you that there could be another explanation?"

"Like what?"

"Like they've trodden on the debris after the crime was committed and carried it innocently into the bus."

The proposition raised a cheer audible on the other side of the police yard, in the main station building. "He's a divvy, let us gan."

"Quiet, gentlemen, please," the detective continued, "PC Catchpole."

"Yes, boss."

"Go and search the coach thoroughly."

"But, boss."

"Try and find some complete flowers."

"But..."

"Do it."

"Dee as ya telt," the miners chanted, ridiculing the chastened schoolboy as he slouched out of the lounge doors past two sheepish draymen beavering in the bowels of the stockroom.

The outer swing-doors of the social club were still wide-open. Minus his enormous headgear Clogger lumbered through them to climb the broad steps up to the police yard. He was feeling pretty miffed about the openly indifferent reception he had just received from the so-called elite. The fight against crime was a relentless affair, akin to digging a hole in wet sand on Seaton Carew beach, and he couldn't understand why his daring initiative hadn't been supported in the traditional way.

Spineless! If he'd gone along with it one of those rocket scientists would have coughed.

Acutely aware the mining community were about to get one over on him, Clogger embarked on the most thorough single-handed search ever witnessed by an expressionless coach driver with a stand-by mentality. He was sucking on an unevenly-packed hand-rolled cigarette, with the Racing Post spread across the steering wheel, when Clogger slipped past the open passenger door on all-fours. The sight of the blue-serge bloodhound checking underneath the vehicle, particularly behind the big wheels, was just enough to distract the pilot from his turf-based deliberations.

"What ya looking for?" he queried with the enthusiasm of a London Underground ticket collector .

231

"Tulips," responded Clogger, eliminating the possibility that crucial evidence had been discarded on disembarkation.

"Ya not still ganning on aboot tulips, are ya?" the driver reacted, returning to Aintree.

"Open the luggage door," Clogger ordered, wiping his hands together to remove the grime.

"Only bait in yon." responded the driver, reluctant to abandon his well-sprung seat.

"Bait! Trimdon is only thirty minutes away, come on, open it."

Reminiscent of an elderly basset hound, the driver drew some smoke through his fingernails, pushed his racing pages to one side, then opened the little gate to his capsule.

"Ya wasting ya time," he advised, following Clogger down the narrow gap between the coach and the brewery lorry. "This lot think two lips are for supping broon."

There wasn't enough room for the driver to lock-open the luggage-hold door in its horizontal position, so he held the aluminium panel aloft at an angle, while Clogger crouched and did his ostrich imitation. Apart from four crates of empty Newcastle Brown Ale bottles, the grey, felt-lined cupboard was bare.

"Breakfast," the driver advised in hum-drum monotone, anticipating Clogger's next question. "They always insist on bait when I tak 'em anywhere."

Slamming the side-panel shut again, the driver pushed home two recessed levers to secure the compartment and wandered back along the near-side towards the hydraulic passenger door.

"Not yet," Clogger called, squeezing by the pilot to climb into the vehicle first.

Determined not to leave any stone unturned, the secret weapon opened the driver's gate fully and scrutinised every inch of space in the little cockpit before courteously stepping aside. By the time the coiled-spring was re-settled with his fag and racing paper, the bloodhound was on all-fours again making his way down the aisle. Apart from a selection of spent cigarette packets and a smattering of screwed-up dog-ends, the search beneath the two rows of forward-facing dual seats proved fruitless, or to be more exact; flowerless. It

232

was on the return journey from the back to the front, that Clogger mastered his bus-searching technique. In strict sequence, he scanned every seat in turn then peered into the overhead luggage rack, occasionally moving a surplus item of personal clothing in his search for floral evidence.

He was back alongside the haze-enveloped driver when the last possible hiding place occurred to him. In the bus roof, halfway down the aisle, a transparent, yellow-plastic sun-roof was partially open on two scissor-type hinges. While very unlikely, it was just possible to squeeze a small bouquet through the gap, so Agent Catchpole straddled adjacent aisle seats beneath the ventilator, then poked his head into the shallow, rectangular convex dome. Despite pushing the nicotine-coated fitting fully open with his head, Clogger's view was restricted by a draught-excluding flange that protruded upwards.

Mmm, can't believe they'd go to all that trouble, but I'll check anyway, he conceded, glancing at the brewery dray sandwiched between the coach and the police horse-box.

If it hadn't been for the convenience factor, even Clogger would have called off the search at that point. In the event though, he jumped off his perch and bounded down the aisle out of the bus, without so much as a glance from the indifferent driver, re-engrossed in the cockpit. Facing in the opposite direction to the other two vehicles, the delivery lorry had its ribbed tail-gate down at the top of the club steps. Doubling as a ramp, Clogger gingerly climbed the creaking walkway and stepped onto the rear cargo platform among well-ordered ranks of crates and beer barrels. Weaving his way towards a nest of modern aluminium kegs at the front, he managed to get himself into a position where he could see the totally barren growing conditions on the roof of the miners' coach. Not really a surprise, the secret weapon was squeezing his way back by a slightly different route when his trousers snagged the side of a hogs-head, the larger of the traditional oak barrels still used in some hostelries.

Shit, Clogger cursed, shaking the heavy material free from the offending splinter.

In no hurry to report his humiliating findings to the acting detective inspector and become the talk of every workingmen's club in the county, Clogger contemplated the precision of the coopers' craft as he carefully eased his way along a neat line of fully charged hardwood containers. Arranged in descending order, when he came to show his affection to a nine-gallon vessel, conveniently sited at the head of the tail-gate, it was two low to stroke so he just tapped it with his foot.

That's a dinky one, the gorilla observed a split-second before he heard a strange metallic rattle.

The strength of the beer it contained fascinated the giant, so he put his paws on the metal rim of the eighteen-gallon cask next to the miniature, and rocked it on its flat base. The recognisable slopping-sound inspired a scientific comparison that involved kicking the little barrel again, but this time a lot harder. Having had their morning delivery schedule severely disrupted by the activities in the city-centre, the dray crew hadn't fully charged the specially adapted vessel, indeed there was only about an inch in the bottom. Without the necessary ballast, the unstable little blighter rattled again, then fell over onto its side and started to make its own way down the delivery ramp.

Oh fuck! grimaced drayman Catchpole, unable to follow the escapee with the same speed and aerodynamic efficiency.

The new delivery-man was only halfway down the creaking ramp when the tiny barrel rolled onto the police yard. It lost some momentum on the flat tarmac and Clogger nearly got a hand to it, but it realigned itself and took-off again down the club steps with a more distinct metallic vibrancy in its bounce. Using his standard triple-jump approach, the friendly giant managed to overtake the rogue vessel mid-descent, positioning himself in front of the wide-open club doors ready for a head-on tackle, but the thing dummied. A finger-tight, black-iron rim was jettisoned, diverting Clogger's out-stretched palms towards the touch-line.

When the tiny winger side-stepped into the club foyer, with only its momentum keeping the modified oak top-plate in place, it was overcome by frictional drag. The hard, green linoleum surface lent itself to space travel, but the giant doormat didn't. It sent the gently rolling piggy-bank into an uneven spin. Like a bird's egg it slowed, circled, then stopped completely, releasing its nose-cone to spill a ready-mix of five and ten-pence pieces across the floor. Clogger was framed in the outer double-doors when the module crashed to earth. The noise brought the acting detective inspector to the inner lounge doors at the same time as two burly, red-faced draymen tried to decamp the stockroom. If someone had come out of the toilet on the other side of the landing area, the security cordon would have been complete, but it didn't really matter because the two-armed bandits just stared at each other and froze to the spot.

The customary startled silence was followed by the senior detective's finely-honed sixth sense, a faculty that Clogger had yet to fully develop. He glanced firstly at the spillage then at the subdued faces of the dray-crew before spinning around in the doorway to pan across the lounge floor. When the hopefully permanent CID head noticed the gaming machine was slightly off-centre, on its stand at the entrance to the billiard area, he guessed it had been replaced in a hurry. A mountain of undetected crime files suddenly appeared in an imaginary balloon above his head, then he hurdled the nine-gallon beer barrel and launched himself at Clogger.

"Get off," the secret weapon insisted, rejecting the sort of embrace only seen in premiership football. "Must be all micey! The last one punched me. Now this one is kissing me!

It was the appearance of God carrying the Bible that brought the game back under control. A very unusual sight, the sub-divisional occurrence book was rarely seen away from the charge-room counter, not least because of its weight and sheer bulk. Some pundits think that the mountain came to Mohammed on VD-Day in recognition of Clogger's record breaking activities, but that was definitely not the case. The old stalwart was simply being expedient in the light of unmanageable numbers. In fact he was unaware two additional scalps had been taken when he shouldered the official, hard-backed document into the club foyer intending to establish a temporary reception point on a lounge table.

"What's this?" the station sergeant queried, toeing the exploded bomb with a three-foot, ink-stained ruler protruding from the current page of the huge book.

"Stash," answered the acting detective inspector in criminal speak. "They've screwed the bandit."

"What, our bandit?"

"Yeah, our bandit," the senior detective growled, savouring the taste of blood. "And there's at least another fifty to clear-up."

"Cheeky bastards...what's the world coming to? Catchpole."

"Yes, boss...I mean sarge."

"Take them to the cells and tell the gaoler to 'cuff them to the ring."

"The ring!" Clogger retorted, confirming the old warrior was referring to a rarely used Victorian wall-fitting designed to restrain particularly difficult prisoners, usually for the purpose of delousing.

"Yes, the ring. Drunk and refusing to fight is one thing, but screwing the police bandit...well."

Clogger had only just got to grips with their respective collars when the strategy paid classical dividends.

"It's a fair cop," one brute squealed.

"I'll make a statement," asserted the other as Clogger frog-marched the twin-peaks out of the outer swing-doors up the club steps.

Why didn't they bluff the miners like that?

In normal circumstances arresting officers are present while their respective prisoners are processed, but Clogger's absence from the club lounge at this point was seen as fortuitous by the station sergeant. In the interests of theatre safety the services of a stand-in were engaged for the final scene. While the old war horse concocted an extended entry in the occurrence book, justifying the block-arrest, the acting detective inspector wandered to the front of the stage to do his one-man show.

"On this occasion the evidence is insufficient to support a prosecution for theft," the compere opened. "But, it's clear," he warned, "that by withholding information from the arresting officer you have collectively attempted to pervert the course of justice, a matter for which you will receive an official caution, recorded against each of your names in the officer's pocket-book."

A few theatre-goers did stand-up to protest.

"Does that mean we can gan?" asked one.

"Pisspotical," spat another. "Flowers were never nicked int first place."

Apart from that one technical challenge to the underlying legal premise, the flexible use of words and procedure, not to mention the criminal law, was a credit to the acting detective inspector's thespian skills. When the curtain finally fell the main body of complaint was about the unnecessary waste of licensing hours, and the pantomime ended without one missile being thrown.

"Where's nearest pub?" queried the first gorilla to reach the lounge door.

"Move that bus first," the sergeant retorted.

The instruction was to no avail because by then the driver was in the land of nod and a private car had started a second unauthorised row, directly behind the coach. Locked-up and unattended, a printed card in the windscreen read; Vet-On-Call, so the thirsty desert nomads charged past their means of transport, across the congested police yard towards the gate. Able to smell a single hop at one hundred yards, they too had a finely-honed sixth sense. The close proximity of the Court Inn was concealed by the police yard wall, but to a man the mob spilled left and hit the bar running.

"Eighty-four pints, landlord" the leading ball of muscle demanded, compensating for lost time.

While the licensee of the Court Inn was achieving his personal best, the station gaoler was studying Clogger's form. With the two draymen banged-up in separate cells, he was back in the charge-room with Clogger, indulging in laborious long division on the cover of his pocket note-book.

"Definitely a force record," he concluded, "that is, assuming you find the first one. I'll tell you what, I'll write to the Police Review and issue a challenge. Eleven-point-two-five arrests per hour, or point-one-nine per minute. It could be a national record!"

"PC Catchpole from foxtrot bravo control."

"Go ahead."

"Location?"

"Charge-room."

"Report to the co-ordinator."

"Roger."

The all-important communications-room hatch was reminiscent of a football-ground turnstile. A build-up of recently demobilised staff, trying to hand-in their pocket-sets before refreshing in the canteen, forced the giant to utilise his full height.

"You want me, boss...I mean sarge?" he shouted over the top of the queue.

"Catchpole?"

"Yes."

"B-Relief, late turn?"

"That's right."

"Your patrol sergeant is indisposed, I'm covering this afternoon. Don't attend the parade. Take a thirty-minute break, then relieve the meat-wagon driver at two. I want you to park-up outside the Market Tavern until they close at three, just in case. Apparently it's heaving."

"Any sign of my first prisoner, boss?" Clogger continued, invigorated by the thought of his name in print.

"Not at Meadowfield or Nevilles Cross," interrupted the communications-room anchor-man. "I haven't been able to contact Sid and Dick, they're out on another call."

"Both brain surgeons! Probably dropped him off at home," the co-ordinator suggested as he tidied away his papers ready to slip into his other role. "Report him for summons."

"Can't, boss...I mean sarge, I haven't got his full details.

"Collator might have them."

"Ah, right, sarge." Clogger sighed, wrestling with decimal points. Straight eleven per hour. Still take some beating!

Students of the Clogger Crisis are divided about the significance of the additional regulation break, insisted upon by the stand-in patrol sergeant during an extended tour of duty. Some think unpenetratable congestion in the canteen and the milling throng in the corridor outside, caused Clogger to stroll out of the front of the building and wander the grounds of St Cuthbert's, with his very last Monte-Cristo in his mouth. Others argue that he only poked his head around the canteen door to satisfy himself his bait-box and pie-encrusted electronic homing-device were still intact on the kitchen table, and the

238

real reason for his amble was a final strategic assessment. Whichever perspective one holds, the fact is Clogger's apparent constitutional was interrupted by a huddle in the Old Elvet entrance to the churchyard.

Frothing and slobbering, a bulging chestnut strutted broadside, instinctively keeping the miscellaneous audience a safe distance from his ailing partner-in-crime. Between the church wall and the gleaming mountain of muscle, Viceroy lay prone on the pavement with his huge head tucked into the bosom of his crouching mistress. Dismounted, with an equally concerned expression, Burt was on the shoulder of a stethoscope-wielding, green waxed-jacket. The vet was still probing when the curious smoke-pole poked his head into the arena.

"What's happened?" he asked, receiving a mournful flash from Viceroy's tennis-ball eyes.

"Been acting strange since we went to the hospital," advised the lady jockey. "Now he doesn't seem to want to get up."

"What do you think it is?" asked Burt when the vet snapped the big clip from his ears and stood-up.

"Nothing too serious, just a touch of indigestion. I'll give him something, then we'll try and get him back onto his feet."

At that late stage in the war it's probable the cause of Viceroy's belly-ache didn't even cross Clogger's mind. Being a responsible military man he was more concerned about the risk of collateral damage and wandered back through the quiet churchyard satisfied the innocent steeds were preoccupied at a safe distance. Back in the police station grounds, with a big, brown detonator burning in his right hand, the secret weapon continued to stroll, slouching past the symbolic blue lamp hanging over the front door. Turning along the Court Lane side of the main building, he could hear the boisterous tones of forty-two underground horticulturists, in the public bar of the Court Inn on the other side of the perimeter wall.

I'll have those bastards, he vowed. There's more than one way to skin a cat!

Had a trained observer been present, Clogger's next move might have aroused suspicion. He didn't walk directly into the police yard, but leaned nonchalantly on the corner of the station wall, cleverly

239

disguising his pre-match nerves by fiddling incessantly in his left-hand trouser-pocket with his Swiss Army knife. Apart from two or three miscellaneous uniformed types crossing the designated battle-site, and Wupert scurrying between the club-house and the back door of the building, conditions were perfect; well almost. All principal central charges were wired by subtle combinations of spilled engine oil and thinly strewn straw, with tightly-packed peripheral incendiary material in every available white-lined parking slot. Even the divisional chief superintendent's private car was occupying its reserved bay. The only available space was the consecrated frontage to the petrol pump, but an unknown quantity lurked.

Puffing studiously on his Cuban monster, the giant ambled over to an unmarked, black Hillman Minx occupying a key place beside the vet in the unauthorised second-row, immediately behind the brewery dray. In a final act of pre-strike reconnaissance, he pondered a rare document replacing the vehicle excise licence in the windscreen. Home Office exemption certificate, what the fuck is that?

The possibility of government counter-espionage officers being close on his tail did cross his mind, but no matter how hard he tried he couldn't reconcile their presence with stolen tulips and dismissed the potential threat as minimal.

Weather seems to be holding Clogger smiled, lifting his gaze from his wrist-watch to feel the dry, westerly breeze on his face. Perfect! I'll collect my helmet from the club and have the last ten minutes on the billiard table.

Agent Catchpole's choice of final bunker, typified his cunning and very successful 'business as usual' approach to his terrorist activities. With the ground floor canteen at bursting point and the coach driver still dozing, in the final analysis he was undoubtedly callous. A standard warning would be given, but all combatants were now expendable.

Ten to two on VD-Day, Clogger leapt down the club steps, through the foyer and into the lounge, essentially to find his helmet. Working at a lounge table, the acting detective inspector was penning an official label for his little treasure. Exhibit No 1 it read, in his best copper-plate script, one modified nine-gallon beer barrel containing twenty pounds and thirty pence in five and ten pence coins.

"How's it going, boss?" called Clogger, his gaze settling on a pristine, brown dustcoat engaged in high-wire trickery on the padded arm of a comfortable chair.

"Couldn't be better, thanks to you," the acting CID head replied, knotting the official court document around the adjustable rim of the barrel.

Clogger grabbed his helmet from a table and tapped the green fibrous contents into a clean ashtray. "Got sufficient evidence this time?" he quipped with a sarcastic glint in his eye.

"Not 'arf," retorted the detective, "they'll need Houdini to get them out of this one."

"Why's that?"

"The bandit has been under electronic surveillance since the beginning of the month. I've just found out about it from Wupert."

"Really!" Clogger declared, glancing again at the brown dustcoat pushing a screwdriver precariously towards the base of an ornate light-fitting on the club wall.

"Upstairs have been keeping it a secret, thought a bobby was involved. Exhibit No. 2 will be full photographic coverage of the interference," asserted the rejuvenated detective, rubbing his hands vigorously together. "Wupert's gone to inform the bosses. Couldn't have come at a better time for me...and you will be a film star too!"

"Well, that depends," Clogger warned. "If we can't find the first one, I'll lose quarter of a point and it may not be enough."

"Mmm," grimaced the mystified real sleuth as he manhandled Exhibit No. 1 out of the room.

The early arrival of police force one for the two o'clock appointment coincided with Clogger's proper use of the billiard table. He was alone, knocking a few balls about with his personal cue, when the four occupants of a readily-recognisable plain red Jaguar landed in the heart of hostile territory, unobserved by the enemy. Judged to perfection the uniformed chauffeur reversed into a privileged position on the broad tarmac footpath at the front of the police station. When he decamped with the grace and formal courtesy of a ballet dancer, it was the rear off-side door he opened first, to allow the heavily-braided lord and master precision access to the front door step. Contrary to popular belief, the chief constable could walk. Indeed, he cut a dashing figure striding into the public reception area followed closely by the assistant chief constable and a heavily burdened staff officer, struggling to catch up.

"Good afternoon, sir," the city-desk constable snapped, abandoning his conversation with an elderly customer to throw his shoulders back.

"Good afternoon constable, inform the superintendent I'm in the building."

Customary but unnecessary, the trio were barging through the internal door when the city-desk man dialled Jenny's extension. She had been on sentry duty for the last half hour, with her office door slightly ajar at the end of the first floor executive corridor. The raiding party were emerging from the head of the main staircase when her office telephone rang.

"Thank you, I can see them," she clipped, returning the receiver smartly to tap on the superintendent's connecting door.

When God formally knocked, Gentlemen Jim and the divisional chief superintendent were standing in the middle of the sub-divisional head's big office, chatting politely with their tunics freshly brushed.

"C...C...ome," Gentlemen Jim called, acknowledging his role as host for the summit meeting.

G...G...Good afternoon, sir. D...D...Do take a seat."

The normally equally refined chief constable didn't move towards one of the comfortable conference chairs pre-arranged in a circle around a low coffee table. Instead he brushed by the reception committee and took Gentleman Jim's own chair behind his immaculately tidy desk. This uncharacteristic move by the head of the entire Durham Force was deceptive. It suggested the executive meeting was really a front for a high-powered bollocking, sending the rest of the hesitation of senior police officers into a routine, best described as a mini bomb-burst. In the few seconds that followed each collided with one another in a desperate attempt to re-arrange the chairs into a more appropriate semi-circle, facing Mecca. When the process was eventually achieved, the allocation of seats was a much more co-ordinated affair with strict protocol kicking-in. Being the next highest rank, the assistant chief constable sat immediately to his leader's right then the divisional chief superintendent, Gentleman Jim and the chief inspector staff officer dropped into place like cascading dominoes. On the chief constable's left a fifth comfortable chair was conspicuously unoccupied.

"Who's missing?" the stickler for punctuality asked, staring across Gentleman Jim's desk at his staff officer, whose traditional role was to arrange such events.

"Nobody, sir," replied the bag-man, taking a note-book from the bulging briefcase beside his chair.

Before the chief constable had the opportunity to query the sub-divisional head's mathematical qualifications, Gentleman Jim stuttered into life from his position amidships.

"I...I...I took the liberty to put the inspector on stand-by sir. There's been more developments in the last hour which I feel you will want briefing on."

"Surely not!"

"I...I...I'm afraid so, sir, b...b...but my initial understanding is that the circumstances are not damaging."

"I'm glad to hear it...I think we deserve some good fortune, don't you?"

The relaxed tone of the final remark rippled through the participants and a slightly more comfortable atmosphere prevailed during the chairman's opening address.

"I'm sure by now you all know my straight-forward approach to management," proffered the chief constable in the preamble to a mild confession. "I had intended to read the Riot Act today, but I must admit to some over-reaction. Since the debacle in the press last week, I've learned from the assistant chief constable that the problem in this sub-division was identified three weeks ago and proper decisions were taken on the information available at that time. I have also received an extremely well prepared synopsis of the current protracted internal enquiries being carried out by the inspector and today, gentleman, I feel that we are on top of the situation."

"Inspector's here," whispered Jenny, poking her head through the connecting door to attract the attention of her master. "Do you want the coffee and sandwiches now?"

Gentleman Jim glanced subordinately at Buddha.

"Yes, bring them all in," the Almighty ordered.

First through the door was an unusually vibrant Wupert hauling a buff-folder, over-stretched with a wedge of loose papers. He waited politely for the royal nod, then sat next to the chief inspector staff officer and nursed his baby. Jenny reappeared seconds later with a large tray and slid a plate of delicately cut salmon sandwiches onto the central coffee table.

"Help yourselves to sugar," she advised, handing out six matching cups and saucers. "Call me if you want any more."

"Thank you," said the chief constable politely, as the secretary slipped discreetly out of the room and carefully closed the connecting door behind her.

"Right inspector," continued the chief constable, holding his saucer to take his first sip of milky nectar. "First of all I want to thank you for furnishing my office with a most thorough briefing document at very short notice, it's a credit to you. Now, if you would like to update the meeting with the latest developments."

"Thank you, sir," replied the beaming young academic. "I must say it's welatively good news. About an hour ago two dwaymen were awwested following an attack on the police club gaming machine, iwonically in no small measure due to the initiative of PC Catchpole."

"So you were right after all, inspector," the assistant chief constable interjected with his coffee cup at his lips and a tiny round of salmon sandwich in his other hand. "As I recall, at our first meeting you weren't convinced he was dishonest."

"That's wight, sir," but I still think your decision at the time was the wight one," Wupert crawled. "The integwity of the force is pawamount."

"Oh, I think we all agree on that," the chief constable remarked, confirming that his deputy had acted properly. "Incidentally what is the position with the covert surveillance equipment?"

"In the ciwcumstances sir, I ordered its immediate wemoval. The Home Office technician came stwaight down from headquarters to dismantle the device."

"Well done, inspector," praised the chief constable. "We really shouldn't monitor our own staff once the suspicion has abated."

"There's just one thing sir, in that wegard," Wupert went on, anxious to tidy-up a loose end. "The acting detective inspector is now aware of its existence and he's anxious to use the photogwaphic evidence in the case against the dwaymen. Appawently he suspects them of a sewies of similar cwimes with the same modus opewandi. I've authowised the matewial to be developed, but I think the decision to use it outside of its intended puwpose ought to be made at a higher level."

"You continue to impress me, inspector," the chief constable glowed, "I really do believe we've now got this affair under control," he continued, glancing urgently to his right for high-level support.

"I don't see why not, sir," the assistant chief constable responded. "Providing it's unedited, the footage is perfectly admissible. The original purpose is irrelevant, indeed if we don't authorise it's release we could leave ourselves open to accusations of withholding evidence."

"Agreed," snapped the Almighty, prompting his staff officer to minute the decision. "Now let's move on. What's the position with your ongoing enquiries, inspector?"

Oozing self-importance, Wupert took centre stage again. "I'm afwaid it will be a few more weeks before I'm in a position to submit a definitive weport to your office, sir" he sighed dramatically, lifting the four-inch thick Catchpole papers for general scrutiny.

"Mmm," muttered the chief constable recognising the scale of the job in hand. "Now that the criminal aspect of this matter has been ruled out, can you give the meeting some idea of your likely recommendations."

"Essentially I think my final weport will catalogue a sewies of policing disasters, justifying disciplinary pwoceedings under the Police Regulations, but I have to say sir, I don't envisage pwesenting you with anything that will wawwant Catchpole's dismissal."

"Thank you for being so candid, inspector," said the chief constable warming even more to his star performer. "Well gentlemen, what are we going to do?"

His part over, Wupert reached for his coffee cup and began to sip. The chief inspector staff officer beside him, continued to scribble while the rest of the shower twiddled with partially gnawed salmon sandwiches. It was the divisional chief superintendent who shuffled his bottom first, cleared his throat and presented the first option.

"You may see fit to resurrect my idea, sir," he ventured cautiously.

"What was that?" the chief constable asked.

"I will create a post of sub-divisional utilities officer."

The proposition that Clogger be retained in the sub-division, albeit as a skivvy, spurred the normally placid Gentleman Jim into an uncharacteristic outburst, but by the time he emptied his mouth and got the first word out a certain amount of impact was lost. "B...B...But..." he spluttered before the chief constable came to his aid.

"No, I think this division deserves a rest, I..."

The final judgement was interrupted by an untimely knock on the other side of Jenny's connecting door.

"W...W...What is it?" Gentleman Jim tried to snap, when his secretary slotted her head into the theatre. "I...I...I thought I said we didn't want to be disturbed."

"Excuse me, but I have a man here from the Home Office technical support group, and he's demanding to see a senior officer."

"Tell him he has my authority to hand the material over to the CID," the assistant chief constable advised, matter of fact, prompting the door to close again and the judge to resume his summing-up.

"Catchpole will be transferred to..."

The door opened again, this time to the annoyance of the chief constable himself. "What is it now?" he blasted at the cowering face peeping in from the aperture.

"He's insistent, sir."

"This had better be important," growled the chief constable from his elevated position on Gentleman Jim's throne. "Send him in."

The instruction from on high resulted in the appearance of the pristine brown dust-coat fresh from the confined bowels of a tiny sub-divisional dark room, used primarily to process mug-shots.

"Oh, I'm ever so sorry to disturb you," quivered a timid boffin, fazed by the heavy crop of shoulder-braid on his bow, "but I do think this ought to be viewed by someone in authority before it's released for court purposes," he continued brandishing a squirming 35mm snake.

"Why?" snapped Buddha. "Has the camera not caught the deed."

"Oh, it's not that," asserted the ministry man. "The draymen have been photographed twice turning the machine upside down. It's the other activity!"

"The club is open twenty-four hours a day for the benefit of all operational staff," the divisional chief superintendent interjected impatiently. "Only the bar closes. How was the equipment set-up?"

"It was triggered by our latest electronic sensor," the boffin replied proudly. "All movement near the gaming machine, outside of licensing hours has been fully recorded."

"Well, there's bound to be unrelated activity on the roll, some officers play the machine in their break-time and during the night," smiled the chief superintendent, convinced he was talking to an operationally naive scientist.

"But, I still think you ought to look at it first," ventured the egg-head.

"Oh, give it here," the chief constable demanded, reaching over Gentleman Jim's desk to grab three yards of contact-printed miniature still-shots. "I can't see that sort of thing without my glasses," he continued, re-directing the serpent to his staff officer after only a cursory glance.

The chief inspector, selected for his discretion, eloquence and attention to detail, put his note-pad away, scrupulously identified the right end, then began the laborious process of feeding the film through his fingers to provide the delegates with a running commentary.

"Legitimate use of the machine," he muttered, when the first two feet coiled onto his lap. "Ah, this looks interesting...two furtive looking draymen turning it upside down...even see the coins falling out...six sequential shots...perfect evidence."

"What on earth is the problem?" blasted the chief constable, irritated by the time-consuming side-track.

"Just various people losing their money," the staff officer continued casually, abandoning another yard of material.

"You're just about there," suggested the nervous boffin. "It's before the second theft."

"Oh, I see what you mean," the chief inspector declared, back-tracking over a foot or so of black and white material with uncharacteristic alarm. "It's the background!"

"What's in the background?" demanded the chief constable, standing to lean over the desk.

"I'm afraid there's activity on the billiard table, sir."

"Of course there's activity on the billiard table, that's what it's there for. It authenticates the evidence you fool."

"With respect sir, you may feel this particular ball game is unsuitable viewing for the magistrates."

"What can you see, man?"

By now the entire conference were on the edge of their seats leaning in the direction of the bag-man. He typically took a second look at the offensive footage to confirm his findings, then continued with his usual diplomacy. "Two very large, hairy buttocks, sir."

"What, someone is taking a shot without his trousers on?"

"You could put it that way, sir. The spider-rest he's using is quite unusual too."

"What do you mean?" the chief constable blustered.

"It looks remarkably feminine to me, sir"

"You mean someone is canoodling on the billiard table?"

"A little more than that, I fear chief constable," the staff officer concluded, slipping an embarrassed glance to Jenny, standing in the background. "I think he's giving her a good seeing to...I speak colloquially of course."

248

"Oh, chief constable," squeaked the prudish spectator, scurrying back into her trap.

"Who are they?" the Almighty bawled, hammering down onto Gentleman Jim's desk-top.

"Hard to tell," replied the chief inspector, closing down on two or three central frames. "She will definitely never sink, and err...well, he appears to have suffered a rather inconvenient injury recently."

At this critical juncture it is worth noting that men engaged in a three-shift-system, albeit at the same police station, often go for long periods without seeing one another. A special overtime detail such as the miners' meeting, is a rare opportunity for a good chin-wag, so when Clogger emerged from the social club, ready for the final action, it wasn't surprising that things were very much as he'd left them. A few had drifted off, but the little canteen was still the forum for extensive debate. Even the chief constable's personal chauffeur found the fine detail of the lunar landing too much and returned to the driver's seat of the red Jaguar to read his newspaper on the front door step.

"I'm your relief," Clogger called, weaving his way through the congested police yard, towards the fuel pump, with the butt of his last Monte-Christo glowing between his big, white teeth.

"Ah, right," answered a tired early-day man, standing at the back of the meat-wagon with the gun in his hand. "Two minutes, while I finish filling-up."

The re-fuelling of police vehicles is a strange, ritualistic affair. Primarily the responsibility of the departing officer, it is similarly courteous for the relief to take over should circumstances permit.

"Anything outstanding?"

"No."

"On your way, then," Clogger ordered, launching his helmet through the wide-open driver's door onto the front passenger seat.

Make no mistake, when the secret weapon took over at the filler-point, he did recognise the danger of smoking in the vicinity of petrol. It was his pocket-set that caused the problem. Intent on savouring the last ounces of Cuban delight, he re-engaged the abandoned trigger, hooked into the rear of the meat-wagon, then held away the stub of his cigar with his other hand.

Chug, chug. chug. Bleep, bleep, bleep.

"PC Catchpole from foxtrot bravo control."

Still a bit left, the giant observed, preferring to use his delivery hand to recover his transmitter from his right-hand trouser-pocket. "Go ahead."

"You're breaking-up PC Catchpole. Location?"

Tucked between the metallic side of the Commer van and the similarly distortive casing of the ancient petrol pump, Clogger immediately recognised the transmission problem and moved into open space at the front of the vehicle, leaving the pistol in its holster.

"Yard," he rattled.

"Make your way to Langley Moor."

"But I'm suppose to be covering the Market Tavern."

"Sergeant's instructions. Your prisoner has been traced to the premises of Ansa Motors."

"Roger."

Eleven-point-two-five enthused the giant, finally flicking the thick, tarry end of his cigar onto the ground.

Clogger was growling through the jaws of the yard entrance when he felt the first physical resistance. It triggered a reflexive fondling of the handbrake between the front seats, but the lever was fully disengaged forcing him to solve the problem with a touch more power. The thick, black rubber tube didn't snap immediately, but it did extend to a remarkable length before developing the properties of a dangerously taught hawser. When the old fuel pump came out of the ground by the roots and fell onto its side there was every possibility Clogger would leave the inevitable spillage behind and tow the whole thing to Langley Moor, but a knot of pipes and other mechanical bits and pieces proved too durable. Firmly anchored, the contraption decided to stress-test a perished area of hose just below the nozzle. When the secret weapon turned the meat-wagon into Court Lane it finally succumbed to superior forces.

Close to the sound barrier, the metal nozzle and its elasticated trailing-end, left the mobile mortar tube and returned to the police station yard with the curved trajectory of a direct free kick. It climbed to about twelve feet, whistled menacingly like a rogue boomerang, then locked onto the electronic homing device in Clogger's bait-box. The petrol spillage was still meandering along a path of least resistance towards the cleverly discarded cigar butt when the missile crashed through the canteen window. Fortunately nobody was decapitated but the smell of petrol, and the crater in the wall, did cause a certain degree of panic. The noise also aroused the coach driver and sent him hurtling down the steps to the safety of the club, just before flames started to dance across the yard.

"What the fuck was that?" one officer screamed, diving for the cover of a kitchen table with his hands over his head.

"Petrol bomb," bawled another, crashing through the melee to smash the glass on the fire alarm.

Bells ringing everywhere the highly infectious news prompted an uncoordinated evacuation of Titanic proportions. A certain amount of minor injury was sustained in the canteen doorway when a collective, urgent exit resulted in a bottleneck, but it was nothing like the problem at the front door. The occupants of every corridor on both floors, converged more or less at the same time. The best part of one hundred personnel, including the scrambled-egg brigade, Jenny and two bewildered draymen, all piled rather violently into the side of the chief constable's car. By the time they all got to their feet again, many winded and complaining of the sort of injuries associated with football stadium disasters, the fire was well alight.

Fanned by the breeze, the horsebox was the first to go, probably because of the straw, but the brewery vehicle and the miners' coach burned equally well, pouring flames into the back of the main building. It wasn't totally shambolic though. Key players in the new station security procedure did function effectively. The communications-room anchor-man called the fire service and reported the attack to headquarters over the dedicated hotline, while his firearms-trained number-two broke open the armoury and raced upstairs to Gentleman Jim's office to get the bullets. His function was to provide armed back-up while the sub-divisional head made a final search for stragglers, particularly in toilet areas and the like, but true to his nick-name, the superintendent refused.

"Give me the revolver," he ordered. "Get out while you can."

For his part the station sergeant herded the walking-wounded to the prison forecourt, a safe distance from the disaster area, and began to work his way through the sub-divisional manifest. He had just started the laborious roll-call when the communications-room skivvy appeared, alone and unarmed.

"You're supposed to be with the superintendent, where is he?" blasted the station manager.

"Ordered me out," the radio operator gasped. "He's doing the final check alone."

Two critical events conclude this story. The first, timed in official police records at 14.17 on Wednesday 23rd April, 1969, is the symbolic end of an era. While the station sergeant was calling out names and trying desperately to account for everybody, a single .38 calibre shot rang out and stunned the haphazard ranks of evacuees into silence. A few seconds later the implications of the discharge dawned and two uniformed constables courageously volunteered to re-enter the premises, but by then flames and smoke were billowing from the roof.

"No," instructed the very dishevelled chief constable from the depths of the assembly. "The superintendent has chosen to go down with his ship."

The second more comprehensive finale is timed on the Durham County Fire Brigade log at 14.29 the same day. Clogger was safely ensconced in the Ansa Motors vehicle compound at Langley Moor at the height of the blaze. It's true, by then he'd noticed the petrol filler-cap on the meat-wagon was missing and he'd even fingered the damage to the end of the filler-tube, but he was preoccupied with a rescue mission of his own. Loco-Len was receiving persistent unwanted attention when the timely demise of the sub-divisional petrol tank rocked the county. The blast could be heard up to ten miles away and when the cloud of acrid black smoke darkened the sky, one hundred ravenous seabirds swept-off on unprecedented migration.

That's about all there is. At nine o'clock the following morning Clogger found himself confined to an isolated Portakabin in the underwater search unit complex at North Dock, Sunderland. Subject to immediate transfer, he was appointed custodian of the flippers in readiness for the setting-up of a national police diving school, but the task proved too boring. On the 1st June that year personnel records suggest he resigned with a view to joining the fire service, but his disappearance coincided with an unconfirmed sighting of a sinister, black conning tower in the mouth of the River Wear, and many believe he is now safely back on foreign soil.

Perhaps the most interesting case-study emanating from the Catchpole Crisis is that of Wupert. One of the few to survive the Three-Week-War, he was undoubtedly numbed by the experience, but with his academic and fast-track credentials he ought to have bounced back and reached the highest echelons of the police service. Initially, in the aftermath of the affair, his prospects of recovery were good. Permanently engaged in follow-up enquiries, he quickly established himself as the force expert on Cloggerism, providing reports, advice and information to agencies such as the Home Office, Police Authority, Fire Brigade etc. at the drop of a hat.

By the middle of 1970 though, it was evident he couldn't manage change. The steam had gone out of the thing, but he persisted with the gimmickry and even converted the box-room of his three-bedroomed semi into a study, where the Clogger volumes are still stored today. In the years that followed, consecutive chief officers systematically conspired with government sources to over-look the boring old fart for promotion. A dangerous obsession with espionage and intrigue are grounds regularly quoted, so at great personal risk he decided to retire and pursue the matter privately, culminating in a novel widely believed to put the record straight.

THE END

Printed in the United Kingdom
by Lightning Source UK Ltd.
106882UKS00001BA/1-24